THE BLOOD
OF THE BEAR

Grahame Fleming

To Amber

For providing the beginning and ending
of my story and putting up with me
while I wrote the bits in-between.

DREICH!

Artos gasps for air, with his feet sliding over the soft and sodden forest floor. The sound of battle fills his ears; the distant calls of friend and foe, weapons clashing or striking against wooden shields, and more immediately the clatter of hooves followed by the call from the enemy to yield.

I will certainly not be yielding.

Instinct forces him down a narrow, thorny path, where thick tangles of branches scratch and tear at his clothes and skin. The escape route is impossible for a horse to penetrate, but it also slows his own progress. Anticipating the impending threat of death at the hands of a mounted enemy, Artos knows he is safer amongst the tight weave of the briar.

His vision is blurred as cold sweat covers his brow and endless drips of rain run on to his face from his matted and soaking hair.

A furious, pain filled yell follows a crash

of branches. A horse has thrown its rider. The animal snorts and brays as the horseman screams and curses at his injuries.

One down.

Artos keeps pushing onward. At least one rider is still in pursuit. A sword hacks at the undergrowth while arching closer with each swing. The pursuant is closing fast. It is possible to escape, but a gruesome fate still looms large.

Thoughts are racing as Artos struggles to focus. The memories of a short life now competing with the present danger. Only muscle memory keeps him from dropping the axe that weighs heavier in his hand with every passing moment.

Balance gives way as his concentration slips. A final misplaced step throws Artos over a small ledge. His descent is painful. There are sharp rocks and tree roots littering the cold ground. As he falls, the world rotates with brief glimpses of a grey sky interspersed with the dark mud of the forest floor.

Fingers tighten his grip on the axe shaft, his hand and arm drag to the side, wrenching out from his shoulder. The pain makes his mind sharper.

Artos rolls into a crouch that turns him back towards the horseman. His opponent descends the slope and pauses. Both men now face each other over open ground.

This is where I stand or fall.

Artos steadies himself. While his heart beats louder, the other sounds of battle fade into the distance. He knows that his opponent sees him as an animal that is ripe for the kill.

The rider sets his position on top of his mount, balances his sword, and tightens his legs to push his steed forward. The horse obeys the command and goes to the canter. As a skilled warrior on the battlefield, it doesn't need much encouragement to charge at an opponent.

I'm ready.

The ground begins to shake. The rider becomes taller and harder to hit while his sword arcs forward, cutting through the air. Artos steadies his stance, while mustering every ounce of strength to leap to the side of the oncoming charge. He avoids the lunging blade by spinning around, and embeds his axe into the leg of the rider. Screams of anger and pain ring out as he holds tight against the forward movement to unseat his opponent.

The weapons fall out of reach as both warriors crash towards the ground. Artos calls out in agony as the rider crushes him by landing heavily on top. A desperate struggle ensues. They reduce the noble arts of warfare to punching, spitting, and wrestling for supremacy.

Artos chokes as a gauntleted hand presses

against his face and blocks the light from his eyes. The stench in his nose is strong with the reek of horse, blood, and soil. The weight of his enemy pushes him into the dirt.

His neck is being pressed on by another hand. He can't breathe. Life is ebbing away. Artos cannot fight back against the opponent's strength and rage. His eyes begin to close.

The cold departs. The landscape around Artos is different. Calm water laps gently against a shore that rises to the summits of rolling green hills. An inviting path stretches out before him. He looks down at himself, dressed in fine, clean clothes. His long, dark hair blows in a light breeze. He feels truly at home in this place.

A dog joins him on his left, while a wolf joins him on his right. He passes through an orchard where he's greeted by a young woman cloaked in black. He walks forward. Now before him is the tumbling, cool water of a spring. Artos kneels and cups some of the liquid in his hands. Drinking deeply, he feels energy coursing through every part of his being. He has never felt stronger or more alive. Then the word repeats in his head, awaken, awaken ...

Awaken. Artos pushes with all his strength against his opponent, causing him to fall to the side, as three dull thuds follow in quick succession. The attacker slumps to the ground in agony. Long, black feathered arrow shafts protrude from his back.

The victor has become the victim. He can only crawl with the faintest hope of making an escape.

Artos leaps to his feet. His near-death experience has given him a renewed lust for life. He rushes to retrieve his battle-axe, turning and raising it to strike.

"Hold that axe and stand back!" calls another mounted warrior arriving at the scene.

The voice belongs to someone from his own warband. MacDuncan MacForres is his commander and the only son of his tribe's chieftain. MacDuncan dismounts with a leap and draws a dagger from his belt.

"For Christ's sake. Do you know who we have here? Cadawg mac Arnall. Get him on his knees. I want him to know that MacDuncan MacForres is taking his life."

Artos drops the axe and raises the slumped body of Cadawg to a kneeling position. Blood escapes from the dying man's back and mouth as he gargles on the trauma of his injuries.

"Who shot him with the arrows?" asks MacDuncan as he pulls Cadawg up against his knife.

"I don't know. We were in a fight," says Artos.

"Doesn't matter," MacDuncan draws the sharp blade of his weapon across the neck of the victim, "this is my kill, you'll be happy to account for that?"

"Aye, I saw that."

Artos has never liked the murderous part of war. A kill on the battlefield creates heroes or martyrs. MacDuncan's action is savage and not worthy of such an honour.

"Right, that'll be another one for me!" MacDuncan remounts his horse, "I'll send someone to take the body back to the wagon. Faither will be pleased to have him as a guest at tonight's feast. Strip him of whatever we can use and get rid of those arrows. Nobody else is getting the claim for the death of Arnall's son."

MacDuncan rides off, leaving Artos alone. The sound of battle is subsiding. He hears a horn in the distance. More hooves and the occasional scream suggest survivors are being captured. The rain increases in intensity as he stands over the body of Cadawg. He sucks in more air, appreciating its sudden abundance, while he draws out his own dagger to remove the arrowheads.

What just happened?

"Artos!"

Another warrior rushes out from the thick of the trees. His mane of blonde hair and piercing green eyes make him easily stand out from the predominantly dark or red-haired members of the warband. He is untouched by the weather or dirt and sweat of battle.

"Alan, you took your time to get here."

"It's not my fault. One minute we're

fighting side-by-side, brothers-in-arms, and the next thing you're running into the distance."

"Aye, all because two over-privileged idiots on horses were hunting me down."

Alan draws his spit in his throat before launching it towards the corpse of Cadawg.

"You got him. That's the main thing."

"No, I didn't get him. I should be where he is."

"Aye, so what happened?"

"He was winning. I was dying. There was nothing I could do. I pushed him aside, and an archer took him out with three quick shots."

"What archer? There were no archers with us."

Both realise they are vulnerable in the open clearing, whoever fired the arrows had some skill.

"Let's drag him into cover," says Artos.

The two men are strong but struggle to lift the uncooperative carcass of a man who has obviously dined well during his life.

"Who slit his throat?" says Alan.

"Who do you think? I was standing here still wondering why I was still standing here, when MacDuncan rides up, jumps off his horse, draws a dagger across the throat of a dead man, and claims the kill. Then he jumps back on his horse, telling me to carry home the things we can re-use."

"Maybe he gets up early to practise being an arse."

"No, he was just born like that," Artos studies an arrow, "he told me this was Cadawg mac Arnall."

"What Cadawg? The son of Arnall?"

"That's usually what it means."

"The son of the King of Galwydell? Jesus! I wouldn't be taking a trip to Ynys Mon anytime soon if I were you."

"Why not? Anywhere else is better than this."

Artos reflects on his surroundings, the bitter chill, the dead body, and the never-ending rain.

"I'm sick of this!"

"Here we go." Alan's heard this talk before.

"Five years I've been fighting for the MacForres family and where's it got me? I'm eighteen. I want to go places, do things."

"Not Camulodunum again."

"What's wrong with Camulodunum? It's the place to be if you want to better yourself."

"So, what then?" says Alan while looting items, "should we fight for someone else?"

"No-one round here. Somewhere where the weather's better. Somewhere that we can get a hope of being promoted or getting paid with coin instead of mead."

"I'm not opposed to leaving Galwydell, but let's concentrate on getting home from here first. I could do with some of that mead right now."

Alan scoops a helmet and some chain mail into his arms. Artos pauses and stands motionless in the rain, staring at the fallen warrior. His daydreams take over and he sees himself wielding a great sword, marrying a princess, and capturing a castle from an evil king.

"Waken up Artos! This might be worth something."

A quick slap on the head pulls Artos back to reality. Alan holds up the victim's left arm. A golden ring adorns Cadawg's index finger, inlaid with a single emerald.

"Yes! That's definitely worth something," says Artos.

He regains his composure and starts tugging at the valuable jewel, but it won't budge. It takes his knife to cut the treasure free, but with the index finger still attached. He holds it up and stares at the gem.

"Decisions, decisions. Do you think I should keep it?"

"They'll gut you alive if they catch you with it."

"I could sell it to someone. Then we'll just have coins to spend. No evidence of the crime."

"Aye, and you having a fistful of coins isn't suspicious."

Alan assumes the persona of two gossiping

villagers, complete with high-pitched voices.

"I saw Artos eating a three-course dinner with wine!"

"Wine did you say?"

"Aye, and he was wearing a fresh shirt made of linen!"

"Linen, not hemp or nettles?"

Artos is still pondering the temptation when he's disturbed by the sound of the horseman sent to pick up the body.

"Quiet, they've sent Redlead," he says, while absent-mindedly pocketing the ring for the moment.

Redlead pulls up his horse beside them. A large and tall figure, ruddy-cheeked, with long red hair and beard. Redlead is the chieftain's cousin and his enforcer when order must be established among the ranks. Feared by friend and foe alike, short in temper and long in leg, he easily steps down from the back of his horse.

"I might have known you two would be the stragglers."

"What d'you mean?" says Artos.

"The battle's finished. Everybody else is away back to Dun Romanach for a drink."

"Aw, that's great," says Alan, "thanks for telling us."

"I just did. Pay attention."

Artos and Alan shift uncomfortably and draw sideways glances at one another while Redlead scoops up the body of Cadawg as if it was made from feathers. His horse protests at the dead weight slung across it. Redlead walks around the front and stares into its eyes. His threatening gaze means the same to man or beast. To compound the horse's stress, he climbs back on and starts to ride off before shouting over his shoulder.

"Better get started back. It's a two hour walk to the mead and the weather's getting worse."

"Is it drier in Camulodunum?" says Alan.

"Never rains apparently," says Artos.

The two friends stride on. Their mood is subdued by the continuous rainfall. The heavy grey of the short winter twilight has disappeared a few miles back and progressed into a pitch-black night complete with a shroud of heavy showers. An uncomfortable saturation creeps through Artos and sinks towards the squelching of his tired and well-worn boots.

"The ford will be up," says Alan.

"I'll be crossing it. Or we'll never get a drink," replies Artos, "I can't get any more wet."

A wind is gathering force, directing icy water and sleet into their faces. The weather doesn't put them off. Most of the year, they work as shepherds in and around their village of Hartriggs. A place where it's normal to experience all four seasons in the space of a day.

It doesn't make it less annoying. It's been hours since they lined up with the rest of the warband and marched to the pre-arranged spot where they would risk their lives on behalf of their leader. On the command, the shield walls would line up against each other. A ritual of jeering, pushing, and shoving, while attempting to catch out your opponent with whatever sharp piece of weaponry you happened to be holding. After a struggle, one side would triumph, leading to the combat breaking down into individual contests. The main rule is don't get caught on the outside, where horsemen can pick you off. Artos found himself in just such a position. He was angry that the enemy had caught him in just this way. The thoughts repeatedly played out in his mind about how he survived.

Who shot the arrows? How am I still here?

He looks over at Alan who has found a stone he can idly kick along the path in front of himself. It creates an annoying rhythm to further build the sense of tension and nerve-stretching frustration within Artos.

A swell of fast running water looms up in front of them. The ford is just low enough to cross, but not without some risk of being dragged off in the current.

"Come on, we've done this before," says Artos.

The friends survey the best point to enter the water. They look for rocks or roots they can use to steady themselves. They search for the shallowest parts to wade into, thinking about where they could end up, further downstream.

It would be hard enough to plan a safe way across in the middle of the day, but on a dark stormy night, it has become far more difficult. The water is devoid of colour. The swirling mass tumbles by at incredible speed. Patches of a thicker substance float by, building in volume until it stretches across the full swell of the flood.

Artos plunges his hand into the darker fluid. He pulls back out immediately. His fingers are dripping in blood.

A scream erupts in the darkness, sending Artos and Alan reeling with the sudden shock.

"What the ..." says Alan.

"Quiet," says Artos, "listen."

The forlorn crying and wailing of a woman can be heard. A mournful call that penetrates through the wind and lashing rain. It is close, upstream, and beyond a bend in the river.

"This is not good," whispers Artos.

The instinct to crouch low feels natural. They draw the axes that have been slung across their backs, bringing them forward into their hands. They begin to creep along the side of the riverbank. All the while, the storm rages and they sense a sudden drop in temperature.

The turmoil of the turbulent river covers the sound of their movement forward, while the lone voice that's howling increases in volume. It is close. They peer between trunks and branches, silently planning their next move forward.

Artos can just make out a shuffling figure as it walks in front of them. A woman with long blonde hair that cascades over her back. She wears a simple white gown and carries a bundle of clothes in her arms. Walking to the river's edge, she bends down and places a tunic and breeches beside her before starting to wash the items in the river. As she works away, her wailing grows, only stopping from time to time before offering a howl into the night sky. Is it a scream or an animal call? It's hard to tell.

Artos and Alan shrink down in the undergrowth. The woman turns, with her back still facing them. She steps through the wet moss and grass to a larger pile of clothes. Once again, she collects more items to wash. Her figure is thin, her hands are longer than normal, with nails that resemble claws. She repeats her journey back to the riverbank, carrying clothes that appear to be stained with blood. Pausing for a moment, her head looks up to the sky. She sniffs at the air and looks around herself, before carrying on washing the clothes at the river's edge.

"Who is she?" asks Alan.

"Or what is she? Did your mother never warn you about the Bean-nighe? The washerwoman who cleans the clothes of those about to die."

"No, that sounds more something your mother would talk about, being the village witch and all. It could be someone who has trouble sleeping?"

"And all the blood-soaked clothes?"

"Yes, you have a point there. So, what do we do?"

Artos spends a moment recounting the tales of his younger days, growing up in a small tribal hut with his adopted mother and twelve sisters.

"We have to speak to her."

"We have to speak to that out there?"

"The washerwoman cleans the clothes of those about to die in battle. If you have the misfortune of stumbling across her, then you can ask her for your clothes back."

"Well, she's not washing my clothes. I'm wearing most of what I own."

"She doesn't have your real clothes. You just have to ask her. I don't know, it's eh, tradition?"

"Tradition?"

A scream causes them to leap with fright. Each become gripped by a strong bony hand, dragging them forcefully through the undergrowth.

The Bean-nighe stands snarling above them. Her long blonde hair frames grey wrinkled flesh, eyes swollen and red, and thin lips that barely cover a row of sharpened teeth.

"Who disturbs the washerwoman?"

Thunder rumbles as if punctuating her question.

"My name is Artos," he says, "and I claim my clothes from you as, eh, tradition demands."

The Bean-nighe smiles with her mouth while the rest of her face remains sorrowful.

"Artos?" says the Bean-nighe, moving close enough for him to smell the stench of death on her breath, "I know of you, Artos," her voice growls and rattles, "you are right to make your claim of me."

She reaches out with her hand and curls her thin, strong fingers around the neck of his tunic, dragging him up on to his feet and pulling him closer.

"I will honour what you ask of me. I will return your clothes and grant you a wish to use before I come to wash your shirt and breeches again."

"Th-thank you washerwoman."

The Bean-nighe turns to search among the blood-soaked clothes that are strewn along the riverbank. A varied choice of styles and sizes that range from the height of fashion to rags stitched together in the rough shape of clothing. She selects a tunic and breeches and places the blood-soaked items into the hands of Artos. The items are unfamiliar to him, but if it's good enough for the Bean-nighe to spare him, they'll do.

"And now your friend."

The Bean-nighe switches her attention to Alan. Once again, she extends her hand out, pulling him closer. He can sense her icy breath on his cheek. Her eyes stare into his with deep loss and longing, and perhaps just an uncomfortable element of lust.

"And you, how should I know you?"

"Alan, eh, washerwoman."

"Alan. You remind me of one that I left long ago," the banshee draws a long sharp nail against his cheek, "tell me what you desire?"

Alan looks nervously towards Artos, who nods encouragement for him to speak.

"My name is Alan from Hartriggs, and I, eh, traditionally claim my clothes from you."

The Bean-nighe pauses for a moment, absent-mindedly flicking her tongue between her teeth.

"Very well. I will accept your claim."

The friends breathe a sigh of relief. Once again, the Bean-nighe searches through the piles of clothes. She seems to select better quality items for Alan before returning.

"Here are your clothes that you have

claimed from me, Alan. I can only offer one gift for one meeting, but I am often at this place should you pass this way alone."

Alan shivers and nods his acceptance while making a mental note to never come here again.

The Bean-nighe turns from them and returns to her work and her wailing. Her now distinctive shrieking call echoes through the forest, along with the sound of two young men fleeing as fast as they can.

THE HONOURED
GUEST

Dun Romanach. Continuous generations have built and modified the ramparts and ditches of the MacForres fortress for over a thousand years.

Perching above the dense Scots Pine, Birch, and Rowan, the fortress itself is large and well protected. Stone constructions and wooden palisades date from earlier years of Roman occupation. Gatehouses set at the north and south stand guard over the only paths in or out.

Within its walls are homes for the most trusted members of the family and their retinue. To the east there are buildings for crafting metals, leather tanning and weaving. A market and small chapel are situated at its centre. While to the west lies the Great Hall itself, an architectural manifestation of the resident lord's wealth and status.

Tonight, within that very place, torches

burn around the walls while serving staff hand out plates of food and jugs of mead across trestle tables. To one side, a troupe of Bavarian minstrels offer the entertainment. Drums, pipes, and a fiddle combine to elevate the spirits of the assembled crowd. On the wall opposite, a roaring fire burns to offer light, heat, and a way for the assembled members of the warband to dry off after the day's battle.

A raised platform at one end of the hall adds importance to the top table, and seated at its centre is the chieftain, Duncan MacForres. Somewhere in his forties, his youth left him behind at least three decades earlier. His lack of beard and short hair distinguishes him from most others. He prefers the classic *Roman look*. He was a handsome man in his younger days, but physical scars from fighting and mental scars internalised by the raw desire for power have gifted him a permanently twisted and angry face.

Duncan scans the room. Taking pride in his success, his brilliance, and his wealth. The one thing he can never understand is how anyone can't love him as much as he loves himself? This includes his ex-wife, who left him, citing that there was a third person in their marriage. Too late, he understood what she meant as he gazed at his own reflection in a mirror, just as she slammed the door literally and metaphorically on their relationship.

A father of two official children, plus another twenty or thirty unofficial *Wee Duncan's* scattered amongst the hamlets that surround Dun Romanach, he never was a traditional family man. Duncan only developed a paternal instinct in the legitimate offspring just before their respective thirteenth birthdays, when they began to have some value. His son as a warrior and his daughter as a bride, to be married off in a political manoeuvre for the advance of his own cause.

MacDuncan was the eldest and, in line with tradition, called after his father, but Duncan extended this vanity to his daughter as well. The fair Duncanna had never objected to the narcissistic part of her name, because she was her father's girl. Intent on the expansion of the family empire under her rule, once her father had passed on and her brother had met with an unfortunate accident.

Sitting to Duncan's left this night, MacDuncan was the only child that he questioned his own role in fathering. Correctly suspecting that his wife had left him long before he ever knew there was a problem.

Tonight, MacDuncan is in excellent form and relays his success of the day to anyone who will listen. As his tales get taller, his roaring laughter gets more pronounced. The wine flies from his goblet as his arms swirl around, recreating the death of Cadawg.

The unfortunate recipient of this version of MacDuncan's story is Andrew, a priest of the new church. A sincere and pious individual who arrived at Dun Romanach as a missionary. A man of learning, letters, and faith, but dogged by alcoholism. He combines his love of God with his love of wine and mead by attending as many weddings as he can. Andrew has presided over a high percentage of the marriages in and around Dun Romanach. He often re-marries couples if it results in more free drink.

On the other side of Duncan sits his daughter's intended, Eochaid. A son of the king of the Dal Riata, who rules the islands to the west of the mainland. The young prince is now only third in line for his family's domain, but with intrigue and murder, Duncan may still promote him through his family ranks.

Duncanna enchants Eochaid with her charms. She has long flowing blonde hair that tumbles in tresses to her waist. Her eyes are of the deepest cobalt blue, and she speaks in soft and submissive breathy tones. Her virtuous demeanour belies the fact that she has murdered three earlier suitors. Two with her preferred method of poison, while the third true love had his heart removed with a small cutlery knife.

"Tha gaol agam ort," says Eochaid, "that is how we say I love you. I will greet you every day and every night with those words, my love. For as long as we are together."

"Oh Eochaid. Am I truly to be the Queen of the Isles?"

"Alas, my mother has that title, which will fall to the wife of the heir, my eldest brother, but you will be a princess whose elegance the bards will proclaim, and whom our monks will portray in their great inscribed works. You will have songs composed in your honour and —"

"Yes, but how many elder brothers do you have?"

"Why two, my love."

"Two?"

Duncanna looks thoughtful as she considers the fate of Eochaid's family members. Meanwhile, the minstrels call a halt to the music. In the gap that follows, a murmur of anticipation circulates around the warriors gathered in the hall. MacDuncan takes his place in the centre of the room, facing back towards his father. He is clearly amused with himself.

"Lord Duncan! Laird of Dun Romanach. Maister of the MacForres Estates and soon to be king of those who dwell in the hills and valleys of all Galwydell."

A cheer erupts from the assembled revellers, amplified by mead infused enthusiasm.

"Faither. Once again, your warband has seen victory on the battlefield against the men of Ynys Mon. Their leader claims our lands as his right, yet his raids have failed. His power lies only within the faded ink on a torn piece of parchment. You are the true leader of our people. You are the one who should rule from the stone halls of the island fortress."

Another rapturous call goes out from the crowd to which Duncan reacts with something approaching a smile.

"I feel there should be a tribute to help celebrate our victory today. For your pleasure, faither, I have brought a guest to join us for the feast. It is with great pride and honour that I invite to your table, Cadawg, eldest son of King Arnall."

The crowd murmurs some more while they look for the enemy prince in the room, but what appears instead is a servant carrying a covered silver platter. The serving girl places the offering in front of Duncan, who rises from his seat with no lack of ceremony. He offers a regal wave of acknowledgement to his son, who responds with a bow, inviting his father to lift the lid.

Duncan places his hand on the cover and looks out over the audience, for whom he is now definitely the centre of attention. The crowd feeds his ego. These moments of triumph add up on his reputation and fame. With a great flourish, he tosses back one side of his cloak and lifts the cover from the plate, revealing the bloodied head of Cadawg, with its mouth slit further open to accommodate a large apple in the manner of a suckling pig.

A loud scream rings out from a dark corner of the hall, but the rest of the crowd reacts with cruel and mocking laughter. Duncan raises his goblet, to which the crowd responds, raising their own cups in toast.

"To Cadawg mac Arnall," says Duncan.

"Cadawg," echoes the crowd.

Duncan remains standing to soak up more glory before settling the crowd with his hand.

"Cadawg is sombre tonight," says Duncan, "was the work of our cooks not to his liking?"

The crowd burst into laughter. If Duncan thinks the joke is funny, then you must join in with the hilarity.

While the joking continues, Artos and Alan arrive, too late to claim a full share of the feast that is allocated to the warband. They quietly take a plate of meat between them and a half-empty jug of mead before finding a place by the fire to listen to Duncan's speech.

"Today's victory over Arnall's raiding party has once again diminished his army. He grows weaker and his friends desert him. I'm sure when we attack the island of Ynys Mon, few will defend the gates. To my vassals, you may know that your loyalty pays for increased land and titles. To the rabble of unruly henchmen that are the soldiers of my army," another cheer goes up, "know that each of you will prosper in your share of the fortune that will come when *we* are the raiders arriving on enemy shores."

The room rumbles with foot stamping and fists banging on tables. Raucous calls from the drunken guests resound around the hall for more war and bloodshed. Duncan clearly approves as he continues.

"To the brave MacDuncan. I give thanks for your gift to me this evening. Cadawg was responsible for the deaths of many, yet it was your skill in battle that saw him meet his end. Good Father Andrew has assured me it was God's will that you, *my son*, triumphed over the son of Arnall.

"You have proved yourself among the ranks and when we launch our final assault on Ynys Mon. and face the raining arrows of their archers, the cold points of their spearmen, and the sharp swords of their footmen, I will have you sitting at the forefront of the charge knowing that God will protect you from almost certain violent death."

The crowd cheer again with the other vassals patting their hands on MacDuncan's back, while his face expresses concern for what his future might hold. Artos and Alan smirk at one another, realising that MacDuncan is possibly regretting his claim of being the one that defeated Cadawg.

"And tonight," Duncan continues, "we

welcome another special guest to our victory celebration. We are honoured to share our feast with our new friends and allies from the Dal Riata. I can now announce that King Fergus and I have agreed terms for the forthcoming marriage of his son, Prince Eochaid, to my daughter, the Lady Duncanna."

Duncan allows a strangely polite round of applause, while Eochiad and Duncanna both stand to share in the good wishes. The stylish costume of Eochaid makes him stand out in the crowd. He obviously comes from a wealthy family, with real status and power. It is marrying down, but Duncanna is skilled in the social graces. She is a good match for a third son with no real chance of taking power.

Artos and Alan begin to move through the crowd, closer to the front. There is something familiar about the prince that they recognise, but they just can't figure out where they've seen him before tonight.

Duncan raises his goblet once more. "As a wedding gift to honour the happy couple, King Fergus has kindly offered his ships to aid our quest for the seat of power on Ynys Mon. He recognises that Galwydell is ours by right and that Arnall does not deserve his throne. This important marriage between our children will form a powerful alliance that few will wish to challenge. To the new alliance!"

A final happy cheer is the cue for Duncan

to sit down as he pretends to offer the head of Cadawg some of his wine. MacDuncan returns to his own chair through the congratulations of his men who line up to offer their support for the forthcoming assault on Ynys Mon.

Yet the crowd wants more. Calls for Prince Eochaid to make a speech grow louder. An awkward few moments of gestures between the top table guests end with the young man standing once again, and clearing his throat to speak. The audience assumes a respectful silence.

"Feasgar math," the greeting goes over the heads of the MacForres warband, "or should I say good evening," polite laughter, "on behalf of my betrothed and myself. May I thank you, Lord Duncan, for your hospitality and your kind introduction. The MacForres line stretches back in history. Your ancestors stood at the gates of Troy and helped to drive the Roman legions from our lands. Those who believed they had the right of rule granted from Rome even walked in this very place until the MacForres forefathers overthrew them. It is a great honour for our families to unite. Your fame supported by the great stories of legend combined with the Dal Riata's actual wealth and power will make for a powerful alliance, I agree.

"Lord Duncan. My heart aches and my loins yearn to join with your daughter, the fair

Duncanna. I hope to provide your line with many grandchildren. The Dal Riata will be proud to know of you as friends, but our loyalty will never break once we are truly together as a family."

Another cheer of encouragement from the crowd. Talk of alliances and power always goes down well. Eochaid calms the crowd before continuing.

"Yet I have a problem. Duncanna is so beautiful, so chaste, so refined, that my debt is too deep in our very first meeting. I must do something in return for you, my future father-in-law. I understand there are those from the battle today who will try to escape back across the sea?"

"It is true. There are always those who choose to run in the face of certain defeat," replies Duncan, not sure where Eochaid is going with his speech.

"I asked my love what she thought of the gift of Cadawg's head on a silver platter," Eochaid briefly allows a small private laugh between himself and Duncanna, "dear soft-spoken and fair Duncanna replied that she would be happy with such a gift if the heads numbered at least ten."

The couple laugh on their own at first until Duncan signals that it's alright for everyone else to join in with them.

"So let us ride out in the morning on a

hunt. Allow myself and my retinue to finish the work of today's battle. We will round up the survivors and stop any from returning to Ynys Mon. The news of the crushing defeat will return to Arnall as a loud message that the MacForres family rule Galwydell. Of those we capture, Duncanna can choose who she wishes served up before her as a token of my love."

Eochaid gently pulls forward Duncanna's hand to plant a kiss, concluding his part of the entertainment. Without further hesitation, the minstrels strike up a rousing piece of music. A suitable call to battle.

The room returns to a myriad of private conversations, and the level of distraction allows Duncan to brood without being noticed. Eochaid and Duncanna only have eyes for one another. Father Andrew has slipped into a wine and mead induced comatose state. Only MacDuncan is aware enough to know that his father's mood is darkening.

"Are you alright, faither?"

"No. Far from it. Come with me now."

With the music still in full swing and the revellers absorbed with the rowdy atmosphere, Duncan and his son make their escape to the private chambers. They are still within the

Great Hall but separated by a thick curtain that hangs down from the ceiling. It keeps out just enough of the background noise to allow Duncan to think.

"Blithering idiot."

"What faither?"

Duncan sits on his chair beside a large dining table. It isn't a throne, just a chair that no-one else dares to sit on for fear of incurring the chieftain's wrath. He looks frustrated as he glances over at MacDuncan.

"The idiot isn't you for once. I'm talking about Eochaid. What was he thinking of? A manhunt for trained troops, desperate to escape. It's not the normal one-sided competition to trap a beast of the forest. The boy is a fool."

"You don't think he can fight?"

"I know he can't fight. He's of no use to Fergus. That is why Duncanna is being allowed to marry him."

"I thought we were joining in a great alliance with one another. Duncanna's hand for a fleet of ships."

"Fergus has offered a single use of his ships in return for taking Eochaid off his hands. The Dal Riata have no interest in Ynys Mon. If we take the throne of Galwydell, then Eochaid's status will survive in some form with an estate and a title. Even if only through marriage."

"Can we not just call off the manhunt?"

"Not now. He called for it in front of everyone. My family, my vassals, my warband. I should have just brought in the dogs and the horses as well, to witness his challenge."

MacDuncan allows a small squeak of a laugh to emerge from his lips, but then retracts it immediately to not further antagonise his father.

"We will have to give him his manhunt," Duncan reflects, "but make sure he doesn't find any quarry. Better that than a levy man of Arnall's destroying our plans to invade Ynys Mon with one lucky swipe of an axe."

MacDuncan draws out the chair opposite Duncan, but still looks for a visual clue that he can sit. Duncan nods and gestures for him to go ahead.

"Faither, we know the direction that the men of Arnall will head. Towards the coast in the south-west. Hoping to find someone who'll ferry them over the sea. We can find them long before Eochaid, as long as his part of the hunting party is, eh, delayed."

Duncan considers the short proposal by stroking his chin and gently nodding in agreement.

"Yes, that could work. So, we separate, sending Eochaid and his retinue in the wrong direction. That's good, but we need a guarantee that he won't suddenly make a right turn. Attach a couple of our levy men to his party. We need them to own enough wit to complete the task yet be expendable. I won't have rumours among the ranks after the event."

"Now you mention it," says MacDuncan, "there's two lads that I could easily expend."

"Then bring them here now."

MacDuncan rises from his chair and departs back through the curtain into the main part of the Great Hall, while Duncan stands up and ambles over to a small hearth where a fire is burning for his personal comfort. Crackling logs on a pedestal made of clay, shaped in the form of crescent moons. A small luxury, its low light gives out just enough illumination to the other treasures in the room that serve practical and decorative purposes. Rich fabrics imported from distant lands are hanging to cover the worst of the cracks and holes in the walls. While the gruesome array of weaponry on display is not the trophies of battle, but on closer inspection, the corroded and blunted tools of an armoury no longer considered fit for use.

Duncan was far travelled, and his private chamber displayed ornaments and art from many places. The historical fame of his family always guaranteed an invitation to the courts of others. Sometimes he would receive a gift for his bard's colourful retelling of the MacForres victories, which credited his family for the legion's retreat to the south of Hadrian's wall.

As he looks around himself, his sense of frustration grows. Time is running out for Duncan to make his own mark on the MacForres family legacy. He has at least maintained the borders of his estates that lie within the Galwydell region. He was the first to accept Christianity for all the spiritual and political advantages that it brought, and he has developed Dun Romanach into a centre for trade that is the envy of other chieftains, not least his rival Arnall who makes a regular claim on Duncan's estates.

Whoever ruled from the island of Ynys Mon was the rightful King of Galwydell according to the historical record. The MacForres lands were generating revenue, but none of it found its way back to Arnall as either tax or tribute. Inevitable conflict had raged between the two opposing forces for many years.

Duncan walks the few short steps through to the bed chamber. A large room with more curtains used to separate out the sleeping arrangements of himself and his family, plus some added floor space for servants that may be required to guard and attend them during the night.

He muses over the thought that the fortress at Ynys Mon is large enough to give his family their own personal rooms, with further space for guests and friends. Duncan presumes he will have people to stay when he is king.

He lifts a dark glass bottle from the floor beside his bed. It's still half full of wine, which he swallows in several large gulps. A warm haze infects him, and his mood lightens. His plans are coming together. He is wise enough to know that a well-placed marriage does more to advance his cause than years of bloody conflict. His only regret is that he has only one daughter, for they are certainly more valuable than sons.

A cough from behind causes him to spin around to see MacDuncan grinning back.

"I've got the volunteers through here."

"Good," Duncan replies as he walks towards the doorway, "let's get this organised, I need another drink."

Artos and Alan are in awe of the lavish surroundings of Duncan's private chamber. They have never been to the other side of the curtain. In fact, many have lived and died for the MacForres family without receiving such an honour.

Duncan stands silently, observing them for a moment. Initially making sure they're not stealing any of his valuables. He recognises these two. The taller blonde-haired one is a distinctive presence in the ranks. He has the strong muscular form of an athlete from Olympus, a chiselled square jaw, and a confidence in himself that enchants every woman in Dun Romanach. If you had a warrior son, you would want him to have the fair face of this man, but then again, he would undoubtedly steal your wife, mistress, and mother.

The second levy man is younger, darker, and shorter. Still strong and obviously suited to his role in Duncan's army. There is something about him that Duncan recognises from his life of a few years ago. The full lips, striking deep brown eyes, and thick black hair, cause a brief flashback. He stirs a memory of an event.

The younger man is examining the few objects in the room that have real value and merit. Duncan's gaze follows Artos, as he traces the contours of a distinctive bronze horse figurine with his long fine fingers.

"Pegasus," confirms Duncan in his most authoritative tone. Artos and Alan react with surprise and stumble to attention in front of their leader, who continues, "the legendary winged horse of the Greeks. It's a magnificent piece that came into my family's possession years ago. I own and collect many treasures and relics from ancient times. I have a bottle of authentic wine from the wedding in Cana, sheep dung preserved from the stable in Bethlehem, and a bag of nails with a parchment that says blacksmiths handcrafted them in Judea. The bronze statue of Pegasus is more magical, more intriguing, more …"

"Genuine?" says Artos.

"Quite so," Duncan shrugs his shoulders, "so on with the task at hand. I'll make this brief. My son tells me you are two of the more reliable foot soldiers in my army?"

Duncan doesn't allow room for a reply. He is in no mood to allow the lowest form of infantry to contaminate his private residence for a second longer than necessary.

"Let me be blunt from the start. Eochaid is to be my future son-in-law. He has many fine qualities, I'm sure, but he is neither wise, talented, nor skilled in battle. Yet the mead encourages his bravery the same as any other man. Under its influence, he can win a war on his own."

Artos raises his hand for permission to speak.

"Granted." says Duncan in response.

"Lord Duncan, sir. When you say war. You mean the manhunt that the prince spoke of?"

"Yes, I mean the manhunt. If Eochaid goes out there and gets himself killed. Then I can forget a fleet of ships provided by the Dal Riata and forget attacking Ynys Mon."

"And you don't want that, Lord Duncan."

Duncan can't help the perplexed look on his face as he turns back to his son with an expression that instantly conveys, *is this the best you can do*? He returns his scowl towards Artos and briefly searches his memories of the young man, but it's a brief consideration as he returns to the point.

"We'll go through with the hunt. I cannot allow even the smallest stain of cowardice on my reputation. Eochaid must meet none of Arnall's stragglers. Tomorrow, once we reach the edge of Caledon Forest, I'll split the party into two, insisting that a pincer movement will help to close in and surround our prey. I will lead MacDuncan and my vassals in one direction. Eochaid's retinue will head in the other. You two will go with him to make sure that he gets lost far away from the actual fight."

"We picked you," says MacDuncan, "because you two know Caledon better than most," he turns to his father, "They come from Hartriggs, it sits on the edge of Caledon."

"Yes, I know Hartriggs. Though it's many years since I've been there," Duncan can now put a place to the face of Artos as memories return, "is the old witch still there?"

"Yes sir," says Artos, "Wren raised me sir. She's my adopted mother, sir."

"Yes, of course she is. We are wasting time. Mainly mine. I am now holding you two responsible for preserving the life of the hopeless fool that my daughter intends to marry. Your task is simple. Lose yourself and Eochaid in the countryside. He will be told you are accompanying him as expert trackers. You must persuade him, that is the case. Under no circumstances should you engage anyone in a fight. If you do, and then have the temerity to survive, then I'll kill you myself. Questions?"

Alan is confused. "What does temerity —"

"I'll tell you later," says Artos.

An awkward silence falls for a brief second, where Duncan exhales a long sigh, and the two Hartriggs friends stay silent in front of him.

"Good. I'm glad I made myself understood. Don't breathe a word to anyone else, and of course the usual terms apply. Do a good job and I won't hang you."

MacDuncan ushers Artos and Alan out of the chamber and draws the curtain behind them.

"I hope you're right," says Duncan.

"These boys are good soldiers. You'll have no trouble with them. Very reliable. Won't let you down at all."

MARE'S TAIL

A watery, lazy sunrise stretches into the sky. It provides light, but no heat. Artos watches his breath rise into the air. A pain in his head sharpens as the glare fills his eyes.

"I'm not ready for this today," he says as he looks over at Alan, standing beside him with not a hair out of place or any sense of a hangover.

How does he do that?

"A long walk will do you good," says Alan.

They continue standing in silence as the rest of the world moves around them. Horses and riders are gathering. A quiet discussion is underway between Duncan and his vassals, with occasional sniggers from his men.

The horsemen of the Dal Riata congregate further away. Unlike their MacForres counterparts, they are more disciplined, better armed, better dressed. They share a drink from a cup that's being passed around and are enthusiastic about the morning's sport. They indulge in their own casual conversation, dotted with mocking laughter and sideways sneering glances at the horsemen from Dun Romanach.

Between the groups of riders, two wagons are being prepared for the supporting levy men who will be required to do the actual hard work of encircling the enemy and subduing them if they dare to fight back.

A small group of Duncan's men emerge together from the Great Hall led by Archie, a walking mass of hair, beard, and teeth. He grins widely at Artos.

"How did you end up with this job?" he asks.

"MacDuncan thought we'd be better off going with the Dal Riata. He doesn't want them to get lost in Caledon."

"Aye well, me and the boys have heard a rumour that's exactly what he wants," Archie roars with laughter, "at least you'll get out of doing the hard work, but I wouldn't fancy my chances fighting alongside that lot."

They stare over towards the group of footmen that have accompanied the retinue of Eochaid. They are older, fatter, and not as fit looking as you would expect a royal bodyguard to be. All of them still seem to be lightly inebriated from the feast the night before, struggling to even get into the back of their wagon.

"Aye, you could be right."

Artos turns to Alan for a sign of agreement, but his friend's attention is elsewhere, with his gaze fixed on Eochaid.

"Ma-tin-va," says Archie.

"What?" says Artos, looking back to the levy man.

"Ma-tin-va. That's how that lot says good morning. Just say that when you go over to them. It's friendly."

"Ma ... tin-va?" repeats Artos.

"Aye that's it. See you at the hunt. Or maybe I won't."

Archie laughs and walks off to collect his horse and join the others who are climbing aboard the MacForres transport.

"What's wrong with you?" says Artos, turning back towards his still dumbfounded friend.

"I've just realised. Last night we thought there was something familiar about Eochaid. It wasn't him. It was his cloak. Where have you seen that lately?"

"The cloak?" the realisation dawns on Artos, "the Bean-nighe had it amongst her washing pile."

"Aye, and you know what that could mean."

A nervous shiver passes through both. Is it fear of the Bean-nighe, or fear of losing Duncan's future son-in-law on their watch? It isn't difficult to imagine that their clothes will end up back with the washerwoman if they don't protect Eochaid and keep him safe from harm. This isn't helping Artos' hangover. His nausea is increasing as the contents of his stomach slosh with growing apprehension.

"Any ideas?" says Alan.

"Follow orders. Make sure we stay away from any fighting. It could have been someone else's cloak."

"Yes. It could," says Alan.

The two friends share a glance as if to say *It's Eochaid's cloak*. Meanwhile MacDuncan rides over to where they're standing. The hunt is obviously about to start.

"Ah, the Hartriggs boys. Ready for your," he winks, "special mission with Prince Eochaid?"

"Aye sir," they both respond.

"I sent out scouts last night. They spotted a small camp, eight men about five miles south. We'll catch them alright, but faither will split the parties before we get there. Do your job. For once, I don't want to see either of you at the fight. Do you understand me?"

"Aye," is the joint reply.

"Good. Then get to your wagon and take your new friends for a nice wee wander in Caledon."

One of the MacForres warband blows on a horn, calling the parties together to move out. Artos and Alan break into a short sprint to catch the wagon that's moving off. As they leap on, two of the Dal Riata help to pull them on board.

Artos squeezes into a corner next to a large old man, who offers an affable smile while refusing to budge an inch to allow him a comfortable seat. He returns a nod and remembers Archie's phrase.

"Ma-tin-va."

"Oh! Madainn mhath," comes the enthusiastic reply, "is mise Iain. Ciamar a tha thu?"

Artos meekly nods in return, having reached his foreign language conversation limit.

The morning passed pleasantly enough. The men of the Dal Riata had shown initiative in providing themselves food for the journey by collecting some of the earlier night's feast in a sack that sat at their feet. They handed out portions of cold roasted goat meat and lamb, along with fruit and a flask of mead. Although Artos couldn't understand what was being said, the men beside him were happy and he supposed they were exchanging pleasantries as they shared the morsels.

He learned that *Is mise* came before your

name, and so each member of the Dal Riata levy politely nodded to a version of the introduction, "Ma-tin-va ees-meesha Artos."

Attempts to speak the language went down well, and so he learned to say *tapadh leat* as a thank you, as well as some words for the food they were eating.

Alan attempted to find out how you asked out a girl in their language, but his mime of a woman became awkward and lost in translation, so the conversation soon ended.

There is a big world out there, beyond these hills.

Artos is happy amongst the company of the strangers. It's interesting and funny. Today's task moves out of his mind as he enjoys the camaraderie.

Horsemen from both sides are up ahead on the road. The MacForres wagon brings up the rear. As Artos looks back, with a chunk of meat in one hand and a cup of mead in the other, he's met with scowls from his black clad comrades, envious that the only nourishment they have minded to bring with them is the black bread that gives you something to chew on as opposed to something you can enjoy.

In a single moment, it sums up his feelings about life in Galwydell; bleak, impoverished, uninteresting. He promises himself that the time to leave will be soon. His dreams will never come true if he wastes his years living within the MacForres lands.

He looks across at Alan, who returns a brief eye roll. The friends have been together since boyhood, working with the goats and sheep around Hartriggs, long before fighting together in Duncan's levy. They don't need to talk to know what each other is thinking. Artos is always dreaming about far-away places; Alan always dreams about far-away girls.

"Hold," the command comes from Duncan at the head of the procession, bringing everyone to a halt.

The great forest of Caledon stretches out before them. As the sun grudgingly lifts itself higher into the sky, it illuminates a picturesque scene. A mixture of trees from bare sycamore to evergreen pines divide the rays into highlights and shadows.

As the leaders discuss plans at the front of the procession, they wave signals back towards the wagon drivers to pull into the side of the road. From this point, the rest of the journey will be on foot.

Artos leaps off the back of the wagon and on to the ground, before helping his slower moving new friend to a safe landing, and then his friend, and then his friend after that. It reminds him of escorting the elders of his village on a day trip to a shrine, instead of preparing to do battle with a desperate enemy on the run.

With everyone alighted and gathering their weapons together, Artos and Alan step away from the crowd.

"We'll take them over towards the Mare's Tail waterfall," says Artos, "it's near to here. There's a stream we can follow. I'd be willing to bet coin that when we get there, they'll all want to stop to take in the view."

"What about Prince Eochaid?" says Alan.

"We must keep him close. Get him distracted. Tell him things about Duncanna. The good things about her."

"Good luck with that." Alan's face is devoid of sarcasm.

MacDuncan has ridden over to the other men of the MacForres levy, issuing instructions. Orders received, they walk on towards Duncan and the other riders, but not before a chorus of *Ma-tin-va's* towards the Dal Riata men. Obviously, Archie has taught everyone his one Gaelic phrase. Meanwhile, MacDuncan rides over to Artos and Alan.

"Right lads. Do you have a plan?"

"We're going to take them up to Mare's Tail," says Artos, "get them to sit down and enjoy the view."

"Good, that's good. The opposite direction from us. Faither doesn't want to waste all day doing this. Just long enough to gather some more heads for my beloved sister. Most lassies just want a ring for their wedding, not our

Duncanna. When we've done the deed, I'll know where to catch up with you."

Artos and Alan respond with a nod as MacDuncan turns and rides back to the front, passing Eochaid with his riders, who are now assembling with their own levy men.

"Let's get this done," says Artos and they wander back into the pack of visiting warriors.

An air of anticipation is forming. Horses that sense tension in their riders are becoming unsettled and difficult to hold still. Several conversations are taking place at once, and none of it in a language that Artos understands.

"Dé 'n t-ainm a th'ort?" says one horseman from Prince Eochaid's retinue.

"Seo Artos," replies a footman.

"Madainn mhath Artos," continues the rider, "An aithne dhut an rathad? A bheil Gàidhlig agad? "

Artos shrugs his shoulders hopelessly. It annoys the rider that Duncan has left them with trackers that they can't converse with. The rider walks his horse away, obviously to have a good moan to some others. Eochaid rides forward to fill the gap. Artos feels more comfortable. The prince of the Dal Riata is at least bilingual.

"Artos? Alan?" asks Eochaid.

The Hartriggs friends raise their hands in response, forgetting that everyone else knows one another.

"Lord Duncan says they know the whereabouts of the last men of Arnall's raiding party. He wants us to approach them from the rear, while he rides ahead to cut off their escape route. We should be on them within the hour and home with our kill by evening. He says you will know the road to take us?"

"Aye, that we do," says Artos, "MacDuncan has given us orders to follow."

Eochaid looks to address his men. Delivering a long speech in his native tongue, sprinkled with various mentions of *Artos agus Alan*, usually followed by some laughter from his party of followers.

He doesn't want to fight anyone today.

Artos realises that Prince Eochaid is not overly concerned about getting the manhunt underway. Duncan's half of the hunting party has departed some time ago and they still haven't set a first foot on to the track for Mare's Tail, but Eochaid ultimately runs out of discussion points and returns his attention to Artos and Alan.

"Right. We are ready to go. Stride forward Artos and lead the way. I will say our horses are still tired from the journey south to Dun Romanach, so don't hurry. If we hear the shouts and screams of the victims, I'm sure we'll get there soon enough. Tiugainn!"

The mounted retinue and footmen make

their way into the nearby woods. Artos and Alan rush to be at the front of the crowd, and with basic hand signals, manoeuvre the group into an organised party, compliantly following their path.

"It's a good job we work with the sheep," says Alan.

Days such as this are perfect to show off Galwydell. Caledon Forest runs on its eastern borders, while to the west lies an abundance of lochs and rivers that cut through rolling hills and green valleys towards a large coastline.

The path that Artos has chosen climbs up to higher ground. Through gaps in the trees, spectacular views present themselves of long stretches of land. The higher peaks are as yet only lightly dusted with snow, but enough to stand out against a cool blue sky.

The men of the Dal Riata are clearly enjoying the sightseeing. There's no sense of being on a manhunt. Most share quiet conversations in their small groups, but as the journey progresses, boisterous calls travel from the back to the front, followed by laughter.

Attempts by Artos and Alan to quieten them down last only a few minutes before the chatter increases once again. If this was a normal hunt, then the prey would be long gone.

"I don't feel right," says Artos, "instinct."

"Aye, I feel it too," says Alan.

"We're almost at Mare's Tail. Once we get them there, we'll look around on our own."

The last stage of the journey is a well-worn path that passes between a natural break in the trees. Sunlight stretches to the ground and reflects in a fast-flowing stream that bubbles and froths over rocks. It isn't unusual to meet others on the way to and from the natural attraction, but today it's quiet. Maybe other visitors have just sought alternative routes given that Artos' party appears to be a small invasion force.

Emerging before the high drop of a waterfall. The Mare's Tail is impressive. The trees circle around the very edge of hill summits that rise sharply before them, creating a natural amphitheatre that amplifies the tumbling torrent of water. It's a spectacular sight, and according to plan, completely distracts Eochaid's hunting party. They waste no time in dismounting and leading their horses to drink from the pool that lies at the base of the cascade.

The visitors find places that offer an enjoyable view. Flat-topped boulders or fallen trees are nature's way of providing seating for all. They duly produce another sack of food for all to share.

How much did they steal last night?

It astounds Artos just how prepared they've been. If only he had understood parts of their conversation, then he might have been able to learn that they only ever wanted a nice day out and a drink or two.

One of Eochaid's horsemen produces a small flask, much to the obvious approval of the others. It passes around each man for a small sip. They follow a drink with a choke or a screwed-up face, then an exclamation or a laugh.

Artos and Alan smile at the reactions, and soon it's their turn. The old levy man approaches them with an offer to drink from the flask.

"Uisge," he says, pointing to the waterfall and then the pool below, "uisge."

"Water?" asks Artos.

"Water," he points to the flask, "uisge-beatha."

"Ooshga-bay-huh?"

The man nods and offers the flask forward. Artos takes it and smells the contents. It seems pleasant enough. He knows that the eyes of all the others are upon him as he tips some of the liquid into his mouth. The taste is sharp without sweetness. As it passes through into his throat, a heat follows, descending into his body and catching him unawares. A quick second sip causes a visible shudder and hilarity amongst his new comrades.

"Ooshga-bay-huh!" proclaims Artos as he holds up the flask.

Everyone cheers in return. Alan repeats the same ritual, and it's obvious that this is the path to acceptance from the Dal Riata. They make the bond.

A short and pleasant time passes, but Artos still feels as if he's looking around himself constantly. He's searching for a sign of another presence. A small movement, or a flash of colour that doesn't sit right with the surroundings. The drink has settled him, but suspicions of danger being close at hand are enough to keep him focussed.

"We should go and look for MacDuncan. Prince Eochaid seems happy to stay here," says Artos.

The two friends walk over to where Eochaid is engaged in lively discussion with his fellow riders. His cheeks are glowing from the effects of the uisge-beatha, and he seems to be content as they approach.

"Prince Eochaid."

"Aye, Artos isn't it?"

"Aye sir. Alan and I are just going to have a look down the road. Lord Duncan should be south of us by now. We just want to see if there's any sign of them yet."

"That's fine lads. Take your time. No rush."

Eochaid returns to the chatter of his friends. Leaving Artos and Alan to shrug at one another and walk off.

As they re-join the main path, the talking and laughing starts to fade into the distance. A single bird sings. Its call is unanswered and seems to draw attention to their isolation and vulnerability. A twig snaps, and did they hear a scrape of metal? The friends squint through the tangle of branches, but all seems as it should. Artos regrets bringing them to a forest full of natural cover and hiding places.

Maybe Mare's Tail wasn't such a great idea.

The coarse call of a lone magpie is never a good sign as it takes off from an adjacent tree, drawing attention up towards the higher branches.

"I can't stop thinking about who the archer was from yesterday," says Artos, as he scans the surroundings.

"Aye, but it wasn't you they killed," Alan responds.

"I know, but I haven't felt that their sight has left us."

"Now you're making me feel nervous."

They look around for any signs of life larger than a bird. Artos unstraps his axe, drawing it forward into his hands.

"Do you hear something?" asks Alan.

"No, I feel something."

Alan draws his own axe, and the two men

stand motionless. The background noise of the nearby river is loud enough to drown out other sounds.

"This is a waste of time," says Artos, "we better get back to Prince Eochaid."

As they turn, a small yelp seems to cut through the air, followed by a roar, then the distinctive clash of metal.

"They're being attacked!" Artos yells.

Running back towards the waterfall makes them realise how far they've walked. As the sound grows louder and the violence clearer, Eochaid and his men are still not in sight. A horse emerges from the conflict, panic driving it forward. It has no intention of stopping as it races past them.

"Quicker," urges Artos as he runs faster.

The conflict ahead comes into view. The noise and chaos of battle transforms the once tranquil stillness of the beauty spot, with men clashing weapons against one another in small pockets of fierce combat.

Artos and Alan charge in upon the scene and into the fray. Axes swing out, hoping that luck helps them find their target, as much as skill.

The fighting is fast and fierce. Artos draws his axe from the shoulder of a defeated opponent, before running to aid Alan, who is being taunted by the point of a spear. Two against one is enough to counter the threat, and the spearman falls to a blow on the back of his head as Artos delivers another forceful attack.

The Dal Riata horses squeal and kick as the desperate raiders capture them. In an instant, the attackers seize their chance to ride off before Artos and Alan can counterattack over the obstacle of multiple dead bodies.

The Hartriggs friends don't drop their guard, but it's plain that they are the only ones left standing amidst the aftermath of a battle lost.

Artos scans the scene. It only takes a few seconds to spy the corpse of Prince Eochaid, separated from its head, and lying trampled into the mud. Displayed for all to see is the fine cloak stained red with his blood.

Fuck!

"What are we going to do?" says Alan.

"What?"

"What are we going to do?"

"What just happened?" Artos gasps in disbelief.

In just a few short minutes, the enemy attack has turned their lives upside down, and they know it. There's too much to process. The fugitives have wiped out the entire retinue of Prince Eochaid.

"We're dead men," Alan gives voice to the thought they both share, "Duncan will kill us for not dying with them."

"Well, he just can't find us. It's as simple as that."

Artos continues to stare at the pile of morbid evidence that proves they've failed in their duty.

"We have to go now, and get as far away as we can, before MacDuncan shows up here."

"This isn't the time for the big dreams, Artos. We're looking at ending today on a noose if we're lucky."

"Aye, well, I can't think of a better day to leave home."

They wipe at their dry mouths and brows that drip with sweat. Their hearts are beating hard and loud, and the adrenaline courses through their veins.

"Aye, you're right, let's go," says Alan.

The two begin to hurry back towards the north. A road that will take them back to Hartriggs. The decision to leave Galwydell for good is confused with the instinct to go home.

"Wait," Artos stops them in their tracks, "we can't just run off. If Duncan doesn't find us here. What do you think he's going to do next?"

"Try to find us. He'll head for Hartriggs, but we won't be there, will we?"

"And if we're not there?" asks Artos, "he'll take out his wrath on someone else. Our families at least."

"Aye, you're right there," says Alan, "what then? We've got no chance in a fight. There's twelve of them."

"No, we can't fight. There must be something else."

Artos scours the site of the battle. His mind searching for an answer, but their predicament seems hopeless as he stands amongst the scattered corpses. Many are so badly cut up and bloodstained that it's almost impossible to identify them as the same happy group that they had led to this place. Several beheadings don't help, but at least provide an inspiration for a way to escape.

"We have to be dead too," says Artos.

"What are you talking about now?"

"We have to be dead as well. If they think we're dead, then they won't have anyone to chase."

"Alright, I see that, but how? I still think we just take a chance and run for it."

"No, we can do this. Look around the bodies. Find somebody your size."

"Eh, why?"

"Because you're going to dress them in your clothes, that's why. Then chop him up a bit more and make sure you take the head off."

"You are off your head."

"That's the only idea I've got, and our time is running out. We do this, get back to Hartriggs to grab what we need, and then off to Camulodunum or anywhere that's far enough away from Duncan MacForres."

"You're mad, but you're right as well."

"Good, let's do it," says Artos with a huge sigh of relief.

Fight or flight is a normal response, but it's not always that straightforward. The two friends stress and sweat as they strip their victims. Buttons are hard to grasp, belts and buckles take time to detach. It's a good job that the selected victims are only simple footmen with no chain mail or other protection.

Artos piles the clothes of his chosen replacement on the ground and then begins to strip off his own clothes. His nakedness adds to the pressure and sense of imminent danger. If Duncan and the others appear now, they have no chance, and their fate will be worse than just being killed. The cold bites deep. Even the weather is conspiring against them and if he thought that undressing the dead was difficult, getting them dressed again in different clothes is even more of a problem.

"How are you getting on?" he calls over to Alan.

"This is a mess. What are we doing? He's too fat for my breeches, I can't get them on."

"Just do the best you can. You're going to use your axe on him. We just need them to think it's us."

"He's got red hair. I'm blonde."

"And who's going to know? You're taking his head off."

Alan works away and curses under his breath, while Artos sits back to inspect his work.

It will do.

He dresses himself as well as he can in the exchanged clothes of the departed, before lifting his axe.

Time is running out, but he briefly allows himself a word of prayer to any of the gods that may be listening. What he is about to do is against all the values he holds dear, but it's life or death, and not just for him and Alan, but any that Duncan might decide to be deserving of his revenge.

With repeated swings, he hacks at the body below him, distorting it into a mass of disconnected flesh and bone. Finally, he removes the head, carrying it by the long hair that its owner had cultivated in life. Alan is completing the same process as Artos steps over beside him.

"What are we going to do with these?" Alan says, lifting his victim's decapitated head.

"Take them with us. We can't have them sticking everything back together. Can we?"

A flock of crows takes off in the distance.

"Someone's coming. We go now."

Racing off into the undergrowth with clothes and boots that barely fit, their one advantage is familiarity of the land. Where to run and where to avoid. Knowledge born of short lives in and around the hills of Galwydell. As they crouch low and descend the high slopes, Artos scrambles through a range of emotions. He never thought this would be the way he would move on from the life he had known. He imagined more time to prepare, to say goodbye, to share a cup of mead over happy memories with friends. Now he must disappear and become someone else. To survive until fate turns in his favour once more.

"Wait," says Alan.

They stumble to a halt. Gasping for air. Their senses sharpened and heightened. In the distance, a tormented cry of woe echoes across the hills. Someone somewhere has discovered Prince Eochaid, and they don't sound happy.

HAG OF HARTRIGGS

Breaking the morning silence, slow steps crunch through a fresh fall of light snow. An old woman exhales heavily with a curse as her back stiffens and aches. She has walked this path many times, but experience has given way to age. Her mind is strong enough to make the climb, her body is less willing.

She pauses briefly to gasp more cold air and looks around herself. Her destination stretches out before her. Modron's Water is a small loch that nestles high amongst the hill summits overlooking Hartriggs.

The woman leans on her staff to steady her stance while surveying the scene for other signs of life. As expected, she has the place to herself. Only a few hardy locals will venture up here in winter, and it's still too dark and early for most of them on the shortest day of the year.

Her steps begin again, and she heads

towards the shore where the water rolls softly against rocks, rippled by the cold breath of a breeze from the east. She follows a small path of pebbles and stones that rises up towards an outcrop.

Placing her staff down, she searches through a bag that hangs from her shoulder and takes out a small pipe and a pouch containing dried herbs and leaves. She carefully places some of the mixture into the bowl while holding the pipe in her mouth. Returning to the bag once more, she produces a small box. Opening the lid uncovers a bright red powder from which she picks the tiniest pinch. Rubbing it between finger and thumb, she drops it into the pipe mix, where it creates a flame to ignite her herbs.

She draws on the pipe. The smoke passes into her body and from the very first breath she sinks into contemplation. In the sky, an eagle has taken to the air. The woman wonders if it's just a bird on the hunt for food, or is it a spirit there to watch over her? Maybe it's her mother, who has long since departed this world.

She has visited this place ever since she was a young child, and it was her mother who brought her in those days. A strong and kind woman, who doted on her *Little Wren* and took advantage of the solitude to school her child in the magical arts. In fact, where the old woman was sitting now was the very place where her mother had offered her a smoke of her first pipe. Wren cackles at the thought.

She continues to inhale the herbal mix, and with each exhale, the smoke stretches out over the water's edge. It reaches out to the centre of the loch. It swirls without dissipating and builds into a dense mist that shuts out the hillside, the bird, and the sky.

Wren cackles once more. The smoke makes you happy; it transports you to another place between the worlds. It allows you to meet guides and teachers that may offer you advice along the way.

Placing the pipe on the ground beside herself, she closes her eyes and takes a deep breath.

She becomes the eagle, soaring high above the loch. From amongst the clouds, she can see everything for miles, including the hilltop fortress of Dun Romanach. She can see a party of horsemen leaving the settlement. At their head is Duncan MacForres, accompanied by his son and the priest, who uses his pulpit to preach against all that she is. Six more riders and a wagon pulled by two horses follow them. A small troop, but important. Why else is she being shown this vision?

She opens her eyes. Her senses are more alert. She can hear insects and small animals moving around from a great distance away. She can smell the cooking pots of villagers preparing the feast for later that evening. The quartzite crystal embedded in the rock sparkles, and she can sense the life force that lies within every blade of grass. It is time.

Packing the smoking kit back into her bag, she reaches for her staff to help herself back to her feet. She now stands straight and unburdened by the painful afflictions that evolve over years. She steps down to the edge of the shore and feels a power that is centred within the water.

The ripples grow larger in front of her, and the clouds of mist created by her smoke begin to move aside. At first, Wren can only glimpse subtle movement as the surface of the loch becomes unsettled, but then a figure begins to emerge. A graceful apparition forms in front of her. Light reflects and dances through the body as the being takes on its chosen human form; the image of a youthful woman who hasn't changed in all the years that Wren has visited this place. The water nymph is exactly who Wren expects to see. The most famed of the Naiad race, known in legend as Nimue, Lady of the Lake. The Guardian of the Sword of Destiny.

"My lady," says Wren, bowing before the spirit, "the time has come. The kingdoms of the Britons will unite under the Bear. Defender of the faiths. Conqueror of those who invade our lands. Under his rule we enter the golden age —"

"Oh P-lease," says Nimue, "It's not the golden age yet. That's years away. Artos has just managed walking and talking. Next, you'll be asking for the sword, won't you?"

The reaction wasn't a total surprise. Wren had conversed with Nimue many times and knew her to be feisty and difficult, but that was just the way of a typical Naiad.

"My lady, I am sorry, but the people need their king, and he must have the sword."

"I knew it. Everybody wants the sword these days. Oh, excuse me Nimue, I've got to sort out a king somewhere, or I've got to find the Holy Grail, or I've got to slay a dragon and it'll be easier if I have the sword. Well, that's not how it works. You know the rules. Only the Merlin can receive Excalibur at the appointed time. Summon me again when he is with you, but still no promises."

"But my lady, we do not have a Merlin. They say the last one went mad after the meteor incident."

"I'm not surprised. No Merlin, no Excalibur."

"My lady," Wren struggles to keep her deference, "can you help me find the Merlin?"

"No! Why don't I just unite the land?"

"Because it's not in the prophecy?"

"Correct."

Wren pauses. "My lady, am I not part of the prophecy?"

Nimue becomes more reflective. "Yes, you are."

"And is it not my part to protect a future king who may yet be the one to wield Excalibur?"

"Yes, I suppose," Nimue says with frustration, "Myrrdin Wylde still holds the title of Merlin. He has not passed through Avalon and is living in your own Forest of Caledon. I imagine he'll allow himself to be discovered when he has sorted out a few emotional conflicts and personal problems. He's not perfect, you know."

Wren smiles a wry smile. "None of us are my lady."

Nimue allows herself a momentary loss of composure and stamps her foot in the water.

"You have summoned me, and I have come, so you may ask me for one gift, though not Excalibur, obviously."

"Then give me sight of my demise."

Nimue looks solemn. "Close your eyes and allow your mind to see the destiny that lies ahead."

The mist thickens again around Wren.

A picture bursts into life. She is at the centre of a splendid party with young people singing and dancing around her, cheering her and thanking her for her kindness. There are tables groaning with food and drink. She is the guest of honour at an important celebration. The scene suddenly becomes dark and her nose twitches under the heavy smell of acrid smoke. Her ears fill with the screams of innocents and the sound of warriors charging into a violent conflict.

"Thank you, lady. I know what I must do. I can see how the prophecy shapes our lives. Many will perish. I must do what I can to remove their torment."

Wren opens her eyes. The mist has dispersed, Nimue has vanished, and the scene has returned to normal. With a heavy heart, she turns and walks away from the loch. The bird of prey swoops low over her, marking her black cloak with its pure white droppings.

"What a complete bitch," says Wren.

The slow walk of the journey home has given Wren time to wrestle with her own thoughts. Descending from Modron's Water to Hartriggs gradually brings her back to the world that most would call reality. Wren views all spheres of existence as part of the same place, but she acknowledges that it requires training to move between them.

The locals are respectful of her knowledge. She has an instinct for when to plant the seeds, when to reap the harvest, how to use flowers and plants to heal, and how to help a mother through childbirth.

Her telling of the future brings outsiders to the village who are seeking a change of fortune, or a perfect love. For those who come and offer payment for her services, she will do her best to recommend choices or offer warnings, but always with kindness and care.

Wren and Hartriggs now share a fate, having shared a life. The brief vision granted by Nimue, pictured the inside of the village's communal large house. Although she couldn't recognise all the faces, there was something familiar about the other people who had appeared to her. Those doomed to share her fate in the darkness, with fire and the noise of battle. A tear rolls down her cheek as she approaches the familiar small circle of buildings that mark the centre of the village. Visions of the future always showed too much and yet never enough. The circumstances that would lead to a violent end were yet unknown. It was still too early to panic the others. Her immediate concern was of her glimpse of Duncan MacForres. He hadn't visited this part of his estates for years. For that, he maybe had good reason. Yet she felt a strong compulsion he was on his way now. All the better that the first villager she ran into was an elder. The short and stocky, fifteen-year-old father of two, Wee Laddie.

"Morning Wren, you're out early today."

"Aye. The short solstice is always a busy day. The summer one grants you more time to prepare."

"You can say that again. Some of just dragged the big log in for the fire. There's food to be organised, and half the forest seems to have gone into the big house. Still, the children love it."

"That's true," says Wren.

Wee Laddie is little more than a child himself, but he is old enough to see, Wren is not acting in her normal way.

"What's wrong? Is there something upsetting you?"

"You know I have the power of the sight. People call it a gift, but it's a burden too."

"Just tell me if I can help."

"Maybe you can. I saw a vision. Duncan MacForres riding out of Dun Romanach with some of his men. My gut tells me he's heading this way, but I don't know why."

"Duncan only appears when he wants something. A tax, a tribute, he'll find something to take. Though I must admit, I thought he had forgotten us. I think I had just started smoking and drinking the last time he was here."

"It was four years ago," Wren reminds.

"Aye that would be about right," grins Wee Laddie, "well just in case I'll let the others know. We'll hide the good stuff for the feast just in case he wants to help himself."

"Aye, you're a good wee laddie, Wee Laddie."

Wren claps him on the head and smiles before walking away.

Pulling the cowl of her black cloak around her head, she limits her contact with the other villagers that she passes. A nod is all she offers to the neighbours who greet her. She is tired from the exertions of the climb to Modron's Water and the summoning of a troublesome water nymph. The cold bites deeper these days. Her skin feels thinner and more vulnerable to the weather. The thought of home and hot tea comes to the forefront of her mind.

Wren's home is on the other side of Hartriggs. Close to where the river runs, it lies secluded behind a twisted hazel hedge. Charms hang from the branches of trees that encroach around the building. Spider webs woven in the high corners of the walls are undisturbed, and little wisps of smoke swirl constantly out of a hole in the roof. A fire is always lit for the inhabitants, who number fourteen when Wren's adopted son Artos is back from the levy.

She pushes a small wooden gate that disturbs the threaded shells and small agates, positioned to announce a visitor. The local witch meets those in need of her services regardless of the time of day, and many prefer the cover of darkness, so an early warning of their arrival is useful to have as well as just making the old house appear a bit more magical.

The wooden door is heavy, but it obediently creaks open as Wren pushes against it. As she steps inside, her eyes take a few seconds to adjust to the dim light. The low glow of the fire casts flickers amongst dark shadows and a single candle burns on the small table that sits in the centre of the main living space. She heads towards it and pulls out a small stool to sit down and take the weight off her feet. Leaning heavily on her staff for support, her attention is first drawn to the gentle bubbling of liquid in the cauldron and then to the pleasant aroma it releases.

"Ah, one of you has made tea. Good."

Wren peers further into the darkness. In front of her is the space reserved for sleeping within the house, where the floor seems covered with black cloaks that rise and fall with the bodies that breathe and move beneath them. A single figure begins to rise out of the group. Pushing herself up from the floor, she stretches cat-like, extending her arms and hands while arching her back before sitting upright on her knees. Even in the low light, her pale skin and long fiery red hair glow and shine. Clad in black like the others, but not with the same choice of cloak. Instead, she appears to be a warrior. Boots and breeches, a black tunic with leather armour for protection, and a short black hood. Around her neck she wears a silver pentagram which glints reflections of the fire's flames. She turns to Wren and yawns before breaking into a soft laugh.

"Have you been out all night, Morganna?" asks Wren.

"It's when I do my best work. I put the tea on before I rested. Should be nice and strong."

"The only way to drink tea," Wren cackles.

Morganna rises to her feet and carefully steps around her sleeping sisters to peer into the cauldron. An assortment of drinking vessels lies nearby. She selects the two that are the favourites for her and Wren and ladles some of the tea into each before bringing it to the table. Wren loads her pipe with a different mixture of herbs from before and once again pinches the bright red powder into a flame. She puffs to make sure that the mixture smoulders away and then draws in the smoke, instantly relaxing herself.

"Did you go up to the loch?" asks Morganna.

"Yes. I always go on feast days, you know that."

"I just wondered if you would make it to the top."

"The ghosts that walk with me lend me their strength."

"And what did —"

"I see? Well, Nimue for one. I can't stand her. Full of her own self-importance. You know

I cannot discuss everything I see, but I can tell you one thing of interest, apparently The Merlin is alive if not well, and now lives near us in Caledon Forest."

"*The* Merlin?"

"I thought that would get you interested."

"I could learn so much from the Merlin. His knowledge and power is legendary."

"As were his mistakes. Everyone knows the story of how he blew up his own army."

"Yes, but by drawing a shooting star out of the sky. It was still magic the rest of us can only dream of creating."

"You care little for the casualties of war, then?"

"If Merlin's spell had worked as he intended, they would talk of him like a god. These men would have engaged in a battle even if he hadn't been present. Death, for many of them, was inevitable. Will you ask Artos how many he has killed this year for the vanity of Duncan MacForres?"

Wren chews on the end of her pipe and silently nods in response to Morganna's point.

"I want to find him," says the young witch, "if he truly is in Caledon."

"Someone should find him," replies Wren.

Morganna knew full well that she was referring to Artos. He had always been the favoured child. The only man in a house full of women, the only non-witch in a house full of witches. She could never work out why Wren always put him first. Artos had never been taught about the old ways. Instead, he had shared in the experience of the other villagers, by learning to farm, working with goats and the sheep in the hills, and when he was ready, joining with the levy and training to fight with axe and sword, and spear.

A silence follows as they both sip their tea. Wren feels sadness for Morganna. She had worked hard to develop her talent as a true elemental witch. She was very skilled at forming ice and cooling the surrounding temperature. She could communicate with the beasts of the natural world, particularly those that were creatures of the night or clad in black, like her. She was older than Artos by three years and could easily move ahead in life without her younger sibling, but that wasn't the plan. Morganna's true destiny was woven into the same tapestry as her brother's. Wren detects a faint flicker in Morganna's eyes.

"Morganna, can you hear my thoughts? This is new."

"I don't hear so much yet. I just know what you are thinking. Is that magic? Or do I just know you too well. Just who is your favourite?"

Wren cackles some more before blowing out a plume of smoke. Morganna sits back from the table. The answer confirmed by the lack of response.

Gradually, in the background, the other witches are surfacing. Small conversations are breaking out around the room, accompanied by the groans and stretches of waking. The tea is being served out to all, and the atmosphere lifts as both Wren and Morganna engage with the general distractions around the house. Tea is another strong point of Morganna's skills, and all enjoy it more when they know she has made it. The compliments ease her feelings of not being the golden child.

As the chatter increases, Wren begins to feel unsettled. Something dangerous is coming. From behind her, she hears the faint rattling of the gate outside the house.

"Quiet," she orders as she spins around.

The other witches freeze on her command, before the door crashes open and Artos and Alan rush in, gasping for breath, and covered in blood, wearing clothes that obviously aren't theirs.

"Artos!" shrieks Wren as she rises to her feet, stamping her staff in front of them, "what's happened to you? How did you get in this state?"

Artos gulps down the smoky air infused with the clouds from Wren's pipe, causing him to choke. He clutches at the cramp in the side of his stomach and collapses to the floor, drenched in a cold sweat. Alan is no different. He slumps beside his friend, gesturing for something to drink.

Two of the witches pass their half-drunk cups of tea. Now colder, but easier to drink down fast.

"Artos," Wren repeats, "what's happened?"

"We're in trouble, big trouble. We had to protect Prince Eochaid of the Dal Riata who was going to be married to Duncanna MacForres and create an alliance that would see King Fergus supply ships to Lord Duncan MacForres, to invade Ynys Mon to capture the right to the Kingdom of Galwydell from King Arnall."

"Artos killed his son the day before," says Alan.

"I didn't kill him. He nearly killed me."

"Well, you know what I mean."

"Slow down. I don't know what any of you mean," says Wren, "close the door, get them up to the table. Morganna, fetch something calming. How did you end up in this mess?"

The witches crowd around the two young men and transport them to the stools beside the table. They replenish the fire with fresh wood, while more candles are lit. Morganna chooses two small pieces of dried mushroom from a small storage jar.

"Eat this," the young witch commands while conveying concern and annoyance at the same time.

Artos and Alan each take the calming

medicine on offer and chew furiously at it. It only takes a few seconds to work. Their breath starts to slow, along with their heart rate. Artos rubs his face with his hands and wipes sweat from his brow. Thirteen pairs of eyes meet his gaze, all staring back at him. Wren sits at the centre, appearing to look within his soul, or at least that's how it feels.

"Now. I'll ask you once more," Wren speaks calmly, "what has happened?"

"We messed up our orders. Duncan had set us a special task, to protect Prince Eochaid as we hunted the last men of Arnall's raiding party who were on the retreat."

"That was a foolish idea to make sport of desperate men on the run for home."

"It was Eochaid that suggested it."

"We took him to Mare's Tail," says Alan.

"To take in the view?"

"Duncan wanted him out of the way," continues Artos, "he wanted to keep him safe for the wedding. We thought Mare's Tail would distract him, keep him occupied while Duncan and his son searched in the other direction."

"Except it turned out that the men of Arnall weren't as far south as we supposed," says Alan, "it turned out they had gone to visit Mare's Tail as well, then stumbled on Eochaid and his men."

"They were old men too," says Artos, "they were no match against Arnall's raiders. They massacred them."

"So where were you two?" asks Morganna.

"We had wandered down the road to look for signs of Duncan returning." Artos replies.

"Duncan knew where you were brother? So now he likely knows that you deserted Eochaid?"

Suddenly Artos and Alan become more relaxed, sharing huge grins and pointing an index finger each into the air to show their good idea. A sense of self-satisfaction combining with the temporary high of Wren's calming medicine allows their fears to evaporate.

"Ah, we faked our own deaths," says Artos, "swapping clothes with two of Arnall's men and then chopping them apart until they were unrecognisable."

"We carried the heads with us for a bit," says Alan, "threw them away when we thought it was safe to do so."

"Is there a chance that they killed Duncan and his party during their escape?" asks Morganna.

Artos and Alan shake their heads and look at one another as the fear returns once again.

"We were still close by when we heard a voice screaming through the woods," says Artos, "it sounded like Duncan, though we can't be sure."

"It was Duncan alright," confirms Wren, "I glimpsed a time to come when I was at Modron's Water. It was Duncan and his son. I'm sure they were riding for Hartriggs with a party of horsemen, their priest, and a wagon."

"Then we'll need to leave before they get here," says Artos, "we can't risk everyone else getting caught up in this. We're going to head for Camulodunum."

"You are heading for nowhere until we know more. I must speak with Duncan before I decide what will happen next. Did anyone pass you on the way in here?"

"No," says Artos, "we kept out of sight."

"Well, something at least. Now get out of those clothes and clean yourselves. If you head to Camulodunum, you'll end up a beggar on the streets, for that's what you look like right now. Morganna, make sure they stay out of any more trouble. None of the other villagers must know they're here. I trust that the secrets of this house stay amongst all of us?"

"Yes Wren," say the other witches.

"Then I must organise a reception for our guests. I'm sure they will visit us today."

TRIBUTE

If the temperature is low in Hartriggs, it's positively balmy compared to the frostiness that has descended in the private chambers of Duncan MacForres. He sits scowling at his son, his servant, and even his breakfast, with only constant refills of wine seeming to ease his mood.

In a corner of the room, a pile of sacks holds three of the victims from yesterday's defeat at Mare's Tail. Prince Eochaid is in one sack, as his status demanded. It was anybody's guess which body parts belonged to who, in the other two sacks, though the assumption was Artos and Alan. The heads were missing and there was maybe an extra hand or leg scooped up with the flesh, but it was basically them.

"Can I have that, if you're not eating it?" asks MacDuncan as he finishes clearing his own plate.

Duncan responds by throwing the food to

his two deerhounds.

"Help yourself."

An uneasy silence falls. MacDuncan goes to say something but stops himself. The tension builds and he summons his courage to confront his father.

"So, what do we do now?"

The rage is building in Duncan. His normal pale complexion passes through different shades of red, his blood is boiling, and even by his own standards, he looks angry and ready to explode.

"What do we do now? What do we do now?" Duncan gives space for MacDuncan to reply, but that's never going to happen, "if there's one thing I hate, it's failure."

An awkward silence falls again, this time broken by MacDuncan pushing a piece of bread around his plate with a knife. The small screeches of metal on metal only aggravates his father's mood even further.

"What a mess," continues Duncan, "weddings are more trouble than they're worth. Picking the date, who to invite, booking the minstrels, where to seat our most detested guests at the feast. Just when you get it all worked out, the groom goes and gets himself killed in a minor skirmish."

"My good sister is inconsolable this morning."

"Duncanna's upset? I'm upset. No marriage,

no ships, no invasion and now King Fergus will demand tribute from us to compensate for his loss. I'll show you inconsolable!"

MacDuncan looks up from his cup of mead. It's obvious that he's had an idea. A series of uncomfortable facial contortions follow as his brain wrestles with the threat of immediate death for speaking out of turn. Instead, he goes back to screeching his knife against the plate. Duncan sighs and his shoulders drop.

"Alright, tell me what your idea is."

"We lie about what happened."

"Oh, you mean don't tell the truth. Oh, well, I never thought of that. Of course we won't tell him the truth, but it's still going to cost me. The one piece of good fortune I have left is that all Eochaid's company died with him."

MacDuncan is undaunted. "Yes, but it's how we tell him. Get our bard to compose an epic. They're all the rage in courts up and down the land, and the Dal Riata are famed for their love of poetry and art."

"Go on," says Duncan.

"The epic will retell how the bravest of his sons met a heroic death in combat, smiting a hundred men of Arnall's warband. He'll get angry with Arnall, not us."

"Maybe we could add a verse in about my generosity to his men while they dined in my halls."

"We can say your mead is plentiful, faither."

"Yes, my mead is plentiful. I like that."

"Then," says MacDuncan, "we make sure the bard keeps repeating the lie."

"The epic," corrects Duncan.

"Yes, he'll repeat the epic everywhere he goes. Once people have heard it a few times, then it becomes fact and in years ahead, it will become history. I wager that Fergus will send us the ships then, just to have his own epic written."

Silence falls within the room, then the smallest gasp of air squeaks from Duncan's rear-end.

"Change the one hundred to three hundred. That's a better number for an epic. Bring me Ifan Gofannon."

"Yes, faither! I'll summon the bard."

MacDuncan promptly leaves through the curtain.

Duncan relaxes back in his seat. His relief is short-lived as his daughter bursts through into the room.

"I hate you!" says Duncanna, "you always ruin my dreams. My life is over and it's your stupid fault. Most of my friends are getting married. I'll be seventeen next year. Call yourself a father? Even Isabel Face-like-an-axe of Dunfaurlin is becoming a Queen. Do you despise me so much?"

Duncan conjures up his best soft and loving tone. "Your brother and I have worked things out. Give me time, you will still be Queen of the Isles, I promise."

"And how, pray, do we do that? If you're thinking of pairing me off with any of his brothers, forget it. The oldest one is five feet tall."

"There's nothing wrong with that."

"Yes, but he's five feet wide as well. Son number two spends his day talking to the flowers in his garden and he stinks of herring! None of them are Eochaid, my true love, my one and only, fiercest of warriors, gentlest of lovers, my broken heart," she pauses, "where is my love's body that I might grieve till this year is out?"

"The sack on the left there," says a perplexed Duncan.

"What's in the other sacks?"

"The bodies of the men who died fighting alongside him," Duncan knows what is coming, "tradition states that we return the levy men who have fallen in battle in the service of me, their lord."

"Tradition! Honestly?"

She reaches into the sack and pulls out a lower leg with foot and boot still attached and casts it toward one of Duncan's dogs. The other stands waiting on its treat as she rummages in the sack again, pulling out another lower leg, foot, and boot, but from a different person. Throwing it to the second dog, she storms back out as fast as she came in, scattering servants and breakfast on the floor as she goes. The servants pick themselves up and collect the spilled food. As they go to take it away on a serving plate, Duncan stops them.

"Just bring that over here. I'll eat it, I'm famished, and bring me more wine."

The servant returns the plate of mashed up food to the table. Duncan lifts a piece of bread and brushes the dirt from it before popping it in his mouth. More wine is then served, and Duncan feels better.

The curtain parts again, and a stylishly dressed man follows behind MacDuncan. He is one of the few in the MacForres court who doesn't wear black. His moustache and beard are in a fashionable form, and his girth is evidence of a long history of entertaining at feasts. Something of a celebrity, who many compare to the great Taliesin, or at least he says they do.

"Ifan Gofannon," says MacDuncan as he ushers the bard through to stand before his father.

"My lord. I understand I may be of service to you."

Ifan bows low in his most theatrical style.

"Yes. A perfect job for a man of your talents. I need you to write a heroic composition. To be dedicated to Prince Eochaid and his legendary battle against the three hundred warriors of

Arnall? No, make it four hundred. Everybody says three hundred in these things."

"An epic, my lord. It will not be my first, but its content may be challenging. We did not widely know Prince Eochaid for his bravery and skill on the battlefield."

"Just include a part about how his love for my daughter inspired him to take up the sword against our enemies."

"I suppose that might work," says Ifan, thinking out loud, "my descriptions of the comely Duncanna have found favour before now. It may distract King Fergus from the less believable parts of the story."

"And mention that my mead is plentiful."

"Indeed, that is standard fare in all epics. It is the fuel of all heroic conquests is it not?"

"Fine. Name your price Gofannon. I acknowledge you will have fees for this kind of work."

"There is indeed great fakery in this verse, my lord. To insure me from the risk of tarnishing my professional reputation, I will need to ask for one hundred gold coins."

"If you dare. Thirty pieces of silver, take it or leave it."

"Why, my lord, it's not just the composition. I presume you ask that I deliver the first rendition of the verses in person to King Fergus. That is not without a certain personal risk on my behalf, should King Fergus wish to take his sword and run-through the messenger."

"Fair enough. Thirty gold for a successful result, but only if I still get his ships."

"Thirty gold was the price I had in mind, my lord. You suffer from no lack of wisdom."

"Indeed. You may leave."

"My lord." Ifan performs another flamboyant bow before turning and exiting the chamber.

"Will there be anything else, faither?" asks MacDuncan.

"Organise some men and tell the priest to join us. We must raise tribute to send with Ifan to the Dal Riata and it will fall to Hartriggs to pay that debt."

The journey from Dun Romanach to Hartriggs stretches for over ten miles. Duncan takes in the view as he and his men pass through a long valley which runs beside a river rushing down from hills that stretch out before them. It is empty and exposed after many years of land clearance during the Roman occupation. Only a few dwellings mark out places where small farms exist. Duncan notes their location for future tax raising purposes.

His son leads the other riders at the front

of the procession, then horses pull a wagon that carries four lightly armed footmen and two sacks of body parts. Duncan and Father Andrew are riding together some distance further back, out of earshot of the others.

"You describe this as God's land, Father Andrew?"

"Indeed. All land is God's land," says Andrew. "you are his custodian, his servant. He charges you with taking care of it. He created it in the beginning."

"And you say that God sees all?"

"God is around and within everything. There is nowhere to hide from the Lord, my lord."

Duncan spends some time looking around himself, not totally sure what he's expecting to see.

"You know, Andrew, this journey it's made me think about a few things that, frankly, I had quite forgotten. Maybe I should converse with God before we get to Hartriggs."

"You wish to confess something, my lord?"

"Yes, I suppose I do."

"Of course, my lord, you may speak your truth. We are distant enough to consider ourselves alone."

The prospect thrills Andrew. Confession from his patron is worth more than a thousand tales of debauchery from the village locals.

"Alright, well, let me see," continues

Duncan, "I once had a good friend. He had a child out of wedlock."

"That is indeed a sin. Did you order that he prostrate himself before his bishop?"

"No. Should I have? He asked me to help with the delicate matter that had led to the premature death of the mother's husband. It embarrassed him in social circles. So, he asked if I could foster the child. Raise him as a family noble. In return, he offered me a regular tribute of gold to fund the child's wellbeing."

"MacDuncan is illegitimate?"

"Maybe, but he's not the child in my tale. I agreed, of course. His terms were very generous. I brought the baby back to Galwydell. but it was poor timing. My wife had just left me and her children. The MacForres estates were expanding out from Dun Romanach. There were people to threaten and oppress. I was just too busy to look after someone else's child. So, I left him with an old midwife."

"Yes, my lord. So let me get this straight. You aided a man driven mad by lust. You carried off his damned-to-hell child. Then you rid yourself of this produce of sinful loins to a randomly selected old woman?"

"Well, you say woman. A witch is a better description."

"Carry on," says Andrew as if totalling the arithmetical value of the unacceptable behaviour.

"Well, I considered his wellbeing. I agreed to a financial settlement, to be paid each year on the same day I received payment from my friend. I admit it was a much smaller value than I was due to receive, but I considered it proportionate with my distant oversight of the child, thus allowing him to grow to full health and strength."

"Yes, yes, I understand that bit."

"Then I suppose I just forgot him. I didn't send any money, I didn't visit, and now he's dead." A solemn pause for thought follows.

"I see. So first are the lustful spoils, the unblessed offspring, the witch. Then there was maybe oath breaking?"

"Yes, I swore an oath, eh, before God as my witness."

"The inappropriate handling of a financial agreement, negligence in the upbringing of a child under God's law, even though he was born out of wedlock, and his ultimate death before reclaiming his father's land, which may add a curse to your fate?

"I suppose so," says Duncan.

Andrew smiles. "Don't worry yourself. It's all fine!"

"Do I not have to flog myself?" says Duncan with surprise, "or climb a mountain with boots full of stones and sharpened metal? Or at least wear sackcloth and ashes?"

"No, don't bother with that nonsense.

That's just for the poor. You're one of the richest men for many a mile and we will dissolve your sins when you leave behind your worldly goods. To the church, of course."

"Of course. Then that's it?"

"That's it. If you wish to offer a token of repentance, then only eat fish next Friday."

"Fish, you say? Oh well, then splendid! Well done! Blessed be, Father Andrew, blessed be."

"We say *praise be* my lord, it's the heathen unbelievers and the witches that say blessed be."

"Well, it's the same thing, isn't it?"

Duncan happily urges his horse into a canter, now released from any further moral obligations. Andrew stays back, deep in thought, and murmurs to himself.

"Land acquisition. There's nothing better than an ecclesiastical property agreement to boost one's status amongst the clergy."

Duncan rides alongside his son as the party begins the final hill climb that leads to Hartriggs. The roof of its large roundhouse is visible on the horizon, and all present detect an atmosphere of mild threat. Strange charms hang from gnarled branches. Villagers have positioned goat skulls on top of rocks almost like lookouts. There's a stillness in the air that seems to increase your sense of foreboding. Goosebumps appear, hair seems to stand on end, and from the rear, Father Andrew is uttering statements in Latin that are clearly concerned with evil spirits.

"Let's get this over with as swiftly as we can," says Duncan, "this place is stuck in the dark ages."

"We can do a bit of taunting though?" asks MacDuncan, "the boys won't be happy if they've come all this way and there's no intimidation."

"Very well but leave Wren Morcant to me."

"The old witch? Should we not get rid of her?"

"Not yet. Not today. Now ride on before me. Kick over a few things, round up the locals and let them know I'm here."

"Yes faither."

MacDuncan waves the other riders to follow. The horses move into a brief gallop, announcing their arrival as they race the final yards to the centre of the village. In a well-drilled manoeuvre, they spread out and immediately encircle the villagers, goading them into a tight group outside of the big house. Rearing horses and jeers from Duncan's horsemen rapidly impose authority.

The wagon follows and the four levy men jump off for even tighter crowd control, pushing the crowd back and holding them behind the shafts of their spears. They punish any insolence by handing out random acts of violence to subdue any thought of retaliation.

"Silence," MacDuncan raises a hand before the villagers to call for quiet, "and pay respects to your maister. Lord Duncan MacForres."

The crowd obey the command, standing still with heads only slightly bowed. Duncan and Andrew ride in together, not disguising their disgust at having to enter the impoverished living space that the villagers endure daily.

Wee Laddie's preparations lie out before them. A meagre fire burns outside, fuelled by damp wood and dung. Over the flames hangs a cooking pot filled with a mixture of foul looking water and solid uncut vegetables including cabbage, turnip and small purple carrots, swimming in a brown unpalatable stock made of more dung. He's littered a final sprinkling of dung on the ground and around the entrances to the buildings.

"You're lucky it's nearly Christmas," says MacDuncan, "I'm in good and fair mood today, but that could change. You find yourself in the company of Lord Duncan MacForres. Now bow to your benevolent maister."

The assembled villagers bow lower towards Duncan, muttering various noises that might express delight or disrespect. Duncan looks on, accepting the enforced grovelling, but still being offended and disgusted at the filthy rabble who have the audacity to live and work on his lands.

"Fine, fine," says Duncan as he waves the crowd into silence, "where is the witch that runs this place?"

The crowd divides, and Wren walks to the front. She is a powerful master of magic and although her body is older and frailer these days, her presence remains strong and threatening. Father Andrew crosses himself from the relative safety of the elevated position on his horse.

Wren smiles with her best toothless grin. With a quick circular motion of the top of her staff, she causes Andrew's horse to turn around and face the wrong direction. The villagers share a laugh at his predicament, before he carefully rotates himself to face both the crowd and the horse's tail.

"You know we don't follow the ways of his God. Why bring him here?" says Wren.

"Why I brought him as an honour to you," replies Duncan, "to bury these sons of Hartriggs and give them hope of salvation."

Duncan gives a signal to the wagon driver, who promptly throws two sacks on to the ground. The footmen allow a gap for Wren to walk through, while MacDuncan leaps from his horse to take the old witch by the arm and lead her to the corpses.

She prods at pieces of flesh with her staff, lifts a loose limb up for closer inspection. She smells it and licks the torn skin before biting a piece. She chews it and completes her post-mortem of the victim. Duncan does his best to hold on to the contents of his own stomach.

"I believe these are your people, Artos and Alan. Victims of a surprise attack. They defended Prince Eochaid of the Dal Riata in a fight to the death. Alas, the young Prince fell in battle. I imagine the sons of your village will have put up a brave if unsuccessful defence."

Wren spits out the small, masticated ball of skin and uses her staff to sort through the remaining contents of the sacks.

"There are no heads."

"Sad but true," says Duncan, "we can only return what the wolves leave untouched."

The old witch stoops to pick up a severed hand. She wipes a tear from her eye as she points the index finger of the body part towards Duncan.

"She's cursing you, my lord!" says Andrew.

"The gods will judge who caused their deaths," says Wren, "they will demand retribution."

Duncan falters under the witch's warning. He knows the eyes of Hartriggs are on him.

"Then may the men of Ynys Mon find their judgement day ahead of them, for they are responsible. Let it be known that I have fulfilled my part and returned the bodies of your dead for burial. I have paid my debt to your people under the laws and traditions of our land, but now I turn to the slight matter of the debt you owe King Fergus. MacDuncan see if you can find anything of value."

MacDuncan draws the large dagger from his belt and grips Wren by the shoulder, pushing her into the crowd.

"Good people of Hartriggs!" he begins, "it pains me to inform you that Artos and Alan were failures and imposters. They made you believe they could bring honour to the hovel you call home by joining the service of our levy, but it gives me no joy," he punctuates with a snigger, "to let you know that their incompetence has brought great dishonour and misfortune to the MacForres name. Under their watch, our enemies killed a prince of the Dal Riata in battle. While he was fighting bravely for our side."

"Oh, get to the point, son." Duncan just wants home.

"Aye faither, eh my lord," MacDuncan bows to his father before returning his attention to the crowd, "we must send tribute back to Alt Clut with the body of the prince. It falls to you to offer that tribute. Riders dismount!"

Pillaging was an essential part of war. The battle-hardened horsemen need no further instruction to carry on relieving Hartriggs of the few possessions it has. Within seconds, buildings are being checked and stores are being raided. There is nothing of any real material value, but a barrel of home brewed mead, a couple of goats, and various items of food preserved for the winter which make it on to the cart. They take a few items of pottery while destroying the rest. Throughout the process, Wren keeps her anger firmly fixed on Duncan and he can feel it.

Duncan does his best to return the stare, but he knows it's pointless. There is nothing in Hartriggs that will appease someone of the stature of King Fergus. He looks to his right where Father Andrew has spent the entire time just trying to get his horse and himself pointing in the same direction. To his left, the other riders are obviously discussing the poor level of seized goods with the cart driver, and in front of him, MacDuncan is among the levy men, handing out slaps and punches to anyone he fancies hitting. Further winding up, the very person who can doubtless take them all out with a lightning bolt. It's a complete waste of time, but then he notices the building that lies further on, separate from the rest. He recognises it from many years ago.

"Search the witch's house," he commands, while trying his best to sneer at Wren.

"Wait," calls Wren, "you cannot enter a

witch's house uninvited. Think of the curses that will befall those of your men who cross the threshold, not to mention their families."

Everyone stops in their tracks. This was a time for decisions from the top. Hartriggs had a well-established reputation for ghosts, demons, and parties with the devil in attendance. Wren's warnings are not to be treated lightly. All await Duncan's response.

"I can leave this place with something worth selling or I can burn it to the ground. Do you have anything of value that you would trade for the opportunity of saving your villager's miserable lives?"

Wren looks downcast and says nothing in return.

"Search the witch's house."

The riders push and shove each other until one of them is forced to volunteer for the duty. A hush falls upon the scene as he nervously steps forward. Looking back over his shoulder, his comrades wave him onwards.

Duncan keeps half an eye on Wren, while waiting to see just what will happen to the man as he reaches her house.

The rider is trying his best not to look too scared but is failing miserably. The worrying prospect of curses is that they follow you home. You might not die right away, but later in a nightmarish showdown with a monster, or an unfortunate accident with something sharp and dangerous, drowning, or burning. All options prey on his mind as he pushes through the gate. The threaded shells rattle and the heavy door opens before him. A procession of black cloaked women emerge, and march in line towards the village centre.

"Now we're talking," calls out MacDuncan.

Eleven witches have walked out and as the rider starts to make for the door once more, a final figure appears. Morganna smiles mischievously before pulling the rider's hood over his face and spinning him around in a circle. As he uncovers himself, he spies a beautiful maiden with flowing red hair walk away in front of him. He conveniently forgets the rest of his instructions before following her.

"Line them up for inspection," MacDuncan barks his command and leers with a lascivious smile.

"Choose something suitable," says Duncan.

"Remove your hoods for your maister."

None of the witches respond, standing motionless and defiant. Stifled laughs from one or two of the villagers embarrass the young MacForres. An open display of public disobedience. In response, he raises his dagger and strides over to Wren. Grabbing her arm, he pulls her into the blade.

"Maybe you'll hear me better from here!"

The villagers are at breaking point. Their

shouts become a clamour as they push against the spears of the levy men, now struggling to control them.

"Silence!" says MacDuncan, "now ladies, I suggest you uncover your heads before she loses hers."

Duncan quietly sighs with frustration and looks skyward as his son forgets his warning to let him handle the old witch. He senses another catastrophe approaching, just like the preceding day.

The witches drag back their hoods and MacDuncan scans along the line; one has the eyes of a serpent, while another smiles back with the sharp fangs of a vampire, two of them have the sharpened ears of folk from the faerie worlds, three covered in painted markings, while four display the scars of battle across their faces.

MacDuncan's wandering eyes settle on the last witch. The hair that curls around her shoulders and back is irresistible to him. Her lips are full and stained red, her skin is pale, and her eyes are blue. Yet Morganna has a terrifying presence. She stands out in a crowd.

"You girl! Tell me your name."

"Morganna is how I am known here."

"Then Morganna you will have the honour of becoming our gift to King Fergus."

He gestures to her with his index figure to walk towards him, and a tension builds amongst the locals. They know Morganna's talents. This will not end well for MacDuncan.

With each slow step she takes, he weakens under her relentless stare. Without thinking, he lets go of Wren and places the long dagger back in its scabbard. As Morganna's long flowing hair moves, twists, and intertwines with a life of its own, he is falling under her spell.

Morganna's presence has a paralysing effect on MacDuncan. His chest and arms become heavy, his breath grows shorter and more rapid, he sweats and shakes from a fast-rising temperature.

"Have you ever heard the expression," asks Morganna, "if looks could kill?"

Duncan has had enough. He casts a perplexed expression towards Wren, who calls out to her young apprentice.

"Morganna, behave yourself, girl."

Wren returns Duncan's gaze; they silently agree a truce.

MacDuncan clutches at his heart and gasps for air. He staggers backwards to be held up by two of his men.

"Give her to the priest," he says, "he knows how to handle the ones that are possessed by the devil."

"And how do you suggest we do that right now?"

Duncan points towards Father Andrew,

who is riding off at speed, screaming and crying as he goes.

MacDuncan turns for support from the rest of the men, but they are eager to leave. The driver of the wagon sets his own horses in motion, forcing the levy men to retreat and climb aboard.

"Get back on your horse's," Duncan orders, before addressing Wren directly, "time to return to normality. though I may need to wash for the first time this year. Back to Dun Romanach."

The party leaves the village and as they ride out of sight, Wee Laddie asks the inevitable question.

"Did anybody piss in the mead?"

Several cries of *I did!* are called out by the assembled villagers, while a dog barks in agreement.

RESURRECTION

"Can you see anything?" asks Alan as he searches through a pile of jars for more of the calming dried mushroom.

"I think they're leaving. It's hard to see from a crack in the door," replies Artos.

"You could go out to the gate," Alan smiles with a sense of triumph as he discovers the treat he was searching for, "they won't see you from there."

"No thanks. I think it's best we keep on the right side of Wren for now, and she said keep out of sight."

Artos returns to sit at the table, where Alan has scattered some mushrooms out for them to share.

"I don't know how much of this we should take," says Artos.

"It's just medicine," insists his friend, "it makes you feel better."

All goes quiet for a while. The two friends

absent-mindedly nibble on the mushrooms. The medicine calms you down. In fact, the stresses and strains of the last couple of days are suddenly lifting from their shoulders and transforming into a slight euphoria. Artos looks over at Alan, who seems to be lost in another world and staring into space. He feels himself wanting to snigger, but tries desperately to keep his silence. Even if for no other reason than to see how long Alan will stay motionless with the same vacant expression. Alan's eyes drop and focus back on Artos, causing the pair of them to burst into uncontrollable laughter. The hilarity intensifies, yet they stay conscious that they shouldn't be making a sound. Attempts to stifle the noise only make it worse. Tears flow from their eyes as they clutch their sides, now cramping in pain. They both slip from their stools on to the floor. Still unable to bring the laughter under control. They punch the floor and roll around the house. Just at the point that they begin to slow down and breath, Alan lets loose an enormous blast from his backside. Filling the room with a putrid stench. The noise and the smell create a climax to the fun, just as the heavy wooden door of the house bursts open.

The world seems to spin around Artos, as many hands lift him from the floor. He becomes encircled by black cloaks, disorientating him amongst what sounds like an angry rabble. Further away he can hear Alan protest and what sounds like furniture falling to the ground. Then the hands let him go. He is back on the stool and the black cloaks move away to show the angry, scowling face of Wren and a silver blade prodding at his throat.

"Put the knife away, Morganna," says Wren, "although a scar may give a good reminder for the years to come."

"Just say the word." Morganna flicks the weapon away.

"I see what you were trying to do," says Wren, "and so far, I have to say that it's worked."

The mood becomes less tense because of everyone's surprise at Wren's reaction.

"Duncan had to think they killed us," says Artos.

"And you were right. He would have burned the entire village down if he thought you were hiding here. You used your brain for once."

"I thought of it too," says Alan.

"I very much doubt that. You're not known for thinking from anywhere much above your waist."

Wren can't help a brief smile as the humour circulates around the room, but she returns to a more serious mood.

"You know I am not your mother, but I made a promise to raise you and look after you, until you could make your way into the destiny that awaits. We almost didn't make it, did we?"

The room is silent. Twelve witches and two young men hanging on for Wren's next words of wisdom.

"The problem is that you're dead and for what I see ahead, Artos, you must stay very much alive."

"We'll get away when it's dark. We won't return. We can head south. There's a place I've heard of —"

"Camulodunum?" Wren raises an eyebrow, "they say the lights go out when you get there. It's not your fate."

"So, what is my fate?"

Wren shrugs and reaches into her bag for her pipe and herb mix. Alan opens his mouth to ask a question, but with one raised finger, Wren silences him. She carefully loads and ignites her pipe. After what seems like an age and several thick clouds of exhaled smoke, she gives her response.

"I can't tell you everything. Too much and never enough is all I ever see, and how great your future may become can always fail if you stray too far from the path."

"Path?"

"The gods have a plan for you. I only know that my part was to take care of you until you were ready. We may be there sooner than I thought. Yet they give me one last task. To put you in a grave and bury you."

"What?" Artos feels his heart jump. The calming mushrooms have stopped doing their work.

"Duncan has left two sacks of someone out there and the entire village thinks that it's you," she responds, "they are digging the holes to put you in right now, and I'll soon be called to say a few words for two fine sons of Hartriggs. I'll need to make it all up, of course."

"Of course?" says Artos, "we'll still have to leave. We can't stay here anymore."

"All I have seen is that you will return to Hartriggs. Stronger, wiser, and maybe at the head of an army."

Everyone gasps at the revelation.

Outside, the shells rattle around the gate and the voice of Wee Laddie calls from the other side of the door.

"Wren, we're ready for you at the burial."

"I'll be there in a moment," she calls out.

"Wait, what do you mean, an army?"

"Later," replies Wren firmly, "Before I must work out how to bring you back to life, I need to commit your souls to the underworld. Now stay quiet and keep away from the mushrooms. I only want to bury you once today."

Wren rises to her feet and turns to leave with the other witches. Morganna finds the time to direct a last threatening look before she leaves, closing the door with a strong thud.

"Army. I'm to lead an army? How could she just walk out after telling me something like that?"

"She said maybe," says Alan.

"Alright, so maybe I'll lead an army. She didn't say maybe I'll be growing cabbages. You heard her the same as me."

An awkward silence descends.

Maybe my visions are about me becoming a great leader.

"What will she be saying about us?" says Artos.

"We could listen," replies Alan as he points over to two unused black cloaks piled in a corner.

"She'll lose her temper if we get caught."

"Better not get caught then," smirks Alan.

The people of Hartriggs stand assembled around two open graves in amongst a small copse of trees that lie to the east of the village. Families stand in small groups, comforting one another. Life can be harsh and short in the villages, but it doesn't make the loss any easier. Morganna does her best to comfort Alan's mother.

Wren seems to keep a quiet dignity even though she has apparently lost a child. In reality, she is now counting the number of sisters of her coven. There appear to be two more than usual. She breathes a deep sigh of frustration as Wee Laddie begins the ceremony.

"Friends, family, fathers, mothers, brothers, sisters, and grandparents. We're gathered to celebrate the life of Artos and Alan. Two of the finest boys to have hailed from our village. Hard workers, good with the sheep, and never ate more than their share. They stepped up to fight for the levy and to serve the Maister MacForres." A grumble circles the crowd, "oh, none of us like him, but they did what we expected for those who live within the hills of Galwydell. We can be proud to have called them family and neighbours."

Artos and Alan nod to one another from their place, standing at the back of the cloaked coven.

"That was very nice," whispers Artos.

"I'm sure we have many fine stories we can share later this evening at our solstice feast," continues Wee Laddie, "but we've got a bit of a mess to fix in the big house, redecorate, dig up the good food that's buried, and bring out the barrels that Duncan's henchmen didn't spot."

The crowd cheers and laughs.

"So I'll hand over to Wren to say a few words. If somebody can do the covering up at the end, that would be a help. I feel as if I've been digging all day."

Artos and Alan share a marginally more disappointed response. As Wren moves to stand in front of the crowd.

"Friends. It is with great sorrow that we gather here today. What could I add to Wee Laddie's fine words of tribute? I cannot speak for Alan so much, although he was always hanging around Artos, like a wee dog you might say."

The crowd and even Alan's mother allow themselves a quick laugh. Artos smiles at his friend.

"Although you do not know of any grandchildren, Agnes. I'm sure it's only a matter of time until the mothers of Galwydell will appear to hand them over to your care."

"Aye, and I'll take them in," says Agnes defiantly.

"And as for Artos. Well, he always thought he was a wee bit better than everyone else. He had ideas of grandeur. People would tell me he spoke properly and sounded very educated. I'll admit he never liked the nickname of Wee Bastard, but we were all just being affectionate, weren't we?"

The crowd laughs once more, with various voices repeating the call of *Wee Bastard*.

Something seems to rustle in the branches high above them. The villagers react as if Artos has heard them speak. They exchange nervous glances about annoying his spirit. Wren casts an eye above her, but nothing seems out of the ordinary, so she continues in the full knowledge of just exactly where Artos is.

"He had such a short life for me to have many good things to say. He was always handy with an axe, whether it was chopping logs for the fire or chopping heads for Duncan. He had a real talent there, but he could be very annoying and ungrateful as well."

The laughs of the crowd continue. Alan nods at Artos.

"He was always getting in the way around the house. He was terrible at making soup, and he always had problems with his big sister. He never saw the funny side if she filled his bed with spiders. Is that right Morganna?"

"Aye, that's right. He would scream like a baby."

Artos is biting his lip with all his might. He knows that Wren knows he's there, and she's going to make him suffer. Alan grins widely in his direction, to annoy him even more.

"So that's it. He might have had a good life with a beautiful wife and children. He might even have made his dreams come true, but now we'll never know. He's dead."

Wren nods to Wee Laddie. The ceremony is complete. As the crowd departs, she casts a smug smile toward Artos, as once more, his sisters direct his movement in amongst a mass of cloaks and cowls that encircle him.

Home and uncloaked, Artos paces the floor. A brief and further humiliation endured by the coven's response to Wren's eulogy has passed, but there's more pressing thoughts on his mind.

What is this army? What does she mean?

He doesn't have long to wait as the old witch enters the house with a wicked smile on her face.

"Did you enjoy that, Artos?"

Artos bites his lip once more. He knows he deserves the ridicule, but now he'll always wonder if Wren would have said anything different if he hadn't been there.

"Ladies, go down to the big house. There's plenty to do to get the place ready for tonight. Morganna dear, you stay with us. We have matters to discuss. Some tea, please."

"Yes Wren," says Morganna, "for everyone?"

"Yes, the boys will need some sustenance too. There's heavy work to be done tonight."

Artos took his place at the table beside Alan, while Wren went through her smoking rituals.

"The army?" says Artos.

"Not just now, Artos," replies Wren. "I will speak with you about it. Like I've said to many who have walked through that door looking for a brighter future. I will tell you what I see in private. It is up to you who you tell beyond that. We will speak before you leave."

"So, we are leaving then?"

"Without a doubt. It seals your fate when you move from one life to the next.

"I'm not dead."

"No? Right now, you are very much dead and no longer able to live anywhere that Duncan MacForres may get to learn of your survival. You will spend one more night in Hartriggs. Tomorrow, your future is what you make of it. I can only point you in what I feel is the right direction. Another will take over from me."

"Another?"

"The Merlin."

A beaker drops and smashes on the floor behind them.

"Sorry," says Morganna.

"The Merlin?" echoes Alan. "I thought he had disappeared. He went mad after the thing with the meteor."

"Well, yes, he was in a bit of a mood. I confess I thought him lost to us as well, but according to Nimue, he is living within Caledon Forest."

"Does he know about me?" says Artos.

"Maybe, but not in a *Hello Artos* way. More of a something is coming way. I've said too much already."

"Yes, and not quite enough," replies Artos.

Wren smiles at her own saying, being turned on her.

"Tonight, we must resurrect you. Tomorrow, you will take your first steps into your new life."

"You'll resurrect us?"

"It's solstice. I'm a witch. I'm going to raise the dead, of course, and that starts with you and Alan digging up the remains of the poor souls we put under the ground earlier."

Smoke spirals upward from the burning log that provides light and heat in the large house. It carries the aromas of the celebration out and over to where Artos and Alan are hard at work, re-opening the freshly dug pits. The muddy earth is easy to shift, but it's dirty and uncomfortable work.

Morganna has disappeared. Something that isn't lost on the others as they stand knee deep in the soft clay, often referred to as *the glaur*.

"Where is she? I might have known she'd avoid the hard work," says Alan.

"She won't want to draw attention," says Artos.

After minutes of furious digging, they

reach the contents contained within the pits. No effort to re-imagine the bodies has taken place. The stench is awful and the various organs and limbs that are still intact are coated in a muddy slime. Much of the ooze has transferred to Artos and Alan's clothes by the time they finish emptying the graves.

"Right, that's it! Where is she?" says Artos, "Morganna, are you out there? Where are you?"

The young witch steps out from the darkness.

"I've been in the shadows, listening to you, but despite your insulting tone, my friends will still help you."

"Your friends?" asks Artos.

Morganna raises her hand, and six of the largest and angriest snarling wolves run out into the clearing.

"Don't worry," she assures, "they won't bite the hand that feeds them," her voice changes to the soft tones of an adoring pet lover, "dinner time."

Artos and Alan are astounded. Within a few short moments, the wolves have devoured the flesh, stolen the bones, and ran into the deep woods for a howl.

"Easy," says Morganna.

She extends a hand towards Artos to help him out of the grave, but on seeing the state of his clothes, she thinks better of it and draws back.

"Come on, you two, we're missing a good feast."

Artos and Alan struggle out of the holes, duly covering themselves in more mud. Only their eyes and mouths are visible as they look down at themselves and one another.

"Well, we certainly look like we've climbed out a grave," says Artos, "Wren will have planned for this."

"Aye, and there goes our chances of kissing someone under the mistletoe," Alan moans.

The three walk together for the short distance up to the large house. The entire village is inside, and it sounds like the party is in full swing. Sounds of drum beats and laughter ring out above noisy conversations.

"I thought it would have been a bit more solemn this year." complains Artos.

"More mead for everyone else," says Morganna cheerily, "you two wait here. When Wren is ready and everything's set, she'll raise a mist. As soon as the clouds start to leak outside, then you can enter. Do as you're told this time."

Morganna parts with a threatening glare that emphasises the danger of disobedience, and as she walks through the door, a welcoming chorus goes up from the crowd.

Artos and Alan both sigh as they remain outside in the darkness. Cold, dirty, and not drinking with everyone else.

For the first hour, the two friends try to stay upbeat and jovial as they await their big entrance. They keep themselves amused with the normal conversation topics; drinking, fighting, girls, plus a few sheep jokes for good measure.

The second hour passes without the smallest wisp of mist appearing through the door. The night temperature is decreasing and to stay warm, they move on to more active entertainment. At first, it's just arm wrestling, before escalating to rock throwing. Points are awarded for accuracy and pain inflicted. By the time they reach end of hour three, they have fully assumed the form of dead men walking.

The roundhouse is a solid construction but has gaps and cracks to peer through and listen. It doesn't help Artos' mood to witness the rest of the village having a great time. He can catch an odd fleeting glimpse of Morganna as she moves around the crowd, giving everyone a welcome hug and a strange pat on the nape of the neck. It's unusual for Morganna, who is unknown for being overly tactile or even that sociable, but she seems to be happy to take her time to talk to everybody tonight.

She's up to something.

From a different crack in the wall, Artos can see Wren, but she hasn't moved from her seat. Happy to be served by the others with her share of the food and drink, the elders keep her in conversation. The only mist she is raising is from the clouds of smoke in her pipe.

"I think I *am* dying now," says Alan as his teeth chatter.

"Surely it won't be long." replies Artos, "I hope she's not forgotten. The drink is flowing in there."

At that moment, Wren rises to her feet and the people quieten, falling silent in anticipation.

"Friends!" she begins.

A rumble of stamping feet and banging of drums welcome Wren to the centre of the festive celebration.

"It is that time again. When I deliver a blessing, a gift from the Holly King to the person who you good people of Hartriggs feel is the most deserving of some good fortune. Mind that I should point out that after a few drinks and puffs on my pipe, my eyesight is neither as good as my insight or foresight and we don't want a repeat of the year I blessed Wee Laddie with a child in his belly."

The crowd roars with laughter as Wee Laddie stands up, raising his young toddler over his head.

"Easy to put in, but a devil to remove," she says.

"You're not kidding," says Wee Laddie.

"So, who will it be?" asks Wren.

A few seconds of silence and then the first

voice shouts out, *Morganna!* followed by others saying, *choose Morganna*, and within moments, they have decided.

"Morganna, my child. Our friends offer you the blessing. What gift may I give you tonight?"

Morganna engages with the sense of drama. Her aura glows as if standing under a spotlight. The tension mounts.

"I ask you to return the living souls of my brother, Artos and his friend, Alan. Make them whole and joined with their bodies once more. Bring them back to life."

A sharp intake of breath follows from the crowd.

"Performing such a feat is very difficult. You ask much of me, Morganna. I cannot do this on my own."

Morganna casts her most mournful expression.

"But maybe," the audience exhales again, "if you all can lend me your power then just maybe I can grant the wish."

The audience grows in excitement, with calls of *Yes* and *We'll help you* in encouragement.

"Let it be so," says Wren, "settle, now settle friends."

Silence falls as Wren closes her eyes in quiet meditation. She speaks in the ancient tongue, sounding repeated rhythms of words long forgotten. It has a hypnotic effect on the audience. The air is electric and charged. Strands of vapour form low on the floor. In a snaking movement, the mist winds around the ankles of the audience. Tiny ice crystals form and hover in the air, reflecting the candles and the flames from the great yule log. The clouds of water vapour thicken and start to bubble and spin.

"Friends," says Wren, "close your eyes, lend me your power and your will. Let Artos and Alan return to us. Close your eyes. Use the love in your hearts to bring them back.

"Artos and Alan, hear the call of your kin, who bind their spirit to this magic. Yule marks the point when the sun is reborn, and we give gifts to one another in honour of the gifts given upon us by the gods themselves. I call on the Moon goddess and her power of rebirth. May the spirits of the Fae lead you from the place between the worlds. Return now to the people that hold you dear. Cast off the icy cloak of death. Come back to the love of your family and friends. I COMMAND YOU RETURN!"

Her words boom across the room and resonate within the bodies of those gathered around her. They are within the spell and experience a great rush of energy overpowering them. Then the room falls still and silent. For those who might risk opening an eye and defy Wren's instructions, they can't. The power of suggestion has taken hold.

Artos steps back from the crack in the wall he's been peering through.

"That's it. Time to go in."

Opening the door creates a draught that covers them in the mist, and coming in from the darkness into the light affects their vision. As they step forward into the room, they collide with people and furniture.

"Sorry," says Artos, "I can't see a thing for this fog."

"Come to the light," announces Wren. "Walk towards the light, let it guide you back."

"There's Wren over there," says Alan.

"Oh aye, I see her," says Artos.

"Everyone, keep your eyes closed," commands Wren, "you must keep them closed until Artos and Alan stand before all of us. Only then will they return. Keep your eyes closed. Keep lending me your power. They are getting closer, closer, closer. Summon every ounce of love from your hearts, draw them here, closer. Now. OPEN YOUR EYES!"

The mist has evaporated. Artos and Alan are standing in the centre of the floor. They are dirty and dishevelled, but otherwise, just as everyone remembers. The crowd goes wild.

LEAVING HOME

Morning. Amid the devastation that naturally follows a party for forty in a confined space, Wren has gathered the village elders in a huddle. Aside from the witch, there's Wee Laddie who busies himself squeezing blackheads, Mother Senga who is the literal mother of over half the children in Hartriggs, Mince who prepares and cooks the communal meals. Then Kenneth, a shepherd and heavy drinker, who is often led home by his own flock.

"I call this emergency meeting," says Wren in hushed tones, "we must agree over an urgent matter."

"Aye," say the others, as one.

"Artos and Alan," she begins, "blessed are the gods for returning them to us."

"Aye, that was good magic Wren," says Kenneth.

"Yes, great," say the others.

"I liked the pies," says Mother Senga.

"Aye," everyone agrees.

"I love your pies, Mince," says Wee Laddie.

Wren taps her staff on the floor.

"Artos and Alan," she reminds everyone, "are back among us, but I fear they cannot stay. The new church frowns upon raising the dead."

"The new church?" says Mother Senga, "they torched a village just for allowing their hens to lay eggs on a Sunday."

"I know what you're saying, Wren," says Wee Laddie, "but Artos and Alan are two valuable members of our village, both healthy and good with the sheep."

"The sheep are safe with me," says Kenneth.

The others stare at their feet in the short and uncomfortable silence that follows.

"They can head south," says Mince, "Duncan MacForres doesn't rule beyond the borders of Galwydell. They'll be safe enough two- or three-days travel from here. I can make up pies for them to get them started."

"Aye, the pies," say the others.

Wren stamps her staff again, but with more menace.

"No more pie talk. Although they are very good," she concedes, "what do you say, Mother Senga?"

"They are lovely boys, but that won't help us if Duncan discovers they've come back to life."

"True," say the others in agreement.

"But if they could raise a warband," says Wee Laddie, "defeat Duncan in battle and free Galwydell from his tyrannical rule. Then they could come back."

"Aye!" say the others while staring at their feet in another awkward silence.

"Very well," Wren acknowledges, "it saddens me, but I agree with your thoughts. I will give them the news that they must leave Hartriggs today. Never to return."

"Aye," say most of the others.

"*Possibly* never to return?" says Wee Laddie.

"Aye." They agree again.

As a group, they spit on the floor to confirm their binding decision before departing the meeting.

Left alone, Wren stares into the flames of the fire. Once again, her mind creates a scene of screaming victims, clashes of a desperate fight, and a raging blaze that may destroy Hartriggs for good. As the vision fades, her eyes focus on Artos, asleep in a corner. She briefly allows herself a look of pride and affection, but only when no-one else is looking.

"Time to wake up," she says, stamping her staff.

Artos stirs from his sleep. The smell of stale alcohol and unbridled flatulence fills the air. He has slept where he collapsed after several hours of drinking the home-brewed mead. The last cup of which was poured over himself, lying around him in a damp puddle. His eyelids fight against the random pattern of stray rays of sunlight that penetrate the roundhouse. Proximity to the smouldering Yule log is causing him to sweat profusely. His muscles ache, his stomach aches, and his head, yes, it aches tremendously. He coughs up the small piece of vomit that has burned away in his throat most of the night and then he starts the long journey towards standing up unsteadily on his feet.

That was a good night.

Other revellers are stirring too. As some of them see Artos pass by, they call out to him and thank the gods for the gift of returning him to life. For a moment he's completely forgotten the events of the earlier forty-eight hours, but then the neurons in his brain re-join the dots. He responds with courtesy, by thanking the gods himself and answering questions about tunnels of light and other things rumoured to be seen when you die. He gives a convincing account as he steps over towards the door.

Outside, in the bright glaring light of a low sun on a sharp winter's morning, Artos is under attack by the elements. His temperature drops, the pain in his head intensifies, and he suddenly feels the need to propel himself towards the edge of the woods to evacuate his stomach contents in a hollowed-out trunk of a fallen tree. He wretches, coughs, and splutters for the next few minutes, and in the gaps, he observes at least four others engaged in the same continuous cycle of perpetual motion. All of them blaming some part of the dinner they communally ate the night before, but ironically, they do this while drinking more mead to take away the awful taste in their mouths.

He gulps down more air as he finally evicts the last of the unprocessed food and drink from the feast. Rising to his feet again, he feels better, but in dire need of a wash, and he knows just the right place to go. He shambles through the centre of Hartriggs, avoiding other staggering and incapacitated locals. Crossing to the side of the village where the river runs alongside a well-worn path. Artos walks along the banking, where small stones extend out to the side of the fast-running water. The river's course meanders along, before disappearing over a small ridge and flowing into a pool that is just deep enough to immerse yourself.

He stops and undresses before venturing in to sit below the drop of the small waterfall. The shock to his body is incredible, but within seconds, his aches and pains are dwindling away. Even the cold seems to disappear after a few short moments.

Hartriggs is situated high amongst the

local fells. From where Artos is sitting, he can look out at an uninterrupted view that extends for miles. Dotted in places, smoke rises into the sky, pointing to other settlements waking from the annual celebration. Facing south, the sun is still some way to his left and still climbing higher in the sky. Its rays are offering warmth and although it's still uncomfortable to look at, he appreciates its healing power.

He gathers water in his cupped hands and throws it over his face, washing away the tiredness and making himself feel alive once again. As he wipes the sun-filled droplets away from his eyes, he can see a blurred figure standing before him. Startled, he stands up in the pool.

"Who is it?"

No reply. The splashing water is all that colours the sound of the scene. Artos wipes his eyes again, and this time, standing before him, is an otherworldly being. A semi-transparent figure of a woman who seems to sparkle and shimmer. Her hair is like spun gold, her eyes are pale and piercing, with ears tapering to a point.

You are beautiful.

Only the smallest hint of a smile appears on the apparition's face. Artos feels as if she can read his thoughts and becomes embarrassed as she stares at him standing naked before her, but her gaze seems to go deeper than the flesh.

He feels as if she's reading every part of his spirit, his essence, his light.

Artos bows awkwardly, convinced it's the spirit that Wren has often described. If so, she is a powerful being that demands respect. He decides that kneeling before her with arms outstretched is the best approach and drops back down into the water with a splash.

"Lady."

The ghostly figure extends her right hand, pointing down to the water of the pool. Small ripples start to appear in the water that lies between her and Artos. As they increase in size, the hilt and blade of a magnificent sword disturbs the surface. Gradually it rises before him, glinting in the sunlight and reflecting the water of the pool, shimmering, dazzling, incredible.

It hangs in the air, emitting a powerful force that Artos has never experienced before. Its energy connects with his and a surge of emotion passes through him. A taste of absolute power.

The lady now clasps both her hands around the sword and holds it as if contemplating its fate. Artos can feel his heart racing, tears well up in his eyes and the power of potent magic crackles in the air round about him. All this time, the figure says nothing, nor gives away any hint of emotion. Every part of Artos is calling for a response, overwhelmed with the experience.

"No, not yet," says the apparition and in a split second, she vanishes.

"What?" Artos rushes back to reality and suddenly the world has become cold again.

Sitting back down in the pool, he plunges his head under the water before resurfacing, desperately trying to summon the apparition back before him.

Except this wasn't a vision, this was real.

"You were there. I could have touched you. Where have you gone? What's with the sword?"

"First sign of madness, talking to yourself," says Morganna as she descends the path that runs by the water.

Artos is now vulnerable as well as confused. Morganna peels an apple saved from the feast with the small-bladed knife that she always keeps close. Her presence is always intimidating, but particularly when bearing arms.

"Did you see it?" asks Artos.

"See what?"

"I don't know, a being, a faerie."

"I saw nothing, but these creatures are hard to spot."

"I think it was the lady that Wren is always cursing."

"Nimue? Wren has learned her craft over many years. She is the seventh daughter of a seventh daughter. She is born to communicate with such spirits. Why would Nimue appear before you? Oh, wait, let me think, you might have been drinking last night?"

"She was here, I tell you. You've told me before that you saw her years ago."

"Yes, when taken to Modron's Water by Wren when I was a child. What did she say to you?"

Artos searched his mind. "She said, No, not yet."

"That was it?" Morganna laughs sarcastically.

"Well, no, she had a big sword. It was immense. It felt like it was part of me."

Morganna is more annoyed than the usual level of annoyed that she expresses in front of Artos.

"You saw the sword?"

"Yes, I saw a sword."

"Not a sword," Morganna's ire was rising, "if you saw Nimue, then you saw *the* sword. I know Nimue as The Lady of the Lake and The Guardian of the Sword of Destiny. It's not just a sword. It is a magical weapon that can smite a hundred men with one swing. It could cleave the summits from these hills. You're seriously telling me that Nimue appeared before you without a summoning spell and gave you a look at the sword. And what then?"

"She said the *No, not yet* words, and vanished."

"Thank the gods for that. Look, it was just a hallucination left over from your breakfast of dried mushrooms yesterday. Less likely, but I will admit possible. Nimue is searching for the champion of legend that will wield Excalibur, and she got the wrong person. Easy mistake to make among the men around here. You all look the same with your long hair and beards."

"Excalibur? It has a name?"

"To some, it's the Irish Blade, because the legends say that's where it first appeared. To many of us who study the magical arts and the ways of the old gods, it is Excalibur. A weapon of great power. I think just all the dying and being born again has been an overwhelming experience for you. You inadvertently ate too much of the mushrooms and then had a night on the mead. I think it's all easily explained."

"I suppose so," says Artos, in a disappointed voice.

"Don't stay in the pool all day. You're leaving for good in a few hours. Eat something. You'll be starving soon."

Morganna tosses the apple for Artos to catch. She offers a smile, but as she turns and walks away, her face darkens. All this talk of Merlin and now Nimue and Excalibur. It was bothering her. If great power was to be granted, she was a better choice.

She walks on, forming plans in her mind, almost knocking over Alan as they pass each other.

"And good morning to you Morganna," says a lightly winded Alan, who watches the young witch wander off while offering a hand gestured insult behind her.

"What's up with Morganna?" says Alan, as he joins Artos at the pool, "oh no wait, it's Morganna. She's like that all the time, isn't she?"

Artos sinks further into the pool. He just wants some peace, but half the village have had the same idea.

"Brought a couple of these," Alan lays two full cups of mead down on the rocks beside them, "a bit of dog that bit you. It always does the trick."

Alan starts to undress. Piling his clothes neatly on the banking, he jumps into the pool to guarantee giving Artos a good soaking of icy water.

"That's me sorted with Gwendolyn. She couldn't resist my charms and how I rose from the dead."

He pushes himself into the choice position beneath the waterfall and commits to an almighty break of wind that releases bubbles of methane to freedom, out and onwards into the river, rushing downstream.

"Oh, that's just pure evil," says Artos as he finally decides that his relaxing visit to the pool is over for today.

He climbs out of the water and uses his tunic to dry himself, before pulling the wet garment over his head. The cold seems to stick to him, and he still feels tired as he pulls on breeches and boots.

"I better head back. We'll have to organise ourselves for the journey."

"I wear most of what I own," says Alan.

"Me too, but maybe I'll find something to take with me and remind me of home."

"Maybe Hartriggs isn't so rotten after all?"

"No, it's terrible," says Artos calmly and with no hint of irony, "but I'm leaving for the big adventure now. I might not return here. I want to find something to keep my family within my heart."

"Does that include Morganna?" says Alan. "I don't think she has a heart."

Home. Four walls and a roof enclosing a clutter of pots, potions, and general paraphernalia required in the day-to-day life of a working witch. You choose where you sit with care to avoid being speared by a poisonous plant or bitten by many of the resident tiny creatures capable of injecting harmful or lethal toxic venom.

Artos takes his time and exercises caution

as he searches for a keepsake amongst boxes of charms and ingredients; crystals of every shape, size, and colour, miniature carvings of gods and goddesses, herb mixes in small pouches intended to be worn, and flat stones carved with ancient symbols that are used to predict the future. All of it is interesting and easy to carry, but none of it has a personal connection with him.

Wren sits observing him from her seat at the table. Chewing on her pipe, she says nothing, but Artos can feel her gaze bearing down on him.

"You said you would tell me about it," says Artos while continuing to search, "when we were alone. You said you would tell me about the future you've seen for me."

"Too much and —"

"Wren. Is there a future for me?"

"Yes, a great future, but a long road to get there," says the witch, finally placing her pipe down.

Artos places his hand on a small, black wooden box. There's nothing exceptional about its appearance, but he's drawn to it, and without realising, he lifts it over to the table, placing it in front of him. Wren's eyes flick between the box and Artos as she expects what he is about to find.

"I won't lie," says Artos, "now that this day has finally come. I'm excited, but I'm sad too.

My whole life is here."

"As we pass through places, we leave a trail, a scent," replies Wren, "something that people may see as a memory or a ghost. That's the sadness and loss that you feel. Now the future, that's the exciting part. You know I am not your mother, but I have raised you since a baby, and for all the times I could have turned you into a toad. I have relished the little joys of watching you grow. Artos. My boy."

Artos is stunned. This is not the Wren that he knows.

Is she dying?

"No, I'm not," cackles the witch. "I never taught you how to disguise your thoughts to those who can read them. So, to business. The prophecy."

"Prophecy?"

"*The* prophecy," Wren corrects, "a prophecy that tells of a king that will be born to rule our lands through a triumphant golden age, where the fields are full at harvest, and the invaders are driven from our shores. A place where the people will enjoy all the favours of the gods and where those that oppress and subjugate will face justice for their crimes against the people."

"People like Duncan MacForres?"

"People just like Duncan MacForres will be driven out by the followers of the one true king," replies Wren.

"I have to go in search of the one true king?"

"No, not yet."

"That's what *she* said."

"That's what who said?"

"The lady. I went down by the river, down to the pool and a being appeared before me. Morganna said it was just the mushrooms from yesterday."

"Morganna was there too?"

"No, she wasn't there when the lady was there, but she came along after and reassured me I was just seeing things, but that's what the lady said to me *No, not yet*, when she was standing holding the big sword."

Wren reached for her smoking kit. It was time for some more calming herbs.

"This was news I wasn't expecting. I didn't think that Nimue would just honour you with a visit such as this."

"You think I saw Nimue? I thought it might be her."

"You know what I say, but I know that your parents, your real parents, were wealthy. I'm sure your father was a lord or a nobleman, someone who had land and titles. Their identity is unknown to me, but not to all in this story. Artos, you may not be searching for the true king, but I believe you could be the true king, and in my sometimes less than agreeable conversations with Nimue over the years, she has said nothing to make me believe otherwise."

A shocked silence descends on the room.

"The king is coming," continues Wren, "I can wager for that, but there are many candidates across these lands. Many already have castles and courts and are in a better position than you to hold power over a realm, but the true king needs only one thing to rule. The Irish Blade. Excalibur. Whoever wields the sword of power is the one true king that all others will kneel to and offer their fealty."

"Excalibur. Morganna said that as well. What does this mean? I feel as if I'm about to burst."

"The prophecy tells of how the one true king will receive Excalibur. When the time is right, the Merlin, the highest rank among the mages, will summon Nimue and take the sword from her."

"The Merlin? Who happens to be living in a forest just down the road from Hartriggs?"

"I admit it's starting to sound less of a coincidence." says Wren, "when you leave here, you must find him. Find the Merlin. He will know what to do."

"And if I can't find him? Caledon is vast."

"Then there's always the Camulodunum choice."

Artos knew that Wren didn't mean that, but this was an incredible story, and it was making sense. The visions that had plagued him for most of his life, were the visions a clue towards his destiny?

Is that what people mean about dreams coming true?

"There's not much time left, Artos. Open the box that sits before you. The item inside is not just a memory of here. It is your only connection with your real family."

Artos removes the lid and looks in at the contents. Enclosed within a soft lining, like a precious jewel, lies a small pendant made of bone. A perfectly crafted head of a snarling bear fixed on to a copper eye and threaded through with a leather cord.

"It was the only thing that came with you when I took you into my care. They had placed it around your arm. No-one would steal it, suspecting a curse on such a thing that was obviously put there as a charm."

Artos lifted the pendant out of the box and let it hang down in front of him. Not for the first time that day, he felt he was near an object of great power.

"Why didn't you tell me about this?"

"To be honest," says Wren with another draw on her pipe, "I thought if you discovered it too early, then you might have left here before the proper time. You would have sought its origins, and that may have set you on a different path. It has always been here, in a simple box that you could always have opened at any time. I'm glad it was today that you stumbled on it."

"Why a bear?"

"You don't need me to answer that, Artos. For that's what your name means. You are called after the bear. Put it around your neck. I'm sure they will have set the cord at the right length for you."

Artos slips the pendant over his head and down around his neck, where the bear hangs perfectly.

"Look after him, and I'm sure he will look after you. I always thought the bone was very ancient. I'm sure that even it has a story to tell."

Artos looks around himself, drawing a last mental picture of his surroundings.

"It's time," insists Wren, "let's collect your friend, who I'm sure is declaring his undying love to someone."

"Yes, at least one."

Hartriggs has turned out in full to say their goodbyes. The elders queue up to shake hands and hug Artos and Alan while offering their best wishes. Only Morganna stands back, observing the scene from a distance.

"I wish I could come with you boys," says Mother Senga with a wink.

"They'll have enough trouble feeding

themselves, without you producing extra mouths to feed," says Wren, "friends," she begins in her inimitable way, "we stand together to wish these sons of Hartriggs well, as they leave the home that we share. Let the gods lead them to a place where they can thrive and grow."

It's an emotional moment. Artos feels he should offer a resounding speech to inflame the hearts and minds of his kinsmen. A first public declaration of the future he envisions for himself. He opens his mouth to speak.

"That's us off then," says Alan.

"Bye," shouts everyone else as they turn their backs and walk off to get back to the normal day's work.

Deprived of his opportunity to say farewell in the manner of a charismatic leader, a brief touch of anxiety overtakes Artos. Venturing into Caledon is a challenge, but then adding in the search for a powerful and insane sorcerer and discovering a legendary sword. It was a serious quest.

No bother.

Wren accompanies them to the edge of Hartriggs. Crossing to the path where the river curves around the village. The water course stretches down into the valleys ahead. In the distance, he can clearly see the tallest trees of Caledon. The witch stops and wipes a tear from her eye.

"Are you alright?" says Artos.

"My son is leaving home. I may be sad."

"I'm sorry this has happened so suddenly. I never thought I would leave like this."

"I'm sorry too, Miss Morcant," says Alan. "I'll look after him for you, I promise."

"I'm sure you'll try your best, Alan."

The awkwardness increases as first Artos and then Alan tries to give Wren a hug goodbye.

"Be off with you. It's time to leave."

"Do you think we'll find the Merlin?" asks Artos.

"If you make enough noise, then I'm hoping that he will find you. I'm sure he will be ready. It could be the very reason he has spent time in Caledon, waiting for your arrival. We must ask the gods that he is in a benevolent mood. Now take care on your journey ahead."

Artos and Alan turn away and continue along beside the stream, disappearing downhill and out of sight.

Wren reaches into her bag for her pipe. Pre-prepared with her anxiety calming herbs. She searches for the red powder to ignite the smoke, but it's missing. Her mind fills with the casual curses that the new church has introduced.

"Damn it!" she chooses. "I must have left it at home!"

Just then, a small lightning bolt sparks

down from the sky above, finding its grounding point in the centre of Wren's pipe. The mix smoulders with its reassuring smoke. Wren draws on the pipe and looks forward. Ahead stands the lone figure of Morganna.

"Thank you, my dear," says Wren, "though you waste such powers on my pipe."

"Why can't I go with them?"

"Why should you go with them? Your path is different. Practice your magic. Perfect your craft."

"Am I to languish here? Preserving the old ones until they reach forty, making love potions to satisfy everyone's lust, or enchanting the mead to stop it from souring?"

"The milk, my dear, the milk."

"Well, the milk then. I know that my destiny lies beyond this village. My power is building and soon it will outgrow this place. For everything that Artos dreams about, I know what I can manifest into my reality. If I can learn from the Merlin, then I will be unstoppable."

"It is that very passion that you need to control."

Morganna holds back. She allows Wren to walk on without her. Turning towards the valley, she steps towards the lip of the hill where Artos and Alan are still descending.

Morganna doesn't suffer from the sentimental afflictions of others, but she has a bond borne out of familiarity with Artos, acting out the role of older sister both for his protection and his chastisement. She now worries he faces more danger without her continued help.

She sits on the grass, watching them go, when a sudden flapping of wings draws her attention. A raven settles on the ground beside her, cocking his head in her direction.

"What do you think I should do?" Morganna enquires of the bird, "maybe you and your friends can tell me?"

The sun is descending once more, and late afternoon frost is settling. Artos and Alan have long disappeared into the distance and the half-light. Morganna sits motionless as, one by one, more ravens gather around her.

Night takes over from day once again. Hartriggs lies still, as the villagers return to the large roundhouse. A cacophony of raven calls echoes out above the rooftops of the village. From inside her home, Wren knows her apprentice has departed.

QUESTS WITHIN QUESTS

Early summer. Artos is sitting alone in a meadow covered in bright, colourful flowers. The sun shines brightly.

He stands up and looks around himself. Behind him lies an entrance to a chambered cairn, while before him, the meadow slopes away, and a worn path in the grass leads towards a gap in a small stone wall. Artos feels pulled in both directions, as if each choice will lead to its own mystery.

He decides on the path through the wall. He steps forward through the gap; the view opens to a lush green valley stretching out before him. A small, fast stream cuts through the centre, crossed by a small wooden bridge. With each stride increasing in speed, he proceeds towards the crossing, descending the slope using a series of stone steps carved out of the landscape.

His heart rate increases. The tranquillity of

the scene departs behind him. Artos crosses the wooden bridge and within an instant he is amid a great battle. Fiery riders encircle him, charging against one another. Overhead, two dragons roar and engage in ferocious combat. One is of the purest white, the other a deep blood red.

His breath is short and rapid as the chaos swirls around him. Oblivious to his own presence, the fiery creatures do battle with one another. At the centre of the mayhem, he sees a cross standing on a hill. He races forward, pushing against the other beings to reach it first.

As he draws nearer, the cross transforms into the image of a great sword embedded into a large stone boulder. The sword glows as he sees a blade engraved with ancient characters. The markings writhe around one another until the words form. 'I AM EXCALIBUR'.

Before he knows it, he has transported to a shoreline. A large rocky outcrop sits just out to sea. Gulls and other birds give an acrobatic display in the skies, then dive to catch an unending supply of fish. As Artos gazes out at the scene, he hears laughing behind him. He turns to see the smiling, graceful image of a raven-haired girl. She dances barefoot on the beach without a care.

Artos reaches towards her, but as her body spins, it disperses into particles of sand, blowing away in a vortex. He turns around to catch another glimpse of her but is now confronted by the image of a large round table surrounded by ornate chairs. Each chair, with one exception, has a flame covered entity in attendance.

The sound of the shore grows louder as Artos circles around the table and takes his place at the empty throne. An object rotates at the table's centre. A shining grail surrounded by an aura of golden light.

Artos shields his eyes from the blinding light of a low glaring sun. He shakes himself out of his dream.

"Good afternoon," says Alan, "I've made breakfast."

He places two full cups of mead down on the ground and thrusts the last remaining mutton pie in Artos' face.

"Do you want this?" he asks.

"No, I'm still full. I must have eaten six of them last night. How many did you have?"

"I don't know. Five? Maybe nine?"

"Have we eaten everything?"

"And drunk everything," says Alan, spraying the campsite with crumbs of the last piece of food as he speaks.

Artos stands up and stretches. The dense forest does not show an obvious path of where to go. He rolls up his sleeping blanket and picks up his equipment, strapping a small axe to his back and lifting the empty bag that used to contain the supplies the villagers gave him.

"What's the plan for today?" says Alan with his mouth still full of mutton and pastry.

"Stay off the well-worn paths. Look for places where sorcerers live. Wren used to tell stories about crystal caves, dark pools of water, or hollowed-out ancient trees."

"So, we're looking for enormous trees in a big forest?"

"How do I know? I've never quested before today. They say he roams with beasts and birds by his side."

"So that makes it clearer. We're looking for an old lunatic surrounded by a pack of animals, hanging around somewhere near a big hole in the ground?"

"Yes? Although that description could match half the people in Galwydell. Let's get moving. We'll not find him by staying round about here."

They drain their mead cups and set off deeper into the forest. The immensity of the task is dawning on them. After only a short while, the usual chatter has faded away into longer periods of silence and reflection.

Artos dwells on his visions, replaying them again and again in his mind. He first experienced them as a young boy. In the last few weeks, they have become more frequent, lucid, and real. It's as if he enters another realm. Somewhere that he might even reach, by crossing an enchanted bridge, or passing through a magical doorway.

"What are you thinking about?" asks Alan.

"If we find the Merlin and he agrees to help us, then what happens next? These dreams that I have. They carry a message that I can't understand, shrouded in mystery. Do you know what I mean?"

"No. sorry," says Alan, "Gwendolyn Nicaskill is the object of my dreams. I've never understood yours."

Artos grins back at his lifelong friend. He knew Alan was incapable of any conversation that required deep thought. As they step towards who knows where, he conjures the picture in his mind of the raven-haired girl of his dreams, conceding that maybe he isn't so different.

Gwendolyn Nicaskill has got nothing on you.

A few hours later, and the noble sentiments of questing are still to show themselves for Artos and Alan. The pair amble along, chatting and laughing at their own jokes. With their stomachs still processing most of Mince's excellent pies and plenty of fresh water to gather and drink in the forest streams, survival in the wilds is yet to become an issue.

Their good mood only starts to descend with the sun as it edges closer to the horizon, just above the treeline.

"We'll make camp again soon," says Artos.

"Aye, the days are shorter here than in the hills," replies Alan, pointing at the summits.

"That's strange. We've been walking for ages. I'd have thought we wouldn't be able to see the hills by now."

They continue in silence, still unable to find a single clue on the whereabouts of the Merlin. The forest is full of distractions; birds calling from the trees, an animal running through the undergrowth, in the distance a call that could be human or maybe the scream of a fox, branches and twigs that snap in the breeze or underfoot?

No-one has passed them all day. No-one to ask or enquire about an old man and his army of beasts. People live in Caledon, but not like the villagers of Hartriggs. Mainly small groups of hunters who live a life of roaming and foraging for food. They are wary of outsiders and protective of their hunting grounds. If Artos and Alan aren't making contact, it's because the forest dwellers are silently permitting them to pass through their territory.

They come upon a place that appears a good spot to camp. A semi-circle of trees gathers around a flat square of ground. A wide stream runs close by and is deep enough to contain fish. It seems peaceful as they approach, but strangely familiar. As they get closer, the charred ground from an old fire causes their hearts to sink.

"This is where we camped last night," says Artos.

"How can that be?" says Alan, "we've walked for miles, not to mention hours."

"Yes, in a big circle."

The pair crash to the ground, suddenly frustrated, tired, and overcome with exhaustion.

"Is there any mead left?" asks Artos.

"No, we finished it."

"Doesn't matter. We can be back in Hartriggs in another hour. We can get some more."

Alan shrugs to show that may be a good idea.

"No," says Artos, "we can't go back. After all the big farewells and the tears?"

Artos casts his eyes around with frustration. He can even see the grasses that were flattened beneath where they slept last night. It's annoying, but he knows he must persevere.

Just one day wasted. There's a whole lifetime ahead. Calm yourself, Artos. Calm yourself.

"I suppose we better get organised," he says. "I'm still full enough. I don't fancy taking on the night-time animals, they've usually got more teeth and claws than the ones you meet during the day. Get a fire started, I'll collect water."

"Sounds like a plan," says Alan.

Artos walks only a short distance from camp, with still just enough light remaining to show the size of the challenge ahead. Last night, in the throes of their big adventure, he hadn't even noticed, but a day on, and a lost one at that, his mood was becoming more serious. He hoped, as Wren had said, that the Merlin might find him.

How can I be the one? I can't even follow a trail in a forest. Yet Nimue has shown me the sword.

Artos felt like a thousand pairs of eyes were on him, as if every living being was looking in his direction, and some of the dead ones. He felt a great weight rest on his shoulders, a pressure to succeed in a task greater than anything he had ever known. If he were to turn these dreams that haunted him into a reality, he would have to be bold and brave. Seize the opportunity that lay in front of him. To become a king, he would first have to become a leader, to inspire others with noble thoughts and deeds. Humble beginnings didn't make the task impossible. He could relate to the needs of ordinary people; he could be a champion for them and aim to change everyone's lives for the better. A true king for the masses, it would start here and start now.

Well, in the morning, at least.

Artos fills two beakers with water that's tumbling over a pile of rocks. He turns back and catches the outline of Alan standing by the lit fire and clearly drinking from a flask.

"He's got mead!"

Artos launches into a sprint with the water flying from the cups in his hands. It doesn't matter, as they've now become missiles. He launches the first for it to smash at Alan's feet. His startled friend looks over as the second connects with his head, sending him flying.

Artos leaps into the camp, grabbing hold of Alan before he's recovered. They trade blows and insults in quick succession and a struggle ensues that sends them tumbling around, while remaining conscious about avoiding the fire. As lifelong friends, they have endured these irregular bouts for supremacy over the years. The intention is never to wound, but maybe just inflict pain to make a point.

Pushing, shoving, and grabbing of clothes usually progresses to face punching, groin kicking, head-butting, neck strangling and ear biting. A truce will be called, but not before a black-eye or bloodied nose determines the outcome of who has lost and won.

The ritual combat has been going on for about an hour when the shout of a stranger's voice breaks the silence and brings their conflict to an immediate halt.

"Stop!"

Artos and Alan prise themselves apart. Instinctively raising their hands and arms in a sign of submission as they face the wrong end of an archer's arrow.

A woman steps forward, clad in elaborate leather armour and a fur covered cowl and cloak. A cloth mask covers her face, leaving only her dark brown eyes visible. Her skin, as much as they can see, is a light olive brown, dark wavy hair creeps out from under her hood. She carries her bow lowered, but with a black feathered arrow, mounted and ready to draw. An arrow that Artos recognises.

"It was you," says Artos, "you that killed Cadawg?"

"The horseman?"

Artos nods in return. "I owe you my life."

"You will owe me, but that will come later. If you are who I believe you are."

"I'm Artos," he drops his hands, as does Alan, but the archer remains standing half-ready to shoot.

"Arktos. Are you a bastard Arktos?"

Alan can't help sniggering, almost with a sense of relief.

"Are you a bastard?" the archer repeats.

"Yes, he is a bastard," contributes Alan with a grin.

"Thanks Alan. It's Ar-tos. My name is Artos."

The archer seems to relax and unloads her arrow.

"Close enough. I am Diana. I have travelled

many miles to join your quest, to get the big sword and become king."

"Wait. How do you know about my quest?"

"Because my grandmother, Baba Yaroslava, mentioned your quest in my quest."

"You have a quest? Baba who?"

"Yes, I have a quest and part of that quest is to aid you in your quest. That is what will come to pass."

"Oh, I see."

"Are you two boys going to continue fighting each other, or can we discuss plans Artos?"

The Hartriggs friends nod towards one another.

"Yes, we've stopped. We're friends, eh, normally."

"I know I can see that. I've been following you for days. You both drink too much and you laugh like children. You can tire me sometimes, but now I am here to help. I'm sure you will appreciate it in the end."

"End? End of your quest or mine?"

"Both."

She lowers her mask, her expression is fierce and proud, her beauty is striking, Artos can't mind read, but he knows Alan's thoughts.

Poor Gwendolyn, forgotten already.

"You are without food, yes?"

"Yes, we're going to hunt tomorrow," replies Artos.

"But with empty bellies, you might die in the cold during the night. I will kill something, but my cooking is terrible, so I hope you can help with that."

"If you get rabbit," volunteers Alan, "I can do that roasted on the fire."

"Good, I like rabbit. We'll eat, then we'll talk."

The mood in the camp improves tremendously with Diana's arrival. As promised, she hastily returns with a fresh rabbit to roast. The archer carries knives, as well as her bow and arrows, so wastes no time with preparing the meat. As they all gather around the campfire to wait on their meal, Diana produces a small flask.

"I have little of this left. I've travelled a long way, but I kept some to celebrate our meeting."

"What is it?" asks Artos.

"Medicine," she smiles.

"I'm not ill."

"It will still make you feel better," she says, "most people mix it with herbs to make healing potions, but I've found that just drinking it on its own works."

They pass the flask around the three of them, and each raise it in gratitude before taking a drink. Artos and Alan immediately choke. The flavour is not the same as the drink they shared with the Dal Riata, but the effect is the same.

"We'll need to make this stuff," says Alan.

After a few attempts where Artos tries to teach Diana the Dal Riata words of *Ooshga-bay-huh*, they settle down in each other's company. The fire cracks and splinters away as the talk turns to quests. Why Diana is here and why now?

"A hundred years before my time. My people lived in the lands around the summer water. They were driven from their home by an invader, King Balamber, and his followers. Fierce horsemen that appeared out of the east and ravaged our villages, killing and burning as they went.

"Defeated, my tribe travelled west over many years, migrating through nations where the Romans ruled, crossing great rivers and mountains to settle once again in warmer, more peaceful lands.

"When I was born, my family lived on an island, in the town of Pollentia. My mother died while giving birth to me. My father was a fisherman, and a warrior who joined the fighting at Carthage. He never returned. From a young age, there was only my grandmother and me.

"She could predict the times that lay ahead. The years still to come to pass. She saw you,

Artos. She saw your quest. She saw a great sword, and she saw you avenge my people. She saw you, and me returning to my ancestral homelands and at the head of a great army, seeking revenge on the children of Balamber."

Artos gulped.

I'm Artos from Hartriggs. What is all of this?

"Are you sure that I am that Artos?"

"My grandmother was Baba Yaroslava. She told me the names of people and places that she did not know, but the goddess Artemis told her, showing her visions of what was to come. Artemis told her of Caledon, of a bastard king who would be called after the bear. He would wield a great sword that could kill hundreds with a single mighty swing.

"I became older before my grandmother passed away. I looked after her and had found love with a partner, but my destiny did not lie there. One night, I gave my love a final kiss as they slept, and I set off on my quest to avenge my people and ride into battle with you."

"And you are sure he's the right Artos?" says Alan.

"I knew where to look. I have been around here for days now. I can hunt well, and I can hunt a man just like a rabbit. I was close enough at the battle a few days ago to hear your name being called. Mainly by him," she gestures towards Alan, "I was at your village. I admit then I was confused, as I thought they were burying you."

"Well," says Artos, "no, it doesn't matter."

"I still wasn't sure until the next day when you were naked in the pool."

"You saw that?"

"Yes, you were cold."

Alan bites his lip to keep a modicum of respect.

"Then I saw her. Artemis standing before you, Showing you the sword. Showing you your future.

"You saw the lady?"

"Yes, I saw her. Then I knew it was you. And now as I sit beside you, I can see you wear the bear around your neck. My grandmother had one almost the same. It marks out followers of Artemis so they may recognise one another when they meet. Yes, you are who I seek. You are The Bear that my grandmother spoke of."

"Did you hear that?" Artos turns to Alan, "She saw Nimue beside me at the pool."

"I saw Artemis."

"Yes, you saw the lady."

"The lady, yes, I saw her."

Thunder rumbles in the distance, but there's no sign of accompanying lightning or rain.

"You are on a quest? That part is true?" asks Diana.

Artos stands up, his faith restored in his

own future.

"The woman who raised me can see like your grandmother. She is a witch and a seer. People visit her and pay her to tell them what fortunes lie ahead. She believes that I could be the one that will wield Excalibur, the sword. She believes that all other kings will bow before me when that happens. She has seen a great future, but she's not so good on times and places. She always says that she sees too much and never enough."

A spreading smile illuminates Diana's face. "I think those that can see the future, all say that."

"My quest, or the first part, is to find the great Merlin. The highest magician in our land. The Merlin has been missing for years but Wren Morcant, the woman who raised me, was told that he lives here in Caledon. When we discover him, she thinks he will know what to do."

"Then maybe it's good that a hunter has joined you."

"I'll drink to that," says Alan, but the flask is empty.

Another thunderclap bursts directly overhead, shaking the surrounding ground. This time it's followed by lightning flashes that clearly illuminate a tall and slender figure clad in black. Instinctively, the group dives for cover, but Artos realises who's chosen to make such a dramatic entrance.

"Morganna? What are you doing here?"

"I've been here for ages. It looks like interested parties can join in with your quest now?"

"I thought I could smell someone else," says Diana, "I could smell these two. They are a bit like cattle, but then I could smell something different. No, not different, I mean nicer. I am Diana."

"Why thank you Diana. My name is Morganna I am on the same quest as Artos."

"No, you're not. Nobody asked you."

"Do you know where Merlin is, brother?"

"She is your sister, Artos?"

"No, she's not my sister."

"As good as," says Morganna, "the stories I could tell you about Artos."

"And have your superior magic powers found out where Merlin is, sister?" says Artos.

"No, but I know where he's been. I've been finding clues while you've been walking, eh, around in a circle."

"Artos, if Morganna has powers she must stay," insists Diana, "anyone who knows anything about quests knows that you need two champions, an archer, and a magician. I don't suppose any of you are good at thieving?"

"I dabble," says Artos, "but look, Wren sent me on this quest. Nimue offered me the sword. Tell her Diana, tell Morganna what you saw."

"The lady appeared to him. I was there."

Morganna wasn't expecting that, so sure she was that Artos was too unimportant to the gods. Artos senses a moral victory, if not a practical one.

"What do we do now?" says Alan, "you know she just won't go away. She never did."

"I can hear you; you know." says Morganna.

"There's enough rabbit for four," decides Artos, "let's eat and see what happens next."

I think that's the right decision.

"Yes, you're right," says Morganna.

Artos frowns at her mind reading.

The campfire burns on for hours and the meal provides a better spirit in the camp with a sense of satisfaction for Alan, who has never cooked a communal meal before in his life. As it grows late, all but Artos have given in to sleep. The light in camp is lower and the cloudless night displays the full canopy of stars. The sound of grazing in the distance means deer are passing nearby. Artos looks over at the others. He is overwhelmed with the events of the past few days, but Diana's arrival has bolstered belief in himself. He thinks of the raven-haired girl dancing in the sand, and the pleasant image of her sends him peacefully to sleep.

A stag looks up from its browsing of the weeds and soft plants on the forest floor as a hand claps the animal gently on its shoulder.

"This is the young king," speaks the voice of

a man who is several lifetimes older than most.

His words, spoken in whispers, blow gently through the leaves and branches.

"It is almost time for me to leave this place. The prophecy is moving forward. I cannot be the one to hold back, for all that I have enjoyed my solitude these last few years. The bear is coming out of hibernation. This world is about to change."

The old man turns and walks away, and the deer herd follows, as do the wolves, the lynx, the owls, the adders, and the bats, then the pine martens, foxes and boars, some crows, a few ravens, and a clutch of starlings.

THE BLACKBIRD
FAMILY

Artos was first to waken the next morning, whether it was excitement about carrying on with the quest or just the usual fear of how many spiders Morganna may have placed on him during the night for a joke, he still arose with an optimistic feeling about the day.

His movements stirred the others and before long the camp had informally organised into a well-functioning team. Diana had caught fish from the river, Alan had kept up his new role of camp cook and gutted the catch, before skewering and laying it out on the dying embers of the fire. Then Morganna shared out salt from a small pouch of essential herbs that she always carried with her. It all contributed to a satisfying breakfast and a happy, if still tired atmosphere amongst the party.

The weather and the intended direction of travel dominated the topics of conversation.

Morganna had done what any normal elemental witch would do in conversing with the nearest crow for clues of where to go. Meanwhile, Diana had discovered a strange mix of animal droppings nearby that suggested a path heading deep within the forest.

Most of Caledon stretched to the north of where they were, and it made sense to all that they should head deeper into the forest. The Merlin vanished years ago; it was unlikely that he ventured near any of the settlements that lay towards more open ground.

"Alright. If everyone agrees, we'll try to follow Diana's animal trail and keep the sun to our back for most of the day. Keep your eyes peeled for the normal signs of a magician. Wood smoke, burning incense, chanting in a language no-one can understand."

"I can understand it," responds Morganna indignantly.

"Alright," Artos sighs, "chanting that no-one can understand except Morganna. Let's hope Wren and Nimue can help to guide our way."

"And Baba Yaroslava," says Diana.

"And Baba Yaroslava who has proved to have a good sense of direction already, by getting her granddaughter here. Everybody happy?"

They all nod and start to walk further into Caledon. Eyes on the trail and caught up in quietly spoken chatter, they don't notice a small and skinny man descending from trees behind them. He stands up as if scenting the air and utters a perfect impression of a blackbird's song.

Motionless, he waits on hearing a faint but similar set of sounds being sent back to him. After a few moments, vaguely discernible from the background of other bird calls, he gets the message he's been waiting to receive. A dark smile creeps across his face. He draws a knife from his belt and crouches low before beginning to follow the party's footsteps.

"None of us have any parents left alive?" asks Diana, as she finds out more about her new friends.

"Only Alan," says Morganna, "his mother is still alive, but Artos and I have no memory of our early lives. He was too young, and I, well I'm sure I was cursed to remove my memories. I can only go back to a night when I was alone on a dark shoreline. Crashing waves and the sound of gulls are all I can remember.

"But you were older?"

"Yes. Wren says she thinks I was about thirteen when I turned up at Hartriggs, but I'm not sure. It makes it difficult to find your parents when any memory of them has gone."

"That's terrible. I can remember my father. He always smiled when he came back in from the sea and saw me. He would make me laugh, even when I could see great sadness in his eyes. I think sometimes he would see parts of my mother in me, and it would bring back the loneliness. Then later I knew the same feeling. It took me years after the wars with the Romans at Carthage to accept that I would never see him again. That he wouldn't walk back through our door, but I have my memories, it's terrible what happened to you."

"One day I hope the memories will return, but will I like what I find? I can't know that for sure."

"Over here!" shouts Alan.

All race over towards him, eagerly expecting a clue, but what they see instead is a corpse, stripped of any item that it once possessed. The body has not been there that long, still lying among a blood-stained carpet of moss, his chest and stomach split open, his organs removed. Not the victim of a normal battle, or even a normal killing.

"Do you think it was wolves?" asks Artos.

"No. Someone cut him open," says Diana, "wolves would have pulled him apart."

"There's been a fire here as well," Alan kicks among the charcoaled wood and grey ash.

Morganna lifts her gaze from the body and walks over to a tree with strange markings carved into the trunk. She continues walking from tree to tree and encircling the scene.

"There are markings on four trees," she says, "I don't know their meaning, but I'm guessing they're marking the four directions. This has been a ritual, a sacrifice, and since I can't say who was receiving the honour, it will be best for us to get out of here. We can't help him now."

A blackbird call breaks the conversation from a short distance away. After another brief moment, the call repeats from the opposite direction.

"Let's keep moving," says Artos, "and concentrate on finding the Merlin as soon as we can."

He unstraps his axe and takes it into his hand, and Alan follows him. Diana takes an arrow and holds it lightly against the bowstring. Morganna only has her small dagger to draw, but her inherent skills remove the need to carry weapons.

The light filters down from the treetops. Bird calls ring out and a breeze rustles the high branches and and causes boughs to creak. From time to time, the blackbird calls again. It comes from two directions, then three, then four. Artos isn't happy. He suspects they are passing through hunting grounds and drawing increasing attention as they press ahead.

A flock of birds suddenly takes off to the

left, issuing an alarm call as they fly away. It causes the party to freeze. Diana tries desperately to scan the landscape, looking for the source of the disturbance.

"It's not an animal that's trailing us," she says.

Now the blackbird calls ring out from multiple locations, and from different distances.

Have we walked into a trap?

Morganna, for once doesn't embarrass Artos with letting him know she can hear his words, but her grim expression lets him know that she agrees.

The ground starts to climb in front of them. A slope where the trees thin out nearer the summit. The top looks bathed in sunlight. At the very least, it might be a place to gather their bearings and decide on their next move.

"Let's get up this hill as quick as we can," says Artos.

A burst of energy from everyone causes them to ascend the hill at speed. As Artos nears the top and turns back round, it's obvious rushing back down at the same pace will not be a choice. For the moment, the constant back and forth of blackbird songs have stopped.

The ground has levelled out, and a ridge opens out to a view of the surrounding forest, which descends again below them. Beyond that, it rolls over two lower hills before rising to a third slope, where a roundhouse sits, small but obviously with a fire smoking at its centre. It is a reassuring sign of life that raises the spirits of the party.

"Do you think it could be him?" asks Alan.

"I don't know, but hopefully whoever is living there will help us," says Artos.

Diana nods in agreement. "If they can offer us a warm place to stay tonight, then I'll catch supper to pay for our rest."

"I don't always say this," says Morganna, "but I have a good feeling about that place."

The feeling is short-lived. As they begin to descend back below the treeline, the sound of metal striking stone begins to echo through the woods. Once again, the party comes to an abrupt halt. They look around themselves as a slow percussive rhythm continues. It comes from directly ahead, amongst the trees stretching out before them.

"We have to go this way," says Artos, "whoever lives between that roundhouse and us already knows we're here."

"All they've done is make blackbird sounds so far," says Alan, "it might not be that bad, but my axe is ready."

"We have to keep going," says Morganna, "I don't think we'll have an easy night staying in the forest."

"We won't fall here," says Diana, "Maybe we'll fall under the charge of the eastern hordes, but not here."

"Alright, let's get on with this," says Artos, not feeling much better about Diana's suggested death, either.

With each step they take forward, the metal sound beats time. Many blackbird calls ring out in an eerie chorus of song. Bushes rustle and ferns move apart, but they still can't get a view of the people causing the disturbance and the noise. Sticking close together, they keep to the path that's woven through this part of the forest for years. It leads through a natural avenue that pulls them forward. The metal clashing against stone is increasing in volume and begins to quicken, doubling its time. Artos and his party have come too far to back down from what lies ahead.

The road leads down to a well of light. A sunlit clearing laid out as a perfect circle. As they approach, they are almost upon the source of the metallic strikes. They can feel it on their chests as well as hear it with their ears. Then a final revelation as they approach the circle. They see bodies hanging from the branches of the surrounding trees. Each one has been mutilated and left to decompose. All tighten the grips on their weapons, and the background clanging stops.

The small and skinny man suddenly appears out of the trees in front of them and ambles around the circle. He sings his beautiful blackbird song. Laughing and giggling, he walks up to one body that hangs low. He turns and faces Artos and the others. He points to the body, then grins and rubs at his stomach. Then, from around him, others emerge from the trees, older and younger. What is beginning to look like generations of the same family. Each one is calling out like a blackbird as they form an ever-tightening circle around Artos and his party.

"Stop!" shouts Artos, "who are you?"

The birdcalls stop and the family halts their advance.

"We don't mean you any harm. We're searching for the Merlin. Do you know him?"

The skinny man who appears to be the father of the group speaks back, but it's a language that Artos, nor any of the others have ever heard. The skinny man continues talking to his family. He mimes stretching up as if casting a spell. Some of the rest of his family join in the fun. They begin to point at skeletons and corpses that are hanging around the circle, conveying a message that maybe some of these other poor souls had been on a similar quest.

Morganna takes the opportunity of the distraction to prepare herself, summoning the force to do battle with magic takes mental preparation. A conjured, icy mist starts to form around her hands.

"Look we mean you no harm. Please let us pass."

Artos knows it's not going too well, but he feels as if he should offer one last chance of a peaceful solution.

The skinny man strokes his chin while considering a response. He murmurs again to other members of his family, all of whom solemnly shake their heads and begin one by one to rub at their bellies and chant in a low hum."

"What are they saying?" says Alan.

"They're saying yum yum?" says Diana, her first arrow now firmly locked in position.

"Yum yum? I think that means the same in any language. Get ready," says Artos.

The party raises their weapons, and the skinny man lets loose a blood curdling scream.

The sound is brought to a halt almost immediately as Diana's arrow slices in through his open mouth, killing him instantly. A stunned silence follows for a few seconds before the family scream their battle cries and charge.

Morganna immediately launches a barrage of stinging hail that knocks several backwards, sending them sprawling on to the ground, but many still leap forward with knives spinning and twirling as they flash in the sunlight. Artos and Alan can only swing wildly with their axes in the face of multiple attacks. Some of the family fall instantly before their blows. The attackers are without armour and depend on the force of numbers to fuel their attack.

Diana falls back and hurriedly scales a tree to provide the cover of her arrows. Though the half-eaten corpse beside her makes for unsettling company.

Artos and Alan continue to defend their position. Standing firm as opposed to advancing, they are conscious of protecting Morganna, offering her cover to deliver icy blasts that freeze the victims to death in an instant. Yet the opponents keep coming, charging in groups of three or four. The ferocity of the attack is wearing Artos and his party down, and gradually they are being driven back to the base of the tree below Diana. A scream of pain rings out to the right-hand side of Artos. He doesn't need to look. It's Alan's voice that's yelling out.

Artos spins around and cleaves the head of Alan's attacker who is still holding the bloodied knife. Alan collapses to the ground with his axe dropping beside him. He can fight no more while he clutches his side in agony. All Artos can do is stand in front of him and hold the rest at bay with Morganna. The attackers surround them.

It can't end here. It won't end here. Great Merlin, we need you.

Suddenly the ground shakes and rumbles,

throwing everyone to the ground and Diana out of her position in the tree. As all recover, the family of attackers back off with fear on their faces. Diana draws her hunting knife, while Artos lifts his axe once more, but the attack has stalled.

The family close ranks together, looking around themselves, suddenly unsure of what to do when within seconds hundreds of little luminous beings in a variety of colours; red, blue, gold, and green emerge from the dark forest to surround them. They fly in and around one another, creating an illuminated spectacle of dancing light.

The family is terrified by the tiny creatures. They swat at them. Then they are repaid with bites or stings. The lights swirl around them like a cloud of hornets, trapping them where they are.

Morganna checks on Alan. Laying on her hands to stem the blood flow. The colour is draining from his skin.

"He's losing too much blood. I can only do so much here."

Artos and Diana stand side by side, preparing to make one final charge on the now cowering family, when they stop in their tracks again. A low and loud incantation sounds through the trees, followed by a gathering rumble and a myriad of animal calls."

"It's a stampede," calls Diana, "take cover."

She and Artos dive backwards just in time as hooves, claws, and wings clatter through the branches. A bewildering array of disarming shrieks and howls blasts through the circle clearing at high speed without stopping It's over in seconds. The noise and force of the charge dissipates and moves off into the distance. Gone with the charge is any evidence of the family, carried off or killed in the chaos.

As the dust settles, out strides a tall figure with long, flowing grey hair and an equally long beard. He wears the garb of a magician, complete with a hat that raises to a point. He carries a staff topped with a crystal orb. His face is grim and angry as he walks directly towards Artos.

"Are you the bastard?"

"Yes, I'm the bastard." Artos was getting used to this.

"Then good, I am in the right place. My name is Myrrdin Wylde, I am the Merlin of the Britons."

Artos wasn't sure what to do, bow or stand to attention maybe, but his first thought was his friend, still lying and clutching his side with more blood escaping.

"Please Merlin."

"Myrrdin will do."

"Myrrdin. Can you save Alan? He's dying."

The magician inspects the wound. "I can stop him from bleeding, but I can't cure him here. The people you fought with use poisons on their blades. I need to get him to my home. I have things there that may help. Get him to his feet and help him. It will be nightfall before we reach there, if indeed he reaches there. Now follow me, there will be plenty time ahead for us to discuss matters more pressing."

They all help Alan to his feet and try their best to support him as he uses all his strength to walk forwards. Each member of the party willing him on as he stumbles through the forest.

Artos is troubled with the weight of the thoughts running through his mind. As the Merlin walks on in front, he doesn't feel excited. He doesn't feel in control. He is still only an observer to events that are happening around him at an incredible pace. Now his best friend is in a serious condition, because of a sense of loyalty that caused him to follow. A woman has travelled thousands of miles because his quest was part of her quest. And even Morganna, who has always grudgingly looked out for him, that much is true, was now risking death for her troubles. The people closest to him were taking huge risks and for what. He looks at Morganna, expecting a reaction, but none appears as they struggle to help Alan with each painful step.

Does the prophecy decide who lives and who dies?

He walks on in silence.

"You are one with the Blessed Isle." Artos hears the phrase repeat in his head as the swirling mists thin. Looking out from his seated position on a grand throne, the round table stretches out in front of him. To his right sits Alan, smiling and clad in bright glistening armour. They clasp a hand with one another, affirming their strong bond of friendship.

Artos looks around at the others gathered. Morganna and Diana each have seats at the table, while indistinct images of fiery beings fill most of the remaining places.

Another chair lies empty, more ornate than the others, with carvings of images and words that stay out of focus.

Artos lifts his gaze. The table sits in the centre of a large, vaulted room surrounded by large glass windows. From its lofty position, he can look out across his entire kingdom.

He can see large ranges of hills, mountains and lakes, towers, and monumental structures of stone. He can see the sea at the fringes of his view and distant islands that lie beyond on the horizon. Beams of light shine and sparkle in the ceiling above him.

"Am I dead?" he asks himself as his

conscious mind returns to win back control.

"No, you're not dead," says Myrrdin, "but I'm afraid that your friend soon will be. Rise now and be with him."

"No!" Artos leaps up from where he has been sleeping.

Myrrdin Wylde's home is much like Wren Morcant's except larger. The smell of burnt incense and charcoal dominates, and all available space is filled with jars and storage boxes, pieces of parchment and candles, plus the obligatory goat's skull and large obsidian scrying glass.

Artos knocks over a few things on the rush over to Alan, but Myrrdin has another thing in common with Wren as he raises an intolerant eyebrow and lights up his pipe.

"Artos, my friend," Alan chokes, "I'll not make it with you to Camulodunum."

"Of course you will. It's going to happen. You'll get better."

Artos looks to the others for comfort. Diana looks away, while Morganna gently shakes her head.

"I'll haunt you. You know that. I won't let you have all the fun without me."

"You can't die now ...."

Alan closes his eyes. His life cut short.

"Surely we can do something, Morganna?" says Artos.

"I do not have the powers to bring souls

back to their earthly bodies, only the very best of mage's could even think about attempting it."

"What. You mean like the high magician? Myrrdin, the Merlin himself. Can he bring him back?"

He turns around looking for a response, but Myrrdin has walked outside and left them alone.

Artos crosses the room in haste. Barging out of the door, he can see the wizard standing amongst his animal horde, handing out claps of affection to deer and wolf alike.

"Myrrdin."

The old man stops him in his tracks with a raised hand.

"What did you see?" he says.

"What?"

"It is important. What did you see? In the vision that I gifted you as you lay in sleep."

"There was a magnificent room filled with my friends. I was in a great tower perched on a high mountain. It let me view the lands of my kingdom."

Myrrdin allows himself a small smile.

"There were beings of fire gathered around me at a vast round table. I felt they looked on me as their king."

"Did you see a grail?"

"No, but I've had those visions before," he pauses, "there was an empty chair, carved and ornate."

"Very well. It seems you are indeed the one," says Myrrdin, "we face a long road before —"

"Before what?"

"Before you, Artos, will become king above kings, uniting the tribes under one banner, commanding great armies on this island and beyond its near seas. Champion for the oppressed, father of the golden age, and the custodian of the Grail. Worlds, both seen and unseen, will come together under your reign. You are one with the Blessed Isle!"

Myrrdin's last words echo throughout the hillside and thunderous explosions rumble across the sky.

"Was that you?" says Artos.

"No, sometimes it just happens."

Morganna and Diana rush out in case the thunder is more than just an effect of the weather.

"Morganna, the visions I've been having are true."

"I know," says Morganna, "I was there in your vision."

"How does that work?" says Artos, "has she always been able to see my dreams?"

Myrrdin shrugs as if to say, *possibly*.

"Hold on though. Alan was in my vision," says Artos.

"I saw him too," says Morganna.

"So did I," says Diana.

"Wait, you saw the vision as well?" asks Artos, "the tower, the fiery knights, and the big table?"

"Yes, I was there, as was Alan," says Diana.

"Then Myrrdin Wylde, Merlin of the Britons, as your king, I command you to return Alan to life."

The old man's face contorts in a rage.

"You are no-one's king yet! Where is your crown? Your queen? your sword of power? Yes, your destiny is great. If indeed you survive the trials that lie ahead of you. For now, you still reek of the dung and detritus of Hartriggs."

"Hartriggs is alright," protests Artos.

Myrrdin mellows. "The river is scenic, I grant you, but that's not my point. We go forward under my leadership. I am not a servant to anyone's command."

"But he was in my vision. He must play a part?"

Myrrdin considers another possibility. "Where was Alan seated at the round table?"

"On my right-hand side. In the chair next to mine."

"I wonder," the Merlin strokes his beard, "Morganna, I will carry out the Rite of the Oak King. Do you know the herbs to collect from my house?"

"Yes, great Merlin," she replies with excitement.

"Don't forget the mistletoe oil."

"I'll help you," says Diana, and the two women rush back inside the roundhouse.

"Artos, do you know how to build a pyre?"

"Are you planning on burning him?"

"We need to lay his body on an altar of pine, oak, and birch. The sun is the flame. Now get your axe and start cutting. Time is against us."

Artos works hard, stripping and piling up the branches and leaves as a makeshift platform. He observes the wizard as he labours. Magicians place great importance on pipe smoking. Wren does it, Myrrdin was doing it. He had even caught Morganna sometimes doing it round the back of the big roundhouse at Hartriggs, but he never understood the attraction himself. Soon Morganna and Diana return, each carrying herbs and oils for the ritual.

"Place Alan's body on top of the altar," says Myrrdin.

Diana helps Artos lift Alan out from the building and over on to the pile of branches, while Myrrdin speaks to Morganna. He instructs her to prepare an infusion with herbs, oils, and water from his well. They work together to organise the ritual to his satisfaction. The sun has begun its descent from its highest point when he commands all to move back.

"Time is running out. This will become

more difficult as we approach sunset."

The wizard walks over and stands on raised ground, allowing him to look over Alan's body. After taking time to compose himself, he kneels with head bowed. Clutching his staff before him with his left hand, his right hand raises above his head. He begins to recite a spell. Artos observes Morganna repeating the chant. She is learning from the wizard.

Inching upwards as if lifting a great weight, the wizard's right hand pushes higher as he uses his staff to steady himself while rising to his feet. As he does so, the whole place is becoming hot. A haze forms. Insects are buzzing around them. Plants and bushes are becoming green and even flowering. Diana has to remove the fur garments she wears, and everyone breaks into a sweat.

Artos notices what is happening. The sun is rising in the sky. As Myrrdin stands taller, the season is changing from winter into summer. The sky is turning to a brilliant blue, without a cloud to be seen. Myrrdin slams his staff into the ground, once again causing the hillside to shake. The crystal embedded at the top illuminates with brilliant sunbeams. It revolves and burns, shooting out small solar flares.

He carefully lowers the searing mass on to the heart of Alan, and the flickering fireball passes into his body, creating an aura of golden light around him and within him. Everything is becoming hotter. The powerful energy builds around Alan, building to a blistering heat. Then suddenly, a glow of sunshine appears around his heart, re-igniting the spark of life. Alan lets out a scream and sits bolt upright, while smoke rises from his body.

"Morganna! Cast the water over him," Myrrdin calls.

Artos and Diana join in to sprinkle the water over Alan. It causes steam to rise into the air. The pale complexion of death has gone and instead he glows with radiant toned skin, as if he's been tanned by the summer heat. Alan breathes and opens his eyes. Standing up, he wipes the sweat away.

"It's boiling today," he says.

Artos, Morganna and Diana rush to embrace him as one, delighted to see their friend returned.

"I never thought I'd say this, but do you know that I missed you," says Morganna.

"And I missed you too," he responds by pulling her forward and kissing her on the cheek.

"It is great to have you back with us," agrees Diana.

"I didn't realise I had been somewhere. Where's all the skinny folk? It's still good to be back." Once again, Alan plants a kiss on the archer.

Morganna and Diana exchange puzzled glances with one another as Artos steps forward, extending his hand to his friend.

"I am pleased to have you back, my brother."

"Where did I go? But I am honoured that you call me brother. You call me brother?" Alan pulls Artos forward, embracing him, "but who am I?"

"Why you are Alan," says Artos.

"A-lance?"

"No, A-lan," the others corrected.

"A-lan. Okay, I can answer to that."

"That explains it," mumbles Myrrdin to himself as he stands up and walks round to face Alan.

"What did you see?"

"It's alright, he asks everyone that," says Artos.

"Well? What did you see? When the world went dark?"

"Lots of light. Yes, a big light. Did I die?"

"Yes, you were dead," Myrrdin confirms.

Alan looks shocked, but the others nod in agreement.

"Well, there was light, and then there was a boat, with some ladies on it. They said nothing, it was all silent. Oh, then they were taking me to an island. Was I dead for long?"

"Not long, an hour or two." says Artos.

"Well, I didn't get to the island, but the boat

journey was very nice, very calming. Then I became warm, and it just felt like I was being pulled through darkness and into light, and then you were all around me."

"You were lucky," says Morganna, "the gods protected you by sending Myrrdin just in time to save you."

Suspicion was intoned in Morganna's statement. She already felt that the Merlin knew more than he was saying, but he had blocked his thoughts from inquisitive minds.

"Thank you Myrrdin," says Alan with an unusual tone of humility, "I have died and came back to life twice in the last few days. I'm getting used to it."

Myrrdin looks confused.

"I'll tell you later about that," says Artos.

"I'll try not to do it again," Alan smiles.

"See that you don't. It puts years on me every time I carry out that spell. It seems right to have done it for the festival of Sol Invictus. So, we'll stay here one more night. I need to recover. We should celebrate our coming together, for tomorrow, we must start our journey together."

"Our journey?" asks Artos.

"Yes, the prophecy. Isn't that why you're here?"

FESTIVE DINNER

Candles flicker in the small chapel at Dun Romanach. Andrew is busy arranging altar pieces and pouring out the prized red wine into a chalice trimmed with gold. He allows himself a small sip and wipes the rim with a piece of cloth. Then repeats the sip and wipe cycle once more.

He places the cup on the altar and moves a candle an inch closer. The flame reflects on the ornate grail, light dancing on the shining metal. He looks at the remaining wine and swirls it within the chalice before draining the cup. With full ritual, he wipes the rim with a cloth and refills the vessel before replacing it on the altar.

Moving to his pulpit, he opens the codex of his own self-penned works, choosing to display a page that is in praise of Duncan's many generous and fictional acts of charity. Beside the book lies a half-completed contract drawn up to gain great swathes of the MacForres lands at the stroke of a quill. He chuckles to himself as he rolls up the parchment. He will present the document when Duncan is closer to meeting his God.

Glancing once again at the chalice on the altar, he admires its shape and form, as well as its contents. His hands shake and he licks his dry lips with anticipation. At first, he hesitates, acknowledging to himself he is succumbing to temptation.

What harm can one more sip do?

Wine has many benefits. Made from fruit, not the evil fig with its leaves employed to cover shame, but the merry fruit of Bacchus. God surely approves of that. Reasoning and contemplation over, he makes a dash for the cup.

"It's a bit early for the sacramental," says Duncan as he enters the chapel, followed by his son and daughter.

"Why it's evening now my lord."

"Yes, but by early, I mean it's not Easter."

"It is a religious celebration. I'm sure we may wet the head of the memory of our Lord's birth."

"Fine, pour me a cup. Remember, I must flog the taxes from the people to fund it. They're not made of money."

Duncan, MacDuncan, and Duncanna take their places in reserved chairs. The other family and high-ranking members of the MacForres warband file in behind to stand in order of importance.

Andrew pours another large goblet of wine, handing it to Duncan. He returns to the altar and mumbles in Latin before swallowing yet another gulp for himself. The congregation gives a small murmur of mocking laughter. Flustered by their disrespect, he then trips and knocks his head off the pulpit, resulting in a louder bout of merriment.

"Keep this up Andrew and we can save money on hiring a jester," says MacDuncan, perfecting his own mocking tones for the sake of the crowd.

"Let's get on with it," says Duncan.

"You are sinners!" says Andrew, launching his sermon with a venomous tone.

The crowd returns a small cheer.

"You may do well to spend this day of celebration without partaking in your usual drunkenness ..." a cheer follows, "... fornication..." a louder cheer follows, "... and laying with the beasts," the loudest cheer follows.

"That's your Christmas ruined MacDuncan," says a voice from the back.

"I told you I was just doing a stock check of the goats."

The congregation collapses in hysterical laughter, even Duncan joins in with the hilarity. The poor behaviour of the flock mortifies Andrew. He regains control by going for the full fire and brimstone rendition of his Christmas message.

"Order, order! Do not succumb to the Lord of Misrule within these hallowed walls. For you, your children, and their children yet to be, will burn in torturous pain for eternity."

It silences the crowd in an instant. The threat of going to hell was always good for crowd control.

"You will not indulge in mirth. You must fast, abstain and purify yourself with self-flagellation."

Andrew leaves a deliberate pause hanging in the air, knowing that his audience is straining to keep their composure.

"Now let us pray."

The congregation bow their heads and close their eyes, but it's then that a high pitched and long-lasting escape of methane pierces the quiet and provides a sudden abundance of aroma to the room.

"Jesus Christ! Who did that?" says MacDuncan and once again the crowd erupts in uncontrollable laughter.

Andrew thumps at his pulpit in disgust with one hand while holding his nose with the other.

"Declare yourself. Who is it? Who dares unleash a demon in this holy place?"

The hilarity in the room continues. The guilty party rises to his feet, head bowed with his admission. Only then does the crowd go quiet, anticipating which punishment will follow.

"For your foul expression of evil, stand in the corner and pray for forgiveness."

The leniency disappoints the crowd as the man squeezes past to move to the back.

"None of you are without sin. Use this day to reflect on your transgressions. Punishable by death or worse."

Andrew's threats subdue the raucous reactions, and the crowd does their best to offer the pretence of respect. Except for one small old man standing at the front. He raises his hand before speaking.

"Aye Father Andrew, it's me, Donal. What does scripture say of unclean food? At the feast for Eochaid, you gorged on a spiced ferret."

A shocked murmur goes around the crowd.

"I assure you the feasting fayre was free of sin. But before you cast your first stone, Donal, may I comment on the sinful way that you style your beard. You should do penance for each day until the shaved parts return to their manly form and you dispose of your demonic countenance."

"Don't you dare accuse my husband!" says Donal's wife. "I love his beard. It's very fashionable."

Another rumble of disapproval moves through the crowd because a woman has just spoken in church.

Undeterred, she continues, "did you not eat with bread, the honeyed jam made by the Lady Duncanna?"

The atmosphere suddenly becomes tense. It's never good to involve Duncanna in any dispute.

"Yes, it was excellent jam. A jam of the highest quality," he says, while grinning at Duncanna.

"Jam from the fruit of a tree planted less than two years ago," says Donal, "that is punishable by death!"

Andrew squirms. He can't pass the blame on to Duncanna. Donal had him where he wanted. The eating of jam made from fruit that wasn't of legal age was indeed a capital offence and so for this evening at least, Andrew had lost the moral high ground.

Seething, he walks to the altar, mutters more Latin and drains more wine, before lifting the collection plate and thrusting it threateningly before the congregation.

"You know how this works. Place coin in the plate to buy the removal of your sinful ways and pass it to the next sinner. I was going to preach on the benefits of fasting, but I waste such lessons on your eagerness to indulge in the manner of your heathen ancestors."

"Aye," cheers everyone in agreement.

Andrew can't disguise his disdain as the great and the good of Dun Romanach leave after placing only a meagre offering of coin clippings on the plate. The congregation shakes Andrew's hand as they leave with enthusiastic words of encouragement, declaring it an excellent service or a wonderful vigil. Andrew reacts with a mixture of enforced politeness and outright contempt for his parishioners.

With the others gone, Duncan drains his cup and walks over to check the contents of the collection plate.

"I'm sure they've sinned more than that," he says. "maybe you should show people how much they're meant to pay for each sin that they commit."

"You want me to write a price list?"

"Yes, an excellent idea."

"Maybe they could do with just committing fewer sins."

"What? The church is here to make money. Don't forget that."

Duncan heads for the door. "Merry Christmas."

"Of course, my lord."

Andrew can't help thinking that Duncan is missing the point. He views the church as nothing more than a commercial enterprise. As the priest's hands stray once again to unroll the parchment headed *Contract*, he experiences a personal moment of revelation. Maybe Duncan is right.

"What are you doing?" says Duncan, as his son presses an ear against the big curtain.

"Just listening in on the conversation. They're coming up with excuses to avoid offering tribute."

Duncan smiles at the naivety of his son. "None of them can open a purse, even to let the moths escape. At this time of year, we must show charity to our family. We can leave torture and taxes for another day. Now get them seated and I'll summon Mona to bring through our festive meal."

MacDuncan disappears through the curtain with his loud and distinctive guffaw. Meanwhile, Duncan turns back towards the entrance to his chambers.

"Mona!" he calls.

After a few moments, the sound of approaching turmoil makes his face drop. Mona's expressive use of Latin interspersed with the demanding tones of Duncanna suggests trouble is coming. Duncan shakes his head and wrings his hands as they enter the chamber together.

Mona is the owner of Tabernae Mona, a tavern that lies beyond the south gate of

Dun Romanach. Her family has lived nearby for hundreds of years since the Romans first ventured north on their occupation of Britannia. Dressed from head to toe in black since the death of her husband, she is not subdued by the lack of colourful clothing. Her hands dance around with every syllable that she fires out. Emotion punctuates every sentence, be it joyous or sad.

She enters the room in full flow, clasping her hands to the side of her head. "No mistress. This dinner is only for men. You cannot be there. What will people say?"

Duncanna is quick to complain. "Dear father, it has been almost a week since they killed my beloved Eochaid in battle and we haven't had a single conversation on who I'm going to marry next."

"My darling daughter. These things take time and organisation. We want to get you a suitable match and we must await the return of Ifan Gofannon. He should be with King Fergus as we speak. Presuming Ifan's performance goes well, there will be others to choose in Eochaid's place."

"Hope! I want more than hope. You have your richest vassals in attendance today. One of them must have a son who can serve me as a husband."

"Redlead has many sons, but they are still children."

"And what of Uncle Torcaill?"

"You want to marry Uncle Torcaill?"

"No, of course not, but Uncle Torcaill knows lots of people with money, land, and sons to spare."

"Yes, but please understand that your marriage must have a higher purpose. Your happiness is important to me and rushing into love seldom produces a good land transaction or military support."

Duncanna waves her hand and grunts with disgust. "It's you that doesn't understand the pressures these days. A charming young man of wealth and good grace is an essential accessory. My friends now call me No-Man-NicForres!"

Duncan sighs. "Very well, I will speak with Torcaill."

"No, I will speak with him. If I'm to fall in love with someone, I at least want to hear the first description."

"Duncanna, you are being unreasonable. It's vulgar for me to discuss your marriage with you there."

"Father, we live in different times. That was in the olden days. It's the fifth century now. You need to keep up to date. Society is changing, and I know my rights."

"Do we have enough food, Mona?" says Duncan in an exasperated tone of defeat.

"My Lord Duncan, you told me the dinner

was for five. I have brought five of everything, not six. This is too much."

"No, it's not enough. Can't you just cut some parts from each? She doesn't eat much you know."

"Which part of the stuffed dormouse?"

"I don't know. The tails?"

"That is the best part."

"Just organise it Mona," he turns to Duncanna, "Does that make you happy my dear?"

"Happy," she replies.

"That was strange weather earlier. The hottest I can remember for a long while."

The man speaking was Torcaill MacForres. Duncan's cousin, and owner of a large estate within the MacForres lands. Older by only a few years. His hair had greyed and thinned out, as opposed to his waistline, which had thickened over his lifetime. A few teeth had survived the skirmishes and battles, and a large wart on the end of his nose completed his look. Torcaill had wealth, status and influence that extended far beyond the borders of Galwydell, so he was considered very desirable by many who would hope to share in his lifestyle.

He stood alongside two more of Duncan's

vassals and MacDuncan as they waited on their leader arriving to take his place for their festive family dinner.

The second member of the group was Redlead, the warband's unofficial leader. Named after the colour of his large beard and the produce of his many mines. Well-built and from farming stock. Redlead had been Duncan's ally for years. His masterful wielding of a great sword had claimed the lives of many opponents in battle.

The third man was Gilbert MacForres. Torcaill's younger sibling. His general look was closer to Duncan than it was to his own brother, leaving scope for a long-held rumour over who his father may have been. He bore the familiar MacForres traits of greed and lust for power and derived his primary source of income from espionage, blackmail, and extortion.

"Aye, the weather gets stranger every year," continues Redlead, "how's yourself Torcaill?"

"It's not been a good year for the farms. Harvests were poor, and the gods cursed the cattle with sour milk. It won't be great when the time comes for my tribute to Duncan, and what about yourself Redlead?"

Redlead shuffled and took in a deep breath before replying. "Aye, I too have had a poor year. You just can't get the slaves these days, and the locals won't go near the mines for the money

I'm willing to pay."

"Or are unwilling to pay," says Gilbert, "gentlemen, we have this conversation every year. The weather, the curses, the slaves. We know we want to enjoy the rewards of our position without handing it straight back to taxes. I haven't paid for them in years. I've told you before, for a small fee I can negotiate with Duncan on your behalf."

MacDuncan fills their mead cups. "There is much to pay for gentlemen. Ynys Mon will not invade itself. Please understand that faither has ambitions for our family. Your investment in his war chest will not go unrewarded. May your mead be plentiful."

"Aye, cheers!" they reply before draining a large part of the ale with two or three gulps.

The large curtain parts and Duncan enters, followed by Duncanna. "Ah, good sirs! I see you have started without me. You know my daughter, Duncanna. She has asked to join us today, and insists that I must modernise?"

"Of course, Duncanna you may join us," says Torcaill, "she is right. We get stuck in our ways when we reach the twilight years of our forties. Do you remember me, my dear? I am your uncle, but I haven't seen you for many years."

"And I," continued Gilbert, "I am your Uncle Gilbert, how I bounced you on my knee when you were a young girl. Do you remember that?"

"How could I forget your fooling Uncle Gilbert, and do you remember I broke your nose as part of our fun? I have laughed many times over that memory in the years hence."

"It still causes me discomfort now," says Gilbert.

A small mocking laughter circulates amongst the other guests as Gilbert taps his squinted facial feature.

The men stand to acknowledge her presence, apart from MacDuncan, who scowls at his sister as the servant places a seat at the table between him and Gilbert.

"And you will know Redlead already," says Duncan, "who operates mines on his estates. He hopes to find gold in the hills one day soon."

"Yet there cannot be a precious metal that matches the golden colour of your hair, my lady," says Redlead.

"Why thank you Master Deadleg. Tell me, what age is your oldest son again?"

"Ten, my lady, and the oldest of ten boys in my family. One day I hope I will have a daughter as charming as you."

"I'm sure your wife will be more than happy to give you a daughter at the eleventh try, so that she may have a rest."

The gathered men laugh together as they usher Duncanna to sit first.

"What are you doing here?" says MacDuncan.

"None of your business. Drink your mead and be quiet."

Duncan signals to the servant. "We will begin our meal now, bring the first course."

"My, a first course, Duncan. You're moving up in the world indeed," says Torcaill, "it's been many a long month since I had courses for my meal."

Three servants enter the hall carrying bowls of soup for the first course. Mona follows them into the room.

"Lady and Gentlemen," she begins, "I have made a sumptuous meal for you today. If you enjoy it, then please visit me at Tabernae Mona, just along from this fortification, where you can sample the best of Roman cuisine at a reasonable price."

The servants place bowls of brown steaming sludge in front of everyone.

"This is my Tisanam Barricam. A delicious soup made with lentil, leek and cabbage, a sprinkling of herbs from the continent and my family recipe of *garum*. Made with the crushed viscera and blood of sardines and anchovies. I ferment it for over two years to develop its unique aroma and flavour. Please enjoy!"

Mona and the servants leave, while the diners stare at the unappetising broth.

"More mead?" asks Duncan.

"Aye, more mead!" the others reply.

MacDuncan fills everyone's cups again,

which they empty before attempting to consume Mona's exotic cuisine.

"Could I ask something?" says Duncanna, "it may not be a surprise, but the untimely death of my intended husband has left me in a quandary. I know not how I can be a perfect wife. Can you share your thoughts? What are the best qualities for someone such as me?"

An exchange of awkward glances passes around the table before Torcaill decides he should give the first reply.

"My lady. What joy my wife brings into my life. Her very presence in the room causes my heart to race. The moments I've shared with her are my happiest. You will adore her Duncanna, she is a full year older than you. I'm sure you will have similar interests."

"Yes, I'm sure," adds Gilbert while licking his lips.

"And what do you say, Master Deadleg?"

"Eh, my name is Redlead, my lady. For me, the best qualities of a wife are loyalty and service. Whether it be looking after the children, cooking the meals, or keeping our dwelling tidy."

"And what of love?"

"Thanks be to God. My wife has little time left for love. I'm not as young as I used to be."

"I see."

Duncanna silently removes Redlead's offspring from her list of possible options.

"I can offer suggestions," says Gilbert.

"No, it's alright uncle, the second course is coming now."

The curtain parts once more and Mona re-emerges with her serving staff.

"Lady and gentlemen. I hope you enjoyed your *gustatio*. Now we will serve your *primae mensae*. Please share and eat together."

They remove the bowls and set out communal plates of wheat porridge, served with bread, cheese, eggs and honey, the stuffed dormice, and other savouries such as snails and pickled sow udders. They serve Duncanna with a tiny plate of fried dormouse tails.

MacDuncan surveys the spread before him.

"Think I just fancy that bread and cheese."

"Yes, me too," says Torcaill.

"More mead?" asks Duncan.

"Aye, more mead!" they agree again.

As they devour the bread and cheese, Duncanna decides the time has come for another question.

"Maybe you can help me again and grant me the help of your knowledge and life experience. Should a wife control the family wealth?"

A condescending laugh circles around the table.

"What need does my wife have for wealth?" says Redlead, "why she has everything she needs. Once a week I will grant her a small allocation of coin and each week I will ask her to buy the same items. It never changes."

"Aye," agrees Torcaill, "maybe my wife is different. She is unconcerned with money, but the things that are gained through spending it. I think my wealth could soon disappear if I gave her control, and then, of course, I might disappear after that," he says, drawing a finger across his neck.

"Fair Duncanna," says Gilbert, "you have brains and refinement, and I'm sure the cunning of a fox. Why rely on another's wealth when you can create your own? Money for services will always keep you in comfort."

"Gilbert!" says Torcaill.

"I merely suggest my lady has access to the courts of kings, where secrets and scandal trade for a high price."

"Yes, I could see myself as a spy," admits Duncanna.

"Then maybe we can discuss this further."

"Lady and gentlemen, *secundae mensae*," says Mona, returning once again with her serving staff, "we have pastries and cake with imported fruit to sweeten your palette and round off your meal."

Once more, the servants exchange the plates on the table for the dessert, while Duncanna directs an angry stare at her father to lead the talk to matrimony.

Duncan shifts in his chair. "Forgive me Torcaill for speaking, with my daughter present, but she is eager to find a suitable marriage partner now that Eochaid is no more. Can you suggest anyone?"

Torcaill is uncomfortable with talking in front of Duncanna, and a pause follows as he first looks at Duncanna's innocent smile, then at Duncan's worried frown, followed by Gilbert's disfigured nose.

"Well, I suppose I can be modern, as you say. There are two potential matches, but both present issues."

Duncanna is excited. "If I can decide among them, then I'm sure we can sort out these issues. Pray tell who they are?"

"I first recommend Owain of the Rheged."

A loud laugh erupts around the table.

"The son of Urien," says Duncan, "I have heard that you should keep your enemies closer than your friends, but Urien allowing his son to wed a MacForres daughter?"

"True," says Torcaill, "but if Owain falls for Duncanna, then maybe his father could yet become an ally."

"Excuse me," says Redlead, "Urien and Owain are best kept at the point of our spears."

"That is true," says Gilbert, "he is powerful. Yet he faces the Angles against his own borders. While the Saxons move closer to the southern reaches of his lands."

"Gentlemen," says Duncanna, "I speak of love not war, If Owain is handsome, virtuous, and wealthy, you can trust he will turn on his own kin long before he will turn on me. I will make sure of that."

Her sweet smile, tainted with malevolence, is plain for everyone to see. This amuses the other family members.

"Owain has the qualities you wish. That is true," says Torcaill, "my other recommendation is a young leader making a name for himself within the Kingdom of Fib."

"Uh oh," says MacDuncan, "you don't mean?"

"The Picts," confirms Torcaill, "Talorc has a fierce reputation, but he is without a wife. He may well consider a proposal from you."

"The Picts are off their heads!" says Redlead.

"Off their heads and uncontrollable," says Gilbert.

"And they always strip down to the nip at the first opportunity," says MacDuncan.

"Really?" Duncanna sounds impressed.

Duncan settles the uproar with a hand gesture. "We can't conduct business with the Picts. The sworn enemies of the Dal Riata, whose ships we need for an assault on Ynys Mon. You see why marriage is difficult to arrange, Duncanna?"

"Is that what I mean to you, father? Getting your hands on a load of leaky boats. Just to invade an island that no-one else is interested to capture. Think bigger."

The table falls into awkward silence. Duncan can order anyone's death on a whim, but Duncanna is dangerous, too. It requires Torcaill to soften the mood again.

"Talorc could offer an army to support an attack against Urien. The Picts have dealings with the Angles and the Saxons. That is where the power lies. A marriage will grant us the opportunity to remove the Rheged and take their land. You and Galwydell will be stronger for it."

"I don't know," says Duncan, "I can see your wisdom, but to take Ynys Mon is the fastest route to a kingdom."

"Very well," agrees Torcaill, "but give it thought. I'm sure Duncanna can control either Talorc or Owain."

A murmur of agreement on Duncanna's abilities concludes the topic as Duncan calls Mona forward with her servants to remove the meal from the table.

"Let's retire to my private chamber. There is a fine wine waiting to finish our dinner."

Duncan and MacDuncan both stand up, followed by Torcaill and Redlead. Duncanna rises to leave, but Gilbert signals for her to stay back. Once they are alone, Gilbert licks his lips again before speaking.

"Are you as devious as your father, dear Duncanna?"

"I'd say more, Uncle Gilbert. My mother and

my father are evil. I have inherited the traits of both."

Gilbert grins. "You know you could do worse than marry me. Your father is getting old, facing dangers that come with age. You have skills with poison; your brother will be an easy target. Life with me need not be unpleasant. I'm sure we could form a profitable partnership."

"Why, Uncle Gilbert, what are you saying? I must confess I am interested in becoming a spy, but," Duncanna grabs a small knife from her plate and holds it to Gilbert's neck, "bounce me on your knee one more time and I will slit you from ear to ear then feed you to our dogs while you still gargle and choke on your own blood."

Redlead has cast his drinking vessel back on to the table, having drained it in one gulp, while Torcaill stands trying to swirl the insignificant quantity of wine in his cup into something bigger.

"You should offer Duncanna's hand to Talorc," says Torcaill, "losing Eochaid will not sit well with the nobles of the Dal Riata. Even if your bard can spin the news of his death to placate King Fergus."

"I think even before that. We should punish Hartriggs," says Redlead, "I didn't beat those two hard enough when they joined the levy. That is easy to see. It is their fault that we are in this predicament."

"Aye. I agree," says Torcaill, "the Dal Riata will expect nothing less from us."

Duncan pauses in thought and looks downcast. "Very well, I'll do it. I'll organise something soon."

"Faither," says MacDuncan, "I can take men with Redlead right now. It will take no time at all."

"I said I'll do it," barks Duncan, "the dinner is over, and I grow tired. Good evening, gentlemen."

The vassals bow and take their cue to go. Duncanna enters as they leave. The brother and sister cast each other suspicious glances. Their father is subdued and preoccupied with his thoughts.

"Are you sure, faither?" says MacDuncan in his most considerate tone, "I'm more than happy to raise that cursed village to the ground on your behalf."

"No. You will go nowhere tonight. There is much to consider first."

"But you agreed."

"Who is your lord?"

"You are, faither."

"So, you will follow my commands, not the

demands of those other fools. Now go to your room."

"Yes, faither," MacDuncan departs.

"What did Gilbert want with you Duncanna?"

"I believe he wanted to propose marriage to me."

"And what did you say?"

"I offered to slice his neck and feed him to the pets."

"That's my girl."

THE TABERNAE
MONA INCIDENT

Steps move through the rough terrain as Artos and the others advance on their next challenge with fresh purpose and grim determination. The endless rain had made the journey more difficult.

With hoods drawn around their faces, four of the five are unrecognisable from a distance, but in contrast Myrrdin's traditional wizard hat, large crystal topped staff and long gaited stride stand out as much as usual.

Earlier that day, Myrrdin had decided they needed transport to help them navigate the prophecy with more ease. That meant fast horses. Dun Romanach itself was the place where they might find enough gathered together. It was too risky to raid Duncan's stables, but there was a less protected location that Artos and Alan knew well.

Tabernae Mona. The tavern sat in a

picturesque part of the forest overlooking the old Roman road to Dun Romanach. It lay out of sight of the fortress and was a popular stopping point. Merchants, soldiers, and other travellers keen to experience an authentic Roman family-run tavern stopped there, and customers meant horses.

The roofed building contained plenty of tables and chairs for guests to be seated. The decor was Mediterranean, comprising authentic artifacts and genuine replicas gathered together during the times spent under the rule of Rome.

Graffiti on the countertop of the bar read, *BIBO ERGO SUM - SEPTIMIUS.* A reference to the last Roman emperor to have set foot in Galwydell.

A kitchen and living quarters were to the rear. Outside lay a landscaped garden that surrounded a waterfall. A large paddock sat to the side to tie up horses.

On summer evenings, Tabernae Mona was always full of visitors. In winter, it was quieter, with only a few regular customers who bought enough mead to justify keeping it open. A warm meal prepared for the family would scent the air and attract the occasional weary tourist.

Artos and his party approach the tavern from higher ground to the rear of the building. They look over at the paddock. Two horses stand beside one another. A third horse, an older mare, stands hitched to the same fence. Then, a few feet along, a wagon containing two barrels.

"I told you there was transport here," says Artos.

"That's disappointing," says Myrrdin, "I hoped for fresh horses for everyone, not just you and me."

"Well, it doesn't matter. Maybe I should have mentioned, I can't ride a horse."

"What do you mean, you can't ride a horse?"

"I've never learned."

"You couldn't tell me this earlier?"

"I was hoping we could find a horse and cart. That's what we used with the warband. I'm sure it can carry us."

"That is not the point," Myrrdin looks skyward, "why do the gods delight in my misfortune? A drover's horse and wagon are not suitable for where we are going. We should ride in on mounts that befit the status of kings and heroes of legend, not as vagabonds cramped between wine barrels."

"There's wine in those barrels?" asks Alan.

"You're not helping," Artos says, dampening Alan's enthusiasm before looking Myrrdin square in the eye, "find transport, you said. You mentioned nothing about kings and heroes of legend."

The wizard stares back. He can read the qualities of the man that stands before him. He has strength, integrity, a strong sense of right and wrong. Admirable qualities for a leader, if you could just ignore the jealousy, a tendency to whine, and a few general insecurities. Myrrdin pauses in thought. Just long enough for the tight ball of rage inside to weaken and dissipate, and his face to crease itself into the form of a smile.

"You are right, of course," he agrees.

"Oh, alright, good then," says Artos, nodding to the rest of the party, "so?"

"So?" replies Myrrdin.

"So, where are we going?"

"Oh yes, of course. Where are we going? Why to the sacred realm, to the spiral mounds of Faerie and their majestic underworld halls, to the mountains carved over time by the crystal waters that rush and flow as blue veins through the body of the land, to the lush rolling meadows with their carpets of cowslip and poppy and endless forest born fields of bluebell, daffodil and snowdrop, to the sunsets that turn the seas from sky blue to burnished gold."

"So, where's that then?" asks Artos.

"Well, it's not anywhere yet. A loose collection of thirty to forty kingdoms made up of different tribes. It's always changing, but one day it will unite as a sovereign isle and take its name from the victors."

"Artosland? I love the sound of that."

"Maybe?" says Myrrdin, "we will begin by travelling to Rheged. To the palace of King Urien, where I pray we can gain his support for an assault on Dun Romanach."

"We're going to fight Duncan?"

"Yes, of course. A king needs a castle. A place to build your power and influence. Dun Romanach is that place. Your people live in and around the fortress walls. This is where the prophecy begins."

A silence follows. Monotonous and grey, the icy breeze and the thick clouds are unforgiving. Artos feels his mouth go dry, his heart races, and fear takes hold. This is no longer a dream. He looks around at Alan, Morganna, and Diana. The thought of the risk they're taking returns to him.

"If the prophecy begins here. Then we must decide to go forth as one. I am the youngest, yet it's my fate to lead. If you cannot follow me, then go in peace. I will understand."

It's Myrrdin's turn to panic. He didn't see this coming. It's too late to influence the minds of the others.

"I'm sure you know I fight by your side no matter what," says Alan, "our years in the shield wall are enough, we are lifelong friends, I will not walk away."

"Artos, you are my brother," says Morganna, "we share a destiny, of that, I am sure. I will not walk away now."

Diana looks at Artos with just a slight hint of frustration.

"Are you shitting me? The years I have travelled. The commitment to the quest. You are the Bastard of Caledon. Now lead us to our glorious fate!"

Myrrdin sighs with relief. "Well, Artos? What do you think we should do?"

"Rheged is not too far away. I'm sure the horse and cart will get us there," says Artos.

"Indeed. We have no other choice for the moment," replies the wizard.

Artos assumes command. "Right, let's get our transport —"

"And the wine," says Alan.

"And the wine. Follow me."

Myrrdin, Morganna, Diana, and Alan all follow Artos as he leads them towards the tavern. They descend the slope at a pace, hoping that the persistent rain will keep the owners of the horses indoors.

There is a raw mix of tension and excitement in the air. The wisps of wood-smoke flavoured with the smell of roasted meat. The muffled sound of drunken voices from within the bar. They must work fast.

Leaping over the low fencing to the rear of the paddock, they cross the open ground. Morganna and Diana make for the two horses that are standing together. The young witch and the archer are skilled at handling animals. They keep both horses settled and calm.

Myrrdin approaches the mare and introduces himself. The old horse snorts and pricks her ears forward, responding with interest as the wizard communicates his intentions.

Artos and Alan know just how to hitch a horse and wagon together. Within a few brief minutes, everything is ready and Myrrdin climbs on to the front to take the reins.

Artos and Alan climb on the back, signalling for Morganna and Diana to join them, but just at that point, two of the voices from within Tabernae Mona sound sharper and closer.

The witch and the archer are still crossing towards the wagon when two of Duncan's warband lumber into view. They are both burly, with the usual combination of muscle and belly. One has black hair while the other has red.

Lost in a good story that has begun a few cups of mead earlier, they notice Myrrdin sitting up behind the mare. They offer a drunken, friendly greeting as they pass. They don't spot Artos and Alan, who slide between the barrels and pull their hoods close around them. It is Morganna and Diana that snap the two well-oiled soldiers back into sharp focus.

"Good afternoon," says the red-haired man

in his most polite, if slightly intoxicated voice.

"Can we be of help?" says the black-haired man.

"Maybe you can. I met this lady as I was walking by," Morganna gesticulates towards Diana, "she's visiting us from abroad. She doesn't speak our language very well. I told her Tabernae Mona was a good place to eat."

The two short, fat, hairy warriors can't believe their luck at running into such beautiful women when they themselves have drunk enough mead to make sure they are desirable enough to any female of the species, or any other species.

"Well, of course," says the red beard, "we always come here. Fine mead and traditional Roman home-cooked cuisine. I am best friends with the owner. She's not here at the moment, but if you care to join us, I can arrange something special to eat."

Red beard offers what he believes is a polite laugh, but it just comes out sounding sleazy and threatening.

"What's going on?" whispers Artos.

"Hold on I can hear her," says Myrrdin, "Morganna can speak with the silent voice?"

Myrrdin, keep going. Diana and I will catch up with you.

Myrrdin can tell a telepathic message when he hears it. He pulls at the horse and tells it to move forward.

"We can't leave them," whispers Artos.

"Morganna is telling us to go," assures Myrrdin, "I can hear her words when others can't."

"How will they find us?"

"She knows where we are heading and says Diana can smell us? They'll find us, I'm sure."

The mare picks up into a trot and pulls the wagon onwards. Drawing its cargo of thieves and wine barrels out on to the main road.

As Diana performs her best version of a foreign tourist, she smiles with kindness and sincerity at the soldiers while she insults them in a wide variety of languages. Meanwhile, red beard and black beard do their best to help the poor foreigner understand with ever increasing vocal volume and theatrical hand gestures.

The conversation continues in a variety of languages and dialects. None of which makes any sense. The two men introduce themselves. The red beard is Rab, and the black beard is Archie. They discover they have a genuine talent for talking, using only hand gestures and a variety of animal noises. They run through a visual description of the enticing menu available at Tabernae Mona. Morganna checks the wagon has disappeared before she interrupts the ridiculous performance.

"Are you handsome lads going to buy us a drink?"

Rab and Archie looked delighted at the prospect and stop their excellent portrayal of blackbird pie served with baked bread. They usher the ladies forward with wide, semi-toothless grins and guttural laughter, while winking their eyes and patting each other on the back.

Entering Tabernae Mona, you were at first struck with a peculiar combination of aromas. Stale alcohol infused air blended with more than a hint of sweat. The strong scent of herbs and spices used in the cooking, wood-smoke, plus a faint sensation of lingering flatulence and manure. Just the way the customers liked it.

"Please take a seat, Morganna. DIANA, THERE'S, A, TABLE, BY, THE FIRE," says Rab.

He describes a chair and flickering flames as he points to a table. Diana responds with a charming smile while denigrating Rab's mother in another multi-lingual insult.

"How will we buy drinks?" says Archie as their two guests choose chairs at the table.

"Felix will let us pay for them later," says Rab.

"You must know a different Felix from me."

The two warriors approach the bar. Rab taps on the wooden counter and Felix walks through to serve.

"Have you two found more coin? I thought I'd emptied your purses today, gentlemen."

Rab looks towards Morganna and Diana. "No, not coin. We have found something else."

A low whistle emerges from between Felix's pursed lips. "My, my. How did you two find them? Are they blind?"

"No, though one of them doesn't speak our language," says Archie, "you couldn't help us out with a wee round of drinks to offer the ladies. You know we'll pay you later."

"I suppose, but it will cost double when you pay me."

"Come on, Felix!" says Archie.

"Take it or leave it."

"We'll take it," says Rab.

Diana covers her mouth as she whispers to Morganna.

"We'll have to kill them, won't we?"

"It is a shame," says Morganna, "they were only out for a drink. It's not their fault that they have fallen into our path at the wrong moment. If I thought they were too drunk to remember us tomorrow."

"And what about the tavern manager?"

"Oh yes, we'll need to kill him."

Rab and Archie walk over, carrying the four cups of mead. It only takes a few seconds for Rab to seal his own fate.

"Wait a minute, don't I recognise you?" he

asks Morganna, "didn't I see you at Hartriggs the other day?"

Morganna forces a smile. "Yes, I'm from Hartriggs."

"Aye, it was you that MacDuncan had a notion to take home, then he reconsidered? Most girls wish to marry MacDuncan. Good looks, money, heir to Dun Romanach."

"Or so he tells us," says Archie.

Both men laugh at their own brilliant sense of humour.

"I prefer a shorter man. I can't be doing with the tall, dark, and handsome nonsense," says Morganna, "give me a stocky man, with a good paunch of fat, and reeking of mead, while he struggles to form words in his mouth."

Rab and Archie smile at each other. The ladies must find them alluring. They splutter out another loud manly laugh, with hair tossing and beard stroking, to turn up the attractiveness level.

Diana speaks to Morganna in her own language and signs that she is still hungry.

"My friend needs to eat something; she has been travelling a long way to get here."

"We might have a wee problem there," says Rab.

"There's no food to cook this afternoon," interrupts Archie, "Felix is waiting for a delivery. His mother, Mona that runs the place, she is away right now, picking ingredients up for later."

Morganna and Diana look around themselves. There is a brace of pheasant hanging next to a box containing salted fish and a leg of venison that lies on a table.

"That stuff is just for show," says Archie, "it's been there for years. You can't eat it."

Diana signals for everyone to stay seated. She lifts her bow and arrows, then walks outside the tavern. An awkward silence follows, before she returns with a rabbit and a magpie. She holds them in the air to a cheer. Rab and Archie can't believe how wonderful their day is turning out.

Diana walks over towards Felix and speaks in hushed tones. "Your friends are idiotic, but I am starving. I can catch wolf, deer, or boar, but I can't boil an egg. I always love someone who can cook me a fine dinner."

Felix grins from ear to ear as he realises Diana can indeed speak the language much better than most.

"Well, let me see. I suppose I could prepare —"

"No," replies Diana, "sign for me. I don't want those trolls to think I can speak to them."

Felix smiles back, showing that he will play along with the subterfuge. He is earning double the money on the mead. If he impresses Diana with his cooking, then who knows? Maybe he will win her affection.

The host attempts to act out different recipes and meal options for the food provided. Rabbit stuffed with figs was an entertaining charade. Pomegranate sauce for the magpie was more difficult. Rab and Archie are in hysterics by now as they watch their friend describe leeks and carrots.

"I'm going to wet my breeches!" roars Archie, "I need to go visit a place right now."

He staggers out of the tavern to find a spot to relieve himself, while Rab drains the remaining mead from Archie's cup.

Felix now believes that Diana is much more interested in him. He is four inches taller and can see his feet when he looks downward. Either Rab or Archie will have to leave.

Archie soon returns to his seat and Rab decides it's his turn to go outside for a toilet break.

"Keep my seat warm," he says, before exiting.

Morganna's expression darkens. "Why do you hang around with that waste of space, Archie? Rab has done nothing but insult you while you were away."

"What?"

"He said he could have had a thousand women, but your ugliness harms his chances."

"No Rab's my friend. That's just a joke."

"He said you were a hedge born coxcomb, a skamelar and a curl, and he didn't stop there.

He said your manhood is of a mandrake. Oh, and every time you fart, a fairy dies."

"Rab's the one with the mandrake manhood," Archie replies, "in fact, even a mandrake mymmerkin. Just wait till I get him."

Archie tries to drink his mead, only to find he has none left. He displays the empty vessel to Morganna.

"The person you call your friend did that."

At that point, Rab walks back into the tavern. Nothing has changed. He watches Felix, still acting out his part in front of Diana. Meanwhile, Archie has moved closer to Morganna. Rab will not miss out, especially as he's paying double for the mead. He staggers over to the counter next to Diana, who places a finger to her lips and winks at Felix.

Diana clutches at her stomach, and gestures that now she needs to use the facilities.

"Let me show you where to go," says Felix. He beckons Diana to follow him outside the tavern.

Time is passing, and the tension is building in Tabernae Mona. Rab frets over how long Felix and Diana are spending outside.

What are they doing?

The thought of Felix stealing his date annoys him, and now Archie is also sending an angry look in his direction.

"What's the matter with your ugly mug?" calls out Rab.

"What's up with my empty mug?" says Archie, holding up the empty cup.

"Sorry my friend!" giggles Rab, "I'll get us another round of drinks, don't worry."

"What will you use for that? Next year's pay?"

Felix returns into the bar, looking far too pleased with himself.

"Where were you?" growls Rab.

"I was just being helpful."

"Well, just remember, she's with me. Give us another round of mead. We need more."

"You have had enough, my friend. It's home time for you."

Morganna whispers to Archie, "your friend is scaring me. He isn't as nice as you."

An air of threat and potential violence descends as Archie draws a dagger from the side of his belt.

"Don't worry, I'll look after you. He's just a fool."

A real argument is now breaking out between Rab and Felix, fuelled by excessive amounts of alcohol and testosterone, it's only ever going to end one way. The voices become raised, as they trade insults against one another. A downward spiralling, mood-killing freefall begins.

"I'll need to find my friend." says Morganna as she hurriedly makes her excuses to leave.

"Don't go," says Archie.

Rab was destroying any chance he might have had of romance with the gorgeous red-headed woman.

"I'll get rid of him. Will you come back?"

"I'll wait for you in the garden by the waterfall."

Morganna stands up and walks out the tavern door.

Archie stares at the dagger before him, before stepping towards the other two men.

"Coxcomb, eh?" he says to himself.

Diana is waiting for Morganna as she exits back into the fresh air.

"The rain has stopped. The scenery is very nice here. Although the weather is terrible."

"You've just arrived at the wrong time of year. The summer lasts for an entire week," says Morganna.

The two of them wander around the outskirts of Tabernae Mona. They stop at the waterfall and talk. They ignore the noise from within the tavern's walls. Raised voices lead to furniture cracks and splinters. Curses, insults, and yelps of pain, are followed by screams, struggles, and shouts. Eventually, an empty silence falls.

"Time to go back in?" says Diana.

The bar is swimming in blood. Felix is bent double, attached to the wooden countertop with Rab's knife planted through his neck. Archie stretches out across the floor. Someone has stabbed him in the back with his own dagger. Rab looks to have become the victim of a series of hurled kitchen implements that have pinned him to the wall.

"It's romantic," says Morganna while surveying the morbid scene, "imagine brutally murdering one another for the chance of a single kiss."

"Yes, romantic, but stupid!" says Diana as she walks over to the cooking pot, "the food is ready. It's a shame not to eat it."

The next two hours pass pleasantly, as they enjoy their meal. They discuss their upbringing, travelling on their own, relationships, magic, and predictions. Both women share a dark sense of humour, chastising the dead men for not engaging in the conversation.

After dinner, they wash the plates and pots they have used, then they steal the kitchen equipment and gadgets that might be useful for their journey to Rheged.

It's another full hour later when Morganna and Diana ride away from Tabernae Mona on the two spare horses from the paddock.

As they canter off along the road, they disappear into a grey mist, unaware of another horse and wagon drawing up to a halt outside of the tavern.

A woman clad from head to foot in black jumps from the wagon and walks inside. Her screams follow a few seconds later, scaring the birds from the trees and pulling several animals out of their winter hibernation.

MACDUNCAN
INVESTIGATES

First light, and the southern gates of Dun
Romanach swing open. Two black-cloaked
horsemen ride out at speed. They descend the
hillside and race to the road that cuts through
the larger settlement. Hooves thunder on the
ground soaked from yesterday's rainfall. Criss-
crossed fallen branches snap under the weight
of horses and riders.

MacDuncan is not riding, he's just trying
not to fall. Another session on the mead has
left him worse for wear. A crushing headache,
heartburn, and an overwhelming sense of
nausea churns around inside him. Every now
and again a stray beam of sunlight breaks free
from the overcast sky to pierce him with sharp
agonising pain. His eyes close, leaving the
horse in charge of wherever they are heading.

A jackdaw peers from a high treetop. Its
normal morning feeding grounds are bustling

with human life. Men move back and forth. Sharp shouts and barked commands mixed with assorted wailing. Horses snort and whinny as they jostle for position.

The jackdaw lacks patience. It watches two more riders arrive and one dismount. It hears further calls and commands from the men gathered. As the figure enters the building below, the wise bird decides that there will be no early wander through familiar woods today. It takes off in search of safer places to forage.

"MASTER MACDUNCAN!" calls a guard stationed outside Tabernae Mona.

"Steady on, son," replies MacDuncan, "I'm a wee bit sensitive this morning. So, what have we got?"

"Three men dead, Rab, Archie, plus the barman."

MacDuncan sweeps into the crime scene with a flourish and stands hand on hips, surveying the terrible tableau of twisted bodies, a floor caked with blood and the stench of death. Or maybe it's just the normal stench of Tabernae Mona.

"Is Redlead here?" asks MacDuncan.

"Aye sir, he's up on the roof," replies the guard.

"Go get him."

MacDuncan is familiar with the carnage caused by an armed fight. The ferocity of this battle has been a few notches higher than normal. He checks for pulses and then checks for coin. There are no signs of life.

"No coin, and body fluids with scented undertones of processed mead. They were drunk." he concludes.

Vomit has been scaling the heights of MacDuncan's oesophagus ever since he awakened. It now erupts out on to Rab's open chest wounds.

"Sorry friend!" he says, while wiping his chin on a sleeve of the dead man's tunic..

"SERGEANT-AT-ARMS!" shouts the guard.

"I told you, stop shouting, my head's thumping!"

"Sorry sir, sergeant-at-arms, Redlead sir."

Redlead enters the room with his usual menace.

"First impressions?" asks MacDuncan.

"We thought it was just a bar fight at first, but now, murder and maybe suicide."

"Suicide?"

"Archie's own knife killed him."

"Aye, but he's stabbed in the back."

"True," says Redlead, "one of the serving girls says items are missing from the kitchen. Small jars, pans, and knives, that kind of thing."

"A robbery as well?"

MacDuncan stands and strokes his beard, to appear intelligent and to check for any remaining spew. His concentration is disturbed from noise outside the tavern. A siren call sounds, an unending wail of anguish, a well-practiced display of grief that takes mourning to a professional level. He winces as the volume increases, and Mona bursts through the door.

"My boy! My boy! What are you doing to my boy? Who could kill my boy?"

"Yes, yes," MacDuncan tries to intervene, "never mind your boy, my head is aching."

"Your head is aching? My poor son's head is attached to the bar with a six-inch blade! What was I thinking, leaving him alone? Dun Romanach has gone downhill since the Romans left. You didn't get murderers in their day."

"That's because they crucified all the locals."

Mona pushes past MacDuncan to get to her son, pulling the knife from the corpse. The body drops to the ground, leaving a detached head on the counter.

"Hey, don't touch the evidence. You're destroying my crime scene," MacDuncan was getting annoyed now, "Redlead, take the deceased's mother outside and keep her there while I conduct my investigations."

The grim man-at-arms removes the murder weapon from Mona's grasp and passes it to MacDuncan while escorting her from the premises.

Outside, Redlead leaves Mona in the capable

hands of two more warband members and makes his way towards the low wooden fence at the rear of the paddock. Something doesn't look right. One of the upright posts is leaning inwards at an angle. It's a small deviation, but Tabernae Mona is a tavern of high repute. Out-of-place fenceposts affect the aesthetic of the establishment.

He grasps at the wooden stake. It's unsteady and dislodged. The soaked grass and mud around its base have suffered from pressure or weight. He considers the options; they don't tie horses to upright stakes, a wagon collision causes more damage, there have been no strong gales.

He ponders the hillside in front of him. Amongst trees and bushes nestles a small clearing on a ledge. He observes it and then turns to look back at Tabernae Mona.

"I wonder," he mumbles to himself.

He continues to survey the ground around the fence.

"Trackers! Over here!"

MacDuncan examines the bodies from every angle. He pays close attention to the wounds by first washing them clean with mead, and then removing the weapons one by one. Felix's body keeps falling back on to the ground, so he organises another two warband members to remove it, stopping it impeding his search for evidence.

The guard helps him sit the bodies of Rab and Archie on to a pair of chairs. Apart from the lack of colour, the stiffened limbs, and the gaping gashes, they look normal. MacDuncan adds a couple of cups of mead to the scene. He does his best to clasp the hands of the dead around a last drink.

"It's what they would have wanted."

With the floor cleared, he looks for more clues. Sifting through pools of blood, patches of dried urine, guts, and diced carrots from his own vomit wasn't telling him much.

He moves on to the kitchen. Remains of rabbit prepared for cooking, not cleared away. The incident had happened soon after they made the meal. Everyone knew Rab and Archie well. They weren't the types to spend good mead drinking money on rabbit cooked at Tabernae Mona.

"Someone else was here. Guard, bring Mona in again for more questioning."

"Yes, master."

MacDuncan moves to the serving side of the counter, underneath the wooden countertop there's a shelf with a small wooden box. It has a small quantity of coin, a couple of rabbit's feet, a small knife, and a carved wooden miniature of a naked goddess. He pockets everything except for the lucky rabbit's feet.

"Not enough here to buy a dinner."

The guard returns with Mona. MacDuncan gestures for her to follow him into the kitchen.

"Come over here. I need your expert opinion."

Mona clasps her hands to her face in shock.

"He was making Coniglio in Porchetta. We haven't served that for years. I didn't even know he could cook it."

"Do you remember who last ordered it?"

"No. A merchant on his way home after selling his wares? It's too pricey for the tight-fisted locals around here, but it's too long ago I don't remember. You eat it with a light and crisp white," Mona panicked, "wine, where is my wine?"

"What wine?"

"It was outside on the wagon. Felix was going to bring it in, but now I realise it's gone."

"Show me where it was," says MacDuncan.

Rushing outside the tavern, Mona shrieks once again.

"They have stolen it. The thieves have stolen everything. Our horse, our wagon, our wine."

The wailing volume increases again. MacDuncan summons two of the serving maids over to comfort Mona and makes his escape into the crowded paddock.

Redlead spots MacDuncan weaving his way towards him.

"Over here!" he shouts.

MacDuncan picks up his pace and vaults over the low fence to stand beside his sergeant-at-arms.

"What have you got for me?"

"There are footprints everywhere. The trackers think maybe five passed through, I'll give you a full report soon."

"Good! Meet me in the tavern when you're ready."

"Master MacDuncan!" Another soldier calls out from shrubs to the rear of the tavern, "we've found a clue."

MacDuncan crosses the paddock towards the soldier who is standing beside one of the tavern's serving girls.

"What have you found then?" says MacDuncan.

"Begging your pardon, sir," says the young maid, "it's where our lady customers go to get rid of the mead they've drunk, or the dinner they ate. It's hidden there, amongst some shrubs."

They step towards a small hollow. Surrounded and masked off from the tavern's garden by wild briar.

"Watch your step," the girl says, as they arrive in Tabernae Mona's public toilet.

MacDuncan bends for a closer look at the

singular thick spiralling snake of dark brown human waste.

"You're sure that came from a woman?"

"It's only ladies that are allowed here, sir."

MacDuncan grabs a twig and prods and pushes the suspect stool. "It's time to send for Blacknail," he says to the soldier, "he can tell us more, and bring the priest, we'll need to bury the bodies soon."

"I'll fetch them right away, sir."

The soldier departs, leaving MacDuncan alone with the serving girl. He prods the offending evidence before impaling it on the stick and lifting it into the air.

"So, have you worked here long?" he says with a smile and a glint in his eye.

Redlead was taken aback as he spoke with two of his trackers.

"You're sure?"

"Two sets of prints are the same as boots that the levy men wear," says one man, while the other nods in agreement.

Redlead makes a cross on himself by touching his chest, his shoulders, and his forehead.

"No, that's not right, sir. You start on your forehead, then the shoulders, then your chest," says the first tracker.

"No, you're both wrong," says the second man, "it's the forehead, chest, left shoulder, right shoulder. Easy."

"I'll cross my boot into your backside," says Redlead, "it doesn't matter. Now keep searching for more clues."

Paying good heed to the threat, the trackers return to their work. Redlead walks back towards the tavern. He meets MacDuncan, emerging from the bushes carrying a large turd on a small stick.

"It's evidence," says MacDuncan, "I've sent for Blacknail to come and do that thing that he does."

Blacknail was the closest person Dun Romanach had to a doctor. A carpenter to trade, he had crossed over into the medical profession, having discovered a talent for surgery. He first coined his motto *Better to live with three legs than die with four,* when he had operated on one of Duncan's hounds, but as he honed his skills on human beings, the phrase still applied. From amputation to trepanation, any procedure performed with woodworking tools was well within his capabilities.

His status had been further increased by the new church. Andrew didn't want the local female witches carrying out any healing, as that was demonic. A nice male medical practitioner was far godlier. The two became firm friends and, to his credit, Andrew had gained Latin translations of Hippocrates for Blacknail to study.

The physician was now a committed follower. An advocate of diagnosis through the study of bodily fluids. A forensic approach that could be useful to the investigation.

MacDuncan and Redlead re-enter the tavern. They are alone except for Rab and Archie, sitting at their mead cups, gazing out over the scene of their own death.

"I need a drink," says Redlead, "d'you want one?"

"Aye, I need something for this hangover."

MacDuncan draws up a chair and sits beside Archie.

"Aye, you're looking pale, son. You want to wrap up you'll catch your death."

He allows himself his first roaring laugh of the day. Mead always lightens the mood, regardless of circumstance.

Redlead sniggers as he settles on the chair next to Rab, while placing two cups of mead on the table.

"Aye, what's up with you, Rab? You love a party."

"It could be worse," says MacDuncan.

They compose themselves and return to the facts.

"Alright," says MacDuncan, "I'm getting a picture. Felix died first. Whoever committed the murders has moved fast. Felix didn't have time to fight beside the others."

"I can agree with that," concurs Redlead, "what's your thoughts on Rab and Archie?"

"Well, they put up a fight. Mona said Felix had been making an expensive meal. Something that they hadn't even served here for years."

"A wealthy traveller?" says Redlead.

"Yes, someone from the south?" they both spit on the floor, "I can't find any evidence of money changing hands."

"Then they didn't have money," says Redlead, "and tried to leave without paying. They stabbed Felix, then Rab and Archie attempted to stop them and lost the fight. Which is very disappointing, by the way. I'd have killed them myself if they came back and told me they had lost a bar fight."

The pieces of the puzzle start to slowly come together in MacDuncan's alcohol impaired mind.

"I think they made their escape using Mona's cart."

"Rab and Archie's horses have disappeared as well," confirms Redlead, "there was definitely a few of them."

"You said the trackers thought there were five?"

"Aye. One tall with a large stride, two women."

"Two women?"

"Aye, but that's not the best part. There are footprints of two men. The trackers recognised them. They reckon they were our own men."

"Our own men? Why didn't you say? Arrest them now!"

"That might be difficult. The men already suspect that it could be Artos and Alan."

"But they're dead."

"Well, you would think so, but I don't remember seeing their heads go into the sacks."

Silence fell, and the lifeless eyes of Rab and Archie burned into MacDuncan's very soul. Every creak in the room signified evil forces were present. You could taste the fear and tension in the air.

"BLACKNAIL AND THE PRIEST!" shouts the guard from outside the door.

"Jesus!" exclaims MacDuncan, as both he and Redlead jump out of their skin.

Blacknail enters, followed by Father Andrew.

"You summoned me, master. How can I help?"

"Come over here," says MacDuncan.

He leads Blacknail to the bar where the faecal evidence is now plated and sitting beside Felix's nose. Andrew crosses himself as he looks at Rab and Archie.

"Show me how you did that again?" asks Redlead.

"This was in the toilet place," MacDuncan explains.

"I am a physician. You can use the Latin master."

"No. The place behind the tavern."

"Oh, I see, I get it now."

"We think it's from the murderer."

"And you wish me to analyse it?"

"Yes, do that thing that you do."

Blacknail rolls up his sleeves. He approaches the plated evidence with care. Revolving it and noting the solid consistency with a lack of cracking on the surface.

"It's a healthy dark brown colour, and a good size, suggesting the suspect has produced nothing else in the preceding three, no make that four days.

"I'd say this person is in good health. Not yet in middle age. They've been travelling, and I suspect from the smell, they have been living on meat. A hunter or raider living on the road for quite some time."

"We think they might be foreign," sneers Redlead.

"I see," says Blacknail, lifting the stool to his nose for closer inspection, "can you pass me the mead?"

MacDuncan hands over his cup. Blacknail places the mead on the bar counter before him, then bites into the stool and masticates.

The others groan, but Blacknail carries on

chewing while taking occasional sips of mead to help it pass. He drains the dregs, gargling before a last swallow.

"It is indeed a woman. There is a continental influence. A spice that I don't recognise. She enjoys eating rabbit."

"They dined on Coniglio in Porchetta," says MacDuncan, as if he knew what it was.

"Very nice." says Andrew.

"Well, there you have it," says Blacknail, "female in her twenties, in good health, somewhere between five foot nine and five foot eleven, a visitor from abroad, the product of a well-to-do family with a taste for the finer things in life. Fell in with the wrong crowd and is eager to rebel against her parents with their orthodox traditions that demand they marry her off to someone twice her age for improved status and financial gain."

"You can tell all that from eating a shit?" says MacDuncan.

"It's amazing what science can tell us, master."

Blacknail grins, revealing brown matter still glued to his teeth.

"Alright, so that's suspect number one, but the four others, including two, that could have risen from the dead. This might be your field of investigation, priest."

"Undead?" Andrew crosses himself again while Redlead tries to emulate his actions.

"The trackers found footprints. They believe they could belong to the Hartriggs boys we buried before Christmas."

Andrew points to Rab and Archie. "Remove these unfortunate souls. If evil is in this place, Robert and Archibald may re-animate in front of us?"

"GUARDS! Get these bodies," shouts Redlead.

A group of soldiers enter and snigger at the sight of Rab and Archie sitting up to meet them. They lift the corpses with no hint of ceremony or respect. MacDuncan and the others gather around Felix's head that has remained staring out from the bar.

"Can you take this too?" orders MacDuncan.

Head removed; he pours more mead to steady their nerves.

"You mentioned another two?" says Blacknail.

"One had a very long stride." replies Redlead.

"Tall then, the same as the woman?"

"Or Beelzebub," exclaims Andrew, "or John of the Long Shanks. Lucifer himself."

It does sound plausible. Since the new church had arrived, the devil got the blame for most crimes in the area.

"Where do you think they ate?" asks Blacknail.

"Look at that table," says MacDuncan,

"they've pulled the chairs out to sit around it."

Blacknail searches around, paying careful attention to the edges of the furniture, checking for marks and further clues. He runs his hand over the back of one chair.

"What's this?"

He produces a long strand of fiery red hair. It dangles from his fingertips, buffeted from the air of his breath. The realisation strikes MacDuncan and Andrew at the same time.

"Morganna, one of the satanic flock of Hartriggs," says the priest, "we should have suspected her evil doings."

"That's it," says MacDuncan, "it needs a witch to summon the devil so that he can raise the dead to rob the tavern and murder Rab, Archie, and Felix. Case closed! Blacknail, thank you for your invaluable help today. You may return to Dun Romanach."

"Thank you, master. I'll just take the rest of the evidence back with me. I may need to chew over the problem more."

He grabs the rest of the plated waste and leaves. The others exchange disgusted glances as he departs.

"Redlead, get the men organised, dig graves, and bury the bodies. Rab and Archie would love it to know they can stay in the tavern forever. Andrew, conduct the burial, then return to cleanse the room."

"Shouldn't the servants do that?"

"I don't want you to sweep the floor. I want you to carry out a bloody exorcism."

"Oh, of course," Andrew smiles.

"Fine, I'll report back to father. I think we'll be heading back to Hartriggs very soon."

THE BLACK OATH

"Ease up on the mead," says an angry Duncan, "I give you a simple job to do. Find out what happened at Tabernae Mona. Now you're telling me the four horsemen of the apocalypse have moved in to Hartriggs."

"It's true, faither. Wait till the others get here. They'll back up my findings. Hell has opened a gateway in one of our villages, and its monsters are creeping out as we speak."

Duncan is perplexed. He knows his son isn't the brightest, but his trackers are experts. To add to his woes, Duncanna enters the chamber.

"What are you doing here?" she says to her brother, "father is spending time with me tonight. We'll be discussing all the details of my wedding plans."

"You don't even have an idea who you're going to marry."

"That's just details."

"Well, you can forget it. The devil is raising

the undead in Hartriggs. We need to do something. Faither?"

"I'm thinking," says Duncan.

"Well, maybe you could ask the devil to get me a decent husband," says Duncanna, "I'm willing to sign up for whatever he wants in return."

"What, your soul?" says MacDuncan.

"No, but maybe yours."

Duncan sits at the table with his head in his hands.

"This has been a terrible Christmas," he says to himself.

A pause breaks out. Just long enough for awkward coughing and forced throat clearing to be overheard.

"Let them in," sighs Duncan.

MacDuncan parts the curtain and ushers in Redlead and Andrew. They look pale and worn out as they both take a seat at Duncan's table. MacDuncan and Duncanna choose chairs at opposite ends, still glowering at one another.

"More mead," says Duncan, and the servants appear with cups and jugs of the honeyed brew.

"Redlead, what say you? Are the hosts of hell beating at the gates of Dun Romanach?"

"Not yet, but the men are *feart*. They're convinced that the Hartriggs boys have returned to haunt and torment us."

"I see," says Duncan, "what is your view,

Andrew?"

"My lord, we have discussed this time for centuries. The end of the world is nigh."

"There will be no end of the world. Certainly not before I become king," says Duncan.

"Maybe," says Redlead in a grave tone, "but half the warband is now sitting in your chapel asking for their lives to be spared. The word won't take long to spread. We must destroy Hartriggs. To end these rumours at least."

"Let me go tonight, faither. I'll take enough men to raise the village with fire. We will capture the witches and bring them back to trial for a guilty verdict."

"Torch flames will not exactly dissuade the devil, but I agree we must do something. Leave me now and let me consider the action we should take."

"Faither I must protest."

"You will do no such thing! We are dealing with superstition and fear. The devil is not sitting on a rock at Hartriggs, lighting his farts and waiting for us to attack him. Begone! Give me time to consider what I should do."

The three men rise from the table and exit the room together. Duncanna maintains her position at the table and is obviously not going anywhere.

"I've seen these incredible pure gold candle holders, which will be fantastic for the top table ..."

The wedding preparations wore on for hours. Duncanna went into every detail of a nuptial ceremony, excluding a groom. Duncan filtered out most of it, except the parts relating to actual costs. He pondered the dilemma facing him. There was a secret that involved Hartriggs. It had saved the village for years from the worst excesses of Duncan's rule. He had looked the other way as it followed its pagan ways in protected isolation. He vowed that good never came from undue leniency.

It's late when he emerges from the darkest depths of his own thoughts. Duncanna has left, content that she was getting everything she wanted. The candles and the dying fire in the room burn low. Long shadows move around the walls. Wood creaks, and out of sight, a mouse scratches away at a new home. The sound of fluttering wings from above draws Duncan's attention as smoke from the fire scatters.

A sense of fear grows inside him as he rises from his chair and squints into the poorly lit corners. An ominous presence has arrived.

"Who is there? I know you're there."

There was no response. Duncan knew he

wasn't alone. The earlier talk of the devil and raising the dead had created a profound atmosphere of evil.

A staff scrapes along the floor behind him. He spins round on the verge of a heart attack when he suddenly recognises his night visitor.

"Wren Morcant?"

"I am, but you know that."

The witch steps forward into the light. Duncan backs onto the table. His hands scramble around for a weapon. In the end, he resorts to crossing himself several times. Each time differently.

"None of you ever get that right," says Wren, "sit yourself at your table. I'm only here to discuss matters, as you might have expected."

"Can't you knock before you enter?"

He pulls himself together and retreats to his seat at the table, inviting the witch to sit herself opposite him. He relaxes, for Wren is at least the devil he knows.

"Can I pour you a cup of wine?"

"Grape is good for the soul."

"Even a damned soul?"

"You have wit, but I wonder which of our souls is the most damned. It's not my actions that have left the prophecy in turmoil, the gods know who is to blame."

"The prophecy is not my concern. An old wives' tale will not make me king."

"And yet I sense your fear. You know the gods meant the bastard to be protected under your care."

"Your care, you mean."

"By arrangement and agreement with you."

Duncan pauses, staring into his cup in a rare moment of self-reflection, leaving Wren to break the silence.

"Do you remember when we first met? When you came to me seeking advice and guidance. The young woman who stole your heart and consumed your thoughts. I offered my help on how to make her your wife. How to ask her, when to ask her. Did I not give you the correct advice and predict that your marriage would happen within the month?"

"You did," replies Duncan, "but it's not a memory that fills me with happiness these days. Why bring it up now? I parted with coin for your advice. It was a trade. You gave me only the answers to the questions I asked and nothing more. Had you mentioned the miserable years to follow, my money might've been better spent."

"Had you sought further advice, then maybe your marriage could have had more value?"

The comment stung Duncan, but in his heart of hearts, he knew it was true.

"It's fortuitous that we meet tonight. Hartriggs has become a problem for me. There are calls to raise it to the ground. They say that your apprentice Morganna has summoned the devil, and that he has raised Artos and Alan from the dead."

"I thought you didn't believe in old wives' tales."

"Everyone else places great faith in them."

"This is your curse, for not observing your proper role in the prophecy. You had a part to play."

"Look, I didn't kill him."

"But neither did you protect him from harm. That was your charge. If ghosts are now haunting Dun Romanach, they are of your making."

The flames of the fire rise higher on cue. The old gods are indeed listening in on their conversation. Duncan drains his cup and pours out more wine.

"My kin, my children, and I'm sure it comes as no surprise, the church, want rid of you."

"Strange that you mention all the people who also wish you dead."

"Me? Dead? Who?"

Wren cackles as she has a moment of realisation.

"I must confess, even I didn't know why the gods instructed me to meet with you. Now the mist clears. Our meeting is business, nothing more."

"Business?" now the old witch is talking in

a language Duncan can understand.

"A trade. The fate of Hartriggs won't change. It may not be your hand, but whomsoever shall follow. I have seen it. I know it will come to pass."

"And the trade? I still don't understand."

Wren stands up from the table. She wanders over towards the small fire burning on the hearth. Reaching into her bag, she picks out a small jar of loose herbs and casts the contents into the flames. Puffs of smoke curl and twist as she traces the shapes with her fingers. She reacts as if gossiping with an old friend. For what feels an age to Duncan, she mutters, winces, and groans. Acknowledgements follow sharp intakes of breath.

"I see, I see, I see."

"What is it you see?"

He can't take any more suspense. He joins Wren by the fire, peering into the flames as if he might witness something himself.

"A warning for you. Just as your lack of attention and inaction failed the bastard you were charged with protecting. You also didn't notice the plots that grow and flourish around you."

"Plots?"

"You don't see them? It is the oldest law. The Threefold Return. Your own conduct with others returned to you. You have angered the spirits, and they have decreed that you will suffer the same fate as Hartriggs. To die before your time."

Wren waves the small clouds away with her hand before returning to her seat and draining the wine from her cup. Duncan stands for a moment, mulling over the threat.

"Wait, you can't stop there. I must know more."

"For endangering the prophecy. Your fate and the fate of Hartriggs are now linked."

"You said Hartriggs will suffer destruction."

"It will, as you will. Which brings us back to the trade."

Wren pushes the empty cup across the table, scraping against the surface. Duncan fills it with more wine.

"I'm listening."

"Hartriggs will pass before you. You may take comfort in that. For as long as it stands, you will stand."

"That's a threat, not a trade."

"Is your memory so poor that you have forgotten my warning so fast? It is in my interest for you to live a long life. I too could suffer by their hand."

"Then tell me their names. I will execute them before the sun rises and I may concede to forget the problems with Hartriggs for the meantime."

"Your executioners will be busy. Those who seek your demise are many in number. They look upon your power and crave it for themselves. Many will perish in civil war if you incur the wrath of their supporters. It is the second sight and wise counsel you need to defeat your opponents, not the hangman's noose."

The room fell silent once more. The aura of magic still hung heavy in the air. Duncan was aware of the dangers that leadership brought. He considered who might be the most likely traitors. As the list of names lengthened, he could see sense in Wren's offer.

"So, what you're saying is, if I'm right," he sighs with more than a hint of frustration, "if I protect Hartriggs, then you will protect me in return."

"I can only offer advice on what you may face. Why, when, and how the stars align. The same service I offered you years ago. I dare not position myself between you and the will of the gods. You could never cover the payment for that," she pauses, "nice try."

"And you don't want coin?"

"No. I do not want your money. Fate binds us. Our reward will be longevity."

Duncan considers how long Wren might live.

She looks the wrong side of one hundred right now.

"I heard that," she says.

It was getting late. Run out of wine late. Duncan had known the witch for many years, and he knew he could trust her words. For many years, she had been the spiritual leader until Andrew walked into Dun Romanach to save the locals.

"Alright. You have my word. I will guarantee the continued protection of Hartriggs. Now tell me, who is behind these plots to kill me?"

"Duncan. your worthless words cannot bind us. There is only one way to swear allegiance. The Black Oath."

Somewhere outside, thunder rumbles across the sky.

"Did you do that?" asks Duncan.

"No, it's just awful weather tonight. Let me get organised. It is a simple yet powerful spell. We need more wine to keep us going.

Duncan's head was spinning. "Am I going to do this? Take the Black Oath? Swear my life to Wren Morcant?"

He enters the sleeping quarters. Where his family lie unconscious in different areas of the room. They sleep alongside guards who should be awake but are snoring in their own slumber. He lays his hands on a full jug of wine and asks himself to remember to flog the guards tomorrow, even though Wren has likely ensured that no witnesses will be present for the ceremony.

Taking a long drink from the jug, he feels better. With the wisdom of the witch at his disposal, he could use her skills to discover more than just the petty plots of traitors. He could murder rival kings with impunity and launch surprise attacks on enemy forces on a violent and treacherous road to the top.

A couple more sips from the jug and a subdued yet satisfied laugh later, he re-enters the main room of the private chambers. Wren sits reciting an ancient mantra with her eyes closed. Items lay before her on the table; a small silver plate, a green apple, a small silver blade with a hilt made from stag antler, a tiny spoon, and a long piece of narrow black silk.

The chant continues and Wren's eyes remain shut, yet she gestures for Duncan to join her at the table. He sits facing her from the opposite chair. More wine is poured into the two cups, and Duncan pushes Wren's drink beside her hand, trying not to disturb her concentration as she mumbles an incantation.

Sitting back in his chair, he makes himself comfortable and ready for what may lie ahead. He raises the cup to his lips just as Wren opens her eyes and shrieks. Duncan throws half his drink over himself and shakes in his chair from fright.

"That's better!" Wren smiles, "thanks for the drink," she says before slurping from the cup.

She spits half-consumed alcohol and saliva on to the small silver plate, before passing the receptacle to Duncan.

"Now you do it."

"Really?" asks Duncan.

"Really," confirms the witch.

With only a modicum of the same effort, Duncan carries out his instructions. Rolling the alcohol around his cheeks, he dribbles his offering on to the plate before placing it back on the centre of the table.

Wren grabs his hand and before he knows it, she has slit the tip of one of his fingers, adding his blood to the plate.

He pulls his hand away to nurse the wound. The witch then uses the blade to cut her own finger, before adding her own blood offering.

"We need a third substance from your body."

"What do you mean?"

Imagining the options made Duncan quite ill.

Wren places her bloodied finger on the side of her nose and projects a lump of off-white mucus on to the plate as the last of her offering.

"That will do," she says in a conciliatory

tone.

"I hope so," says Duncan before taking the plate.

"I find it helps not to look."

Duncan does his best to summon an equal volume of mucus from his nostril. Wren lifts the spoon, she blends the ingredients together until it resembles a sticky red paste. She lifts the blade again, chopping the green apple in half, then in quarters, then into eight equal and indistinguishable parts.

"Choose a piece of the fruit of transformation. Hold it in the palm of your hand."

Duncan selects his part of the apple before Wren follows suit. She then clasps her hand to his and uses the black silk to bind their hands together. She closes her eyes once more and murmurs more of the spell. Duncan doesn't know who she is talking to or what she is saying, but he can sense a powerful energy coursing through his entire body.

Wren looks content. She unwinds the silk cloth and places the silver platter below their joined hands.

"Now we complete our part. We open our hands and drop the fruit on to the plate."

Duncan takes his cue from Wren's nod.

The two pieces of apple drop on to the mixture.

"Is that it then?" asks Duncan.

"Not yet."

Once again, she picks up the spoon, dowsing the apple with the paste. As she does so, she performs a strange chattering sound.

Two white rats scurry on to the table. Each rat grabs a piece of apple from the plate before darting off into the darkest parts of the room with the stolen fruit.

"What part do rats play in our oath?" asks Duncan.

"The rats are stewards of our agreement, and they are now the heralds of our death. If either of us break the oath or when indeed it's our natural time to leave, then each of our rats will return to us. They will produce the apple before us in its undigested and pristine form, and then we will have one day to sort out our business before we meet our end."

Duncan nods. There was no going back.

Wren stands up without saying anymore. She turns and leaves the room. This time by walking through the curtain. Duncan rests in his chair, tired but satisfied. He considers that he was a man of God who is now in league with the devil. What could possibly go wrong?

JACOBUS AND SARA

The sound of seabirds fills the air. Oystercatchers, Gulls, and Curlews, search the shoreline for a morning meal.

Artos is enjoying the view. Low-lying grasses blow in the breeze and geese settle on marsh that surrounds mud flats exposed by the low tide. Behind him to the north are the familiar hills of home, before him across the water rise the peaks of the mountains of Rheged.

Light footsteps approach Artos from behind, drawing him from his meditation. Herbs brewed into a soothing drink, break through the dominant backdrop of the invigorating sea air. He looks up to see Morganna standing above him, smiling back, and offering the cup of hot tea.

"Drink this," she says, "it's better than mead."

Artos takes the cup and sips. "What does

this do?"

"Not everything I make has to do something," she laughs, "although it will calm you and give rest in your heart before we reach Rheged."

"Have you been to Rheged?"

"Yes, when the storms swept me north, and my only company were ravens or the wolves. I never met the people," she pauses, trying to remember something from that time, "there are wonderful mountains, hills, and valleys. Great lakes surrounded by white peaks of snow. One of the highest mountains in the land lies there. I'm sure you can see Hartriggs from it on a sunny day."

They both look out to sea and across to Rheged. The light changes as large white clouds pass by, painting the landscape in different shades, sparkling, and reflecting on the water. It's good that they are together on this quest. They rest shoulder to shoulder on one another, looking out towards their future.

A hacking cough interrupts the moment, along with the large swirling clouds of Myrrdin's strong pipe mix.

"I believe we are ready to break our fast before we head further south."

"Good, I'm hungry," says Morganna, rising to leave, "Alan's become a great cook. Maybe he's not as useless as I always thought he was."

As she walks back to camp, Artos holds

back.

"Can Morganna see the future?"

"No," says Myrrdin, "though she will be a great and powerful sorceress."

"And me?"

"You will be a legendary king."

"Though here I am. Only a day or so travel from the place I have spent my entire life, and I'm looking over the water at land I have never known. I worry I am not the king. That maybe I just share his name."

Myrrdin drew long on his pipe before releasing a tiny and perfectly formed circle of smoke.

"Even a king begins life, scrabbling for his mother's milk and learning to stand and walk. Everything comes in time. Just keep learning. In that way, you will keep moving towards your destiny. I know you can be king."

Artos contemplates his fate as he stands up in silence, simply nodding to Myrrdin in acknowledgement before both of them walk back towards the campfire and breakfast.

With plenty of wine, an expert hunter, and Alan's newfound culinary skills, camping wasn't so bad. The company was good, and the mood was filled with optimism and excitement. Yet Artos was deeply apprehensive for himself and his party. His visions were becoming more intense and more regular. The violent scenes of death and battle on an unprecedented scale were increasing. Something the mind readers in his party didn't seem to be able to detect. They were his experiences alone. They set him apart even from a great magician like Myrrdin.

I still don't know why I've been chosen, but I must accept this version of myself. A king in the making.

Myrrdin enjoys the best view as he steers horse and wagon on the track that will lead them on to high roads and long stretching valleys before they reach their destination.

His mind concentrates on the immediate matter of acquiring horses. Morganna and Diana have kept their mounts, so Myrrdin is even more conscious that the wagon is slowing their progress.

The road runs parallel to a river, with long lazy curves that match the route of the flowing water. Gentle sounds of the horses at walking pace and the wooden rolling wheels of the wagon create a pleasant rhythm. The normal spirals of smoke show the scattered locations of the locals, but they haven't passed a single soul that morning.

They cross a small ford, where the water flows to the main river. Myrrdin raises his hand and brings everyone to a halt. In the distance, along an old track, they can hear raised voices. Two people are arguing while a mixture of animal sounds adds to the backdrop.

"I think I hear the calls of an old friend," says Myrrdin.

He turns the wagon towards the farm track and drives onward. Rounding the bend, Myrrdin roars with laughter at the sight before him. A farmer trips and slides through mud. He is surrounded by most of his animals, that have obviously escaped their pens. His wife is chasing him with a rolling pin and using language as foul as her mood. Geese honk and flap their wings as they chase the couple in circles. The sheep and the goats have scattered in every direction. The dogs are trying to get between the couple to stop any potential assault. While a cow has wandered off, looking for a quieter spot.

"Jacobus Brooker," says Myrrdin.

"Myrrdin? Is that you?" The farmer stops in his tracks just long enough for a flying, rolling pin to connect with his head and send him sprawling into a burn.

"Get rid of him, Jacobus," says the farmer's wife as she turns and storms into her home. She means to slam a door shut, but it falls from its hinges and lands on the ground.

"Let's clear this up," says Myrrdin.

Artos and Alan jump from the wagon and start working with the dogs to round up the sheep and goats. Diana has taken hold of the cow and walks it back to the small patch where it grazes, and Morganna uses her best instincts with birds to calm the nerves of the high-strung geese, encouraging them back into the farm.

Myrrdin extends a hand to Jacobus and pulls him up from the water. The farmer looks as if he has aged twenty years, although it hasn't been over six years since Myrrdin last set eyes upon him.

"Sara is missing her usual sweet mood today."

"Her sweet mood left us a long while ago, Myrrdin. It is good to see you, friend."

Jacobus tries to wash the dirt from his face and wipe the excess of the water from his clothes. He has developed a belly fuelled by mead. His nose is bloated and red, his hair thinning and his eyes bloodshot. He doesn't look well.

"What's happened here? You've changed Jacobus."

"Aye, and not for the better, I daresay?" Myrrdin nods in response, "times have changed. I'm longer in years and quicker to temper, and the wife is a perfect match, except she's handier with a rolling pin than me."

He rubs at the bright red lump now rising on his forehead. The others in the party finish their tidying up of the animals and assemble around Myrrdin.

"My thanks to your friends. I admit I staggered home drunk this morning and opened a few of the gates, thinking they were my front door."

"The mead must be strong in these parts," says Myrrdin.

"Not strong, but plentiful, and I know I partake more than I should these days," he sighs, "but here I am, being rude and bothering you with my problems. Tie up your horses and let them have water. Please, you are welcome into my house, please come in friends."

Jacobus walks ahead into his home. Voices raise in anger, but then the shouting settles. As the others organise their horses, Myrrdin lights up his pipe and surveys the surroundings. The farm is in a poor state of repair. No workers, and the animals are fewer than he remembers. You could tell that the Brookers had fallen on harder times.

Myrrdin leads the party into the dwelling, chapping on the frame where the front door used to hang.

"Come in," says Jacobus, "take a seat. We're happy and honoured to have your company."

A loud crash of pots in the background suggests maybe Sara isn't as enthusiastic.

"Thank you, Jacobus," says Myrrdin, "allow me to introduce my friends. This is Artos, Alan, Morganna, and Diana. My friends and myself are travelling south. Heading for the court of Urien."

Jacobus nods in acknowledgement. "Delighted to meet you. On behalf of my wife and myself, welcome to our home. I must tell you though that Urien is fighting against the Angles. The roads are not so safe as you near his palace."

Myrrdin raises an eyebrow. "Then I'm glad I came. Your warning will keep us alert and ready."

Sara arrives at the table and serves each person the hearty meal of one boiled egg each. Jacobus looks embarrassed at the meagre offering.

"Is that the most we can offer our guests, Sara?"

"I have cooked the food we have. Do you expect me to magic a meal out of thin air?"

"An egg is just exactly what I wanted," says Artos, and the others agree.

"We should tell the Merlin our story," says Jacobus to Sara, "maybe he can help us. You know that."

The tears form in Sara's eyes as she nods in silent agreement. Jacobus sighs and his shoulders drop as he begins his tale of the merchant and the magical trade that changed their lives forever.

"We had a good life once. Each week, month, season, and year passed as expected. I put in an honest day's work for an honest day's pay. The one luxury I allowed myself was a long, drawn-out single cup of mead on a Friday night with friends at the tavern. On one night, I chose instead to join the company of a well-dressed stranger.

"The man introduced himself as Dionisi, a successful merchant and trader. He had frequented the courts of many kings and queens. He made his money from trading in relics and great treasures. The stories he told were incredible. He had seen the Great Pyramids, the Parthenon, and the Coliseum. He told me that one legendary treasure had eluded him throughout his life. That most famous and sacred object, the Holy Grail. I had never met such a man. My life felt dull in comparison. His exploits were so inspiring.

"It grew late. The rest of the tavern had emptied. The owner slept in a corner. We nursed a last drink, and the conversation turned to what I had achieved. He surprised me with his reaction to my boring life.

"I am jealous, he said to me, you have achieved what you wanted, but I still hunger for what has escaped me.

"No, said I, Sara and I always dreamed of having three sons. To bless us with grandchildren and take over our farm. So, our marriage could mean more than just toil. A chance to spend our twilight years with a large family around us.

"Dionisi smiled and said to me, Jacobus, I knew when I saw you that our meeting was no accident. We are not so different. Successful, but unhappy.

"Dionisi then told me a final tale set on a mysterious island, surrounded by dangerous bogs and marsh. On the island was an enchanted spring. The water that flowed from it blessed by the goddess of fertility. Any woman who drank the water gave birth within one moon cycle. Dionisi filled a flagon with the water. Over the years, he sold it to those rich in coin, but barren of child.

"Why don't we exchange lives? said Dionisi.

"What do you mean? I asked.

"Dionisi opened a pouch that he wore on his belt, and he drew out three small crystal phials of the water. This is the last, he said. Enough to give you and Sara the sons that you seek. Remember, though, I am a merchant. I must make a fair trade. Otherwise, the water will have no effect.

"Well, I couldn't believe what I was hearing. Name your price for this magic. What can I pay you?

"Dionisi said my price is simple. For each of the three bottles, I will ask for one third of your savings, whatever that price may be. You must pay it without regret and consider it a fair price. Present each third, so I might judge the weight and know they are even.

"But it will leave me with nothing! I pleaded.

"Then he said. What will you lose but the wasted years of misguided dreams? It is your turn to take on the quest. To experience the gifts that the gods can bring. It will be my fate to rest with the riches you have saved and enjoy years of contemplation and introspection. For I now know that the Holy Grail lies inside us. Within our hearts.

"So, I said to him. If I bring you my savings, you will trade me for the water that brings forth life?

"I will, he said, but your pact is with the goddess of the water. You must raise these sons until they are adults. For their fate will be great. Your sons will serve in a great army. When they leave to join the ranks of a righteous king, your part in this bargain will be complete. You will receive three times the coin you saved, to compensate you and Sara for your good work in raising fine children.

"I told him his offer was incredible, but I must speak with Sara. The savings that he wanted me to part with belonged to both of us.

"The merchant agreed. He promised to visit our farm one week from that night. If we wanted to trade, then our savings should be ready as he asked.

"I made my way home and told Sara of the chance meeting with Dionisi. Over the next few days, we discussed the matter further and often. We had never had a worry. Not in any of our years together. Was the chance worth taking?

"Before we knew it, six days had passed. Sara slept that night and fell into a dream. Why don't you tell them this part, Sara? It was your dream."

Sara leans forward and clears her throat.

"It was a warm spring day. The animals and birds were chattering and feeding their young. The flowers stood out as bees hovered between them. I walked by a stream. It wasn't deep, but it teamed with life such as water voles, toads, dragonflies, and pond skaters. A snake slithered through the grass and as I followed its winding trail, I could see the field that lies behind our home. The single hawthorn tree stood at its centre, surrounded by lush green grass. Wooden fencing kept it separate from the rest of the farm. I could hear calls from around the tree, the cries of newborn babies. I panicked and let myself in through a gate, running towards the sound. As I arrived by the thorn tree, there they were. Three male babies lying on the soft warm grass before me. Beside each baby was a casket filled with gold. I felt the hand of Jacobus on my shoulder. I turned to look at him. His face beamed with happiness. He put two babies into my arms and then lifted the third. The children were at peace. Smiling and cooing as we cradled them.

"Well, I woke up and shook at Jacobus to wake him too. I told him what I had dreamt. It must be a good omen."

"So, then we decided," says Jacobus, "we just had to wait until Dionisi returned to us.

"Next day, the sun set before the sound of hooves approached. We rushed out to welcome Dionisi, as he sat on the saddle of a fine-looking chestnut gelding. He leapt on to the ground from his horse and bowed low with a kind smile. Giving the hug of an old friend to me, he kissed Sara's hand.

"We ushered him into our home. Sara had cooked a meal, and we brought out wine we had saved for a special occasion. Cheerful conversation continued for hours. Each of us recalled our childhoods, wonderful memories, and the values of family. We spoke of ancestry and the traits we inherited from our elders.

"We had talked so long that the candles were burning low. The mood of Dionisi became more sombre. Are you ready to decide? he asked.

"We looked at one another. I'm ready, said Sara, and then I spoke to say, my wife is happy, so I am happy. We are ready to shake on the trade.

"I will give you one last chance to consider, said Dionisi, for you cannot go back on this word. Once I have gone, your pact will be with the goddess herself. Commit to raise your sons until they are ready to leave. To take their place beside a king and his champions. Only show them kindness and raise them and teach them to the best of your ability. Allow your hearts to grow and make room to share your love for each one of them.

"We will! You can see that? said I.

"Yes, I can see that, my friend, he said in return. Then he agreed to make the trade.

"Dionisi produced the small containers filled with the magical water. He looked at Sara and told her. It is you who must drink this water, Sara. On the next new moon, drink the first phial of water and before the moon has completed its waning crescent, then the goddess will present you with your first child. Repeat the magic on the next new moon and the one beyond that. By the time three cycles have passed, you will receive your three sons. Then he paused and spoke. Now you must offer me your savings in three pouches, so that I may judge that the payment is fair.

"I went and collected the purses. They were heavy with coin saved from the profits of hard work and our life's dedication. Dionisi lifted them and weighed them in his hands.

He smiled across at us and thanked us for our generous payment. Then we shook hands on the contract.

"We clasped our hands together. I thanked him again and told him our meeting was a blessing.

"Good fortune, my friend, he said, before leaving our home and departing into the night."

The room falls silent.

"Where are the children?" asks Myrrdin.

Jacobus and Sara draw each other an anguished look.

"Show him," says Sara.

"Follow me," says Jacobus.

They follow the farmer outside and walk to the rear of the building, where they can see a small field of lush grass surrounded by a wooden fence. In the centre grows a hawthorn tree and grazing around it are three horses. A grey, another as white as snow, another as black as jet.

"These are our children," says Jacobus with a great sadness in his heart, "something has angered the goddess, or we fell under the merchant's trickery. Each time Sara drunk the water, within the cycle of the moon, the goddess delivered a young foal to this field. We prayed for a human child, but it was only the colour that changed."

"So, we kept to our part of the bargain," says

Sara, "I looked after the horses as if they were our sons, fed them when we had nothing. We trained them to race as fast as the wind, kept them safe, and watched them grow strong. Even as our own lives suffered.

"Whether he'll admit it, Jacobus became lost to the mead, and I became consumed with anger and frustration. Before long, not a single soul worked for us. It became difficult to run the farm. Word went round that we had dabbled in magic. Long friendships ended. We found ourselves shunned and left alone with our ... children."

"Can you help us, Myrrdin?" asks Jacobus, "if nothing else, can you tell us why this fate became ours? We had only ever wanted children, was that so bad?"

Everyone looks to Myrrdin for his wisdom. The story was tragic, and it touched the hearts of all.

"Let me speak with your children," he says.

Myrrdin opens the gate to the field and heads for the horses. The animals watch him approach without fear, and the grey steps forward to meet him. He walks beside the horse, locked in conversation. Meanwhile, the black horse has wandered over to the fence to stand in front of Artos and the white has walked towards Alan. They were fine horses and bonded with the two friends.

Jacobus and Sara were proud of them

and discussed their distinct personalities, their talents and maybe sometimes when their behaviour was disobedient or challenging. Artos, Alan and Diana listened, but the talking fades away for Morganna.

With the others engrossed in conversation, they don't notice her stepping into the field and walking over to the hawthorn tree that lies at its centre. The young witch knows how to detect spirits around her. She circles around, touching branches with her fingers, experiencing the life within the tree. She circles a second time. The temperature lowers. She circles a third time, then stops. Looking at the tree, she can see the faded image of a man, his arms outstretched amongst the branches, his legs merging with the trunk. He looks asleep, but then his eyes open. The figure reaches out to her with his hands.

Dionisi? says Morganna in her silent voice.

The figure's response sounds within her head.

Have you come to complete the trade?

Meanwhile, Myrrdin has returned to the rest of the party and the mood has deteriorated.

"I can't just let you take the horses," says Jacobus.

"I have spoken with the grey," says Myrrdin, "he assures me they must leave with us."

"That one will leave with anyone, if you offer him an apple or a long piece of grass," says Sara.

The grey whinnies in response, as if annoyed.

"I thought Dionisi told you," Myrrdin reminds them, "your children are to serve at the front of a great army."

"Yes, with a king and his champions. I see none here."

Artos wants to volunteer his opinion, but Myrrdin bids him stay silent with a gesture of his hand.

"I promise you, Jacobus, this will end well for you and Sara. I have told you we seek Urien to call on his aid in battle. Is he not a king?"

"I suppose you may be right, but with the horses gone?"

"Our children!" says Sara.

"With our children gone, it will leave us with nothing. Is that to be our fate, Myrrdin?"

"The trade is not complete," says Morganna as she returns to the group.

"What?" says Jacobus and Sara.

"I have spoken with the spirit of the hawthorn tree. It is Dionisi. His body has lain below it for many years, before either of you lived in this place. A wife who loved him planted the tree in his memory."

Sara sobs again. "I can't take this anymore. I don't want your magic. I just want back what I had before they tempted us to part with everything we had earned. Those days were hard, but they were happy."

Jacobus hugs his wife. "You see Myrrdin. This is what our life has become."

"Hear Morganna out," says Myrrdin, "she has talked with those who move between the worlds throughout her life. You must trust her. Go on Morganna."

"Dionisi told me that the trade is not yet complete. We must exchange our possessions for the horses. That is the first part. Your youngest child. The third horse."

"That is Hengroen, the black," says Jacobus.

"He goes to the king, who will protect the Holy Grail."

Thunder rumbles overhead, and they turn to Myrrdin.

"Wasn't me," he says as he puffs on his pipe.

Lightning flashes again, illuminating the figure of Dionisi who suddenly appears before them.

"It is good to see you again, my friend."

Dionisi steps forward and hugs Jacobus before lifting Sara's hand to offer a kiss. His presence calms them.

"Please allow me to negotiate the trade on your behalf." he turns to face Myrrdin, "you must trade what you have. The mare and the wagon, what's left of the wine that it carries. Then the three coins that lie forgotten in your purse." Dionisi smiles.

"My only three coins?" says Myrrdin.

"Give him what he wants," says Morganna.

"Very well, I will trade."

"Then seal the contract." Dionisi extends his hand and Myrrdin clasps it with his own.

"Is that it? What happens to us now?" asks Jacobus.

"It is Morganna's destiny to complete the ritual," says Dionisi, "she will represent the goddess and bring this enchantment to its end. You have done well Jacobus and Sara. I knew you were the right choice to raise these fine children, gifted by the goddess."

"Do not worry," says Morganna, "We will not leave until the trade is complete. You will not be alone."

"We have no choice but to offer our trust," says Sara.

Dionisi approaches Artos. "I owe you everything, my king. You will be the one who will hold the greatest treasure in your hands. Remember, I will be close when you are on your own quest for the grail. You will always find me wherever the hawthorn tree grows."

Dionisi drops to his knee and bows before Artos. The others look shocked, but they follow the actions of Dionisi, falling to their knees and joining him in tribute.

"Rise," says Artos. It felt awkward, but good.

Dionisi fades away into nothing, before the eyes of everyone.

"Let us make the trade," says Morganna.

Artos, Lancelot and Myrrdin walk the horses out from the field while Jacobus, Sara, and Diana collect the saddles and reins. The grey was for Myrrdin. The white was for Alan. The black stallion, Hengroen, was the mount for Artos.

"I still don't know how to ride," says Artos.

"This isn't any old horse from the local village," says Myrrdin, "it's the magic beast of an ancient goddess from a far-off land born to carry you towards the Holy Grail. Just climb on to him. He will do the rest."

They made the young stallions ready. Then they walked the mare into the field with the hawthorn tree.

"Your coins Myrrdin, give them to me," says Morganna.

Myrrdin took his time opening the purse.

"Now we gather around the tree."

They follow the witch into the centre of the field. She arranges them in a circle with the thorn tree in the centre. Morganna walks around the tree, singing the sweetest song. A haunting lullaby to induce sleep.

As she completes the first circle, she lays a coin at the foot of the tree. She circles a second time. Then circles a third. Each time laying a coin among the tree roots. She checks everyone has fallen asleep. Then she lays down and closes her own eyes.

Artos sees the round table before him. He is alone and the room is lit by four different moons that shine in through the large, ornate windows. Slowly he walks towards the chair which always lies empty. The air is calm, but he can feel his heart beating faster as he draws closer.

Tracing his fingers over the wood and its intricate carvings, a thought enters his mind. The chair has a name. The Siege Perilous.

Suddenly Artos finds himself in a desolate landscape. The moons still shine down from the north, east, south, and west. The white orbs are reflected across the frozen ground. Up ahead in the distance a golden glow draws him forward. He feels tired, hungry, and weak, but a force pulls him on, and he is soon bathed in its golden rays. He reaches out with his hands towards the source of the light.

The energy causes a shock within him, and he is transported to a hill surrounded by a mist covered inland sea. There in front of him is a solitary hawthorn tree. The vision fades to darkness.

Artos wakes with a jump to see those

around him stirring from their spell induced slumber. They dust the frost from their bodies, although they don't feel cold. There beside the hawthorn tree, Jacobus and Sara stand cradling three infants between them in their arms. They are younger looking, happy, and beaming with joy. Around their feet lie three caskets brimming with gold.

Morganna is the first to offer her congratulations.

"Now your fortune has returned. You have served the goddess well. Your life will be long and happy as you watch these little ones grow."

"Thank you Morganna," says Sara, "thank all of you for helping to make this happen."

Jacobus walks over to the others to show off his new son. He is brimming with emotion as he looks at Artos.

"Dionisi honoured you as the true king. I have learned that his wisdom on such things cannot be challenged but let me give a friendly warning about Hengroen. Be you an ordinary man or a glorious leader, it is Hengroen who will decide on your direction of travel from now on," Jacobus pauses, "should we wet the baby's head?"

"I think you've done quite enough of that," calls out Sara with a beaming smile.

"And I think It's time for us to leave you and your new family to enjoy some well-earned peace," says Myrrdin.

Everyone pays their respects to the new Brooker family before walking to their respective horses. The party mounts up, except for Artos, who looks nervous.

"Go on," says Myrrdin.

With one leap, Artos is sitting atop Hengroen, in the saddle and ready to go. He looks pleased with himself as he surveys the world from a horseman's point of view.

"See, you're a natural," says Diana.

"He'll still need to learn to do it without my magic," Myrrdin mutters to himself as they ride off.

THUNOR'S DISCIPLES

Rheged was a spectacular wilderness. Outwards to the west, snow dusted peaks stood against the blue sky, and white cotton clouds painted serene pictures across the vast lakes. To the east lay steep hills, tall sentinels marking out territory controlled by the descendants of the mercenaries, once employed by the Romans.

Artos rides at the front of the party, with Myrrdin by his side.

"Is this my kingdom?" he asks.

"Part of it, at least. If the prophecy comes true."

"How can you be sure?"

"The prophecy is not a bedtime story. It is before us, around us, and behind us. It is real. You have shared your own visions. You have seen much of what lies ahead."

"I think I'm still in a dream. I mean, everyone knelt before me last night."

"Well, don't expect that every day," grumbles Myrrdin.

The path twists and turns along, lined by hedgerows, and trees that arc over from either side. Dark green tunnels that open out into patches of pastoral land. The party makes polite exchanges with friendly locals. They start to become hungry as a large and inviting tavern looms into view.

"We should stop here," says Myrrdin, "rest the horses, give them water and let them graze."

The tavern is busy with travellers arriving and departing, checking horses and wagons, stretching their legs, and taking time for a smoke or chewing on the familiar dark bread. Many drink where they stand, others head inside, and you can hear the customers long before you see them. Mead always inspires hearty laughter, shouting, occasional fighting, and even more shouting.

A large sign outside declares 'This Is A Family Establishment - No Weapons Allowed During The Day'. It takes a few moments for the party to secure their horses and their range of armaments before heading inside.

The five enter the hostelry and the multitude of chattering voices stops as one. You can hear a pin drop. Myrrdin scowls as he surveys the crowd, and the other customers return to their discussions. The party pushes through, between the various bodies gathering around the bar. Many dialects and languages are being spoken, but it's easy to sense hostility. They are the strangers in town.

A large and friendly looking man, full-bellied and face flushed from drinking his own profits, comes to serve them.

"Hello Master Merlin. How can I help you today?"

"You know who I am?" says the tall and distinctive looking wizard.

"I don't know you, master, but plenty do that have passed you this morning. Word gets around fast. What brings you to Inglewood?"

"A rest on the road. A place to stop and make use of your services, and find refreshment."

"And glad we are, Master Merlin. Five for mead, is it? We're doing a special today. If you buy one of our delicious stews, you can refill your mead cups for free."

"That sounds very good."

"Find a table. The girl will bring your food and drink over when you're seated. My name is Gareth and I'm the tavern manager. Just let me know if you need my help."

They file through the packed, noisy crowd and pull five chairs around a table that is intended for two.

"This is a nice place," says Artos.

He scans the room. Potential bandits and

thieves talk out of the side of their mouths while passing furtive glances. A strong, intimidating group of men occupies the space nearest to the bar. To their left, a small, muscular woman, painted in blue woad, stands out. Her steely gaze fixed on Artos. He notes she is the only one allowed to carry a weapon. Sheathed at her side is a short sword, no doubt once recovered from a fleeing or dead centurion.

Well, maybe not that nice a place.

The serving girls arrive with bowls of stew, a communal loaf of bread, and jugs of mead. After instruction on claiming refills, they leave the group alone to enjoy their meal at the now overladen table.

"So how far now, Myrrdin?" asks Artos.

"We'll be there by nightfall. A few more miles. We'll follow the route of a small river that leads to Urien's Palace."

"And you are sure that he will help us."

"No, but he despises Duncan MacForres, so it's a good place to start. If he's caught up with fighting to the east, as Jacobus suggested, then his northern territories are vulnerable. Duncan is not without ambition. Capturing even the northernmost parts of Rheged will aid his own aspirations for kingship, but he still needs allies if he is to expand his reach from Dun Romanach and Galwydell."

"I think we've foiled that plan," says Artos,

"Duncan meant the marriage of Duncanna to Eochaid to win him allegiance from the Dal Riata, but now the son of King Fergus is dead."

"Don't forget we're dead," says Alan.

"It is good he doesn't know you are alive," says Myrrdin. "you are not here, you are food for the worms."

"Alright, alright," says Artos with a shiver.

"At least you didn't get killed," says Alan, "unlike me."

"I BROUGHT YOU BACK TO LIFE!" Myrrdin exclaims, "talk about ungrateful."

"Quiet," says Morganna, but it's too late as the entire tavern falls silent and stares towards them.

"Ha ha! Very good joke!" says Diana, her acting as terrible as her cooking.

Myrrdin puffs a large plume of smoke that obscures them from everyone else in the room.

"Time is on our side. He cannot arrange another suitor for his daughter so soon. We will have until then to strike and secure our first victory."

"And he won't just accept that I'm king?" says Artos, "I mean you lot accepted it when a ghost told you last night."

Alan spat out the mead he was swallowing, showering everyone at the table.

"Duncan! Accepting you as his king? A Hartriggs boy? That's never going to happen."

Once again, they draw unwanted attention

from the crowd. The other drinkers return to conversations at their own tables, but there's a strong sensation that the whole room is still listening.

"We should leave this talk until we're somewhere more private," says Artos.

"Agreed," replies Myrrdin.

The rest of the meal is consumed in silence, but Artos is sure they're the current topic of discussion for most of the other customers. The intimidating gang of men and the woman covered in blue woad stare directly at them. It's not a welcoming look.

Artos waves over towards the serving girl to get her attention.

"Can we pay for our food, please?"

She nods and walks over towards them.

"Five lunches with mead. That will be three coins."

"Ah," says Myrrdin, "I gave away my last three coins to someone else just a short while ago."

"That's no problem," replies the girl, "we take jewellery, wheel pottery, ornaments, or grave goods."

"Maybe I could cast a spell of good fortune?" suggests Myrrdin with a weak smile.

"Sorry, sir. We don't accept magic. It wears off after the magician has left."

An embarrassed pause follows as the serving girl awaits a response from the group.

"Is this an adequate payment?" Artos reaches into the small pocket on his tunic and produces a small emerald ring that is loosening around the blackened and shrivelled, rotting finger of Cadawg.

"That'll do nicely sir," says the girl, placing the jewellery on her tray and walking away.

Rising from the table, Artos and his party form a slow line to leave between the packed tables.

"Thank you for your business. Do come again," Gareth waves from behind the bar counter.

His kind farewell contrasts with sinister grins and smiles from the five large men that have been watching them. Each one wears a piece of red cloth tied in a knot around their necks. The men jostle with one another, drunken and threatening, they leer at Morganna and Diana.

Artos keeps his head low as he leaves the tavern. Strange new emotions overcome him. The unacceptable behaviour towards women is eating away at him. He himself has been boisterous and drunken plenty of times. In fact, he recognises the loutish behaviour very well, but now he is raging inside with a burning need to punish them for their lack of respect towards his sister and his friend.

Outside again, they make their way towards the horses with a quiet sense of urgency.

"Friends!" comes the call from behind them, "good friends, I do not recognise you. What brings you here to our part of the world?"

Artos turns back first, even although he is sure he's stepping into a dangerous predicament. Alan turns to stand at his comrade's shoulder.

"We are heading for Urien's palace."

The rough-looking men are unimpressed. The lead man speaks to his friends in a hushed tone and with a thick dialect. Three of the group stagger off towards their own horses. Leaving the leader and one more to face off against Artos and Alan. Then the woad covered warrior emerges from the doorway of the tavern.

"They are not of the Rheged tribes," she says, "they are Angles. Get yourself out of this place."

"And you are not Rheged either, Brigid," the man responds, "just a remnant of Iceni scum, the last dregs of a forgotten tribe."

Myrrdin, Morganna, and Diana keep walking and make it to their horses, releasing the tethers and making ready to leave, in a hurry if necessary. Meanwhile, customers from the tavern have emerged, forming into an audience. The growing crowd is obviously expecting a scene to develop, and this emboldens the Angle leader, who nods towards the Iceni.

"The blue girl over there, she serves Urien, but she sups her mead in my tavern, so I let her live," he laughs at his own humour, "I'm sorry, good friends, where are my manners. I am Theo, the leader of Thunor's Disciples. This is our land, our tavern. Urien does not rule here. When you offer tribute, it's offered to me."

"Do you hear that?" asks Theo's accomplice, "you offer tribute to Thunor's Disciples, or else."

Theo slaps the back of the other man's head.

"My apologies," continues Theo, "He is my most trusted associate, Odo. He's stupid but faithful and will kill on my word, should I choose to give it."

"Come along Artos, Alan!" Myrrdin orders.

"Artos? Alan? Your grandfather wants to leave, but the roads around here are dangerous. It is important to have protection from raiders."

"Vicious raiders," says Odo.

"Leave this place now," says Brigid.

The crowd groans with disappointment.

"They don't need your advice Brigid," says Theo, "I am only offering my services to the grandfather and his grandchildren," Theo turns his attention back to Artos, "do not listen to her. She once tried to break my heart," he pauses as if for comic timing, "literally tried to break it," pulling aside his shirt, to show a huge scar across his chest. The audience laugh and applauds his efforts at humour.

Brigid walks away, tired of the show. Her transport is an impressive war chariot. A traditional biga, drawn by two chestnut mares. She prepares to leave but keeps half an eye on the proceedings. She knows Theo well. His theatrical display is a well-practiced form of menace. A forerunner to an inevitable violent climax.

One of the other members of Theo's group mounts his horse and rides off at a gallop, while the remaining two unstrap axes and saunter back to their leader, flanking him at either side. It's obvious to all that a fight is approaching, including most of the other tavern customers who are placing bets with one another.

Diana collects her bow and arrows from her horse, but Myrrdin holds her back.

"We can't use explosions or missiles here. It could hurt the innocent children."

"I promise you I will not miss," says Diana.

"So, my friends," continues Theo, "Will you consider paying a reasonable fee for an offer of protection from me and my men as you travel these very dangerous routes towards Urien's palace. A terrible gang stalks the very roads you will travel. They are ruthless killers."

The crowd offers oohs and aahs in response. "Get on with it!" some of them cry.

Artos has had enough. Alan can read his friend's body language well. They know when each other will strike.

"And I suppose you are that gang?"

"Yes, we are," replies Odo, without hesitation.

Alan places his arm around the shoulder of Artos.

"Let's go. We don't need this today."

Alan turns Artos back and they step towards their own horses and the others. In response, the audience jeers and whistles. Many call out insults, while others make loud chicken squawks to taunt them into action.

"Don't leave us, my good friends," says Theo, "I'm sure the redhead and her friend wish to stay drinking with us."

Artos stops and closes his eyes for a moment.

He is surrounded by the sounds of battle. Fire, horses, the sound of metal striking wood. He stands amongst a circle of opponents who edge towards him. Then into his view appears his hands holding a mighty sword. Its power surges through every fibre of his being. He raises it and swings it in a single arc, felling all opponents before him.

The red mist continues to rise over Artos. In a split second, he spins around, connecting a hefty punch aimed at Theo's chin. It sends the leader of Thunor's Disciples sprawling into the dirt.

"You're barred!" shouts Gareth

Artos continues his attack. He pulls Odo forward by the collar before head butting him and sending him hurtling backwards amongst the assembled crowd, scattering the audience that surrounds them.

Theo wastes no time calling his two other henchmen. He spits the dirt from his mouth and springs to his feet, dagger drawn and ready.

Alan launches a flying kick at the first axeman. The other drops to the ground as one of Diana's arrows pierces through his wrist.

Theo and Odo respond by rushing forward together with blades in hand, encouraged to retaliate by an excited crowd who are baying for blood. Artos and Alan make ready to fend off the armed attackers with nothing to defend themselves but their bare hands.

Myrrdin drives his staff into the ground, sending out shock waves that scatter through the crowd and send everyone reeling. As the combatants from both sides pick themselves up and recover, the sound of large cracks fracturing the earth below them sends the crowd into a panic. Ruptures in the ground twist and turn, snaking towards the tavern, before finally opening a sinkhole that swallows the building whole.

Artos looks back at Myrrdin.

"Too much?" says the wizard.

Clouds of dust envelope the stunned and choking crowd. The swinging sign suspended from a single upright pole is the only part of the tavern remaining. It creaks as it rocks back and forth. It slows, splits, and drops on to a small boy. The tension mounts. Then the child bursts into tears.

"GET THEM!" shouts Gareth, and everyone charges. Racing forward, the crowd leave Theo and Odo standing as they surge towards Artos and Alan.

"Time to go!" shouts Alan, grabbing his best friend by the arm and running towards their horses.

Myrrdin, Morganna, and Diana all mount up, while Hengroen takes it upon himself to barge into the crowd, scooping up Artos on to his back.

Alan scrambles to make it to his own steed as the mob attempts to pull him back. His white charger works its way between him and the crowd, giving him the opportunity to leap into the saddle, but the rabble continues to surround them, stopping them from getting away.

A horn sound signals a charge. More Thunor's Disciples have appeared at the scene. A complement of men that now resembles a full mounted cavalry of around twenty riders is descending on them with swords and axes drawn.

The three enchanted steeds break free from the angry mob, but Morganna and Diana's horses do not have the same magical prowess. The people hem them in, and both are pulled from their saddles, disappearing in amongst a sea of bodies that close in around them.

Artos charges into the crowd. Many hands grasp at him, trying to unseat him. He hangs on to Hengroen as the horse begins to make the decisions. The calls of the enemy charging towards them start to drive the crowd apart. Artos can hear the protests of Morganna and Diana, but in the confusion there's no sense of where they are. The battle becomes a struggle to stay upright. Myrrdin and Alan are doing their best to fight from their horses, but the crowd is angry and undeterred. A mob bent on revenge.

Artos is within a few feet of more heavily armed opposition when Myrrdin directs another pulsing shock wave into the crowd. It clears just enough space for Artos to ride up beside the wizard and Alan. He hesitates, but Hengroen decides for him. Charging out of the crowd, he leads his equine brothers and their riders away from the tavern. The screams of Morganna and Diana ring in their ears, but Artos can't turn his horse around, now it has decided the course of action. He casts frantic glances over to Alan and Myrrdin, and their grim expressions speak volumes. This was a loss in battle that they weren't expecting, nor one that they are ever likely to forget.

Hengroen and the other horses carry their riders as fast as the wind for miles without halting or even breaking the pace of the gallop. The horsemen in pursuit couldn't match their speed and have given up the chase, but the furious escape only comes to a stop when they reach the skeletal cover of an oak wood in winter.

An enraged and emotional Artos leaps off his mount and roars with anger at himself, at the sky, at the gods, or any person within earshot of his anguish.

Alan dismounts and attempts to place an arm around his friend, but Artos pulls away.

"Give him this time alone," advises Myrrdin.

"I know how he feels," says Alan, "why did that have to happen? Aren't the gods on our side?"

"The gods don't take sides. Trust me. Morganna and Diana won't meet their end today."

"But the longer we stay here, then surely the longer they will be in danger?"

Myrrdin doesn't answer but retreats into

his own thoughts as he contemplates the next steps ahead.

Artos continues, walking away from the others. The silence and the sadness have become overwhelming. He needs to seek solitude for a while. He finds his space. A fallen tree trunk provides a place to sit. The forest is quiet with no bird song or breeze. Before him there lies a pool of dark water, a small well disconnected from any visible source of supply.

He closes his eyes. His mind races along with the adrenaline charging through his body, and it floods with images of the events of the past few days. The low temperature and sheer exhaustion cause him to shift in and out of consciousness. Small wisps of mist form around him, but lost in his own despair, he doesn't notice how the frozen vapour wraps around him. Obscuring him from the sight of Alan and Myrrdin.

He gathers water in his cupped hands and throws it over his face to wash away the tiredness. As he wipes the droplets away, he can see a blurred figure standing before him. Startled, he stands to his feet.

"Is it you?"

There is no reply, but Nimue stands before him. Once again, her face doesn't offer an emotion as she stares deep into his soul. Then the ripples begin to form on the water that lies between them, and gradually the hilt and then the blade of Excalibur breaks the surface and rises higher. Nimue clasps her hands around it. Artos feels his heart thumping, the tears return to his eyes. The power of a potent magic surrounds him. Nimue is contemplating her decision.

"No, not yet," says the Lady.

"Still no, not yet?" says Artos with frustration.

"You cannot bear the weight of grief over a friend lost," says Nimue, "then how can you expect to bear the responsibility of an entire nation?"

"But my lady, with the sword by my side, I will vanquish my enemies."

Nimue looks skyward and inhales a frosty sharp gasp before pausing and sighing out a more calming breath.

"Excalibur is a blessing and a curse. Be mindful that I must judge anyone who might claim this sword. It is a weapon of mass destruction that will lay waste upon thousands. I must be sure you can win the hardest battle if I am to consider passing it into your care."

"The hardest battle?"

"The battle with yourself. You must destroy everything you have been before you create everything you will become. You must rule in the kingdom of your own mind before you are anywhere near ready to rule over the Blessed

Isle."

Artos understands her words, but the legendary sword transfixes him, only inches from his grasp.

Nimue appears to soften her appearance.

"Excalibur is truth. Truth cuts through everything. Not the version of events that you wish to be true. Truth is order, balance, and judgement. When you can accept truth in its purest form, then you will be ready to wield the sword."

"But not yet?"

Nimue becomes grim as she shakes her head. "I have appeared before you. You may ask one more thing of me before I leave. Not the sword, obviously."

Artos ponders for the briefest moment. "Will we get Morganna and Diana back? And what else will go wrong?"

"That's two things at least. I don't have all day. You will face your enemy again soon, be brave, and subdue their flame. As for your friend, Alan? When he next dies, you and the Merlin must bring him to me."

"Oh no, that's happened."

"The next time he dies, bring him to me! Only I will have the gift to return him to you."

The image of Nimue and Excalibur fades into the mist, which then evaporates before him.

"Wait. What flame? Lady? Lady?"

Alone again, Artos turns and can see the others in the distance, locked in discussion, maybe hatching a plan. As he walks back, thoughts of Morganna, Diana, and now Alan are weighing heavily on his mind.

He has no time to think, before the sound of fast rolling wheels pulled by galloping, braying horses shatters the stillness. A whip cracks through the air and a shrieking battle cry prompts Artos to break into a run towards the others.

Myrrdin makes ready to stand his ground. The crystal orb that sits atop his staff is glowing with a revolving golden aura of shimmering sparks. Meanwhile, Alan rushes towards the horses to grab the nearest weapon.

The charioteer looms into view. It's the same woad covered warrior from the tavern at Inglewood. It doesn't look as if she intends stopping. Artos and his comrades gather to confront the oncoming danger.

Myrrdin lifts his staff high into the air. Alan readies his axe. They can feel the breath of the horses. The ground shakes with the thunder of their hooves.

"Wait!" shouts Artos, "it's Diana!"

The chariot pulls up to a dramatic halt. Diana leaps from the back, still holding a javelin in her hand. Battered and bruised, but very much alive.

"What happened? How did you get away?"

asks Artos.

"With the help of the Iceni, I'm glad to say. They were holding me to the ground when she just charged in with her chariot at full pace. Scattering the people and grabbing hold of me. With one arm, she drew me up beside her. I grabbed a spear, and we cut our way through those who tried to block our escape."

Diana looks on with genuine admiration of her saviour.

"This is Brigid. I owe her at least one of my lives for what she did for me today."

The gushing praise embarrasses the charioteer.

"I'm sorry I couldn't save the other one," she says, "do you often run from a fight?"

Artos and Alan look at their feet. Myrrdin attempts to offer the first crumb of comfort.

"I am Myrrdin Wylde, Merlin of the Britons, seer, and battle mage. I know that Morganna's destiny goes beyond this day. We will rescue her. Of that, I am sure."

"I only saw an old man ride off to avoid a fight with merchants, crooks, and annoying families."

"Don't forget the ruthless gang of killers," says Alan.

"Thanks Alan! Morganna's still out there," says Artos.

"Alright stop it everyone," Diana calms them, "listen to Brigid. She rides into battle with Urien and the Rheged. She can take us to him now."

Myrrdin becomes more animated. "You must know of me. I have fought alongside your chieftain many times."

"I have heard stories of you, Merlin. They even say that you fought alongside my great grandmother."

"Ah Boudicca. Yes, of course. I was just starting out then."

Myrrdin looks wistful, with memories of his youth.

"Can you take us to Urien's palace?" says Artos, "We intended to ask for his support against the tyrant that rules over Galwydell, but we have a more urgent problem with these Thunor's Disciples."

"Artos speaks the truth," says Diana, "his quest is part of my quest. If he fails, then I will fail. I cannot let that happen, or we will never avenge my people."

Brigid considers her response before bowing towards them. "My first impression of you wasn't good, but Urien speaks with high regard for you, Merlin. Diana, we share a bond. Warriors far from home, searching for a greater prize. As for you other two? Maybe you can fight, although I've still to see proof."

An awkward and uneasy silence falls.

"I will take you to Urien. Thunor's Disciples have been raiding his supply lines for a long while. I'm sure he will be happy to accept your services dealing with the matter. Mount your horses, I have seen how fast they can gallop. I'm sure it will not take us long to reach his palace."

"Then again, maybe we should try to get Morganna back now?" says Artos.

"The Disciples like a hostage and Theo likes your friend. They will take her back to their camp. It is well protected. We will need more than just us to attack."

"We have the Merlin," says Alan.

"Yes. Was it you that blew up your own side in a battle?" an uncomfortable silence follows, "then I think you'll need the help of the Rheged to save your friend."

DUNCANNA'S PLAN

Ifan Gofannon sweeps into the great hall of Dun Romanach with the artistic presence of a minor actor who believes he should have been the leading light. He strides with purpose towards the curtain, to be met by MacDuncan, standing by a table with a sign on it that reads 'Leave your weapons here. Collect on the way out'.

"It's a new rule," says MacDuncan, "father fears assassination. He met with a fortune teller."

"Not a very fortunate teller," Ifan replies.

MacDuncan allows himself a small chortle. "No, I suppose not. Still, you'll need to leave your dagger here."

"Pah! The blade is not but six inches. It is a stage prop, not a proper weapon."

MacDuncan's stony faced look confirms that this isn't the time for mirth.

"Sorry Ifan, you're an excellent bard, but I'll

have to kill you."

"Fine, take my offending article if it makes Lord Duncan more accommodating. The news is not that good."

Ifan places his dagger on the table and passes through the curtain along with MacDuncan, where a frosty mood permeates the chamber. Duncan and Duncanna are both sitting in silence, post-argument.

"Ifan, you have returned," says Duncan, rising from his chair with some relief, "I thought that only your head might make the journey back."

"Had it not been for my finest theatrical performance, my great oratory powers, and my ability to lie through gritted teeth, then I may well have fallen foul of the wrath of King Fergus. I told him Eochaid was dead, but not before slaughtering two hundred. I felt that was more realistic."

"So how did Fergus take it? I don't need the poetry version, just report what happened without those other more fanciful expressions that you do."

"He took counsel for two days while they confined me to a cell. Left without food or water. On the third day they brought me before King Fergus. They offered me a fine meal with wine —"

"Not mead? Wine, that's very generous."

"His executioner served the meal. My fate

was obvious if I did not give an excellent account of Eochaid's death. I summoned the *awen* of my life and told my tale. His priest recorded it on vellum as I spoke. My lord, please allow me to recreate the scene. I'm sure I will impress you."

"I'm sure, but the short version will suffice. Did he believe you? That's what I want to know."

"He did. At first, he struck the table and wrung his hands over the loss. He cursed Eochaid's retinue for falling in battle and not having the decency to return for their own execution. Then there were particular points he noted."

"Go on," says Duncan, with an overwhelming sense of approaching losses.

"Eochaid's bravery impressed him, having never seen it himself. He confessed it surprised him that his third son even knew which end of a sword to wield. This amused his other sons, who were present."

"How did the sons receive the news?"

"Happy. Their inheritance now one part of two as opposed to one part of three. They will race to murder when Fergus is no more."

The MacForres children draw each other looks as if to show that similar thoughts of fratricide and sororicide had crossed their own minds.

"T'was then that Fergus noted that Stoirm

Gheimhridh had not arrived home with the bones of his son."

"Storm what?"

"Stoirm Gheimhridh. It seems he had named his sword and that it had some material value. Fergus suggested you return as a matter of priority the equivalent weight of the sword in silver as recompense for its loss."

"The crafty old devil," says MacDuncan, "he's trying to rob us blind. What else does he want?"

"A new warhorse from your stables. A stallion that he shall name Eochaid, so that his name at least will continue to charge into battle as bravely as the departed third son."

"Fine. Is that it?"

"King Fergus expresses genuine remorse for the loss suffered by the fair Duncanna. He wishes it to be known that through his sense of charity and lack of any thought for himself, he is prepared to accept Duncanna as his own wife."

"He has a wife already, does he not?"

"King Fergus assures me my lord, that his current wife yearns for a life of solitude and self-reflection at his settlement on the Isle of Hy, many miles north of his fortress in Alt Clut, and that her dreams can come true in the blink of an eye if you will only agree to his terms."

"Will I be Queen of the Isles then?" asks Duncanna.

"Certainly, my lady. King Fergus admits to himself that he is not in the best of health. What with the drop, the flux, regular bouts of sweating sickness, Holy Fire, leprosy, and a history of syphilis. Yet he is sure he will meet expectations on his wedding night by using herbal preparations."

"There's no chance of that!" says Duncanna, "father, I have my own conditions for this arrangement. You will make sure he drinks too much at the banquet to delay his affection. I will need a lady-in-waiting to attend to me. Skill with a blade will be an essential qualification. Finally, fit my wedding garter with a sheath for a skinning knife. In case I must defend myself against my new husband."

Duncan and Ifan nod to one another in collective acknowledgement of Duncanna's demands.

"If we agree to these terms Ifan, will Fergus still give me the ships and men for an assault on Ynys Mon?"

"He assured me once the marriage is consecrated, he will adhere to the original bargain."

"I'll marry him, but he can forget consecrating anything," says Duncanna.

"My lord, Fergus has no direct quarrel with Arnall. The current King of Galwydell enjoys a fine reputation among many tribal leaders. Fergus will make demands of land and tribute in return for supporting your own ambitions of kingship. Until he has a son with Duncanna, the lands and titles will pass to his other sons, and you could lose many of the gains from your alliance."

"Excuse me, I am here," says Duncanna. "I'm sure I can produce a red-haired child with no trouble, if it's related to Fergus or not."

"You're just like your mother," says Duncan, "very well Ifan, we will take King Fergus at his word. I will organise the silver and the horse. Go now and write the best description of Duncanna that you can."

Ifan often wrestled with the ethics and morals of life as a bard. His lifelong ambition was to write a long story. A bound codex telling of his life among high society. A real page turner, exposing the secrets of the establishment.

For now, life confined him to write dishonest news for an honest day's pay. Working for the MacForres family provided employment, but at what cost to his artistic reputation? He drains the mead from his cup before pouring another from the jug. He exhales a deep, disillusioned sigh, and a disturbance draws his gaze towards the curtain that separates the people from the power.

A guard sits by the new weapon table. He yawns and stretches his arms out every now and again. Muffled curses echo across the hall from behind the divide. A fist knocks it three times, followed by a sigh and a foot stamp. The guard jumps from his half-sleep to part the curtain for Duncanna.

"Where were you? I've been knocking for ages," she says, "you just can't get the servants these days."

Duncanna skips towards Ifan. She can be pleasant when it suits her, and she smiles at the bard as she sits beside him.

"I hope you have written fine words to describe me?"

"You are indeed fair, my lady. I'm sure the descriptive text of your refinement and virtue will be the finest prose. Yet I must weave matters of court into my verse. If King Fergus allies with your father through your forthcoming marriage, then it will strengthen his hand against Arnall but might make an enemy of Talorc and the Picts."

"The Picts hate Fergus?"

"Not just Fergus, all of Dal Riata. They have fought each other for years over the places where their kingdoms meet. The spies of both courts pass unnoticed between them. Whatever I say to King Fergus will reach the ears of Talorc within weeks. I must portray the alliance in a light that may dissuade the fierce tribes of the far north from an attack on Dun Romanach."

"And can you persuade them?"

Ifan allows himself a self-satisfied grin.

"I am a bard. My words carry a message as opposed to a truth. If a man slays a few? The bard can add hundreds to his tally. What if his mead is in short supply? It is the bard's words that make it plentiful beyond imagination. The sword captures land. The quill captures glory."

Duncanna nods and looks thoughtful. "Do you know the Lord Talorc?" she asks.

"Yes, I have toured to his Broch. The Picts enjoy a feast night like any other."

"So, their mead is plentiful?"

"Oh yes, very plentiful, my lady."

Duncanna sits fiddling with her blonde tresses.

"You're very good with words, Ifan."

"Thank you, my lady."

"Describe King Fergus to me with your, words."

"Well, he has long lost the youthful representation of his body. Bright red hair not as thick as it once was. He has a bronzed complexion dried out from years of sailing in the salt filled air around his island kingdom. His height from head to toe is less than yours. The circumference of his belly is moderate and acceptable. Kind. reliable, though mean with coin. He has afflictions, but who doesn't? His breath is foul only on days he has consumed mackerel."

Duncanna nodded. "And Talorc? How do you describe him with your words?"

"Talorc is young, wild, and fierce. He has covered his body with painted markings and images of ancient symbols, monsters, and mythic beasts. Much taller than you, my lady, muscular yet lithe. A fine swordsman, rider, and hunter. He is charismatic and strong, brutal, and unforgiving of his enemies. His reputation travels of his triumphant victories in conflict. He likes his meat raw with the blood still oozing from its flesh and he has sharpened his teeth into points."

"Talorc sounds amazing!" says Duncanna with no lack of sincerity, "how large is each other's kingdoms?"

"Fergus wins on that point. Talorc's territories are not the largest in the Pictish lands. I think through marriage, political negotiation or —"

"Murder?"

"I was going to say battle. Talorc could rule over the largest part of the north."

"That is interesting?" says Duncanna, "then I must consider the options before making my final decision."

"My lady, your father will have calculated that Fergus is the established leader of his people. Talorc needs to incite much slaughter amongst other Pictish tribes to achieve the same supremacy."

"I know, isn't it romantic?"

There was a charm in the brightness of Duncanna's smile as it contrasted with the darkness of her soul.

"My lady, Talorc has never shown a want to take a wife. His lust for power is without compare."

"Well, he hasn't met me yet, has he? Thank you, I shall have further discussions with my family. My betrothal will unite tribes as never known before in history. I cannot leave the final decision to my father and certainly not to my annoying lackey of a brother."

The large curtain parts once more. Duncan and his son enter, mead in hand, and locked in conversation.

"Father," says Duncanna in an unnervingly bright tone of voice, "I've been talking to Ifan."

"I'm sorry my lord," says Ifan as he hurriedly gathers his parchment, ink, and quill.

"No, please stay Ifan. I do not want to disturb you in your work," Duncan is not known for subtlety. It's obvious that Ifan could suffer a random punishment, depending on what Duncanna says.

"Now the wedding," she says, while the others groan, "I'm having second thoughts on who I might want to have as the groom —"

"What?" Duncan's rage overflows into

every spare corner of the Great Hall.

"I've been speaking to Ifan, and the political repercussions of a marriage between King Fergus and myself may complicate our relations with Talorc and the Picts."

Duncan smirks back at his daughter with her sudden interest in politics; then glowers at Ifan for introducing her to the subject.

"Nobody has a relationship with the Picts, and Talorc especially," says Duncan.

"Aye, you're playing with fire there," MacDuncan's smug tone is squarely aimed at undermining his sister.

"And doesn't Talorc have the ships you need to besiege Arnall at Ynys Mon?" she asks.

"He does," says Duncan, "but their navy must navigate past Fergus first. That is disastrous for our plan."

"And?" Duncanna can't understand the problem.

"I know you favour war," Duncan continues, "but both tribes have skirmished over their borderlands for years. Neither has an appetite for long campaigns."

"We cannot please both, regardless of who you marry," says MacDuncan, "if we side with the Picts, then Fergus will not supply us the ships we need."

"He's right," agrees Duncan, "your match will be with Fergus. Poison him and his older offspring as soon as you bear him a son. That's a nice simple plan we can control."

"Why don't I marry both of them?"

"What?" echoed Duncan and MacDuncan. While Ifan spat a mouthful of mead on to the floor.

"Sorry," says the bard.

"If I marry Fergus *and* Talorc, both the Dal Riata and the Picts will ally with Galwydell. Then, father, you will find yourself in command of the largest force north of Hadrian's Wall. You will have a navy and fierce warriors to complement our cavalry. Then you can defeat Ynys Mon and sweep south against Urien and then whatever place you arrive at after that. No-one will deny you are the mightiest of kings, across all the lands."

MacDuncan protests, "don't be ridiculous."

"No, wait a minute," the audacious plan excites Duncan, "I think you just might have something."

"And how can we marry my dear sister off to both?" says MacDuncan, "won't they know?"

"I will have a twin sister," says Duncanna, "neither of my husbands will wish to visit each other. They will never know that my twin is me."

She sits back, arms folded, content that her work here is done.

"What kind of plan is that?" says MacDuncan, "how do you plan to live with both of them?"

"I won't. I'll spend a few days with one, then just say I need to return to Dun Romanach to cope with my homesickness, visit my family, carry out alms giving and charitable work. I'll live with husband number two for another few days, then go back to husband number one."

"Charitable work? Your plan is falling apart."

MacDuncan and his sister exchange hateful and disparaging looks at one another.

"And what if one makes a child with you dear sister?"

"Both will be assured they are the father."

"And when the child grows older?"

"Any child of mine will be extremely well schooled in subterfuge before then. Murdering relatives will be part of their basic education."

Duncan has been wandering around the hall, lost in thought.

"Your plan is dangerous, and your lack of morality is above comparison. Yet it might just work."

"Faither, news will get out."

"What news? We control the news. Nobody records any events these days, apart from bards and the church. Throw in a miracle or supernatural act and it becomes believable. Duncanna could have a twin that your mother kept secret from us. In fact, I have no problem believing that story."

"What will Father Andrew say? Will he

even agree to carry out these marriages?"

"I'm sure he will have no problem, if it doubles the quantity of my wine he can consume."

"We agree then," says Duncanna, "we have two weddings to plan."

Duncan shudders at the thought of even more hours spent on the minutiae of table decorations, but the end justifies the means.

"I think this calls for wine and more talk. Carry on Ifan. This might have ended badly for you, but I'm actually quite pleased."

"Thank you, Lord Duncan."

Ifan bows low as the MacForres family head off to hatch their plot.

Andrew sits alone in his chapel. An odd-shaped hole in the wall casts light on to the parchment on the desk before him. He takes great time with his quill to transfer his thoughts into the written word, as he details a weighty personal account of the good works of his mission.

It was rare for someone to achieve sainthood in life. So, it was always prudent to prepare a curriculum vitae for future reference after you had gone. If you had performed miracles with snakes, serpents, or dragons, then that was useful. Healing the sick earned you credit, as did the number of conversions. He faced increased competition from new priests arriving every day. Many claiming to have a family connection with Jesus to boost their status.

The door to the chapel creaks open and Duncan enters.

"Ah, Father Andrew. What are you up to today?"

"Writing my lord."

"Ah yes, writing. Very good. Don't let me stop you."

Duncan edges up to behind Andrew's shoulder and peers over at the script. It's meaningless to him, but he is always keen to appear educated.

"Are you writing a list of my good deeds?"

"Not today, my lord. I felt compelled to record the details of the wicked child Morganna, daughter of the devil."

He crosses himself for protection at even uttering her name.

"I see, so tell me, what is it you say?"

"In partibus infidelium —"

"No, tell me in a language I know, you fool."

"Oh, of course, my lord. I'm telling the story of the young witch of Hartriggs. Daughter of a harlot queen, mother of her brother's child, purveyor of evil who will seek to destroy the very foundations of this angelic isle."

"It's very, eh, demonic, isn't it? I didn't even

know she had a brother."

"I'm sure in time, the history of these years will confirm my God given truth."

"Yes, but it's a lie. If the people who —"

"Read it my lord?"

"Yes, if the people who read it don't believe it tells the truth, then they may not believe your accounts of my own successes. That's not good, considering the generous funding I give for your —"

"Small chapel, my lord," interrupts Andrew, but he acknowledges the point, "very well, my lord. What if I add a section where you resist her comely temptations because the Holy Spirit takes possession of your body just in time to save you from your own lustful weakness?"

"Yes," says Duncan, "that works for me."

An awkward pause follows, and Andrew returns to his work, while Duncan fidgets, shuffles his feet and drums his fingers on his chest.

"Was there something else you wanted, my lord?"

"Look, I've been thinking," continues Duncan.

"Oh dear, I am sorry my lord."

"I think it's time I allowed you to go out into the wider world, convert the masses, grow your flock of followers. Life on the open road. A simple diet of black bread and water fresh from the stream. What do you say?"

"Maybe if I was younger, my lord. I dedicate myself to study now. Recording my experiences for those that may follow. I suffer from many conditions helped by modest consumption of wine and regular hot meals."

"Nonsense. God will offer the sustenance you need. Is that not what you preach?"

Andrew touches his forehead to mop up the beads of sweat aligning above his thick eyebrows. His complexion has gone pale.

"Missionary work is for a younger man. It can take many years to convert a population to follow God."

"You misunderstand me," says Duncan, "I don't want you to convert followers to God, I want you to convert followers to me. I need new allies and so I have a plan. I want you to travel to the Kingdom of Fib and present yourself as my emissary."

"The Kingdom of Fib? The Picts?"

"You will seek their chieftain, Talorc. Visit his fortress and if you survive your first meeting, by grace of God, then bring him round to your point of view, as well as mine."

Andrew was in a panic. People often regarded Talorc as being insane, but Duncan's reputation excelled at levels of sheer cruelty. The dilemma that faced the priest was which power crazed warlord was worse.

"I agree Talorc could be a powerful ally, but we will need to offer tribute before we even enter his hall."

"And you shall. Coin of course, a cask of wine which I will expect to be delivered unopened," Duncan's accusing look was enough to underline importance of what he was saying, "and of course you will offer the hand of my daughter in marriage to Talorc."

"Your daughter, Duncanna? I thought she was to marry into the court of the Dal Riata?"

"Yes, no, I mean you don't understand. We will offer Talorc the other hand, of her twin sister of course."

"Her twin? Sister? You have never mentioned this before, my lord. Duncanna really has a twin sister?"

"No, she doesn't have a twin. Talorc won't know that."

The mist clears in Andrew's mind. "You intend to marry Duncanna to Fergus *and* Talorc, but that's bigamy."

"Yes," Duncan shrugs, "but not if they're marrying sisters, of course."

"But she doesn't have a twin sister."

"Oh, for goodness' sake. Am I talking in a different language? Who knows if Duncanna has a twin? If I say it, you say it, or Ifan recites it to music.

"This is a way of bringing peace to our land. Can you not see that? The Galwydell, the Dal Riata, and the Picts gathered under one banner. My raven banner that will lead a vast army and navy, first against Ynys Mon, where I will assume my rightful title as King of Galwydell and then onwards to the lands in the south. To crush any that might oppose me, one tribe at a time."

Andrew could see how his own destiny might transform with such an audacious plan. Duncan ruling over more land meant more for the church to inherit. Then he, Andrew, could be an absolute certainty for living sainthood.

"It's maybe a strange peace that leads to such war, but may I say that it's an inspired idea, my lord!"

"Splendid, I knew I could count on you being as immoral as everyone else," says Duncan, "of course, you will need protection on the journey, or at least the money and wine will. I'll send four of my warband with you. They will make sure that you reach Talorc's fortress."

"When do I leave, my lord? I will need time to prepare."

"Grab your good book and off you trot. We have prepared your transport. Ifan has written descriptive text of Duncanna's image on parchment, which you must give to Talorc. I recommend you do not read it yourself, being a man of the cloth and all that."

"But, my lord, someone will need to deliver the weekly service. I need to organise sermons and the taking of confessions."

"We can live without that for a couple of weeks. We'll not burn in hell, will we? Now begone, I need time for quiet reflection and contemplation with, eh, Him."

"Of course, my lord," says the priest as he picks up his pre-packed religious travel bag, "just one thing, my lord?"

"Yes?"

"What will I say is the name of Duncanna's sister?"

"Hm, good question. I hadn't thought of that. I always found naming the children difficult."

"May I suggest Duncella, my lord?"

"Duncella, that has a ring to it! I'm sure that Duncanna will remember it when spending time with husband number two. Yes, Duncella, that's settled. Now make haste and my usual terms apply. Be successful, and I won't hang you."

"Yes, my lord, of course my lord."

Duncan sneers with satisfaction as Andrew exits the chapel. A quick search is all it needs to find the supply of consecrated wine. As he settles down in his reserved chair, he offers a word of wisdom to his God.

"Christmas is always terrible, but I have to admit the new year is looking so much better."

URIEN RHEGED

"I need more drink," says Urien as he looks grimly across the table at Myrrdin. He empties the last drops of liquid from a mead jug and drains the cup in a single gulp.

The pair sit alone in Urien's private chamber. The atmosphere is cordial but strained. They have talked through the night, recounting their shared history. Around dawn, Myrrdin broached the subjects of the prophecy, the sword and the coming king who would rule over all the tribes.

Urien hasn't received the news well. Myrrdin has told him he is not the king to unite the land. Instead, he should support a young unknown warrior from an unknown village. A place that lies amongst the estates of a despised enemy. If he didn't know Myrrdin as a loyal friend, then he might have suspected a plot to rule his lands with a puppet king. with Duncan MacForres lurking in the shadows as the actual power behind the throne.

"I don't know my old friend. I understand you know of things that happen between the worlds, but it will be very difficult to convince my nobles to follow this lad. They'll question my sanity by ordering them to do such a thing."

Myrrdin knew he was right, Urien was every inch a strong and noble king. Age hadn't affected his physical presence. A deep, commanding voice meant he always spoke with authority. He wore the ornamental trappings of victory and the scars of battle. His people loved him and served no other. The Rheged were proud and independent, but all served Urien without question.

"And then," the king continues, "Rheged cavalry have fought to keep back invaders from the east. Battle hardened. More used to fighting from the saddle. Do you think they will follow someone who has just learned to ride?"

"He rides Hengroen," replies Myrrdin, "an enchanted horse that no other person can handle or guide. None will ever unseat him from his mount."

"I understand that. He may be charmed, but king and then further? The king who will unite the whole of these isles under one banner? I cannot support that at this stage. I am king here, and wise enough to know that I cannot show weakness. As for the Irish Blade, many will seek to claim it. If not me, then my son

Owain has rights to its possession."

The two men sit in silence, contemplating an amicable solution for both. Joint wisdom will find a way forward. Myrrdin inhales an extra-long draw on his pipe, hoping to draw inspiration from the smoke.

"Urien. You are indeed wise, benevolent, and strong. I have dwelt in the wilderness, and removed myself from the matters of court and politics. I can understand your caution. Nimue is not yet ready to part with Excalibur."

Urien's expression was fraught, but thoughtful. "The captured witch. Is she ..."

"Yes, the daughter of Gorlois, Duke of Cornwall and the Lady Igraine. Half-sister of Artos, who, of course, is the son of none other than Uther Pendragon."

"Aided by your magic, I heard?"

"My advice that is true. He used his own abilities to deceive Igraine. You understand that the son of Uther has a legitimate claim to Excalibur."

"Does he know?"

"None of them know their parts yet."

"I can understand you are reluctant to say too much too soon, but if we must follow him? He at least needs to know who he is, so that he may lead."

"That brings us full circle," says Myrrdin, "he will first need to capture the titles and estates of Duncan MacForres. He must hold authority over a people, a castle, and an army. Can you spare at least the military support for that venture?"

Urien sits long in silence before giving his response.

"Had I not known you all these years, then I might have locked you away to protect others from your madness, but I confess I know all the characters in your play and the prophecy has long been a favourite topic of my bard Taliesin. The Rheged are ready for a king to come, but it's not for me to convince them about your young prince's heritage," Urien breathes deep, "but I agree that an assault on the MacForres family is good for us. You know that we go back into history as enemies, and that Duncan MacForres has something of ours that we want returned. We likewise have land to the west of his territories, so I'm sure my nobles will agree to supporting an attack that can expand the borders of Rheged territory further north?"

"I'm sure that is acceptable as a fair price for your cavalry," confirms Myrrdin.

"Then I will allow you at least the opportunity to present your case to my nobles, though Artos will no doubt still have to prove his prowess to even engage the support of a few of my army. We don't want you having to cast a spell over everyone. That doesn't work out so well."

"I agree," says Myrrdin, staring at his feet.

"I will need to call my elders together. Those that call themselves Thunor's Disciples have been attempting to compromise my supply routes. An attack on their camp is well overdue. I will lend support for a rescue of the daughter of Gorlois. Let us confirm the gods seek to protect Artos in the face of our common enemies. If he is successful, then I will issue a challenge. My cavalry must believe he can lead them into battle, but that can wait until I know he will live out today. Now find the rest of your party and meet with us in my Hall. My nobles must have a part in the decision."

"Thank you for your wise counsel."

Myrrdin offers a small but courteous nod of respect before leaving, while Urien continues to brood in silence.

Artos and Alan are at the centre of many conversations within the Great Hall of Urien Rheged. The vassals nod or raise a cup in courteous welcome, but none have approached the young men yet, choosing instead to queue for a few words with the celebrated figure of the Merlin.

"He's loving this," says Alan.

"A lot of them know him well. The older ones, at least," Artos replies in hushed tones.

Myrrdin was enjoying the attention. He was laughing like they had never seen, greeting old friends, and exhaling vast quantities of his pipe smoke. Urien's Hall was not so rowdy as Dun Romanach, but knowing few people made Artos feel more isolated and vulnerable. Again, his anxiety over his role in this adventure was testing his nerve.

Many of Urien's nobles had just returned from a battle in Catraeth, where they appeared to have won over the Angle enemy. They were sharing their stories of battle in just the same way that the levy of Duncan did, but this battle sounded far larger than anything Artos or Alan had experienced.

I hope none of them ask about our little battles.

Artos drank more than usual and shrunk into a darker corner away from many of the curious looks of the hosts. Absent-mindedly, he drinks from a jug instead of a cup.

"You better go easy on the mead," Brigid calls over from behind him, "they might ask you to speak."

"Do you think so?"

Brigid nods in return and smiles at Diana.

"You'll be fine," says Alan, "you did a good speech when Wee Laddie got married."

"I don't remember."

"I don't think most folk remembered anything after that wedding, but I'm sure I laughed."

"Great," says Artos, while his heart sinks even lower.

"Artos," says Diana, "you have already led us among enemies. These are friends. Show them you are a leader, and they will follow. I promise. Think of Morganna right now and what she must be thinking."

"It's thinking of what Morganna is thinking is the reason I'm drinking, but you're right, this is for her."

The group return to their people watching when a tall commanding figure enters the room. An athletic physique and darker skin, marks him out as he clasps hands with the other vassals. He doesn't show any scars of battle, but is undoubtedly a warrior, exhibiting the self-assured confidence of a leader. He notices Artos and makes straight for him.

"It's Prince Owain, Urien's son," says Brigid.

Before Artos has said anything, Owain has already taken his hand and clasped it inside his own iron grip.

"I believe you are Artos of Galwydell. I am Owain of the Rheged, son of Urien, and for my sins, commander of the forward camp at Catraeth."

"Yes, I am Artos of Hartriggs, eh in Galwydell. I'm eh, honoured to meet you Owain."

Over-privileged?

"And you are?" continues Owain.

"Alan Owain, I mean Alan of eh, Galwydell, same as Artos. Owain."

"Are you brothers?"

"No, we're just brothers-in-arms." replies Artos.

"The best kind of brother. I think you'll find."

"Yes, your Grace."

"Save that for my father. I always answer to Owain," he turns to Diana, "And welcome my lady to our court. Are you also from Galwydell?"

"No Owain. I am Diana. I am from Pollentia."

"Is that true? My mother's family came here from Palmaria. We must talk about the island. I would like to travel there one day."

"It is a wonderful place. The weather is much better and warmer than here."

"Good to see you again Brigid," says Owain, "Urien keeps you here by his side, but I could have done with you in my army over the past few weeks."

"You know I would be there, but your father insists that I train the new recruits."

"Just try not to kill so many in training," he laughs, "Artos can we have a word together."

Owain puts an arm around the shoulder of Artos and walks away from the others.

"I only killed one," says Brigid quietly,

"What do you think of him, Diana?"

"No, he's not my type," Diana smiles.

"Really?" says Alan, "I quite fancy him myself."

The mood begins to become more serious as the vassals gather around a large round table that dominates one end of the Great Hall. There is no single chair marked out to give authority. Servants set each place with a simple meal and a cup. They disperse jugs of mead around the various attendants who are stationed behind the nobles.

Owain draws Artos away from the crowd and whispers. "Before we take our place, I want to let you know that I have spoken with Myrrdin Wylde already. I know what is about to be proposed and I am pleased to have your aid with these raiders who have been plaguing our villages and merchants, but the task beyond that is my main interest. We despise the MacForres family. Their success has led to our struggle. We fight to secure the borders of our lands, but we were weakened by the ancestors of Duncan MacForres. I just wanted to say that I will be glad to join with your warband to avenge my people. Now good luck convincing our elders, they're friendly, but stubborn."

Owain pats Artos firmly on the shoulder and walks over to take his chair at Urien's right hand. Artos turns back round to face Alan.

"I really don't know about this," he

whispers, "look at him. Why am I the chosen one when there are men like Prince Owain?"

"You're the one with the dreams," Alan replies, "I know you better than anyone and I would trust you over any prince to have my back in a fight. Artos, people are drawn to you. Diana travelled thousands of miles, not to mention the highest mage in the land is on your side. Even Morganna is following you, does that not tell you something?"

"You're right," Artos took a deep breath, "and this is for Morganna, but my stomach is still churning."

"Artos," came the booming voice of King Urien, "come sit here at our table. Join us as our honoured guest."

The room turns as one to look at the young warrior. He can see the years of experience and knowledge written across the faces of the vassals. As he steps forward to take his seat, all who are assembled clatter their mead cups or bang their fists on the round wooden table. They cheer as once again he clasps a hand with Owain as they sit next to each other, and then a quiet sudden realisation follows. He has seen this scene before, in a dream of many years ago, but now the dream has moved into his reality.

Do I have the sight now?

Alan and Diana sit across the table from Artos. The archer is used to the attention her presence generates at meetings full of men. She has spent time with many tribes on her journey and she knows that a full mucus laden spit usually settles everyone down and earns their respect.

As they break bread and share out the mead, only one person remains standing. Brigid is on duty as Urien's bodyguard and keeps a watchful eye as she stands behind the shoulder of the king.

"At least I'm not the only woman today," Diana whispers to Alan, as she smiles over at the charioteer.

Brigid returns a small smile before grinning and ejecting her own full-throated gob of spittle.

"Welcome to our gathering," says Urien, "we have shared food. We give our thanks to God for the gift of our land, our families, and the plentiful mead."

A chorus of responses signals everyone's agreement until Urien strikes at the table several times with his hand, restoring silence and reverence to the room.

"Today we are in the company of our old friend Myrrdin Wylde. Who most will know as the Merlin. He has arrived with his party of fellow adventurers from the north to seek the help of the Rheged."

The gathered nobles thump on the tables. Issuing another fearsome thunder of welcome to their hall.

"While we have concentrated on repelling the Angles," Urien continues, "another threat has emerged on our northern border. The pretender, Duncan MacForres, has his sights set on alliance with the Dal Riata, intending to launch an assault on Ynys Mon to claim the seat of power that will grant him the title of King of Galwydell."

Urien allows disapproving comments to circulate.

"I wager his ambitions will not stop there and that we can expect to fall under his jealous gaze, with or without the continued support from Fergus. The strategic location of Ynys Mon will leave our own ports vulnerable to attack, while Duncan too has horses and cavalry that can sweep in over land where we share a border."

"Yet as you said," interrupts Owain, "we have committed our armies to war against the Angles. We cannot spare the men for a war in the north."

"Which is why, my son, I will stop talking. Myrrdin, the Merlin will offer a solution to this issue. It may suit our needs and his own. Please Myrrdin, speak."

Myrrdin stands to his feet. His wise eyes peering out from under thick eyebrows. He meets the gaze of the nobles with the calm authority his title brings.

"Friends. After the incident ..."

A round of coughing covers inappropriate laughter.

"... I retreated to the great forest of Caledon. A sanctuary for my mind and my soul. A place where I could devote my life to study and contemplation. I shut myself away from the affairs of men. The politics, the battles, the success, and the strife born of war. I had killed many. Too sure of my power. Too confident in my own abilities. It took until that terrible time to make me realise we do not win wars on the battlefield, but in the hearts and minds of the people," he pauses for dramatic effect, "only then will we unite under one banner, under one king."

The nobles strike the table and stamp their boots.

Urien makes a quiet note that the Merlin hasn't mentioned which king can unite the land. So, his years in Caledon haven't removed all his political skills. Most around the table assume Urien will be the chosen one.

Myrrdin continues, "but, my friends, that age of perfection, that land of plentiful mead and honey, is under threat before it's even born. Even as I speak, a dark force is rising. A despot who will enslave your people. Duncan MacForres will unite those who share his appetite for destruction. Raising villages to the ground and slaying the innocent in the pursuit of power. The Pretender of Galwydell, will look to Rheged with its magnificent mountains and lakes, its winding rivers, and lush valleys as nothing more than a picturesque obstruction in his own rise to greatness. Prepare for hell to be unleashed upon your tribe if we cannot stop him before he takes Ynys Mon."

Myrrdin pauses again to let his words settle. It astounds Artos and Alan how Myrrdin depicts Duncan MacForres, realising that until a few weeks ago, they themselves had been part of this dark army of the north.

"You have given us much to fear," says Owain, "now can you share any hope? What is your plan?"

"Time is still on our side. A small warband now, can achieve our goals. It will demand a large army if we let the months pass by with delay. Duncan MacForres only has a dream. He has only one fortress at Dun Romanach, with a military force that concerns itself with subjugating the local population and collecting their taxes.

"Yet even now, that time is short. He had planned to marry his daughter to a prince of the Dal Riata. A marriage that could have formed an alliance to threaten Ynys Mon and indeed your own lands that lie around the coast.

"The three warriors that are with me today foiled that plan. Their part in the death of Eochaid, Prince of Dal Riata, was brave, courageous, and devoid of thoughts of personal gain. The blow they delivered has weakened the advance of Duncan MacForres. They have performed a great service to the Rheged whilst putting their own lives in great danger."

Urien marvels at Myrrdin's skills of persuasion as he observes how the wizard lays out the case for following Artos. It impresses Artos, Alan and Diana as well. Myrrdin's play on words has turned a disastrous event into a stunning victory for the righteous.

"And so," says Myrrdin, "we come here to ask for aid from your cavalry. A warband, to support us in an attack on Dun Romanach. Aiding us to capture the stronghold of Duncan MacForres will defeat the growing danger on your northern borders and serve your people well."

Myrrdin can sense the excitement wane in the room. The nobles are reluctant to engage in further conflict, as Urien has forewarned. All fall silent as Myrrdin retreats to his chair. The vassals look to their leader. After a pause purposely inserted to add weight to his consideration, he then offers his opinion.

"Myrrdin, Artos, Diana, and Alan. Your noble cause stirs our hearts. We hear what you say, but the Angles challenge our borders every day. Unless we hold them back, they will cover our land. Even our language will change, our history forgotten, our family lines will fade into nothing, and our era will become an age of darkness. People will seldom remember us around the hearths. Yet, a way forward may be possible. You have my word that the Rheged honour their debts. So, I ask you first, help us against the Angles who threaten us even at our own gates."

"Thunor's Disciples?" asks Owain,

"Thunor's Disciples," Urien confirms, "tell us Myrrdin of your chance meeting with these criminals."

The room becomes interested again. Something the nobles can support. The Angle bandits are skilled and fast. Their camp has strong defences, and they have created a reputation for themselves that instils fear in the local population. The raiders don't number enough for a direct attack on Urien's palace, but their role as parasites satisfies them. They live off the local people by extorting their own taxes and raiding traders for supplies of food and mead.

"I must confess a shame at our confrontation with them yesterday," says Myrrdin, "we had to run from a fight at the tavern at Inglewood. They and the locals who aided them overpowered us. In the conflict, we lost one of our own. Morganna, the sister of Artos, captured. I presume she now languishes within their camp. If it was not for Brigid ..."

The nobles turned to look at Urien's

bodyguard.

"... we could have lost Diana as well."

"Myrrdin," says Urien, "we now walk on common ground. It troubles me that our own people side with such men. That is indeed something that deserves our attention. We have let them thrive too long if our own folk are treating them as their masters. We know where their camp lies. Wooden gates and fences that can be put to the torch."

Urien then turns his attention to Artos.

"You have arrived in my court seeking help and your case has been adequately presented by no less than the great Merlin. That is worth our attention at least, but the bond that will be struck is between you and me. So, I offer you the floor before my nobles. Present yourself so that we know we are all on the same side and tell us how *you* wish to lead this assault on Thunor's Disciples. Each man at this table leads a warband and more are based to the south and the east. We are hemmed in and forced to ride out to shield our land from danger, but my nobles are not so different, we all seek to drive out the invaders and reclaim the land. If we aid you, how will you aid us?"

The sound of stamping and thumping echoes around Urien's Great Hall once more. Artos is urged to his feet.

"No pressure," says Alan, quietly to Diana.

Artos feels his mouth go dry as all the

eyes in the room fall on him. Owain is aware of Artos' discomfort and hands him a cup of mead. As the honeyed fluid slips down his throat, his nerves begin to disappear he feels a power coming over him, the same force that he felt in the sword's presence.

"Friends," he says, "I thank King Urien for allowing me to stand before you. I am a soldier, and I am a shepherd. I have grown like any other to learn the ways to support my village and how to defend my lands. I cannot lie, even a few weeks ago I could not have foreseen myself standing before you in this way. My life was in the ranks and indeed in the service of Duncan MacForres ..."

A slight murmur goes around the table. Alan feels himself sinking uncomfortably back in his seat and looking for a quick escape route should he need it.

"... I would let you know that the people of Galwydell are good people. Don't judge them because of one man that seeks his own advancement. I can see King Urien how you rule. This very table shows that all can be equal in this place. Duncan MacForres could not conceive of such an idea. Good people thrive under a good leader, where they suffer under one that is bad.

"A short time ago. I served in an army to put food and mead in my belly and to bring home a pittance in coin for my mother and twelve sisters ..."

The impoverished part of the speech returns some warmth in the room for Artos.

"Does he really have twelve sisters?" asks Diana.

"Well, they're not all related, but yes he calls them his sisters." replies Alan.

"... I thought I was doing the right and the honourable thing. Little did I know of how I was only serving the cause of a tyrant. Aiding his personal ambition while my people, the good people, suffered from his oppression the same as any he would call an enemy. Whether it's the work of the gods or fate that lays out our paths before us, my life has changed. The people I now lead, I could easily have followed in another life. It is their belief, their loyalty, which has transformed me. And now with the goodwill of all I can raise a party of heroes to write the wrongs committed by your Angle raiders, I can raise a warband to rid Galwydell of its tyrant, then raise an army to be with you in battle as we vanquish the invaders together."

The crowd delivers a rapturous response to Artos' words, standing at their places and applauding. Alan's face is in shock, Diana is happily smiling, and Myrrdin appears to be the proud father. Even Brigid has broken her stern bodyguard look to join in with the response. Artos catches himself using his hands to settle the crowd, encouraging them to sit for more.

"And so, friends. It is time to turn these words to action. My sister —"

"Which sister?" shouts a voice from the room.

"My sister Morganna is held captive by these Thunor's Disciples. Tonight, I will ride to their camp whether alone or in the company of allies. I will face down as many as needed to release her from captivity. I know that I cannot charge towards their gates. I know that we must get to her before they know we are there. I only need a small party to help me break in and rescue Morganna. Once she is safe, we will open the gates if you can provide the horsemen to ride in and help us with their final destruction.

"My men will ride out for you," shouts one noble.

"And my men will be there too," shouts another.

Soon the room is full of nobles offering the support of their horses. Some walk over to pat Artos on the back. He can't quite believe it, as King Urien silences the crowd.

"Friends, my lords. It seems as if you all want to go. I don't think Artos offered free mead as I would to gain your support," the audience laughs, "we will choose forty to go with you Artos. There are woods nearby their camp. We will take cover there until you send a signal."

"Are you going father?" asks Owain.

"It's beginning to sound like a good night out. Yes, I think I will go," he laughs.

"Then can I join Artos and his raiding party. I wish to be in the vanguard."

"What do you say, Artos, can my son join your party?"

"Aye, I would be honoured for Owain to join us."

"King Urien, your Grace," says Brigid, "Can I join with Owain and Artos. I know these raiders. I can help."

"Well, Artos, you are a good speaker. Two of my best warriors wish to join your ranks. I should end this gathering now lest I lose all my army to you."

"Owain and Brigid beside us will guarantee our victory, of that I'm certain."

"Then so be it," says King Urien, "we ride out after sunset, and we will not accept prisoners."

A final cheer goes around the room, and as the hall empties Artos is left with his party; Alan, Diana, Myrrdin, Brigid, and Owain. They all sit at a chair each, around the round table, and a vision appears in the mind of Artos.

He sits at his own round table with Alan at his right. Scattered around are all the other party members, including Morganna. The other seats are still occupied by fiery beings and the great windows of his court look out at all his lands, each quarter of the view is a season of spring in bloom, summer skies, the colours of autumn, and winter snows. The large shining grail revolves in the centre, casting light out into the room.

He comes back to full consciousness and gazes at the others, awaiting his words.

"Let's plan our attack," he says.

THE WRATH OF
MORGANNA

Odo shivers in the sub-zero temperature of a small storehouse. The gang has stationed him here to guard over Morganna. Volunteering for what he thought was an agreeable task meant he could be alone with the beautiful red-haired witch long enough for her to fall under his irresistible charms.

He thinks his fashionable braided beard, or the roundness of his stomach, are his most appealing features. His sense of humour is legendary amongst his comrades. He knows it normally attracts the ladies, but nothing works with the witch. He sulks when his best tales of theft or assault don't elicit a response.

As the hours pass, the bouts of silence increase. It forces Odo to pass the time. He reflects on the highs and lows of his years with Thunor's Disciples. His mood plummets with the temperature, and he focuses on the way his comrades treat him. His feelings turn upside down.

Maybe my jokes aren't funny? Maybe they just laugh at me? Maybe I am the joke?

He is becoming tired, but he carries out his duty without complaint. Reminding himself that he is a Disciple first and a mere mortal second. He can't waiver or show weakness, even though the temperature is becoming unbearably cold.

His eyelids flicker, but he fights against the impulse to sleep. As he wipes his watering eyes, the tears harden into frost and scrape against his rough and drying skin.

Again, he tries to engage the witch in conversation. This time presenting his sensitive side. He talks of being a well-behaved son for his mother. Or else there was the time he saved a kitten from drowning. Yet the witch's expression is unchanged. Not even a glimmer of appreciation.

What am I saying?

His confusion grows. Even he can't understand half of what is coming out of his mouth as he stumbles and slurs over his words. Looking at the empty cup now frozen in his hand. He feels he must have lost his touch. First, his attractiveness to women and now his ability to hold his drink. He's had only one cup of mead, yet he feels drunk.

He sighs as his breathing becomes more

laboured. The urge to drop off to sleep is growing into an irresistible force. He can't hear his own words anymore, only faint noises that his mouth is making. His mind rambles until one final thought appears into sharp focus.

I am dying.

Now too frozen to move, he can't resist any longer. Morganna appears to be as an angel before him. Present as a witness to his redemption before his gods. He looks at her one last time. Gulps a final breath of air and closes his eyes. His life is at an end.

"Where have they got to?" says Morganna.

She creaks the door open to peer outside the storehouse. The Disciples have posted guards at regular intervals, as if expecting a reprisal from her friends. She has worked through various stages of anger, but she knows Artos must return for her. Footsteps crunch on the ground nearby, and she closes the door over once more. She turns and looks to the dead body of Odo as if he might suddenly give her information on the size of the guard, where the camp is located? And where her brother is?

"I should have asked questions first," she whispers.

Her anger rises and falls in waves. What if she had been rescuing Artos? Would she have left him for what was rapidly becoming a second night? Then she begins to question if they had made it away from the tavern, but then wouldn't Odo have said? After all, he hadn't stopped whining all day long.

One small candle lit the inside of the storehouse. If she was going to break out, then her eyes would have to be used to the dark. The wave of a hand extinguishes the light, and she becomes cloaked in gloom.

Sound took over, to guide her on the world outside her poorly constructed prison. The camp was busy. Shouts and other drunken calls came from various distances and directions. The crunching footsteps came past at regular intervals, maybe a sentry? A few minutes would pass between the cycle. Timing an escape correctly would avoid the guard. Further in the distance was the sound of goods being piled up, along with mocking laughter. The Disciples didn't sound concerned. Capturing people as well as stolen items from merchants was just normal business.

Morganna runs through her options, but most will cause a confrontation especially once her cellmate is discovered. It has taken the leader Theo too long already to return for her. He will have some fate in mind, whether for him, or the highest bidder.

She must go. Artos will be near, and if not, then Duncan MacForres will be the very least of his worries.

Morganna waits for the footsteps passing one more time, before creaking open the door once again. Most of the camp is without light. A high watchtower has torches burning around it, illuminating the figures of more guards. Other than that, there's a well-lit space near the gate, but it dips below a slope that puts the scene out of sight, it's also where most of the noise is coming from, so that's the last place she wants to go. Whatever is down there, it's keeping her captors busy as she steps out into the night air.

Drawing her black hood around her helps her merge with the night. Apart from removing her favourite dagger from her possession they have so far left her untouched. She will prepare herself for a fight in good time, but for now she wants to concentrate on finding a way out.

The camp is in disarray. Small ramshackle buildings, separated by debris that covers the spare ground. Broken carts, piles of wood and rubble. The unused remains of captured items. Then there's the smell. A pungent stench of a rotting carcass. Ever-present undertones of the reek of diseased meat. Shifting ground beneath her feet, rendered into mud by disgusting waste. It at least provides places for cover as the odd figure shambles out of a doorway. Drunk men, incapable of seeing much beyond themselves.

Then the footsteps appear again. Only two boots. Fight or flight? It's so tempting to choose this particular Disciple to receive the full force of her wrath, but her head for once rules her heart. Crouching low behind barrels is the better choice until the steps have walked off again.

On she goes in short bursts of movement, making sure that her way forward is safe around corners before choosing a direction to run. She's moving higher and can see from the random position of torches that the camp is on a hill in three tiers. The light is concentrated around the bottom; she is in the middle, and a roundhouse occupies the top tier. If Theo is holed up in a drunken stupor, it will be there. She can see part of the walls that surround the camp. Enormous trunks of wood bound together and sharpened to points at the top. It's at least double her own height and impossible for her to climb.

Huddled on the ground and feeling isolated. She can't remember a time when she didn't have the company of her beloved ravens and wolves. Stranded far from home, isolated, and vulnerable, a tear rolls on her cheek as she looks over towards the centre of camp. Many small buildings obscure her view, but the abundance of torchlight and noise highlights the place to avoid.

"Whatever fate has planned for me. I'm sure it lies down there," she says to herself.

A voice plays out in her head; rhythmic,

familiar, annoying. Words keep repeating, again and again.

"*Can you hear me? Can you hear me?*"

"Myrrdin!" she says out loud, before realising the wizard is speaking with the silent voice.

She closes her eyes tightly. Reading minds is one thing, but sending thoughts back is another.

"*Myrrdin, is that you?*"

"*Morganna!*" says the voice in her head, "*Morganna, are you alright? Are you safe?*"

"*I've had better days Myrrdin. Where are you?*"

"*Not far. We're at the rear of the camp. In a small group of trees. Diana killed the guards that were posted there. She's asking me to say hello by the way.*"

"*And Artos and Alan?*"

"*They are here with me. We are coming to get you. Where are you now?*"

"*Wait. Everyone survived the fight at the tavern. You left me behind on my own?*"

"*Well, eh, yes, well, no? I mean, the small blue girl rescued Diana. She's called Brigid.*"

"*That's very nice. HOW COME I'M THE ONLY ONE LEFT TO ROT IN THIS DUNG HEAP?*"

"*Ouch, that hurts. Don't scream your thoughts.*"

"*Sorry, I'm annoyed. I'm sure you can understand.*"

She takes a quick pause from thinking before continuing.

"I have escaped, but I'm still in the camp. I think I'm on the opposite side from you. I'll make my way back. Their guards are useless. I'll get there."

"That's good news. I'll wait until I see you and then I'll create an opening in the wall. You'll see a glow of purple light from my wand. Follow the light."

It relieves Morganna to hear a friendly voice, even Myrrdin's. Forgiveness was going to take more time. *"I'll be expecting grovelling apologies when I get back."* she thinks.

"Yes, of course," comes the solemn reply.

Morganna keeps low and out of sight, continuing her tactic of running from cover to cover. Her anger has dissipated again. She just wants back to her friends. Her clothing is dirty and has taken on the pervading aroma of the camp. Crouching at the side of a small, ruined building where the roof has crumbled half towards the ground, she notices closer voices and footsteps. The men speak in agitated voices. They're calling out for Odo, and obviously annoyed at not getting a reply. Morganna can see the palisade that runs along the rear of the camp. She scans left to right, looking for a purple glow. Frantic cries are coming from nearby. She knows they have discovered her escape. Roars fill the camp, followed by the blowing of a horn, sounding the alarm.

"Come on, where are you?" she whispers to herself.

Horses are being mounted and ridden out at speed. Orders barked out for instructions to search. Doors are being kicked in and her chances of rescue are disappearing.

Then a purple light appears, glowing at a section of the wall. It burns through the wood with a single hot beam of light, turning the wood black and smouldering, weakening the fencing. There is no time to think. She has a short distance to run and get to the others. Maybe she can help destroy the wall. She takes the risk.

Rising to her feet, she starts to run, only to be charged at and knocked off balance with the side of a horse crashing into her. As she shakes herself from the fall, more horses encircle her, the view of the fence now obstructed. She can no longer see a purple light, only the angry and gloating faces of the Disciples that surround her, snarling with hatred, amidst calls of *murderer* and *witch*. A violent strike to her head knocks her out cold.

It can only have been a short time that passed

before she opens her eyes again. Her hands are tightly bound behind her back, and she is being dragged to her feet. Surrounded by a noisy procession amid the mob, she is pushed and pulled in every direction. She tries desperately to summon the energy to attack, but the constant blows and the tugging forward by her captors, along with the noise and hatred directed at her, impacts on her efforts to summon a magical response.

Then, through the buildings that run to her side she glimpses Artos, following along in the darkness. In the confusion, she is sure that other figures move with him. They are inside and near her. Knowing they are with her is all that she needs as the Disciples drag her down to the lowest part of the camp. She can walk with more strength knowing that she isn't alone and Myrrdin's voice has once again taken up residence in her head.

"Morganna we are near you. We can see you. We are taking a position to strike," comes the voice.

"Hurry!" thinks Morganna.

Myrrdin is silent for a few moments. It worries Morganna that he hasn't replied, then his voice returns, sounding solemn and fearful.

"Do not worry Morganna, about what you see next. Do not worry we are surrounding them."

"What I see next? What are you saying?"

Finally dragged into the light at the lowest

part of the camp her intended fate becomes obvious.

Theo stands before her, a lit torch in his hand. A few yards behind him, a stake is erected on top of a pile of straw and thick branches. He grins as the other Disciples force her on to her knees before him and he lowers the torch close against her face, just enough to torment her with its heat. Morganna can tell that Theo has gone through this ritual before. It is more theatrical entertainment for the masses. Theo enjoys pleasing his crowd.

"Bring Odo out to witness his killer's fate."

Some men appear, lifting the dead body of their comrade, still frozen to his chair. They carefully position the corpse for the best view of the burning.

"Burn the witch!" is called out amongst the jeers and curses of the crowd as they demand fiery revenge for their fallen comrade. The assembled mob of Thunor's Disciples reach fever pitch as their leader turns to face Morganna.

"Witch! We do not need a trial. Each man here has condemned you to your fate. Odo, our brother, was killed in cold blood."

The crowd break into laughter, with the irony of Theo's words not lost on them.

"If I was merciful. If you had fought as equals on the battlefield and caused his death with axe or sword then I may have had you strangled first out of respect for your talents, but you killed Odo only by your black and evil magic and for that I will show you no forgiveness. Now you will burn. Tie her to the stake!"

Once again, the grasping hands of her captors drag her forward, hauling her up and pinning her to the timber where they bind her tightly. Her head is full of the noise from the crowd. She searches for any sign of her friends. Only Myrrdin's voice persists amongst the rabble.

"Morganna, we're just about to launch our attack. Nearly there, most of us are in position, we're coming."

"Hurry! What's keeping you?"

Then comes the first sign. Just as Theo builds the tension by walking back and forth, passing the dry branches with the flames of his torch, something is happening behind him. A small figure is climbing up the outside of the watchtower.

"Burn the witch! Burn the witch!" chants the mob.

Theo, with no lack of dramatic tension, lowers the torch to the straw only for the flames to extinguish, causing the mob to let out a tremendous groan of disappointment. Theo angrily stabs the torch into the straw with frustration, but it sets nothing alight.

"Get me another!" he barks.

A second torch is handed to the leader. Theo examines it before returning to the pile of straw. Once again, the flame extinguishes as soon as he lowers it. Morganna smiles in defiance at her captor.

"What trickery is this? You only delay your fate. I can stand here until dawn. We have plenty of torches. I just need your cursed powers to fail once," an inspired look dawns across Theo's face, "archers, line up before me with flaming arrows. Let us have sport. Plentiful mead for an entire month for the man whose arrow ignites a purifying fire beneath the witch."

The crowd cheers their leader's ingenuity and now Morganna's face expresses fear as the archers assemble and take their positions before her.

"Where are you Myrrdin?"

"Archers! Take aim!" commands Theo.

"We're ready now." comes Myrrdin's reply.

As the archers stand awaiting the command to shoot, a small, red-coloured ball of light rises above them into the night sky with a crackle that draws everyone's attention.

The glowing sphere sparkles like a small star and splits into ten equal parts, each arcing outwards and descending through the air. Each light spiralling towards a landing spot on the flames that lick from the burning arrowheads. As the ten spheres land and sparkle on the tip of each arrow, Theo realises the danger too late.

"Everybody take cover!" he shouts.

Ten simultaneous explosions blast through the archers, scattering each of them into several pieces and showering Theo with blood and flesh. Frozen to the spot in shock, his men begin to collapse before him as Artos, Alan and Owain emerge from the shadows, swords whirling and glinting as they catch their victims by surprise.

Morganna struggles at her bonds, trying to loosen them. Further In the distance she can see the guards plunge from the watchtower and from behind she is surrounded by a barrage of what she hopes is Myrrdin's incendiary spells and Diana's black arrows. The missiles whiz past her, hitting their targets with ruthless efficiency.

Theo gathers men around him, ordering them into a counterattack. "Get their leader." he commands, and his men charge as one at Artos who disappears amongst a crush of seething Angle enemies. Meanwhile, Theo grabs one final lit torch that lies within reach.

"You will still burn," he says to Morganna, "I will be the first person to greet you when you arrive in hell."

He tosses the flame before lunging into the fight with his men. This time it stays lit, igniting the straw and the branches around the base of the stake.

As Theo rushes forward his fellow warriors battle against Artos, Alan and Owain in a ferocious fight to the death. As swords and axes clash in close combat, a vicious struggle for victory ensues.

Artos can see many enemies before him. The faces of all those who will fall in the battles that lie ahead. He will be called on to fight against overwhelming odds. The images switch between his present and his future. His strength is coming from a source of power that is present deep within his soul. The swords of his enemies rain down, but they cannot touch him. Then suddenly before him the sword of power stands clearly ahead, embedded in stone at the summit of a hill where the dragons duel for supremacy. Their fiery breath destroying all in their path.

The heat of the flames draws him back to reality. His victims are laid out before him. He hasn't halted from the fight while under the influence of his vision. Every fibre of his being is alive. He can sense every trace of metal that draws through the air. He can twist and turn to avoid every attack and deliver his own strikes with deadly accuracy. He has never fought like this in his life, as he claims more and more of the enemy in an unrelenting onslaught.

"Get Morganna," shouts Artos, as he battles on against the last Disciples that are protecting Theo.

Morganna struggles at her bonds. She is

breaking loose and is about to be free when she spots a large and powerful warrior making his way towards her. He slices through the last enemy that blocks his path and rushes through the flames to cut her free. In one move he lifts her into his arms and leaps from the burning pyre on to solid ground.

"Who are you?" says Morganna.

"Owain my lady, son of Urien, King of the Rheged."

"Doesn't that make you a prince?"

"Yes, it does."

The battle is lost for the Disciples as their camp fills with forty horsemen of the Rheged and Morganna is once again free to deliver her own magic. Brigid has raced back from the watchtower and with a series of whirlwind strikes is scything through the final few with her gladius sword. The bandits who have run are easily picked off, but although his rule is over, Theo is determined to take one last life.

As Artos defeats another opponent, it allows Theo the space to charge into the gap. His sword is perfectly aimed, and he delivers a series of powerful blows. Yet he stops in his tracks and allows his guard to drop. He is aware he is putting on his very last show.

The fire now burns bright from the fuel that sits around the stake. Theo can see he is surrounded as the Rheged horses circle and the other warriors stand back, allowing their leader to deliver the final assault. The rage on the face of Artos is plain for all to see. Theo doesn't see a man before him. He's looks upon a demon, blood covered and full of wrath, lit by the flames of a fiery hell.

Artos hesitates. Theo senses a weakness for a brief second and makes a final charge. As he lunges forward, he misses his target. Artos steps beyond the reach of his opponent's blade and in a single fluid motion cuts through his wrist, stabs towards his body and arcs the sword around to cleave into the side of the last of Thunor's Disciples. Theo falls to the ground, gasping for breath.

As Artos lowers the point of his sword, Urien dismounts and stands beside him.

"You have caused me much trouble over the past few years," says the Rheged king, "this is how it ends for you tonight."

"I am happy to fall in battle," says Theo.

"Then you get your wish. You have fallen before a mighty warrior."

"Him?" Theo spits blood from his mouth. "I curse him with the evil company he keeps. I swear on what's left of my life that my kin will always oppose you, Artos? Your bloody end will be what they seek. King Urien is wise to not carry the blame for this carnage. Will your people be happy, Urien, that you have ridden out here to save a witch?"

Artos steps forward. The noble talk doesn't

come easy to him yet, but he can sense something turning in his stomach, something awakening in his heart. He holds his sword to Theo's chest.

"And how will your people know me? A traveller who picked the wrong tavern for lunch. A raider from the lands beyond the Roman wall? Did I fight with enough skill to bring your end? Or were you a victim of your own overreach? You chose a brawl with one who fights alongside the Merlin of the Britons, a Prince of the Rheged, an archer sent by Artemis herself, is brother to the most powerful of witches, friend to a warrior who has never lost in any fight, and Brigid, descendant of Boudicca. The Iceni who once broke your heart. It is not just me that your kin should fear. Indeed, it's the company I keep that will drive them from these shores."

"Very good, Artos," says Myrrdin.

"It is time to end this," says Artos.

He draws his sword up, but before he strikes, a fork lightning bolt passes straight through the body of Theo, rendering him to nothing more than a smouldering black mass on the ground.

Everyone assembled turns to look at Morganna.

"What? You owed me that after everything I've been through the last couple of days."

No-one dared disagree.

THE CLOSEST THING
TO CAMULODUNUM

Artos wanders alone in a peaceful part of the woods that surrounds Urien's palace. Life has become more settled in the days since the battle. While living as a house guest of the king, he is free to wander, and has discovered a favourite place to sit and contemplate his future. Purposely he has chosen a view that sits beside a small body of water, just in case Nimue joins him and tests his readiness once again. The ripples today are only made by a gentle breeze.

The weather is milder, although it's early in the year. On this morning, there's a sense of spring approaching in the air. Artos has spent the best part of his life roaming the hills of Galwydell, observing the changes that move through every season. Today takes him back to Hartriggs. He inhales deeply, his nose filling with a familiar perfume, a flower essence favoured by his sister.

"I hope I'm not disturbing you," says Morganna as she sits herself on an adjacent rock, "it's a nice place."

"Part of me could just stay," says Artos, "it's like home, but the air is different."

"Maybe it's you that's different, especially in this place. You're quite the talk of Urien's court. I hear that Urien has encouraged Taleisin to compose some words to celebrate our battle, but don't be surprised that his son may feature more in the finished piece."

Morganna smiles gently, with no hint of the sarcasm or disrespect Artos has become accustomed to over their years of them growing up together in Hartriggs.

"You've changed as well," says Artos, "you've spent long hours in the company of Owain. I think it's done you good."

"He is pleasant company, but this is not where our story ends, brother. We should be careful not to overstay our welcome. It suits Urien to have us around right now. The heroes who vanquished the Thunor's Disciples are boosting his own reputation amongst the other tribes. He has us where he wants us."

"I think Urien has a plan," says Artos, "he has summoned nobles back from the war with the Angles. Myrrdin says that he will declare his intention soon."

"There is something that Urien wants from

Duncan MacForres. I think they will ask us to get it."

"Did Owain tell you that?"

Morganna nods. "He said something like that to me."

A crow descends next to Morganna, turning its head to look at the witch, it squawks for attention. Morganna laughs in response and brushes the bird's feathers with her hand.

"Can you speak to him?"

"It's her, and yes. Crows are not as eloquent as my beloved ravens, but they still hear much from their perches around this place."

"Do they speak the same language?"

"Similar, just differences in accent."

"So, what have they told you since we've been here?"

"Diana and Brigid have fallen in love."

"Even I know that."

"And they say that Alan falls in love with a different girl every day."

"I'm surprised they can see him. He moves around in the centre of an adoring pack of admirers. You can tell he's in amongst them somewhere. I can't get close enough to ask, but I'm sure he's happy ..."

Artos finishes speaking with a long sigh. It's obvious that something is on his mind.

"What's wrong?" asks Morganna.

"Nimue appeared to me after we left you at the tavern."

"Don't think I have forgotten."

"I was alone. I had walked away from the others to calm down when she appeared."

"What did she say?"

"That Alan would die once again. When it happens, I should bring him to her along with Myrrdin. She said that only she could return him to us. I know he's happy here, I wonder if it's better to leave him here in Rheged."

"Have you spoken to Alan?"

"No, you're the only person I've told."

"Trust Nimue. She is powerful and can move between worlds, including the place we go when we pass. I'm sure Alan will never be content to be left out of the adventure. His first thought is always to defend his friend, and he is now a hero in a Taleisin epic, do you really think he would settle with giving up on the dream we all share now? If he is to fall, then it's better he falls at your side. A jealous lover or angry father could kill him when you may be miles away."

"You're right. So, do you think I should tell him?"

"No," says Morganna, "you must trust Nimue. She has told you what to do when this death occurs. If you try to alter events to your own preference, it could make you stray from the path that the gods intend you to walk."

"Would you tell me? If you knew I was going to die?"

"I don't have the sight any more than you, but no I wouldn't tell you. Maybe I would just let you off with less teasing for a few days before you went."

"Thank you."

"You are very welcome."

They both smile and fall silent, gazing out at the mountains in the distance.

Urien's Great Hall is buzzing with anticipation. More days have passed. As Morganna had observed, Urien was not in a rush to let Artos and his party leave. The story of their victory against overwhelming odds had already been spread through a network of Urien's spies and contacts at other courts. Their presence would make other tribes think twice before attacking him.

As his vassals draw chairs to sit around his table. He looks over at his son, talking with his new friends. Encouraging Owain to be part of the heroes was a wise position to take. Especially regarding the Irish Blade. Should Myrrdin be wrong, then Urien wished his son to be next in line. Close to the seat of power.

He lets the conversations build for a while longer. His vassals are more animated than they have been for some time. They have moved away from the mindset of defenders threatened at home. Now the talk is of the Rheged rising once again to dominate the Blessed Isle. The timing is right to deliver the speech he is about to make.

Urien lifts a hand to signal the servants to withdraw. He doesn't need to speak a word; the gesture is enough, as he pauses and looks around the table.

"Friends. I want to thank our honoured guests for their time amongst our company. I will be sorry to see them leave. Even though they have drunk a year's worth of mead with great vigour and haste."

A roar of laughter prompts embarrassed looks from Artos and the others.

"They have performed a great service for us in removing the Angle raiders who were a blight on our lands and so near our gates. I'm sure Thunor's Disciples could have confronted us as their numbers swelled. Including, I'm afraid to say, men and women of our own tribe."

The crowd reacts with heated emotion at the thought of traitors in their midst. Calling for revenge on those who have aided the enemy. Urien raises a hand again.

"I'm sure many will regret their actions, the others who don't will face justice when we uncover their loyalties."

A ripple of approval passes around the table

again.

"The Merlin, with Artos and his party came seeking our support. Requesting our aid to overthrow the Pretender of Galwydell. After their victory and how they achieved it, I for one, will be happier if we help to install them as custodians of Dun Romanach, against the tyrant Duncan MacForres, who is no ally of ours."

The Rheged leaders rumble in agreement. Artos can hear mentions of *The Horse* and the name *Pegasus* in amongst the uttered responses.

"Aye, he has the horse too," says Urien.

"Pegasus?" responds Artos, "Do you mean the bronze statue of the winged horse?"

"We do," answers Urien, "stolen from my ancestor by his ancestor. To our tribe, the horse is as powerful a magical item as the sword that everybody searches for these days."

"Excalibur?"

"If you wish. Or Caladbolg, as the Irish call it, for it first appeared there centuries ago, cared for by the spirits of the water. Those same spirits created the statue that Duncan MacForres possesses. It grants him a power that I'm sure he does not even understand. The Irish Blade can protect the man who wields it, but the bronze Pegasus aids armies. They who bring it to the battle will not see defeat."

"But I've seen it!" says Artos, "It sits on a

plinth in his private chambers. He treats it as an ornament."

"Then we are fortunate that he does not know its proper use. The dying Medusa, a Gorgon, a winged monster with venomous snakes for hair, foaled the legendary flying horse Pegasus. Legend says that anyone who looked at her and met her gaze turned to stone.

"The water spirits enchanted the statue with Medusa's power. Carried at the head of an army, it doesn't turn people to stone. The tales say that enemies will freeze with their own fear. I confess, for this reason, we have never threatened the Pretender of Galwydell. I cannot risk my people facing a massacre."

"Duncan MacForres doesn't know the statue grants this power," says Artos, "he doesn't realise what he possesses."

"Then whether by the grace of my God, or indeed the older gods that others worship, we have been fortunate that he has never understood how his family could seize Dun Romanach from the Romans? A family against a legion? They prevailed because of the power within that bronze statue."

"You said that it once belonged to the Rheged?"

"It was how our tribe rose to power in our land. An ancient warrior who fought for the Greeks against Troy had taken the bronze as his spoils of war. He brought the statue to our shores and settled here.

"Legend says that he made home amongst the mountains of our lands and that our entire tribe descends from him. The Rheged built their kingdom on the back of the magical power contained within Duncan's ornament.

"The problem with God-given power is that it's often discharged by fallible men. It brings out the worst of a person as opposed to the best. This is where I must delve into our history. I do not have the words of Taleisin, but maybe things are best explained in simpler terms."

A hush falls upon the room. Respect for the telling of a tragic tale that all in the Rheged know well.

"Duncan's ancestor, the original Forres, forefather of his tribe. I'm afraid to say he was one of our own, a Rheged warrior who had earned the trust of his brothers in many conflicts. It was Forres that was granted the right to carry the Pegasus into battle. He knew the great power the statue could unleash. He knew that it could turn the fate of any war in our favour, but over time he began to consider that it was his presence that counted more than anything else.

"Forres started to believe that he should lead the Rheged, but he was not part of the line that ruled. His ambition was plain for all to see, but he wasn't strong enough to mount a challenge, having little support from other vassals. He must have been planning to leave for some time, but he would need to take the Pegasus with him. Obviously, such a treasure was guarded when not in use. He was merely its host when on the battlefield.

"His chance came when returning from another victory among fifty of our cavalry. On the road home, they encountered a swollen river in the middle of a storm. To go around would have added many hours to the journey. They decided to cross. The misadventure cost every man and beast their lives as a huge swell carried them off while they attempted to make the crossing. Or at least, it was assumed that all had perished that day.

"The storms continued, causing great floods and affecting many settlements. When the water finally receded, many of our kin were dead or injured and had their homes and livelihoods destroyed. When our people discovered that the Pegasus had also been lost, they assumed the gods were angry with how we had used its power. They decided that Zeus himself had sent a storm to punish us. It made sense that Forres had met his fate at the same time.

"Whether he crossed the river first or didn't cross it at all, we will never know, but after many years had passed, news began to arrive of Roman defeats north of the wall, and the rise of a family that were laying waste to the legion of Septimius Severus. That family's name was MacForres, the sons of Forres.

"Since losing the horse, we have become weaker. Our tribe fights as others do, but we can no longer be confident that those who oppose us will fall before us so easily."

The mood in the room was sombre. Artos could sense the despair amongst a proud people who had seen their own golden age falter and desert them.

"Now you will understand me when I ask you, my honoured guests, for one more favour —"

"You want us to recapture the Pegasus?" says Artos.

"A few might succeed where an army could suffer many casualties," says Urien.

Artos looks at his own party. It doesn't surprise him that the challenge excites them. Myrrdin takes a long draw from his pipe and nods his approval. Artos beams as he turns back to Urien.

"I think I can speak for everyone. King Urien, you have made us welcome and given us a home from home. In return, we will offer to capture the treasure and bring it back to your people. But your Grace, I must ask. If we succeed in our task, can we count the Rheged amongst our number? Will you help us defeat the tyrant of Galwydell?"

Urien returns his widest smile.

"Artos, if you can return the Pegasus to our tribe and grant us the power to use it at the head of our cavalries, then the Rheged will *always* ride out to support you wherever your battles may be. And you will be forever sure of victory where our horses are present."

The two men stand and embrace, and a mighty roar erupts within the Great Hall.

Hengroen was aware of the newfound status of his rider. More than ever, he led from the front, while controlling the other horses if they dared to walk beside him. As they journey north back towards Galwydell, his authority is absolute for navigating the road ahead.

They had left Urien's palace several hours before, with periods at a gallop, a canter, and a walk. Taking in the scenery and stopping now and then to let the non-enchanted horses have a rest.

A few people that the party passed bowed low to show respect or raced to get their children to witness the sight of Artos and his warriors. Families offered food and rest as an enticement for the party to stop awhile and hopefully share their stories first hand.

On the journey, they had retraced the same road they took south. The demolished tavern at Inglewood was still doing good business as a tourist attraction. Families and other travellers were obviously being led on a conducted tour by Gareth the tavern manager, and as he spots Artos heading along the road, he waves furiously to attract attention.

"You're not barred, you're not barred." he shouts, as the party ride onwards.

Artos and the others ignore his appeals, for which Gareth instantly barters more payment out of his visitors, because of the unique and once in a lifetime experience provided.

Considering their earlier visit to the tavern had not ended well. Artos was in good spirits at passing the landmark. So much had happened since then. Ranging from the depths of despair to being acclaimed a hero. From hanging on to Hengroen for fear of falling off, to knowing every twist and turn on his horse and understanding his ways, his moods, and his eagerness to charge. Then from hiding in a darkened corner in Urien's palace, to counting a member of the Rheged royal family as one of his party.

The same confidence extends to all. Artos can feel the force of them travelling along the road together. The energy and optimism as they set out on their next quest. The bond of fellowship is strong. It makes him ready to take on whatever is coming next.

Owain had arranged for them to stay at Cair

Ligualid. A traditional former Roman town, which he insisted was the closest thing they had to Camulodunum, and worth a visit.

It was very much part of Urien's kingdom. They would be safe there and with Owain amongst them their accommodation was not amongst the other travellers or merchants, but inside a private residence that lay within the walls of the stone-built fortress itself.

Artos was astounded by his first visit to a big city. There were streets and many buildings, a population of what might have been hundreds of people, but he hadn't seen that many in one place before, so he couldn't tell. They rode the horses and Brigid's briga into the fort between two well-protected stone towers and through to a square surrounded by an impressive villa built by the previous owners. The villa had an unusual feature that Artos had never experienced before, separate rooms for everyone to stay in, places intended for only one or two to sleep in at a time. Owain guided everyone to their personal accommodation before suggesting they walk to a favourite tavern for the evening once they had rested for a while after the journey.

Artos tries to settle himself, but he can't. His dreams are turning into reality. Once alone, he returns to the cool air of evening. With the light fading, torches are being lit. There is so much to take in as he walks around the fortress. The tall and impressive stone walls and towers, an aqueduct and even a fountain lie within the complex. Large long buildings for workers or soldiers. The sheer size of everything takes his breath away. He walks towards the gatehouse where all have agreed to meet. Myrrdin is already waiting, chewing on his pipe as ever, standing under his own little cloud.

"I've seen nothing like this before," says Artos.

"You better get used to it," says Myrrdin, "Dun Romanach and Hartriggs have given you a very underdeveloped view of the world."

"I thought that was the world for so long. I'm sure if I even tried to describe this to half the people in Hartriggs they would suspect I was on the mead," he pauses, "well on the mead again. Dun Romanach doesn't compare with this place. Has Duncan seen this?"

"Oh yes," replies the wizard, "that's why he isn't satisfied with his lot. He inherited a fort that has been lived in for many years before the Romans. The legion of Septimius added a few parts to make it more homely, but nothing like this. Ynys Mon has an even larger fortress. That's why Duncan is so desperate to seize it."

"Duncan causes trouble just to get a bigger house?"

"A bigger house than his peers, something he can brag about, yes, that's about it."

"Where will my castle be?"

Myrrdin thought long and hard before answering.

"I don't think you'll go straight to the big castle. That will take time and bloodshed along the way, but we aim to take Dun Romanach soon. At least you know it well. Still better than sharing a room with another thirteen."

"They'll want to move in with me."

"You'll manage. There's room to extend."

The footsteps of the rest of the party approach. The collective carefree atmosphere is such a contrast to every moment of tension and danger they have passed through in the last few weeks. The guards at the gate are polite to all as they let them out on to the main street. Locals bow towards Owain and so to all his guests as well. The chatter is happy and full of laughter, and after a short walk to the tavern and an even shorter talk between Owain and the tavern owner, they are told that the mead is *on the house*.

"Free drink!" says Alan, "I'm getting used to this."

"Duncan gave you free mead," says Artos.

"Yes, but we don't have to kill anyone tonight to get it."

Artos smiles at Alan's comment. The thought of his friend still facing death levels his sense of humour for a while, but the general and infectious mood is distracting. As the night goes on, he forgets the pressures of living out the prophetic visions of otherworldly beings.

A fiddler and a piper play music for the customers and in the party atmosphere, the word travels about the celebrities in town. The locals are friendly and inquisitive, wanting to know more about Owain's guests.

Myrrdin is entertaining the crowd by blowing interesting shapes with his pipe smoke and Morganna is apparently using *dice skills* to relieve some merchants of their coin clippings in a gambling game.

Artos and Alan wander outside for some fresh air.

"What a night," says Alan, "you wanted to go all the way to Camulodunum, and this is on your doorstep."

"Do you like it here?"

"Do you not? Would you prefer sitting on a rock looking at a big field of grass in Hartriggs?"

"Well, of course, this was always my idea remember?"

"Well then. Let's get this job done and we can come back for another few nights."

"What about Gwendolyn?"

"Oh aye, Gwendolyn. She can come too."

"Look I'm just saying. There are risks ahead for us. If you feel you would be happy somewhere else ..."

"Now, Artos, you've been drinking."

"As have you."

"Indeed, as have I. Now drink makes us say stupid things, so I will forgive your misguided attempts to offload your best friend just when the good times are starting."

"I didn't mean that."

"I know that my friend. If you ever really think that I lust, no, not lust, yearn for the domestic life, then you have my full permission to kill me."

Artos winces at the reply, but Alan doesn't notice.

"No, you're right," says Artos, "brothers-in-arms."

"Indeed. You for another cup of the free mead?"

"Aye, get me another cup, I'll follow you in shortly."

A crowd of fellow revellers nod towards Artos while pushing one of their number to the front. An overweight and friendly looking man, dressed in the robe of a monk of the new church and hair styled with a tonsure.

"Greetings friend," says the man, "my associates are volunteering me, because like you, my accent originates north of the wall. My name is Aedan, and you are?"

"Artos, from Galwydell."

"Artos, good to meet you Artos, and from Galwydell? Where in Galwydell?"

"Hartriggs, and yourself."

"From Glaschu at first, then part of my life amongst the Irish, before ending up here."

"You are a monk?"

"I know I look more of a sinner," Aedan laughs, "but it's not my life that my friends want to know. They have asked me to ask you, about how you live. Everyone is gossiping about your party. Great warriors from afar we hear, fighting under Urien's banner. It's very exciting."

"I never thought about it like that. It's true though, we have allied with Urien. He is a good and noble king."

"Ah yes, all of us would agree with that. We are settled under his rule. So do you intend to stay in Cair Ligualid?"

"No, we continue our journey, when we recover from tonight," both men laugh together.

"And where do you head for next? Against the Angles at Catraeth? Or the Saxons in the south?"

"No, we head north to Dun Romanach, seat of Duncan MacForres and his family."

Artos knows as soon as he has spoken the words that he has already said too much, but Aedan presses further in his friendly and persuasive manner.

"Duncan MacForres is a scoundrel. Surely you will not serve in his court?"

"No, no, of course not," replies Artos, "we have business to conduct there, that's all."

"Well, watch yourself my friend. Doing business with a man such as him can end badly. Yet you said you came from Hartriggs. Was he not then your lord?"

Artos is suddenly in a battle of wits that he can't escape. How to answer while saying nothing?

"Yes, I was very young then, just a boy. I didn't become a legendary warrior until after I left," Artos laughs to keep the conversation light.

"I think I see," says Aedan, "Your business with Duncan MacForres will not be to his liking. I will ask you no more my friend. I have taken advantage of you enough. Can I get you a drink?"

"No, I'm stopping drinking for the night. It's been nice to meet you, Aedan."

"And nice to meet you Artos. I will buy you that drink if you pass this way again."

They nod to one another and part. Artos turns back briefly to see Aedan already imparting the details of their conversation to his friends.

What were you saying Artos? You talk too much.

He re-enters the now riotous inside of the tavern. The party has split amongst the locals. Conversations are happening everywhere.

Artos now realises the danger of careless talk. Deciding that the night should end, he takes on herding his party together. Easier said than done.

Retrieving Alan from within the centre of a group of ladies was never easy, but he has at least had some practice of this. Diana and Brigid were next. They had found a secluded corner of their own but had remained sober enough to agree with Artos that it was time to leave. The magicians turned out to be the worst. Morganna is having a good time, as well as growing wealthier by the minute. Owain is recruited to draw her away from the gaming table. It's Myrrdin who is the last to leave, but not before he has entertained the crowd to a display of flashing lights and bangs in the sky. Then taking several minutes of applause and adulation before joining the others for the walk home.

Artos is relieved to see all his friends stagger in through the fortress gates. If only he had turned around one last time, he may have seen the recognisable face of a man on horseback in the middle of the street.

Gilbert MacForres manages a sneer as he watches the warriors disappear inside the fortress, before turning his horse to the northern road and riding off into the night.

SEEDS OF
TREACHERY

Ifan chews greedily on his breakfast of black bread and broth. He swallows it down at speed, covering Duncan's table with soup stains and crumbs, every now and again pausing for a deep swig of mead.

"Doesn't Fergus feed his guests?" asks Duncan.

"His guests maybe, his servants sparingly. I am of the working class to King Fergus and my body has needs that his sense of adequate reward does not meet."

"In other words?"

"I was left starving my lord. I am much obliged to be back in your court."

"Well, I've only got so much food myself, so when you're ready, stop eating and start talking."

"Yes, of course, Lord Duncan."

Ifan stops to take a breath, a drink, a burp,

a breath, break wind, a burp, and a final deep breath, before sitting back to tell his tale.

"King Fergus kept me waiting for three days once again, before I was summoned to his rooms. You are not so much a guest of his as a prisoner in a better accommodated cell. I admit it does not encourage a good mood and aggravates any aches and pains that a man can suffer. I was not at my best when I was brought in front of him. When his guard came for me, I remember thinking that he didn't look quite so poorly fed."

What his guard had for supper the night before doesn't concern me," says Duncan, "what happened next?"

"King Fergus welcomed me and offered his thanks for your gifts and your acceptance of his offer for the hand of the Lady Duncanna. He only raised a couple of issues."

"Go on."

"He remembered Stoirm Gheimhridh to have more weight than the offer of silver provided, but he accepted what he referred to as *your version of events* and the horse measured up to his expectations if not to the size of his frame as of course it's still a foal."

"He'll get more years of use out of it," says Duncan.

"Then came the topic of land."

"What land?"

"His land. Which, of course, is your land

right now."

"Explain."

"King Fergus realises the advantages of an alliance between you and him. His kingdom is hemmed in with the Irish tribes to the south-west and the Picts to the east and north. If he is to help you advance against Ynys Mon and then even the Rheged, he see's little territorial advancement for his own tribe."

"As we advance, then titles and estates would be created. That would be acceptable, I'm sure."

"I think King Fergus is more concerned if you lose. He feels there should be a price for, eh, taking part. Namely, the northern half of your territories that run beside his borders."

I see," Duncan taps the table with his fist as he thinks, "most of that land is under my cousin Torcaill's control. He will not be happy to give it away. He's rarely there, maybe it would take him some time to notice."

"But he would notice."

"By then, we might have made gains. I can grant him other lands in the future. Somewhere on the coast with a more pleasing view. Very well, I suppose for the moment I have no choice but to concede. Rights to land and inheritance can easily be changed at my own discretion."

"And if Duncanna will provide a grandson for you, that will also help."

"Yes well, I won't rely on that," Duncan sat back in his chair, "when can we complete this arrangement?"

"In a few days, my lord. King Fergus is excited to meet and marry Duncanna. He became very aroused with my descriptive text of her form."

"Yes fine, I don't need to know the sordid details."

"King Fergus asked only for some time to arrange his existing wife's travel to the island of Hy. He will ride south to Dun Romanach with his retinue once that is done. Just time to decorate Dun Romanach for a wedding."

Duncan looks as if he is straining something out as he considers the complicated worlds of politics and law, who owned what, who was married to who, but it really all boiled down to him getting the ships he needed to attack Ynys Mon. A smile of satisfaction appears.

"Splendid. Thank you, Ifan. Prepare some good words for the celebration. I'll tell Duncanna the good news."

Within minutes of Duncanna discovering that her wedding was just days away, the whole of Dun Romanach was ordered into action.

The hilltop fortress was always active, but the sudden need to spruce the place up and bring in extra supplies had caught everyone by surprise.

Duncanna had now assumed the role of a commander of an army. Even taking Duncan's favourite chair in his private chamber to organise her bridal troops.

"Mona says we don't have enough meat," says Duncanna, "we need more meat."

"What kind of meat?" asks MacDuncan.

"I don't know any kind of meat. We have farms with animals, just get them."

"We can't just take all the animals from our farms. What about husbandry? We can't kill everything."

"That's what I'm saying I need meat for my husbandry at the wedding."

"Oh, good grief!" says Duncan, "MacDuncan instruct Redlead to take some men out to collect what they can, within reason. If he can't get enough, then he has my permission to raid some of our neighbours, but during the night. I don't want angry pitchfork wielding locals deciding to visit during the ceremony."

"I'll tell him to raid the cattle and only kill those that witness the theft."

"That sounds fine."

MacDuncan departs, relieved to get off so lightly.

"I have all those holes in the fences being

mended," Duncanna continues, "the Great Hall decoration is underway. I need to find a bridesmaid that is skilled with sharp weapons and can offer me protection. Can you think of anyone?"

"Your mother would have been perfect, but unfortunately, she is gone. Or fortunately, depending on how you want to look at it. I'll see who I can find."

"Not as beautiful as me, of course."

"Yes, my daughter."

"The invitations!" I'll need riders to be despatched with those. They'll need to go out tonight. Tell Redlead not to take everyone on the meat gathering. Too much to do and not enough time. Who's ever organised a wedding like this?"

Just then, the curtain rustles once more and MacDuncan reappears with a look of panic.

"Father Andrew is back. He's almost dead."

"What? Where is he?" says Duncan.

"They've laid him out in the chapel. You want to see what the Picts have done to him."

"Oh, that's all I need," says Duncanna, "I can't have the priest dying before the wedding. Why has everything to go wrong at once."

"I will see for myself," says Duncan, "you stay and organise things from here, please."

Andrew is not dead, although he is wishing he was. Naked and face pressed against the floor. He jolts and pulls his head up, as an excruciating pain runs across his back. His skin feels as if it's burning and cracked open. As his eyesight clears, he can see the familiar walls of his chapel around him.

He pushes himself up to a sitting position. Each move exacerbates the agony that stretches between his shoulder blades and spine. He struggles to reach around with his hand to the source of his suffering. His skin is oozing and swollen, sensitive even under the lightest searching of his fingers.

He stands up and looks around himself. His robe lies beside him. With the gentlest of movements, he pulls it on, but each point of contact between the coarse wool and the wounds on his back result in shooting pain that brings tears to his eyes and the urge to scream.

The door to the chapel opens, causing Father Andrew to jump and inflict more torture upon his body.

"You're not dead," says Duncan as he enters.

"No, my lord. Wounded certainly," he says, sitting on the first available chair.

"What happened?" asks MacDuncan, "did the Picts take offence? Did you anger them?"

"No, the Picts loved me, that was the

problem."

"MacDuncan, pour him some wine," Duncan pulls up a stool used by the normal congregation and sits down to interrogate, "tell us what happened."

"We arrived at the Broch where Talorc lives with his closest family. Guided to his door by a horde of fierce spear carrying warriors that had spotted us on the road. They were wearing clothes at least, I thanked God for that. Talorc himself greeted me at the tower entrance. He gave us all a warm welcome and was eager to discuss the new church. He asked me to baptise him almost straight away. Fortunately, I had all I needed to perform the ritual. After I had welcomed him into the family of the church, well, let's just say the drink flowed. Religious fervour mixed with mead can impair the mind. Before I knew it, I had agreed to be marked and painted as a true priest of the Picts.

"Talorc explained that marked in this way I could roam their lands and find acceptance to carry out conversions wherever I went. I admit, my ambition for sainthood and maybe an inclination to avarice made his offer most tempting to me. I agreed to take part while forgetting that progressing to an exalted holy state often involves pain.

"You entered into this wounding willingly?"

"It seemed like a modest price to pay."

"I'll never get the self-inflicted pain part of this religion. The witches never did that. What about the reason that I sent you there? Did he like the text describing, eh, Duncella?"

"Yes, my lord. He was most pleased. He assured me he had been kept up half the night reading Ifan's words and said he was very keen to enter a betrothal with her. He slapped my back several times to express his happiness," Duncan and his son snigger at one another unsympathetically, "he said Duncella was one of the finest women he had ever read about, that she appeared gentle and loving."

"What did Ifan write?" says MacDuncan.

"He is a good bard," says Duncan.

"And an excellent liar," continues MacDuncan.

"Talorc's mood was most unlike his reputation, though I would not recommend bringing him to anger. He said he was happy to have converted from his heathen ways, and he was sure that Duncella would help to *settle him down*, so that only left the small discussion of a dowry."

"Yes of course. I am happy to receive his tribute."

"No, my lord, he expects dowry from you."

"Do they all think I'm made of money?"

"He knows of your estates my lord. They are smaller than his. Yet he is sure that the summer weather is better in Galwydell. He is prepared to accept only half of your land along with the hand of the fair Duncella."

"Half my land? King Fergus wants half my land."

MacDuncan tries to calculate in his head. "That's two halves. That's all your land. You can't do that."

"Well, of course I can't," says Duncan, "did you say that he only wished to use it in summer? Fergus will accept Torcaill's land," considers Duncan, "if Talorc accepts the same arrangement, but only visits in summer?"

"The Dal Riata would never agree to the Picts just turning up for a bit more sun," says MacDuncan.

"They invade each other all the time. What's so different if they fight over Torcaill's estates."

"What will Uncle Torcaill say?" asks MacDuncan.

"I'm thinking Torcaill may have to be murdered."

"Talorc made one promise," says Andrew.

"Thank God," says Duncan.

"He assured you that the marriage would bring an alliance between the two tribes. That the spears of the Kingdom of Fib would always rally to your cause whether in defence or attack. I asked him if he would join your assault on Ynys Mon. *Nae bother*, was his reply."

"Good, good," says Duncan, "Does he know

the story that Duncella is one of twins?"

"I said she had an identical sister as you asked. Talorc insisted that he should marry the better-looking identical twin. I assured him that was Duncella."

The door to the chapel was flung open again. This time, Duncanna entered.

"Father, I want to have some servants flogged, but then I worry that they might not be fully recovered to carry out their duties on the big day. Can we hire extra workers?"

"I would recommend not flogging them until after the wedding, but we will recruit more servants as well."

"Perfect," she smiles, "what's up with him?" she says, pointing at Father Andrew.

"The Picts marked him with their paint."

"Oh really," Duncanna was delighted, "go on, let's see."

With no sign of gentleness, she pulls Father Andrew's robe from his shoulders revealing an angry and weeping back. Red, and partially infected, it barely allows her to make out the twisted body of a dragon that climbs his spine and splits into two heads across his shoulder blades.

"Oh yuk!" says Duncanna.

"I say!" says Duncan, "that's very impressive. Looks worse than crucifixion. No wonder the Romans couldn't intimidate them. If I get that drunk at the wedding, put me to bed before I get one."

"So Talorc also wishes to marry me?" says Duncanna.

"So it would seem."

"Yes," she says while punching the air, "you all thought it wouldn't work, didn't you?

"He is indeed keen to join with you in matrimony," Andrew groans as he pulls his robe back on, "he thought the bard's description sounded very desirable indeed."

"I would expect no less," says Duncanna, "is he as strong and handsome as they say?"

"I'm sure you will be pleased to decipher the markings across his face and body."

"So, a decent chap, then?" says Duncan.

"My lord, he's given to becoming a renewed figure with this marriage, but I received the impression that his journey south on his *stag-do* will account for many sinful acts along the way. Not least the theft of gifts to give to you. He promised unnecessary bloodshed and drinking for his men."

"So, when is he planning on arriving for the wedding?"

"Many reasons could waylay them. Talorc thinks a few might die on the road. They'll arrive in a few days."

"Perfect. Make ready Duncanna. You will marry Fergus this weekend. He can spend the night and then send him back home. You'll stay here for Uncle Torcaill's funeral."

THE BLOOD OF THE BEAR

"Torcaill is dead?" says Duncanna.

"Not yet. You'll need to give me a day to arrange that."

The sun is at its highest point for the day as the guards open the southern gate of Dun Romanach, just in time to allow a horse and rider to gallop at full pace toward the central grounds of the fortress. Even at speed, the horseman's trained eye observes unusual activities.

Dun Romanach is being transformed; fences and gates repaired, the ground swept and cleaned, the Great Hall decorated and prepared for an important event.

As the black hooded rider dismounts, he hands the reins of his horse over to the nearest levy man, whilst knocking several others out of the way. He forces his way through into the Great Hall.

Duncan sits at his top table, overseeing the many servants as they busy themselves with Duncanna's demands. His worst nightmare is spending time with the lower classes, but it's preferable to keep a safe distance from the bride-to-be who is back to fussing over every detail.

As the rider approaches, Duncan's face

creases as he recognises his cousin.

"Gilbert! To what do I owe this displeasure."

The rider throws back his hood. "You may first want to know what you owe me in fees. Your ambitions are causing me more work than usual."

"Yes, yes, I'm sure, but sit with me and share the mead first. Tell me what you know of Arnall and Ynys Mon. What news is there of my foes?"

Duncan empties the best part of a jug into a large goblet, which Gilbert drains rapidly after his long ride.

"I'll take another. Though it won't lower my price."

A servant carries over two more jugs to Duncan's clicked finger command.

"What of Ynys Mon?"

"Arnall will *not* pose a threat again before the summer fighting season. He is still in mourning over the death of his son while his depleted forces must reinforce and train."

"Still in mourning? That was a month ago. Surely, it's time for him to get over it."

"The death of his son has caused great sadness. Not yet turned to revenge. You could attack his fortress in the spring. If you can persuade the Dal Riata to ferry your cavalry across the water."

Duncan grinned. "That should be possible. We're organising a wedding now."

"Who is she to marry this time?"

"Fergus and Talorc."

"She doesn't know which?"

"No, you misheard me. I sent proposals to both, and both have agreed."

Gilbert sat back with a rare look of admiration. "I am intrigued to know how you might achieve this deception. Has Duncanna agreed to this?"

"It was her idea!" Both men shrug at one another with a lack of surprise on their faces.

"Fergus and Talorc loathe one another," Duncan continues, "even on the same side of a battlefield, it will be easy to keep them apart. We marry her to one, ask her to return home under the pretence of family business and then have a second wedding, where she will use the identity of her twin sister."

"The twin sister no-one knows of?"

"We can say she's quieter and doesn't appear in public so often. A recluse, yes, that's it."

"Risky, but not impossible," considers Gilbert, "such alliances will help protect you for an assault from King Urien and the Rheged cavalries."

"The Rheged?"

"The Rheged."

"Yes, yes, don't just keep saying The Rheged."

"Do you wish to pay me for more words?"

Duncan looks skyward. Why did everybody want something for themselves? Did nobody value family and loyalty these days? But then he reminded himself he was talking to Gilbert, a man who had never indulged in such moral weakness or indeed a sense of integrity.

"Very well, I will meet your expenses."

"I have travelled from Cair Ligualid. There is much talk of warriors who defeated an Angle army. They number only seven. They say that the Merlin rides among them.

"The Merlin?" Duncan rolled the thought around in his head, "he's not the best ally. Everyone knows the meteor story. He's not as good as he once was."

"Maybe, but he's out of retirement and living in Rheged, where he now serves Urien."

"Urien, Urien, I'm sick of hearing Urien's name! Urien's got Taleisin the bard, and now Urien has the Merlin. Everyone else has a fort or a camp, but oh no, Urien has a palace, doesn't he? What else does he have?"

"He has two of your own warriors. Those from Hartriggs, and the red-haired witch from the same village. Morganna is her name."

"The witch maybe, but the dead men? It can't be, we transported their bodies home for burial."

"Did you see them being buried?"

"No, but they were dead."

"You saw the corpses?"

"Not completely. Their headless body parts lay in sacks in this very hall."

"Headless? Ah, the oldest trick in the book."

"What?"

"The old body switch never fails."

"No, that's impossible. They're dead. My men reported that their ghosts had killed three people at Tabernae Mona."

"Ghosts was it! These ghosts have plenty of life within them. Certainly, they have more wit," says Gilbert, throwing his head back in a loud, mocking laugh.

Duncan feels uncomfortable and starts shifting in his seat. A tight ball of rage is gathering force inside him, which his more experienced servants recognise as a potential threat to life. They disappear to carry out essential work somewhere else, or anywhere else for that matter.

Duncan now realises he has fallen for a trick. Its architect is the crone that serves as leader of the damned village and its heathen ways. He considers the body parts in the sacks. How could he have known if they were his levy men? Duncanna had fed half of them to the dogs. Then there was the burial at Hartriggs. He could have blamed himself for not overseeing the funeral, but no, it was MacDuncan's fault for taking on the red-haired witch, causing him embarrassment, and making him want to leave early. Then the incident at Tabernae Mona. Well, that was everyone else's fault by falling for their own superstitions. He reminded himself that he had never believed the fact that the devil was amassing a dark army of demons in one village just a few miles from Dun Romanach. He had seen through that part of the deception, at least.

Finally, there was the sheer audacity of Wren Morcant. Visiting his own hall and persuading him that his life was at risk if he didn't protect Hartriggs. She knew he had not endangered the prophecy if the son of Uther Pendragon still lived. The Black Oath? Nothing more than a con trick.

"This isn't my fault," he blurted out in a childlike manner, "the crone Wren Morcant deceived me. She will pay for this and her village. She must have known the truth from the very start."

"Maybe I should recruit her," says Gilbert.

"That will be very difficult when she's dead."

"Then you better hasten. Urien's warriors are now bound for Dun Romanach."

"You're certain."

"I saw the party in Cair Ligualid with my own eyes. Urien's own son is with them. My spies told me they were planning on heading north to Dun Romanach and although they didn't know the exact reason, it didn't sound good."

"And Artos is among them?"

"I don't know him, but his name was mentioned. My informant spoke to someone called Artos. That is where he got his information."

"Then I didn't break my oath."

"What oath?"

"It doesn't matter, and he travels with the Merlin?"

"Yes. Why?"

"It doesn't matter."

"Does he have a big sword with him?"

"I didn't see a sword. They were in the tavern. No weapons allowed. Why?"

"You're maybe too young. Did you know of the business with Uther Pendragon?"

"The little bastard?"

"Yes him."

"Artos, he's the little bastard?"

"Well, he's bigger now. If I had remembered, he may have grown up to love his Uncle Duncan."

"No, he hates you. The bastard son of Uther Pendragon definitely hates you. That's not good for your plans, Duncan. There are still plenty loyal to Uther's legacy. Artos must be removed. Couldn't you have told me this earlier?"

"I forgot."

"You forgot? That's it."

"We'll get him."

"Well, get him soon." says Gilbert.

"I'm in the middle of a wedding being planned. No, make that two weddings being planned. Redlead has been dispatched with most of the men to get meat."

"Meat?"

"It's a long story."

"Duncan, they could arrive tonight, though I would give you a chance that it will be tomorrow, the state they were in when they left the tavern."

"They won't come straight here. I'm sure they'll head for Hartriggs," says Duncan.

"And remember two of their party can control unnatural forces, they can cause you problems."

"It's timing," says Duncan, "in a few days we will have the Dal Riata as allies, a few days later the Picts will come to our defence. If Urien is planning an assault, he will find a stronger army than he bargains for. If his warriors attack, then he's likely to have to pay a hefty ransom for the return of his own son in a single piece."

"And if they attack before the weddings?"

"Duncanna will probably individually strangle them. Our family has not lost a single battle since we took Dun Romanach, it will not start now. I'll tell MacDuncan to recruit as many new levy men as he can, but we will need to delay the advance of the warriors that's true. How long is it since you've been to a burning Gilbert?"

"Some time, not since the new church took over these things. It got a bit too religious for me then."

"Time to go back to the old ways. We'll ride out for Hartriggs before the sun sets."

SAD ENDINGS

Artos feels a cool sea breeze upon his face. As his vision sharpens, he stands on a shoreline looking out at the gentle wash of the waves. From behind, he hears the laugh of a young woman. Turning, he sees the smiling face and long raven hair blowing in the wind. The same person he has seen before. She extends her hands out to him. Artos reaches out. As soon as their fingers touch, he feels himself being lifted into the air, spinning around, his body dissolves into particles of sand blown apart in the breeze. He is becoming nothing. The image changes around him and he feels as if he is among the stars. Then all goes dark. Once again, the sound of the waves takes over, He is face down on the wet sand. The sound of gulls around him. He pulls himself to his feet. The stars still glow. As he looks up into the sky, lines form between the distant points of light. They create two constellations, one becomes a bear cub, the other a figure with a stag's head. For a moment, it's as if the power of these distant suns flow through him. He feels as if the gods themselves are touching him. Then his attention is drawn to a cliff-side ahead of him, a promontory supporting a large castle linked to the shore by a narrow bridge, beyond which, a blood red sun begins to rise. Its light creeps towards him, spreading red, gold, and orange rays across every surface. The light raises fire on every place around him.

Artos wakes up suddenly. A golden glow is cast into his room from the dawn light. For a moment, he is still half in his dream and a brief panic causes him to sit upright. Everything is still.

Sounds start to feed in from the outside world as the people in the fortress are stirring and starting their work for the day.

He dresses and heads out into the courtyard of the villa. Myrrdin is already standing, enjoying his first pipe of the day, and looking over at the sunrise. Artos walks over beside him.

"Good morning Myrrdin," he says.

"Maybe," comes the reply. "we have stayed here too long. We have to return to Galwydell today."

"I agree. We've celebrated our first victory enough. We can't do this every time. There isn't enough mead," says Artos, "you know I have visions. I had another just now."

"What did you see?" asks Myrrdin.

"I saw the woman again."

"We often see love in our dreams."

"There was more. So many stars. Some formed into a bear cub and a horned god."

"That's more interesting. That sounds like a message."

"From whom?"

"The gods speak quietly to us. Often, they can only be heard at the point that we move between sleep and our wakened state. The messages you receive then are to inform you, to help you. I believe your visions show that the gods are on your side. They want you to succeed. They offer the gift of power, but it's up to you to bring what they offer into your own reality. You must act on these messages. You have trained yourself to follow your dreams. Is that not why we are here now? How did you feel when you awakened?"

"Panic, if I'm honest. The end wasn't good. It felt like I wanted to go home."

"To be honest. I feel the same way. Let us press on with the task that Urien has set."

The unmarked borders heading into the south of Galwydell were familiar territory, but it saw a shift in public reaction. The passers-by were more cautious. A small group of well-armed riders could be easily taken for bandits patrolling amongst the rolling hillsides. Artos was very conscious of the wariness they were encountering. A passing comment on the weather in the local accent helped. Politeness wasn't common from raiders, so it satisfied most that the greeting offered by the warrior was friendly.

After much discussion earlier in the day, the party had decided they would return to Hartriggs. It was still the best place to base themselves since it was rarely visited by outsiders, apart from Wren's fortune seeking customers. Even that had dwindled though, with Father Andrew declaring all such things the work of the devil.

Artos still doesn't feel as if he's heading home.

Maybe home is a different place for me now.

Morganna is quiet too. Owain feels that he has said something or done something wrong to upset her. In a quiet conversation, Artos assures him that Morganna is prone to long periods of sorrow.

"Don't worry I'm sure it's not you," he says, "Morganna needs to retreat to the darkness, to be alone in her own world now and then. Even in a small home with fourteen people she has always been good at cutting herself off. In fact, I've never seen her so happy before the last few days she's spent with you."

"Thank you Artos, that means a lot to me. Morganna is gentle, kind, and loving, tender and giving."

"Well, maybe I know a different Morganna. To me she's just an annoying older sister, but I'm sure she wouldn't be happy if I thought anything else."

"I'm sure you're wrong," Owain smiles and lets his horse fall back in the procession to be closer to the witch.

I'm sure I'm not.

Alan then rides forward to take the place just half a step behind Hengroen, to avoid upsetting the lead horse.

"Are you alright, Artos?"

"No. not really. Is it nerves again? It sounded good in Urien's palace when I was agreeing to his challenge, but as we get nearer, there's a thousand thoughts in my head."

"I'm the same, but we've done this now. We have almost a warband. Once Urien's men join us for an assault on Duncan, our forces will match.

"But only if we capture the Pegasus first. Duncan doesn't know what he has that's true, but if we're attacking Dun Romanach that's where it sits. Its power may still work for him. In that case, we will lose."

The two ride on in silence, each forming plans in their own minds. They both know the fortress well, so at least that's an advantage.

They know the weaknesses and the gaps in the walls. Where the guards on duty would sneak off for a sleep or a midnight feast of mead and more mead.

The road begins to climb into the hills. The summits start to flatten out before them as they gain height. Hartriggs is just beyond the horizon. A stronger breeze is picking up around the hilltops and bad weather is closing in with dark grey clouds forming. The temperature is dropping, and the air is changing. A solitary bird of prey circles in the surrounding sky. Morganna rides to the front beside Artos.

"Something's wrong," she says, "I've been thinking about Wren all the way home."

"I feel the same. I wondered if it was just nerves about having to go back to Dun Romanach. There is only seven of us, heroes or not."

"Urien is clever," says Morganna, "to get such a prize back for his people and risk little in return."

"His son, his bodyguard?"

"You saw how his vassals had no appetite for war in the north, the death of their prince might change that. Urien may well strike back against Duncan even if we fail, no make that especially if we fail. You may be a king one day, but for now others rule, and it's still their decisions that we follow."

"But it's going to stay that way until we

can claim our own lands. I can see why Myrrdin wanted us to take these actions. Why he's manipulated this whole alliance with the Rheged. He's a magician yes, but he's also skilled with the workings of court."

"He knows who hates who," says Morganna

"Yes, he knows who hates who," Artos pauses, and raises his hand to stop the party, "can you smell that?"

"Something is on fire," says Diana.

All peer ahead on the road. Rising above the last hill before them, a narrow patch of lighter grey smoke stands out against the vast skyline. Buffeted by the breeze, the small swirling clouds are obviously the source of the acrid smell.

"That's Hartriggs!"

Hengroen begins charging without being asked. The horse knows his master's intention, to race for the village with as much speed as he can.

Artos can see the devastation. His heart is thumping out of his chest. It fills him with dread over what he will find. He races on to save someone, anyone, from the burned-out village. Yet as soon as he dismounts from Hengroen, and his feet land on the scorched grass, the realisation overtakes him that Hartriggs is far beyond rescuing. Artos slumps on the ground in despair. After a few long minutes of eerie silence, broken only by the faint snap and crackle of dying embers, he can hear the others arriving around him with gasps and words of shock.

Artos closes his eyes, hoping that the surrounding scene will have vanished when he opens them again.

It is Morganna's hands placed on his shoulders that strengthen him to stand back on his feet. She surrounds him with a comforting hug. The others have already started searching through the debris, looking for victims.

Brigid stands amongst the charred remains of the large roundhouse with wisps of smoke rising and swirling around her. She chokes as she pushes aside the timbers that have collapsed in on themselves.

Artos joins the rest in a desperate search. Broken pottery and furniture litter a blackened mass of torched wood and straw, but there's no-one to be seen.

"I can't see any bodies," says Brigid.

"Did they get away?" says Alan.

"There were bodies, but *we* buried them."

The party turn around, startled. It's Wee Laddie, surrounded by other younger folk of Hartriggs, emerging from the cover of the trees.

"Wee Laddie! Are you alright?" says Artos.

"Aye, I am, but not others. Wren knew what was coming. She sent us away before Duncan MacForres descended on the village," he pauses, "she didn't make it, Artos. None of the older ones did. I'm sorry, but your mother too, Alan."

"Why now? Why did he destroy the village?" says Artos.

"We don't know. Wren brought the whole village together yesterday as the sun was setting. She told us of her last prophecy. She knew she was going to die, and she knew how her death would occur. She told us that Hartriggs would end with her, and she wanted to make sure that most of us would survive the attack."

Alan pushes out of the group that surrounds him, stepping aggressively towards Wee Laddie. Artos grabs hold of his friend to restrain him.

"You just left them then?" shouts Alan.

"We didn't want to leave Wren or any of the others. They chose to stay with her, and Wren promised to us all that those who couldn't make the journey would not be aware of their ..."

"Their what?" says Alan.

"Their deaths," Wee Laddie is downcast and anguished, "Wren planned to transform them. Make them immune to the pain and the fear.

Your mother, Alan, she asked me to pass on her love to you, should I ever see you again. She smiled as she spoke about you. She talked about how you always made her proud."

Tears were being shed amongst all that were gathered, and the rain finally broke free from the dark clouds. Owain walked over to comfort Morganna. Although she stood firm, the darkness of her emotions crept out of every part of her.

"Did Wren say anything for Morganna or for me?" Artos asks.

"You know Wren, even amid the despair she had a comment or two to make us smile. She was mother of neither, yet mother to both. She asked me to say both of you are on the right path and that the old gods are with you. She said that all her years of scolding had paid off."

Wee Laddie smiled sympathetically and hugged at Artos then Morganna. Then he walked to Alan who pushed him away, still full of anger.

"We could have been here," says Alan, "we should have been here before this happened. What say you great Merlin? Didn't your magic tell you what was going to happen? And you, Artos, with your dreams and visions didn't they tell you that Hartriggs was going to be burned to the ground. Wren knew. She knew. Why just her?"

"Alan, I'm sorry," says Wee Laddie, "Wren

told us she had performed a spell, something to do with a rat that predicted her death."

"A what?"

"A rat. A white rat."

"So where did you go when you left?" asks Artos.

"Near to here. There's a clearing surrounded by a thick circle of trees. Almost impossible to enter with horses. We felt we would be safer there until we could move to another home, beyond Galwydell. I'll take you there now."

"Wee Laddie," Artos pauses, "what is your name?"

"It's Alistair," he smiles. "I'm called Alistair."

"Alistair, I'm proud to have you as a friend, a neighbour, and an ally. Wren always trusted you."

Artos inhales and faces Alan, who is inconsolable with grief. The others stand back as he walks towards his lifelong friend and pulls him into an embrace. They hold each other, both with heads bowed, both genuine in their sorrow for one another's loss. After a few seconds, Alan pulls away and begins walking to his horse, which he immediately mounts.

"We will take our revenge. Duncan MacForres cannot live another day. We beat the Disciples. I reckon the odds are the same at Dun Romanach."

"No! We can't charge into the fortress without a plan," says Artos, "innocent people live within the walls of Dun Romanach as well. It is not the bandit camp in Rheged."

"Have you lost your gut?" protests Alan, "we know this enemy. We fought beside them for long enough! There is not one of them we can't beat. Ask yourself which of them killed your mother? I am sure that I will find the cowards that killed mine. We must end his rule now. It's as simple as that. The hours I have spent listening to your stories of being a king. Now is your chance to claim your kingdom. Or are you just another sheep awaiting your own slaughter!"

The comment drew a wound deeper than any enemy could have made with a blade.

"Alan, trust me. We will break into Dun Romanach at dawn and retrieve the Pegasus. We will return it to Urien, and within days, the finest cavalry of the Rheged will be here to join us in our assault. Duncan's reign will end then. I promise you that."

"Horses can fall against a shield wall," says Alan, "I'm ashamed of your cowardice. Duncan MacForres has destroyed everything we've ever known."

"Horses can fall surely if Duncan still has the Pegasus. Do you think I loved my mother less than you? Do you think I am without pain or any of us here? Listen to me. We are not enemies. If we become so, then Duncan MacForres has already won, our efforts will have been for nothing."

"You have got everything you wanted. We fight for another lord and do his bidding, but we are horsemen now, so you got your promotion, we've eaten well, we drink well, and we're treated as heroes amongst the Rheged at least. Yes, you have got your dreams, and now it has become a nightmare. If we had been here. Their deaths would have been avoided, but we were all too busy celebrating your high and mighty visions coming true.

"We all decided."

"No Artos. You are the leader. We all follow you. So do not shrink back now that it's time to lead. Join me, all of you. Let us take our revenge."

All stand in silence, averting their gaze from Alan.

"Just like I said. They follow you Artos. When you do nothing, so do they."

Alan turns his horse and gallops away from Hartriggs. The rain lashes into his face and mixes with his tears. His anger is all-consuming as he charges along the road that leads back to Dun Romanach. He has lost his mother, lost his village, and probably lost his lifelong friend. There is nothing left for him but the death of Duncan MacForres, and if they come within reach of his sword arm, his whole sorry family will perish.

He rides for miles at full pace. His mind made up about where he's going. How he would get into the fortress and through the Great Hall to Duncan's private chambers. He knew who he was likely to face on duty in the guard. Those who didn't yield would die. What happened beyond killing Duncan didn't matter. If the fates were with him, then he would find a route of escape. If not, then he would fight with any life left inside him.

Although his plans are made, there's also an opportunity. As he nears Dun Romanach, he travels along the road that passes Tabernae Mona. As he approaches, he pulls his horse to a halt. Ahead he can see four black clad riders dismount and head for the tavern, one of whom he knows well. MacDuncan MacForres.

Alan walks his horse on at a slower pace, allowing the time to let Duncan's son settle down with a cup of mead. He rides into the paddock and dismounts, carefully unstrapping the sword that he has been gifted by Urien. As he stands alone outside, he weighs the weapon in his hand. It is crafted perfectly. A natural extension of his arm. Alan moves forward, his footsteps quickening, he is completely focussed on the kill. Violently pushing the door open he can feel the energy of a crowd parting as MacDuncan stands at the bar with his back to him.

In a single move he has reached out with his spare hand to grab MacDuncan's long hair, tugging it back and raising his sword across his victim's neck, ready to slice his throat.

Then comes a crushing pain at the back of his head as a blunt weapon bludgeons into his skull, sending him sprawling amongst the tables. Hands grab at him as MacDuncan barks orders. Alan fights back for all he is worth. In the scramble, bodies scatter while others leap upon him. The fight is desperate, but he is outnumbered. There are too many to defend MacDuncan. Soon, Alan falls, too wounded on the floor to offer any more resistance.

MacDuncan's face appears in front of him; snarling, angry, spitting. He kicks Alan's body, and aims a mead cup at his face.

"Take him to Dun Romanach."

Cold water brings Alan back to full awareness, along with his head getting pulled back and the sting of his jaw being slapped. He has made it into Dun Romanach, but as a prisoner. Held outside, he is in front of the Great Hall and surrounded by what looks like half the levy, all pointing spears towards him. He is bound tightly, but the men of Dun Romanach all still look nervous and strangely they look disappointed. Alan is not long from being one of their own and popular among the ranks. They stand silent as in the distance two figures approach. MacDuncan and his father, both wearing expressions that more than convey their intentions.

Duncan walks straight up to Alan and punches him hard in the mouth, removing some teeth. The force of the blow sends his head spinning. When he refocuses, Duncan is rubbing his fist and collecting a dagger from his son.

"That tap is for what you have cost me in added aggravation over the past few weeks, but that is the least of your worries right now. Where is the other one? Artos?"

Alan's head bows low. He realises what he has done at last. How his anger has led him to making this choice. If it was the last thing he could do, it would be at least to lie on his best friend's behalf."

"We are no longer friends."

"When did this happen?"

"In Cair Ligualid. He liked it too much. He always wanted the big city life."

Duncan considers the fact that Alan was confirming their last known location."

427

"You are telling me you returned on your own? Back to Hartriggs, or what's left of it," he sneers.

"Aye, I saw what you did. Be sure that was enough to make me come here on my own, craving your death, and all the rest of your sorry family."

His call is addressed to everyone, and they feel it. Grips tighten on the spears that encircle him. He raises his bloodied face towards MacDuncan in defiance.

"What did you tell your faither MacDuncan? Have you claimed me as your kill? Just like Cadawg. Slitting the throat of a dead man doesn't count."

"He's off his head. Don't listen to him," says MacDuncan as his father looks on suspiciously.

"Am I? Your men all know you. They might fear you MacDuncan. They don't respect you."

"Faither let me —"

"Be quiet!" Duncan leans into Alan's face, "you are about to die. The manner of your death depends on how you answer my questions. Tell me what I need to know, and I will slice your neck cleanly. If you don't, then my son may take longer to finish you off."

Alan attempts an insolent smile towards MacDuncan.

"My spies tell me you have joined with the Rheged and now serve their King Urien?"

"Aye," replies Alan.

Then are they also right that Urien means to attack us?"

"He doesn't even know you exist. He fights with an army of hundreds. His camps and his cities make Dun Romanach look like a sheep pen. Be happy. You are safe because you are nothing to him."

Duncan smiles. "Then we will surprise him. That is good. You know Alan I suppose I could spare you. You and your friend deserting your duty. I presume that's what happened. You've done me a favour. Now I won't just ally with the Dal Riata, but with the Picts as well. Yes, the fearsome Picts are now my friends. What an army we will make marching into Urien's lands. Be sure when we get there your friend Artos will be the first we seek out amongst Urien's men. He should have died a long time ago. The world will be more straightforward without him in it."

"Is that it? Are your questions answered?" asks Alan, "my people are gone, and I wish to join them."

"Oh yes, your people. They didn't stand a chance I'm afraid. It was almost too easy to block their escape from their roundhouse and put it to the flame. Something else I should have done a long time ago."

"And you think you have killed Wren Morcant and escaped without a curse?"

Duncan seems unsettled for a moment. His

thoughts are churning around in his head with memories of the ritual of The Black Oath.

"Grant him his wish my son," Duncan passes the dagger back and walks over to one of his guards. Against a background of cries and screams, he issues his orders.

"Double the guard tonight and from now on until the weddings. I don't believe he travelled here alone."

Finally, a silence falls, and Duncan turns to see his son covered in blood.

"Do you claim the kill?"

"Yes, I claim the kill faither."

"Well, at least this time there are witnesses to your account. Take the body and strap it to the watchtower. It can rot there as a wedding decoration. I'm sure Duncanna will love the gesture."

PEGASUS

Six horses negotiate the forest trails that lead towards Dun Romanach. Artos wonders if it's an unlucky number and whether the others share his dismay. They have felt invincible since destroying the Thunor's Disciples camp, but Alan's absence has changed all that.

They ride past the ledge that looks over into the paddock beside Tabernae Mona, where the group's shared quest began. The tavern hasn't changed. Morganna and Diana are still riding the horses they captured that day, but Artos doesn't recognise himself. Recent events had affected life more than he could ever have imagined.

They carry on without speaking. Slowing the horses as they near their target. Only gentle hooves break the silence now, as they manoeuvre between the outlying buildings that surround Dun Romanach. The scattered places where the locals are sleeping. Small footpaths with fenced off areas for farming, and small areas of trees that offer cover from a chance of discovery.

Artos raises his hand to signal they've reached their destination. A safe place beside the river to dismount. Simple nods between the group coordinate their movements.

They carry out a last check of blades, arrows, and magical supplies. The horses walk to the river's edge where they drink from the water, but Hengroen becomes unsettled. His ears shift direction, as he holds his neck high. Artos peers into the night and spies a ghostly white shape approaching them through the trees.

"It's Alan's horse!"

His whisper is loud enough for everyone to hear. Brigid runs forward and collects the reins, while Diana checks for signs of injury. The horse settles when reunited with his brothers, but Alan is nowhere to be seen.

"Do you think he's went in on his own?" Owain asks.

"I hope not," says Artos.

"We do stupid things in anger," says Diana, "I just hope he's lying drunk somewhere. That is the Alan I know."

Myrrdin and Morganna use the silent voice to communicate their thoughts to one another.

"Something's troubling me," says Morganna, *"Artos told me he met with Nimue before you*

reached Urien's palace. He said she warned him that Alan was to die."

"He died, remember? I brought him back to life."

"No, not then. She meant he was about to die once more. She told Artos to return Alan's body to her."

"How long have you known this?"

"For a few days. Artos told me before the last banquet with the Rheged nobles."

Myrrdin forgets telepathy, calling out with his voice instead.

"And you didn't think to tell me!"

"Sh," the others say as one.

"Artos," Myrrdin projects his whisper, "when were you going to tell me you met with Nimue?"

"Met Nimue?"

"How many times have you met her? Does she talk to you every day of the week?"

"No, no, she doesn't. She came to me when we had stopped in the forest before Brigid returned with Diana."

"And the part where she told you of Alan's death?"

Artos directs an annoyed stare at Morganna, who has looked away. He realises he has been wrong to keep the warning to himself.

"Yes, she warned me. She insisted we were to take him to her when it happened, but he was there beside me. It wasn't the right moment. Then we were with Urien. Well, I thought she might be wrong."

"I don't think she's ever wrong. Let's hope we find Alan in a single piece."

"We don't know that he's dead yet," says Owain, "we just know that he's here."

"We need to get on with the job," says Artos, "If we come across him, then let's just hope he's able to help us."

The adrenaline is racing as they make steady progress towards the footpath that leads to the southern gate. The darkness only offers limited protection. Burning torches line the last part of the approach.

The gate looms into view. Four guards are visible, standing on the watchtower. Below the MacForres sentries, more torches flicker in the breeze, illuminating a grotesque adornment suspended from the tower. They have stretched the cruciform shape of a blood covered body out as a warning to others. It's obvious who the corpse once was.

Shock strikes through all in the party as they set eyes on the lifeless image of Alan. Myrrdin places a hand on the shoulder of Artos. Applying a magical force to keep the young warrior back.

Artos strains against the hold. "They are going to die."

"They will die, but not tonight by your hand. Think. How can you take him to Nimue if you charge into a battle that you cannot win?"

"I can reach Duncan at least. I know where he sleeps."

"And then what?" says Myrrdin, "his son survives, or his daughter. You risk yourself and everyone else here. How many more must die. Nimue has only said she can save one. The one that is already dead."

"You can let me go," says Artos.

"I will, but we stay with our plan. We use magic to break into the fortress. Unbridled rage will not serve our goals. Do we all agree?"

The others nod silently even though they all exude a shared anger. Myrrdin is more than aware they would have willingly followed blindly into a change of plan driven by Artos' need for revenge. He releases his grip, and Artos sucks in a long breath to steady himself.

"We'll get the body when we take the gate," says Artos.

"I can carry him back to the horses," says Brigid.

The others return a disbelieving look at the Iceni warrior, who is much smaller than Alan.

"Don't doubt me now! I can carry him to the horses if you and Owain can carry a small statue between you."

Everyone nods in agreement.

"They're waiting for us," says Owain, "they know you won't be far away, if Alan is here."

"That won't help them," threatens Artos.

"It is time to begin," says Morganna.

The wizard and the witch step on to the footpath leading to the gate. Whether they're invisible or whether they're diverting the guard's attention in another way, they make rapid progress to the bottom of the watchtower without being spotted. Myrrdin holds out his staff. Drawing a circle before him, he whispers a spell that extinguishes the lights around the gate.

A sudden plunge into darkness is followed by an icy gust of air that lands ice particles and flakes of snow around the watchtower. The guards are disturbed by the instant weather change, but for now that's all they think.

"That wind is freezing," says the head guard, "get a torch lit again, can't see a thing now."

His men grumble, huddling around a fresh spark of flame. They don't notice they have company. A raven lands on the edge of the guard tower behind them. Its eyes observing their every move.

Another powerful burst of wind rattles the gates below them. A large timber bar rattles on its iron rests as it strains to hold the two halves of the gate together.

"What was that?" asks another sentry.

"It's just the wind Hamish," says the head guard, "don't go making us jump every five minutes, or it's going to be a long night. Make yourself useful. Grab something to warm us from the Hall."

"MacDuncan said we weren't to leave our post."

"Aye well, it's my order you'll obey now. I think my fingers and everything else are going to drop off."

"Aye right you are."

Hamish descends the ladder and speeds off into the darkness, towards the Great Hall. The raven takes note. Only three guards remain in the south gate's watchtower.

A second burst of wind rattles the gate again. This time it raises the timber that holds the gates together, causing it to fall to the ground with a crash. The gates swing open.

"What's going on tonight?" says the head guard, "someone check the gate."

Another sentry descends to find the timber has ripped the rests from the gates.

"The iron brace is broken," calls out the sentry, "there's no way we can fix that right now. We'll need the smith to forge new parts."

"Then move the wood and get back up here."

The guard lifts the large piece of timber at one end and drags it into the corners of the fence below the gatehouse. As he turns back, Owain's face looms out of the darkness. The raven counts two guards to go.

The remaining men huddle closer to the single torch they've lit again, while the temperature plummets further, and causes their toes to nip within their boots.

"Where's Hamish with the drinks?"

The gate moves below them, followed by footsteps. The head guard squints his eyes, peering into the shadows cast around the ground.

A firm hand grabs on to his tunic, catching him by surprise. Artos pulls him over the side of the tower. The raven calls out, causing the remaining guard to spin round in fright. There is no time for him to raise the alarm before Owain connects a solid punch to his chin, sending him flying and knocking him unconscious.

Artos and Owain drag the three unconscious guards into a darkened corner beneath the watchtower, while Myrrdin and Morganna dust them with powder that will keep them asleep for several hours. Meanwhile, Diana and Brigid work together to untie Alan's body from the ropes that bind his corpse. They lower him downwards, where the group then gather to receive the body. Even in the darkness, all can clearly see the brutal wounds that Alan suffered before he died. Myrrdin catches a glance from Artos once again.

"Promise me. We will only carry out the task that is set for us," says the wizard, "it's the only way that you may see your friend again."

Artos bites on his lip and closes his eyes briefly, drawing in the cold air once more.

"You have my word. You're wise, I have much to learn. May the gods keep Duncan in peaceful sleep tonight, for if he stumbles in front of my sword arm. I know I will strike."

Together they hoist the body of Alan over Brigid's shoulder, as she takes the weight upon herself.

"Don't return Brigid. Guard the body until we get there," orders Artos, "this will not take long."

Brigid nods her understanding before turning and descending the path back into the trees. Diana then takes up her observation point on the watchtower, with an arrow loaded on her bow. The remaining party members make their way on towards the Great Hall.

Slumped near the entrance, the guards are in a mead fuelled stupor. They offer no resistance as Morganna once again douses them with the sleep-inducing powdered herb.

Within seconds of leaving the south gate, they are inside the Great Hall. The fire that burns inside casts its light over Duncan's men as they sleep, scattered across the floor.

"Half the warband is in here," whispers

Artos, "if they wake, we are in trouble."

"They won't wake," says Myrrdin, "Morganna and I will see to it. Get the statue."

Myrrdin and Morganna set to work, carefully stepping among the unconscious soldiers, and sending them into deeper sleep. A snore or a cough or turning over is enough to summon a magician to subdue any chance of an individual soldier waking up and raising the alarm.

Artos and Owain move with great stealth towards the curtain and pass through into the private chamber. The only light comes from the clay hearth. The dying embers of a fire. It has the atmosphere of a tomb filled with artifacts. In the half-light, the bronze Pegasus reflects even the smallest licks of flame. Standing out amongst the other treasures.

Artos rushes over and lifts the statue from its plinth. The very sight of the object triggers something within Owain. Its power awakens something in his soul, something ancient and primal. As Artos turns to make for the opening in the curtain, Owain stops him in his tracks.

"May I carry it?"

Artos experiences the energy of the bronze statue coursing through his body.

Looking down from the verge of a hill. A vast army gathers together on either side. Some men are visible, but most of his troops are represented by burning flames. The roar of a dragon overhead causes Artos to raise his sword. The sword of power. He signals a charge into the midst of battle. The angry faces of the enemy surround him, but they fall in vast swathes before his weapon. Explosions burst around him, along with the trails of the dragon's fiery breath. Suddenly he is back on the summit of a hill. Ancient stone rings are laid out towards the east, snowy peaks to the west. The bodies of his enemies lie stretched out in the valley below, extending for miles. Artos turns to see Myrrdin. The wizard is chanting in the ancient tongue. The crystal orb at the top of his staff bursts with light as Myrrdin slams his staff into the ground.

When Artos returns to reality, he is already handing the Pegasus to Owain. The son of Urien is transfixed with the object. He handles it with care. Hypnotised by its presence.

"We should go," urges Artos.

They make for the curtain when a clay container smashes on the floor behind them, causing them to turn on their heels once more.

"Hamish?"

"Artos? It is you. They said you were back, and you're stealing Duncan's horse?" says Hamish.

"Retrieving it for the Rheged," says Owain, "its rightful owners."

The Rheged prince draws his sword forward to emphasise the point.

"What are you going to do, Hamish?" says

Artos.

"Well, let me think? If I side with Duncan, you'll kill me now. If I let you go, he'll kill me, and not as quick."

"There's a third choice," says Artos, "side with us and fight at our side."

"It still might only give me a few more days to live."

"Hamish," says Artos, "I know Owain's sword arm grows twitchy. We don't exactly have much time."

"Aye, you're right enough. I'll side with you."

Hamish drops the alcohol he's holding and follows the other two through the curtain to where Myrrdin and Morganna are waiting. They're startled to see a recruit between Artos and Owain.

"It's okay, he's with us," confirms Artos.

As they emerge back out into the night air. Diana observes their passage back to the gate. She notices Hamish as well, keeping her bow trained on him just in case.

We've got the horse," Owain calls out to her quietly, "come and join us now."

Diana climbs down from the tower and joins them to pass back through the gate, moving downhill under cover of the high tree line that extends around the fortress.

Dun Romanach remains silent behind them. With Myrrdin and Morganna's sleeping powder, it's likely to stay that way for some time.

Brigid has just finished strapping Alan's lifeless body to his horse when the others return. She draws her blade upon seeing Hamish, who lets out a squeal as she points her gladius at his throat.

"It's alright," says Artos, "I know him. He's joined us."

"Did he have a choice?" says Owain.

Hamish shows remorse at the sight of Alan's body.

"Poor soul!" he says, "I swear I was nothing to do with it. I wasn't on duty when …"

"When what Hamish?" says Artos.

"I'm sorry to say, the news about Alan spread through the fortress quick enough. MacDuncan executed him. He couldn't fight back. Bound and half-dead from beatings he had already received."

"You ride my horse," says Morganna to Hamish, as she jumps on to Alan's white stallion to take the reins.

"We have what we came for tonight," says Artos, "may the gods bless Duncan MacForres and his son with premature deaths before we return for them."

Hengroen announces the departure as he

rears up and leads the party home. Losing Alan has diluted the night's success. Their only hope is to reach Modron's Water before it's too late. The black horse senses this when setting the pace. His instinct is to make quick progress within reason, he doesn't charge out of control.

Artos now knows that Hengroen will carry him anywhere and into any danger without flinching. He trusts in the heat of battle that Hengroen will be as important as the sword he wields.

They pass no-one on the road. They feel alone with the spirits who haunt the old paths, and the creatures of the night that are drawn to Morganna during times such as these.

Howls in the distance sound the watchful ways of the wolves. Bats skim around them in an ever-rotating cloud that charts their journey forward.

After less than an hour, they reach a crossroads. Ahead of them the rubble of Hartriggs and beyond that, the temporary home of the survivors. To the left the road climbs towards Modron's Water. The high loch was well established as a place where the veil is thin and contact between the worlds is possible.

"Myrrdin, Morganna and I will take Alan to the water. Nimue has appeared before all of us before. I'm sure she will appear again if we limit who is there. Owain leave as soon as you need to with the horse. Return with your father's cavalry."

"I'll get myself ready. I would like to see Alan returned to us before I leave."

All nod in agreement and part their separate ways.

Artos leads the climb. The path is easy enough to manage, especially for enchanted horses. Their hooves tread a cushion of air that lies somewhere just above the ground. Making the ride to the top both steady and smooth.

Ahead in the sky, wisps of green and yellow, colouring the darkness. The large streaks of light are always considered an omen when they appear.

"That is the sign that war is coming," says Morganna.

"War is coming," replies Artos.

They reach the top and Morganna leads them to the spot that Wren would sit. It felt right to summon the water nymph there. Myrrdin wastes no time in preparing himself for the ritual of summoning. Raising a mist is the first step. Wading into the water up to his knees, he sweeps his staff on the surface before him, unsettling its state, turning it into a gas that forms small clouds that rotate and spin. Each sweep creates more mist, creeping outwards into the loch, covering it from edge to edge with a cloud.

"Artos, Morganna, bring the body before me. Place him where the mist will support him. Then stand behind me, for I can sense Nimue approaching. Her mood is not good."

Unsettled by Myrrdin's warning, they run to unstrap Alan's body and struggle to hold his weight between them as they wade out to the water's edge. Artos directs a curious look at Myrrdin.

"Just lay him down?" says Artos, "let him go?"

"Trust me just do it," replies the wizard.

The mist swirls below Alan in a dense mass. Artos and Morganna let him go, almost as if they are laying him out on a soft bed.

"Is Nimue dangerous?" says Artos, moving behind Myrrdin's left shoulder.

"Imagine being within the thunder when it rumbles, not just below it. That may give you a glimpse of the wrath that she can summon."

A green light spreads out from below the mist, within the water. The scene is more reminiscent of a mystical island than a mountain top. Every part of Morganna's body is tingling. It's as if the light is filling her, charging her with great power. Whatever is being summoned is becoming part of her, inside her, around her.

Artos was becoming used to his body as

a vessel, filling with the energy of ancient times. He couldn't harness it like Myrrdin or Morganna, but it made him feel more alive, strong, unbeatable.

Myrrdin continues chanting his ancient incantations as Artos watches Morganna copy the movements of his mouth. As before, with the Rite of the Oak King, she is committing the magic to memory.

A silence falls as the clouds of mist rise around them. It encloses them in a space that is hidden from the outside world. Then an opening appears as part of the cloud parts, revealing Nimue as none of them have seen her before.

The Naiad kneels before them while suspended in the air. A hand touching her brow as she weeps, mourning for the departed. She places her other hand on her heart and, without lifting her head, she floats closer until she is above the body of Alan. Then she bends herself across, covering him with her grief.

The others stand silent in both respect and fear as they wait for her words. After a time, the lady moves upright to face them. Her form twisting and reshaping within the clouds until she meets them eye to eye."

"Myrrdin, I thank you for returning my son."

"Your son, my lady?"

"Yes, my son. Sent to protect the vessel of

the prophecy. He was given to one of the village to raise, as was Artos and Morganna."

"The Vessel?" says Artos, "is that what I see in my vision?

"No, *you are* the vessel. You must be protected. You face danger from forces that will oppose you. I sent my son to carry out that task. I allowed him to become too ... human. That was my error of judgement. I allowed him to have qualities that did not befit his true nature."

"Can you save him, lady?" Morganna sought her own response from the water spirit.

"His soul has returned to the Fae. He will need persuasion to return to your world, yet the prophecy requires his presence. He shares a fate with everyone. Artos, you must be patient. The trials ahead are tests you must pass. Many will stand against you, although they cannot wield the sword of destiny themselves."

"Morganna, I have given you a gift. A new power is moving through you. I know you are aware of its presence. You must use this power for good. Learn from those who have passed. You can now call on their wisdom to aid your own learning and growth."

"And Myrrdin, you know your own fate. You are courageous to go forward with that knowledge. Unveil the other players in this story. They must know who they are. Do this before the next challenge. Will you do this for me? It must happen before my son can return to you."

"I understand, Nimue."

Myrrdin bows. Artos and Morganna follow with their own mark of respect. As they lower their heads, the clouds of mist swirl and dissipate. They look up once again to see that all has vanished. The mist, Nimue, and Alan.

"Let's head for the forest," says Myrrdin.

"She spoke of players?" Artos asks. "She said you must tell us something?"

"That's best done when we are back amongst our friends. I hate having to repeat myself."

They mount the horses and start the winding route back to the forest beyond Hartriggs. Myrrdin and Artos continue discussing Alan, but Morganna rides on in silence, experiencing a new strength inside her.

My power grows.

Glancing around at Myrrdin, they catch each other's eye. There is no doubt he has overheard her thoughts, but he carries on speaking with Artos.

"Thank you, my lady," Morganna whispers.

THE BLOODLINE

Entering the hideout that the villagers of Hartriggs had used wasn't easy. A network of solid and low branches extended out from a dense thicket of hazel and silver birch. You had to enter the clearing on foot. It was just possible for a horse to enter if led through carefully.

It was a peaceful place to guard or prepare for invaders. The Hartriggs villagers were familiar with the creatures of the forest, and they had so many witches among their number that there was always something scurrying around with sharp teeth or slime dripping from green skin. They were used to it.

Artos walks Hengroen into the clearing, followed on by the others. The villagers have spotted them coming and gathered in a semi-circle about thirty strong to receive the news.

To the front stands Diana, Brigid and Owain. Their faces are solemn, waiting for news of their friend. Wailing amongst the crowd begins. It's obvious Alan has not returned.

"What happened?" says Diana, "did the Lady Nimue carry out her promise?"

"Yes," says Myrrdin, "but Alan has passed between the worlds. It will take time for him to return to us."

"But he will return?" asks Brigid.

"I believe so."

"Hamish, come forward" Owain interrupts as he ushers the Dun Romanach guard to move to the front, "tell Artos what you have told us."

Hamish still looks nervous among Artos and his warriors, but no-one has killed him so far.

"Owain told me how you plan to attack Dun Romanach, but you know the guards do a good job there. Dun Romanach has never been taken since the MacForres family became the residents."

"Not the right time, Hamish," says Artos, "but I'm certain we've weakened their chances."

"Well, it's just that there's no point trying to break through the gates. In a couple of days, the gates will be wide open. Duncanna is getting married to King Fergus of the Dal Riata. She is planning a huge celebration and wants Dun Romanach to be open to all the villagers from across the MacForres estates in Galwydell."

"What do you think Myrrdin? If the Dal Riata are there in numbers, then we will have more to defeat."

"When is King Fergus due to arrive?" asks Myrrdin.

"Anytime, we know he is on his way."

"Hamish, do you think we might get near enough to Duncan if we are hidden in the crowd." says Artos.

"I think so. I think Duncanna plans to walk around the fortress to take everyone's admiration and applause. Duncan will follow her, then MacDuncan, then Redlead and the other vassals.

"We can get them all if we surround them," says Owain.

"It will be dangerous," replies Artos, "we need to be sure that Urien and his cavalry will be close."

"We will be here," says Owain, "you have my promise."

Artos continues. "If we can attack the family then it's likely that the fight back will be disorganised. I'm sure the people won't turn on us. They hate Duncan as much as we do."

"What do you say, Artos?" interrupts Owain, "I need to leave now if I am to return with our cavalry before Duncanna's wedding reception."

"Yes, go now. We must seize our chance. Return to the Rheged. Ride as fast as you can."

Owain finishes strapping the bronze Pegasus to his horse. Before leaving, he stops to whisper quiet words to Morganna before placing a kiss on her hand.

Artos smiles as he witnesses the gentle goodbye.

"I wonder when I'll find a princess."

Diana laughs. "Baba Yaroslava told me you will have the most beautiful queen."

"That was in her prophecy?"

"Yes, she told me."

For a moment, Artos relaxes, shutting out the noise of other conversations. His dreams were creeping into his reality more and more. He had to believe his first war was not to be his last.

Artos looks around the flickering flames of the campfire and those gathered around him; Morganna, Myrrdin, Diana, and Brigid, the villagers from Hartriggs, and now Hamish, who has settled in the crowd.

The food is plentiful. Diana always improves the quality and quantity of meat that is available. It's no wonder that many tribes over her long journey have welcomed her. It occurs to Artos that she must have known long before he did about his destiny.

She always sits near Brigid. They have become inseparable and have shown how they can fight as a formidable duo. Defending the honour of their ancestors while looking for a place to call home. Their meeting has ended the years of isolation and loneliness for both.

Morganna, as usual, sits apart from the crowd with a raven for company. Artos always wonders how she converses with the black birds. She can speak wolf and bat, snake, maybe spider. She never sits by the fire, preferring to be surrounded by colder air.

Myrrdin needs the heat for his aging bones. Nobody knows how long he has lived, but people use the word ancient to describe him when he isn't listening. The wizard pulls his hat and cloak around himself while lost in thought. Meditating, or planning for the battle ahead, it's hard to tell. As the communal breakfast finishes and the morning wears on, he decides it's time to speak.

He throws a powder into the fire that makes its flame dance with the colours of the rainbow. It attracts attention from all assembled. He positions himself on a rock that gives him a good view of the audience.

"It is time," he pauses for effect, "for a tale of kings, treachery and deceit, and the prophecy that binds all who seek the sword, with its power to unite these lands."

Morganna makes eye contact with Artos.

Myrrdin is enacting Nimue's instructions.

The villagers gather closer around the Merlin, sensing a power around them in the forest. They push Artos and Morganna to the front. There is a communal notion they might feature in the story. The villagers have long suspected they came from wealthier families and have always felt sure the gods placed them in Hartriggs for their own protection.

And those among the crowd who are witches. The many sisters of Artos who have watched him and Morganna grow, raise their hands to the sky and whisper incantations to invite the creatures of the Fae to be present for the Merlin's words.

As normal, Myrrdin takes a long draw of his pipe and breathes out a cloud of smoke, as he starts to speak.

"As all pleasant tales begin, a long time ago, when I was younger, though not young, the gods gifted the kings that ruled these lands with special talents. Great wisdom, great strength, and powerful magic to help drive the Roman legions back from our shores. These heroes set out to claim and then defend the kingdoms of your people. Yes, beyond Galwydell, your brothers and sisters farm, fish and build their lives far across this Blessed Isle and further still.

"Across the narrow sea, one such place is Armorica, where a leader known as Cynan led his army and his people to victory. Providing them with a home in which to grow and prosper. This is where the prophecy began.

"Cynan defended his people from warring neighbours who coveted the lush and fertile ground. It was a land of plenty. To aid Cynan in the wars, the gods had granted him the power to return after death. He could be reborn if war or enslavement ever threatened his people."

Morganna pinches the arm of Artos, and a shiver runs along his spine. His sister can read minds, so he wonders does she know the story in advance.

"No, he's blocking me out," whispers Morganna.

Myrrdin carries on with his tale. "Cynan fathered three sons before he died. The oldest, Constans, became king in his place, returning from Armorica to the lands of his fathers, leading the Britons against the Saxon hordes. Constans won more ground than his father, but man's greed can wreck the work of gods. Constans had a trusted adviser. Vortigern, served as the power behind the throne. Granted his role through the accident of fate, he was not of the golden line of those chosen to rule, but he seized his opportunity. He incited the Picts to murder Constans, but in his haste to gain power, he didn't consider the consequences of allowing the dead king's brothers to escape back to Armorica. After all, they were still but children. What harm could they do?

"To protect his position on the throne, Vortigern agreed with the Saxons to grant them lands of their own. Each year, the Saxons returned to Vortigern, claiming they needed more land to feed their people and grow their tribes. Vortigern lacked the wisdom to see through the plan. In time, the Saxons had reclaimed enough territory, and Vortigern's permission was no longer required. Their armies drove him back west until he could retreat no further. He built a last stronghold. To protect himself, not his people. A prisoner in his own kingdom. He languished there for many years, until the return of the two brothers Aurelius and Uther.

"And so it was that Aurelius arrived with an army to besiege Vortigern's fortress, burning it to the ground along with all who were trapped inside its walls. Yet Vortigern had a final victory. Knowing that he could not survive an attack from his opponent, he ordered the water that flowed around his stronghold to be poisoned. Aurelius fell ill in the days that followed, as did many of his men. They died in burning pain, just as Vortigern had perished."

Myrrdin pauses, but the audience urges him to continue.

"What about Uther? Where was Uther?". Myrrdin raises a hand as the crowd returns to silence.

"Uther differed from his brothers. The gods had a role for him. Cynan's kin had lost the kingdom once more, and so it was then that Uther summoned me to his court in Ireland. He was on a quest for the sword. The same blade we speak of as Excalibur. He searched for the water nymphs, who were custodians of the blade. They came to his call, and he convinced them of his destiny, his right to wield the sword."

"Once Uther had Excalibur in his possession, he began to be tormented by visions. This is how the gods communicate with men. The images aren't easy to translate. Isn't that right?"

All the eyes of the audience fall upon Artos.

"I met Uther and translated the visions so that he could be sure of their meaning. The visions spoke of a single task. Uther was to raise giant stones and carry them to the great plains that lie to the south. Giant stones arranged in a circle, marking the place of his own burial. For the great distance they had to travel, the stones themselves granted the power to defeat any foe they encountered. Once again, the descendants of Cynan drove the Saxons back to the east. To mark his success, the gods rewarded Uther with a magical enchantment. The power to change his form at will. It would protect him from the likes of those that had murdered his brother Constans, but it was also then that Uther tired of the battle. He stopped his advance to drive the invaders back across the sea and rested at a fortress owned by his ally. Gorlois, leader of the Dumnonii.

"Gorlois had a beautiful wife, the Lady Igraine, and when Uther set eyes on her, the twin headed serpent that is known as love and lust consumed him. Gorlois saw that Uther coveted Igraine. A fight broke out, spilling out of his Great Hall on to the battlefield. For weeks, the two armies fought for victory over one another.

"To break the deadlock, Uther retreated from his siege, tempting Gorlois and his men to pursue them. And so, Uther's trap was laid. He had set a great ambush, with only one purpose. Gorlois was to fall in battle. Then Uther could claim Igraine for his own wife. I'm sorry I have talked long and have such a thirst!"

The crowd groaned, but soon a goblet of fresh water is passed and Myrrdin drinks deep before finishing his tale.

"The gods aligned on Uther's side, but it was for one last time. When he used Excalibur to run through Gorlois, he destroyed himself. After the battle, he rode to the fortress of his opponent. Using his shape-shifting powers to take on Gorlois' image, he entered the bed chamber of Lady Igraine and acted as her husband, satisfying his passion, and fathering a child. A short time later, word reached the fortress. Gorlois lay dead on the battlefield. The Lady Igraine was distraught. Was it a ghost or demon that had visited her?

"Uther never admitted his guilt, but wed the Lady Igraine, for he loved her as well as desired her, but his own corruption had now damaged him more than any blade could. He could never unite this island now. Allies didn't trust him. His sickness increased. The Saxons began calling him the Half-dead King and once again, their territories began to expand.

"Igraine, who had raised the daughter of Gorlois for three years, now gave birth to a son, but by then Uther's power had waned and many gathered around his death bed, awaiting their own chance of glory. It was then that he summoned me again. Many battles had passed since I had told him what his vision meant, but he had never forgotten me. I was told he entrusted his newborn's care to another. A lord that lived far from his lands. The Lady Igraine and her daughter travelled to a monastery in Armorica. They could live there in safety, in the homelands of Cynan.

"Then he ordered me in his last few days to return the sword. To cast it into a lake, returning it to the great water spirits. The custodians of the blade met with me and carried it below the water. It now lies awaiting the next soul pure enough to bear its burden.

His last request of me was that when his son grew old enough to lead, that I should come to his aid and translate his visions. Guiding him to his destiny as I had guided Uther. I'm afraid once I returned the sword, I did not keep to the rest of the bargain. I had my own demons to meet, and I'm not without fault.

"Many years passed. The Lady Igraine had died. Her daughter had a distant claim over the titles of others, but close enough to worry them. They sent her back across the narrow sea and, in the darkness, left her alone on an isolated shore. No-one risked the wrath of the gods by ending her life and so they abandoned her to chance.

"She travelled north under the cloak of darkness. Her only friends were beast and bird. They guided her to this place, to Hartriggs, though she didn't know why. She found a home when she arrived at Wren's door."

Everyone looked towards Morganna, her face displayed a warm glow. Myrrdin stared into her eyes.

"Morganna, you are the daughter of Gorlois and Igraine. descendant of the Dumnonii and sister to the inheritor of the prophecy."

Everyone, including Morganna, turned in shock towards Artos, who fixed his own gaze on Myrrdin, now standing in front of him, extending his hand.

"Artos. You are the son of Uther Pendragon

and the Lady Igraine, grandson of Cynan, and the one destined to rule over all within the Blessed Isle. Rise and greet your people, for they are the first of your great nation."

The silence holds as everyone takes in the enormous implications of Myrrdin's story. It's Hamish that ends the tension.

"May the gods bless Artos! The king is among us!

"The king is among us!" echo the others, followed by a cheer that shakes the surrounding trees.

Artos and Morganna embrace one another as their fellow warriors and the Hartriggs villagers gather around them. All wanting to lay on hands of congratulation.

The entire forest appears to spin around Artos. Some of those around him sense his unsteadiness and support him as he turns to Myrrdin.

"Why tell me now?"

"In the words of the woman that raised you from a baby, all the characters in this play knew too much and never enough. The gods have decided and stated their intention to Nimue. All that you have been, is now stories for old friends and those who still have to enter your life. All that you shall become is legend. The journey will be long, but I believe you will achieve this destiny."

There was excitement amongst everyone following Myrrdin's tale. The people had split into small groups, some talking about their thoughts of when Artos and Morganna had arrived in Hartriggs, while others talked of plans for the assault on Dun Romanach's ruling family. Many wondered what it would be like when the Rheged cavalry returned with Owain. All were eager to discuss the revelations with Artos and Morganna, but for the moment those two had sought quieter spaces to take in the news. Morganna walked deeper into the forest to be closer to the beasts and the birds. While Artos walked with Myrrdin to get answers to the many more questions he had.

The wizard was already regretting the invitation to translate the mystical visions. It transpired that Artos had experienced many more of these than Uther. In rare moments of silence, Myrrdin contemplated that Artos could be the greatest king, doing more to rule over the Blessed Isle than those before him.

One more question occurs to Artos.

"Who was the lord? Who did Uther ask to raise me?"

"I thought it best not to mention him by name when telling the story, but yes I can read your thoughts, and you are right to be considering none other than Duncan MacForres as the lord who served Uther's request."

"But I was in his levy for five years. Duncan said nothing. He was my adopted father all this time?"

"He neither adopted you nor claimed to be your father. Duncan based his friendship with Uther on a gambling debt. He owed your father a large sum of his wealth. Uther absolved him of the money owed and offered to pay for your upkeep. Duncan could not refuse such an offer. He left you in the care of Wren Morcant. Enough to appease his conscience, that he had kept his side of the bargain."

"Then why did my adopted mother never tell me?"

"Wren knew from the beginning. Your destiny lay in opposition to Duncan. She couldn't teach armed combat. The only way to learn was to join the MacForres levy. Wren had a dark sense of humour."

They walk on in silence for a while, under the cloud of Myrrdin's pipe smoke, as Artos starts to focus on the next set of tasks ahead.

"Yes, we should get back to talk with the others. We need to act soon," says Myrrdin.

"Myrrdin."

"Yes?"

"Stop reading my thoughts all the time."

"Sorry."

They carry on the short distance back to the centre of camp, where Morganna has reappeared and sits with Diana and Brigid, already locked in discussion.

"How are you?" asks Diana as Artos approaches.

"I'm fine now."

"I'm happier now," says Diana, "I no longer have any doubts that my grandmother gave me the right advice."

"You doubted me?"

"Several times."

Artos waits for her to say more or add some humour to her statement, but the awkward pause that follows has the effect of bringing him back to his old self. He wasn't a king yet and there was a battle to win. Alan still hadn't returned from wherever he now roamed, and he couldn't help but feel weakened by the sudden loss of his best friend. The cold seems to bite a bit more. He looks around at the people who are depending on him, believing in him to seek the revenge that they all crave. Duncan MacForres has destroyed their lives and Artos has become the champion of their cause. He remembers the words of Nimue regarding responsibility, about becoming a new person. The person who might wield Excalibur.

Artos rubs at his face with his hands and looks across at the others all staring back, waiting on his first proclamations.

"Alright, let's plan. We have a wedding to attend. Brigid, how many will Urien bring?"

"His personal guard of twenty, plus Owain, but we know that others of the tribe will offer aid. There could be a hundred horsemen in his cavalry."

"Good numbers," he pauses, "though, as Alan said, we can't just charge. There will be villagers with guards wandering between them. The enemy may be hard to pick out in the crush."

"We've had another idea," says Morganna, "poison. There will be a banquet. We poison the meal before the celebration. Then they may just live long enough to see us walk into the Great Hall."

"There will be food tasters for both Duncan and Fergus. If they fall ill, then it will alert the enemy."

"So, then we have to make sure that the food they taste is untainted?" says Diana.

"We'll need to be guests at the wedding," says Artos.

"Not guests, but servants handing out the meal," she says, "none of them know Brigid and me. We can turn up at Dun Romanach today, looking for work at the wedding."

"I don't know," says Artos, "it's dangerous, and I can't risk losing either of you before the battle. We don't even know if they'll accept you as servants."

"Two foreign women looking for serving jobs? We won't be the first to do that in these lands."

"True enough," says Artos, "what kind of poison?"

"Everything I need grows near here," says Morganna, "how would you like them to die?"

"I'll leave the details to you. With Diana and Brigid inside the Great Hall, we need to control the south gate so that Urien's horsemen can ride in without a fight.

"Our sisters can play their part in that," says Morganna, "they can distract Duncan's guards before removing them."

"From their posts?"

"No, from this world."

"That leaves Myrrdin and me with ten from Hartriggs who can put up a decent fight."

"And me," says Morganna, "I don't just make poisons."

"Won't you stay at the south gate."

"That's a waste of my talents. When we were with Nimue, she strengthened me."

"I knew she had done something," says Myrrdin, "does she intend to aid you in becoming a Merlin?"

"There can only be one, Merlin. Though it's true that one day I might assume the title."

"Yes, that maybe true," answers the wizard, "but be careful where you aim your bolts of magic. I don't want an unfortunate injury."

Morganna smiles in response. Myrrdin knows how his end will come. Not by Morganna's hand. That still didn't bar her from mischief making. He makes a mental note to have magical protection during the assault, and Morganna makes a mental note as well.

"If we are outside," says Artos, "we'll need to know when the poison has taken effect. When to launch the attack and order the charge of Urien's horsemen."

"When the wedding guests start to fall," says Brigid, "I'll give the battle cry of the Iceni."

Without warning, Brigid roars at the top of her voice, sending the birds from the trees, scaring the horses, and putting the fear of the gods into everyone, maybe including a few of the ghosts that lurk nearby.

"That's fine, I think we'll all hear that! And I'm sure it will scatter those who are not amongst the guards. When we hear your call, we will rush towards the Great Hall to reach Duncan and Fergus. If the poison doesn't work or something else goes wrong, just get out of the Great Hall as fast as you can, without being noticed, and lose yourself in the crowd. We'll be watching for you. If that happens, we will go back to our first plan to surround the family when they walk through the crowds."

"That will be a fiercer battle," says Myrrdin.

"I have to count on Urien and Owain being

there when we need them," replies Artos.

"When will Alan join us?" asks Diana.

"I have done as Nimue asked," says Myrrdin, "we can only hope that she can keep her promise."

"He has to be there," says Artos, "I've never fought in a battle without him. I don't intend to start now."

UNDERCOVER ICENI

Duncan had gone to bed satisfied that his plans were bearing fruit, including the bonus of having killed a trussed-up prisoner in cold blood. This had cheered him. A long sleep had led to the day starting later than normal. He had just dined on a fine breakfast of fresh trout with mashed barley in a vegetable broth. The omens were good. Then he saw it or didn't see it. The bronze Pegasus is missing from its plinth.

"Guards!"

Four still half-asleep men of the warband, that had been tasked with security for the private quarters, duly appeared in a dishevelled and disorganised manner. It wasn't apparent if there had been any actual guarding taking place overnight.

"Who was in charge last night?"

The smallest of the four men is volunteered to the front by his three larger companions.

"Eh, it was me, Lord Duncan."

"So, did anything unusual happen last night?"

"No, no. It was silent where I was, my lord."

"Silent?"

"Oh yes, my lord. Quietest I can remember."

"Quiet enough to hear my bronze Pegasus suddenly flap his wings and take off."

The guards are equally shocked to see the empty plinth. Sensing that at least one of them is about to face capital punishment, they bicker with one another about who was most at fault. The commotion wakes MacDuncan who appears from the sleeping chamber.

"What's going on?" he says.

"What's going on?" says Duncan, "my Pegasus has disappeared, gone, vanished. The only thing in life I can ever say that I liked."

"Aw, you don't mean that —"

"The only thing."

"I'll discover the thief faither. I'm good at that."

"And who pray tell is going to be the culprit this time amongst Beelzebub's various minions? Maybe it will be the ghost of Medusa herself!"

"I was right about Artos and Alan in the end."

MacDuncan looks down at his own feet with self-pity.

"I suppose so. Order a search now. No-one

gets out the gates without being questioned."

MacDuncan bows and leaves through the curtain, just as Duncanna appears in his place.

"What's going on?" she says.

"My Pegasus is gone. That's what's going on."

"Father. It will turn up somewhere," says Duncanna, "but I need to get on and you're taking up too much space in here. Find your horsey while I set my servants to work, there's only so much they can do before hunger stops them from being useful."

"How can I host a wedding when my Pegasus is gone?"

The room suddenly plummets into an air of tension. Duncanna has been challenged.

"How can you think about a wedding?" she begins, "I expect you to think about nothing else. This is the finest hour of the MacForres family. Well, the finest two hours when we do it again with the Picts. This wedding, for all that it seems to matter, is your only chance of doing something worth remembering. All I've heard for years is Ynys Mon this and Ynys Mon that. Now you have a chance at last and your more concerned with a dusty old ornament, which to be honest has always looked out of place in here. You should have melted it years ago and turned it into something useful.

"Now look here," protests Duncan.

"No father. You will look here. Your

daughter's wedding day is the most important day of your life and don't you forget it. Now organise something."

"Organise something?"

"Security, the meal, the entertainment, the seating arrangements, what you're wearing, your speech. Do I need to ask if you've done any of those things yet?"

"I'm sure everything is in hand. Do not worry my dear."

"Then go."

Duncanna dismisses her father with the wave of a hand as she steps back into the sleeping chamber. Had there been a door she would have slammed it.

Duncan looks sheepish, but then remembers the guards and his face turns red with rage.

"Find my Pegasus. Now."

The guards remain frightened to even breathe too much in case it annoys Duncan further, but the smallest one plucks up the courage.

"Wine my lord."

"What?"

"Wine, my lord. Whoever took your Pegasus tried to take your wine as well."

The guard points to the dropped containers and the puddle of red liquid that has spilled and stained the floor. Duncan briefly examines the mess, as the name of a single suspect rolls across his mind.

"Follow me to the chapel!" he orders.

MacDuncan strides towards the south gate with a purpose. He loves subterfuge and intrigue. Mysteries of disappearing objects or relatives rank at the top of his personal interests. Though most crimes can be solved by pointing the finger towards his Uncle Gilbert.

As he nears the guards who have been on duty all night, he spots them gathered around the broken gate, watching the smith carrying out the repairs.

"What happened here?" calls MacDuncan, causing the guards to spin around in fright.

"Just gate maintenance, sir," says the head guard. "there was a big gust of wind last night. It damaged the gate, and it seems to have blown Alan away as well. We just thought with the wedding and everything that you would want it eh, looking nice."

"Wait, wait. What was that? Alan managed to just blow away in the wind?"

MacDuncan peers around them. It's unusual for anyone among the guard to show initiative, so that's suspicious for a start.He can see that the smith is attaching new latches, but then his gaze is drawn to the massive black eye that the head guard is sporting.

"So, what happened to you then?"

"I walked into a post. You know what they say. Sometimes it's so dark out here you can't see your hand in front of your face."

"What d'you mean? You're a guard. Even I know that's not a job for someone that's half blind! There was a burglary last night. The thief stole a precious item from faither."

"Stolen?" says the guard.

"Aye, stolen."

"None of us stole nothing sir. We were out here in the watchtower the whole night."

"I'm not asking what you stole. You're a guard, the clue is in the name. Did you see anything unusual?"

"Nothing happened here last night. Quiet throughout the night. Isn't that right, lads?"

"Aye!" agree the other sentries.

"Apart from the big gust of wind?" says MacDuncan.

The sentries nod.

"That blew Alan away?"

They nod again.

MacDuncan's cross-examination complete, he peers at the other two guards. One has a large lump protruding from his head, while the other sports a swollen ear. He offers his most suspicious and enquiring look at the two men, making it obvious he is considering their potential role in the crime.

"So, none of you two saw anything suspicious either?"

The guards shake their heads in response.

"Well, keep your eyes and ears peeled," he looked at the head guard, "well keep your eye peeled at least," he looked at the guard with the swollen ear, "and you keep your ear peeled. Oh, never mind."

He strides off, back towards the Great Hall.

"Should we have said about Hamish?" says the sentry with the swollen ear.

"No, we keep quiet about that," replies the head guard, "if Hamish is the thief, then we could end up dancing on the rope beside him, but if I see him again soon, you mark my words," the head guard half draws a dagger from his belt, "he'll be sorry alright."

Duncan bashes through the chapel door, seeing that Andrew is still suffering from his Pictish makeover.

Laid out face to the floor. Stripped to the waist. The double-headed dragon twisting up his back remains a fiery mass of ruptured skin. Andrew groans as Duncan orders the guards to scoop him up, sitting him on the small throne.

Pressing his face up against the priest, Duncan sniffs around his mouth and nose as if to detect consumed wine. A pointless task as Andrew always has alcohol on his breath, but given his poor physical state, it's obvious even to Duncan that he's not the lead suspect for the theft. He orders the guards to search the chapel. The surrounding disruption and noise cause Andrew to come to his senses. As his eyes come into focus. His patron looks back at him with an annoyed glare.

"What does God do?" Duncan asks.

Andrew is half awake with an aching back and thumping head. Half dressed, he pulls his habit back over his shoulders and arms before attempting to answer Duncan's question about the ultimate omnipotent being.

"God is in everything, my lord. He sees all."

"Well, can you ask him then, who stole my bronze Pegasus last night? I know he doesn't speak to me, but he could at least tell you."

"God speaks to us all if our hearts are open."

"What are you blithering about, Andrew? I thought thou shalt not steal was a commandment! Someone has made off with my Pegasus. and God doesn't look too bothered from where I'm standing."

"God will deliver his punishment to the wicked sinner my lord, of that, I'm sure."

"When? When he's dead? If I get my Pegasus back, then I'll be the reason for his death. Just dropping whomsoever into the burning pit after they steal my treasure is not a disincentive for the thieving rabble that live around here."

"Punishment for all eternity is not to be treated lightly."

"I ask again. What does God do for me? I just burned the most heathen village in the whole of Galwydell. Executed one of their own undead last night. And I'll get the other one when he shows his face ..."

Duncan's voice trails off. His mind searching for a name. Suddenly he recalls the scene from the night before Eochaid died, when the two levy men from Hartriggs had the rare privilege of an audience within his private chamber. He remembers Artos studying the Pegasus and no doubt planning even then to steal it.

"Artos!" he says out loud. "I should have killed him when he was a baby."

Andrew draws the sign of the cross over his chest.

"My lord, you should not use this language in a house of God. Remember, he sees and hears all."

"Why the concern about someone who has made no useful contribution, financial or otherwise, to the church?"

"Religion is not about doing business, my lord. The children are innocent."

"Well, I wasn't, and Duncanna isn't. She committed her first murder when she was only thirteen."

"Ah yes, her first husband. As I've said before, supporting the influence of the church more than atones for less Godly actions by you and your family."

"And what of Artos? He grew up a heathen, raised by witches and other devil worshippers."

"Oh yes, that's fine. You can do away with him now. You can even torture him first if it pleases you, my lord."

"Yes, that pleases me Andrew, that pleases me indeed."

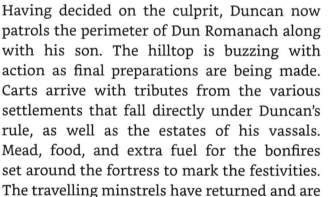

Having decided on the culprit, Duncan now patrols the perimeter of Dun Romanach along with his son. The hilltop is buzzing with action as final preparations are being made. Carts arrive with tributes from the various settlements that fall directly under Duncan's rule, as well as the estates of his vassals. Mead, food, and extra fuel for the bonfires set around the fortress to mark the festivities. The travelling minstrels have returned and are busy carrying their drums, pipes, and fiddles into the Great Hall, while Mona moves in with her own small army of cooks and serving staff.

"Alan blew away in a gust of wind?" says Duncan, "the same night as my Pegasus goes missing."

"It is a coincidence. You've got to admit."

"Coincidence, of course it's not a coincidence. Is it a coincidence that we find out that they're still alive? That we perfectly reasonably burn down their village and everything in it, and then Alan suddenly reappears?"

"Ah, but we killed him."

"We killed him, but then someone else steals my Pegasus and Alan's body mysteriously blows away in the middle of the night. Can your great criminal mind not work it out?"

"Artos has returned and eh stolen, the Pegasus?"

"My thoughts exactly. Could they not have had the decency to wait a few more days until the wedding was out of the way and my alliances consummated?"

"Weddings, faither."

"Yes, I know. Weddings. Good grief. If it's not stressful enough, making your daughter's happiest day, eh, days. We need to boost the levy. If he's around, there's bound to be more trouble. Fergus will be here soon, so at least we'll have his men to support us. I'm sure once I tell him that Artos was involved in the loss of his son, he'll be just as keen as me to see him dead."

"Maybe he'll want a manhunt," sniggers

MacDuncan.

Duncan returns an icy stare, no more needs to be said on the subject. Just then, a horn blows at the north gate. A guard announces that a messenger is arriving.

The heavy gate is unbarred to a rider dressed in coloured plaid, not the usual black worn head to foot by Duncan's men. The rider dismounts, handing parchment to the guard, who looks at it, but reading isn't his strong point. He hands the parchment back and calls on foot soldiers to escort the stranger towards Duncan.

"My lord," says the messenger, "I bring news from Fergus, King of the Dal Riata."

The man hands the parchment to Duncan, who pretends to read it. He looks at it for a few moments before MacDuncan points out that it's upside down. Duncan squints at the strange-looking scribbles for a few more seconds. It might be words, but not arranged in the normal way. He thrusts the parchment back at the messenger.

"Just tell me what it says. I can't understand a word you people speak to be honest."

The messenger rolls out the scroll of parchment.

"Lord Pretender of the Galwydell, my future father-in-law, please accept my apologies. The old wife didn't move out as willingly as I hoped. We're on the road, but a fierce night on the uisge beatha has left us all feeling tired and emotional. Going to take it easy today, but we'll be with you tomorrow in plenty time, sober enough to get through the ceremony. Please pass on my regards to my intended and assure that I only wish to be fresher for the after-ritual events. Don't start without me, your new son-in-law, King Fergus of the Dal Riata."

"The ooshga what?" says Duncan.

"It's a drink, my lord, made with grains and peat."

"Sounds disgusting."

"Aye, but you don't notice after the first one. King Fergus is bringing it to you as a gift for the celebration."

"I hope there's some left when he gets here. I suppose we can indulge him with the delay. How many are in his party. Just for the catering, you understand."

"He is travelling with other nobles and kin and his best guard. Forty men and personal servants in all."

"Forty, I see." Duncan looks at MacDuncan for confirmation that forty is manageable if a fight breaks out, "return to your master and let him note our disappointment that he will miss the feast planned for later tonight and the minstrels I have paid for two nights of entertainment. It's our pleasure to receive him by noon tomorrow when the wedding shall take place. Please arrive on time. It's possible our priest will be too drunk to conduct the ceremony, should it be much later in the day."

"I will carry your message back my lord."

"Be off with you," with his customary wave, Duncan dismisses the messenger, "they better show," he whispers to his son, "if he wishes to avoid your sister's murderous ways."

"We're still down by forty until they arrive," says MacDuncan, "What will we do about Artos?"

"Head out into the settlement. Anyone over four feet tall that can hold a spear is now part of the levy. Recruit them and bring them back. Then select the guards to take over at the gates. Those that know Artos best. Tell them there's a bounty on his head. Gold and mead for the man that slays him first."

"You'll pay them? Not the usual, we won't hang you?"

"I know. I'm becoming soft in my later years. Tell them that the bounty will double if he's captured alive. An execution as part of the marital celebration will add to the thrill of the entertainment."

MacDuncan starts to walk away to carry out his orders.

"And one more thing," calls Duncan, "if Duncanna asks, you're just organising for the wedding."

"What was that father," says

Duncanna, standing immediately behind and accompanied by Ifan.

"Nothing, my dear, nothing. I'm afraid we have had a message from King Fergus. He will be delayed until just before the wedding ceremony. It creates some extra duties for your brother that's all."

"Perfect," says Duncanna, "the less I have to see of Fergus before the wedding the better."

Duncan and Ifan draw strange glances at one another.

"Well, I'm not doing this for love after all. Ynys Mon father? Try not to forget."

"Yes, of course, but I thought you were looking forward to the wedding at least?"

"The wedding maybe, but not the husband."

"You will like Talorc, my lady," says Ifan helpfully.

"Well, maybe Ifan. He sounds more pleasing."

Back at the south gate a fight seems to break out between a small woad covered woman and the head guard. Mona is present and is shouting in Latin at the sentries as another woman attempts to hold the smaller one back. The head guard lunges at the woad covered woman who promptly kicks him in the groin, before head butting him.

"What is happening now?" says Duncan with frustration.

The head guard is still being thrashed by the small woman when Duncan, Ifan, and Duncanna arrive on the scene. Mona seems to be encouraging the assailant.

"Stop this now," shouts Duncan.

"My Lord Duncan," says Mona, "Your guard is an animal, pawing at that girl."

"It was just a body search," complains the head guard, now sporting even more bruises.

"You did not search me in such a way," says Mona.

"I know who you are, Mona. I drink in your tavern!"

"Let him go," orders Duncan, "What is your name girl?"

"Brigid, eh, Lord Duncan, I just came looking for work at the wedding with my friend Diana."

Duncan smiles at his daughter.

"I think we may have found a bridesmaid for you. Does she fit the job description?"

Duncanna's face lights up, unusually.

"Yes, she may be perfect, well from what I can make out under all the blue stuff. That will need to come off."

Duncanna walks forward and around Brigid, weighing up her fitness for the role.

"You are small, so the dress will be cheaper. You can obviously handle yourself in a fight, and you're not as gorgeous as me. You make me look tall, and if any man declares that I am not fit to marry, then I'm positive you can silence them before the words of objection even leave their lips. Am I correct?"

"I am Iceni, my lady. No man has beat me in a fight."

"Yes, I thought so. Come with me, Brigid, we must hurry and get you measured for your bridesmaid dress."

Duncanna grabs Brigid's hand and whisks her off towards the Great Hall. Duncan looks contemptuously down at the fallen guard.

"Take him to the kitchens with you, Mona. He's not much use as a guard."

"Lord Duncan sir. I only wished to protect you in my duties," protests the guard.

"Yes, and not very well, by the looks of things. Just be glad I'm short of people today and can't spare you for a flogging. Take him out of my sight Mona."

"Yes, Lord Duncan."

"Maids, girls, maid-girls, come here!" Duncanna sweeps into her private bed chamber, still tightly gripping Brigid's hand. Her servants rush to her side.

"This is Brigid, and she will be my bridesmaid. I need her dressed to look the part."

The maids pounce on Brigid before she can launch a protest. She is battle hardened, but no match for determined dressers who know the price of failure. In an instant, they strip her to just the small shift that serves as an undergarment to the heavier wool of her peasant clothes.

"Burn those rags," orders Duncanna.

Brigid panics. A poison pouch is attached to the fastenings of the dress and is now out of her reach.

"Please, my lady, please no. This is the only thing I have left from my great grandmother, Boudicca!"

"Boudicca wore that pile of stinking rags. No wonder she killed herself. Alright, throw it underneath where my brother sleeps, he won't smell it."

One maid lifts the pile of clothes and moves them to MacDuncan's corner of the room. Brigid makes a point of noticing where everything lies, while she also commits to memory the insult just delivered to her ancestor.

The rest of the servant's tug and pull, placing Brigid into a variety of costumes until they find one fitted enough to just allow breathing space for swift movement, just in case she needs to kill someone, as Duncanna has ordered.

Exhausted and overwhelmed. Brigid's mind is racing. Her normal instinct is to kill first and ask questions later, but this is different. She must be calm and choose her moment. She never counted on being separated from Diana. Suddenly the plans are not so straightforward.

Duncanna dismisses her maids, sending them to help with the setting out of places in the Great Hall. As they leave, her father enters the room.

"I like my new bridesmaid father. Her Iceni accent is quite cute, but I think she can be ferocious as well."

"Yes, Iceni," says Duncan, "I didn't think there were many of your people left."

"Few, my lord," says Brigid through gritted teeth, "my tribe is all but gone."

"Yes, I thought so. Maybe then it's time to lose the war paint. For tomorrow, at least."

"But I am Iceni, my lord."

"Yes," interrupts Duncanna, "I'll take care of your make up in the morning, after your bath."

"You bathe my lady?"

"Well, not normally, but you'll need to get the blue off."

"This talk of bathing irritates my skin," says Duncan, "does Brigid know the plan?"

"I was just getting to that. Honestly, I have so much to do and so few slaves to do it for me."

"I know my daughter. I have told you. Once I rule from Ynys Mon, you can have all the slaves you want."

"Fathers eh, Brigid! Oh, I'm sorry maybe you don't have one, there I go again putting my exquisite foot in it."

"You know you are to become Duncanna's bodyguard for her marital events?"

"Bridesmaid," corrects Duncanna.

"You are to become Duncanna's bridesmaid and bodyguard for all her weddings."

"All her weddings?" responds Brigid.

Duncanna sighs. "Brigid, you will act as a bridesmaid more than once. Tomorrow, I marry fat Fergus. Next week I'll come back and do it all again with Lord Talorc."

"Do they allow that here?" asks Brigid.

"Maybe not allow," says Duncan, "it's a new idea we've had. We're very modern and free spirited here in the Galwydell. We see the advantages of forging good relations with our neighbours and allies."

"But your allies don't know that they're both marrying the Lady Duncanna?" asks Brigid.

"See, father. I knew she was a good choice."

"No, they don't know, and they never should. When Duncanna marries Talorc, it will be as her twin sister, Duncella. It's very important that you remember that."

"So Duncanna will lie with Fergus and then

Duncella will lie with Talorc."

"Well, I've still to decide if I'll do any lie-ing with," says Duncanna, "but that's the right names for the right people, yes."

"So, do you have any more twins?"

"No, that's it for now," says Duncan, "but if it all works out, who knows! I'll take my leave. There's a jug of mead with my name on it. I'll retire to my table and leave you ladies to discuss the arrangements."

Duncan wanders back through the short passage that leads to the place that serves as dining room, war room, and private drinking den. He is still annoyed about the absence of his Pegasus. With times like this in the past, the bronze statue would be the recipient of his most private thoughts. In fact, he was always sure that it listened.

He pours himself a large goblet of mead and pushes his chair back, lifting his feet on to the table. The potential for Artos to reappear is a threat, but he can cope. With every plan, there are inevitable bumps along the road.

He's sure even his plan to rule through his daughter's bigamy can unravel. Gilbert's silence might become more expensive to buy, but by then, it could be too late for his ambitious cousin to oppose him. He closes his eyes and belches his way into a total state of relaxation.

"Life is good," he says.

"Yes, life was good!" comes the sound of Wren Morcant's voice in his head.

The surprise makes him jump and fall from his chair, bashing his back off the cold floor. He sits up, to the sound of small teeth chattering. A noise coming from above his head. Cautiously, he moves on to his knees, raising his head until the point that his eyes are level with the edge of the table. Then, it's in front of him, a white rat with pink albino eyes, swaying its head from side to side, focusing in on Duncan. The rat considers if he is indeed the right person to receive the important delivery.

"No!" shouts Duncan.

Scrambling on to his feet, he hammers his fist on the table repeatedly. He doesn't connect with the rodent, who is efficient at evading capture. As Duncan draws his dagger, the rat reaches into its throat with its claws and casts the small piece of apple across the wooden surface. It squeaks in anger and speeds away into a dark corner, just as the point of Duncan's blade embeds itself deeply into the table, splitting the tiny piece of apple into even tinier crumbs.

Duncan's screaming and cursing can be heard all around Dun Romanach, but then that's just a normal day.

THE PAINTED MEN

Once again, Artos sits on the back of Hengroen at the head of a great army lined up before battle. He looks to his right and Alan is there, along with Morganna and Owain. He turns to his left where Myrrdin, Diana and Brigid are stationed. He looks ahead at thousands who face them on the battlefield, at their centre a man carried above them on a large platform, borne by giants, surrounded by monsters. The men of the army are painted and fierce. Their anger creating a force of energy that shakes the ground as they step towards Artos.

Brigid sounds the battle cry and both armies advance, colliding at speed. Artos swings his sword, and the hordes fall before him. He is aware of his friends beside him and the battles they are facing. He fights his way through until no opponent stands before him.

The image changes, and he stands at the mouth of a cave. He can hear the battle still raging around him, but as he steps through into the darkness, all is silent. The cave is lit by a line of candles that mark a route forward. He walks on and with each step descends lower and lower. Heat is increasing around him. He passes a cool dark spring that emerges out of the rock, where he stops to take a drink of cold, refreshing water. Then he is distracted by the sound of chanting from his left. It begins as a whisper, but as he moves closer, the chant appears to echo, as if it slithers on the walls that surround him. After some time, he walks into a room full of books and jars of herbs. Incense burns in the air and in the middle sits a witch, smoking on a pipe and muttering incantations. It looks like Wren. Artos reaches forward, lifting the cowl. Only to reveal the face of Duncanna laughing back.

Morning. Artos is leading his war party past the blackened remains of Hartriggs. They keep their heads bowed in memory of those of their kin that have fallen on the whim of Duncan MacForres. Their anger for the moment is contained, their tears restrained. Before the day is out, there will either be victory or defeat. They are not afraid to face their destiny.

"I expected Alan to have returned by now," says Artos, and Morganna just nods silently in agreement.

"Nimue will regret it, if she cannot have her son at your side," says Myrrdin, "that has been her intention throughout these years, from the very beginning."

"Do you think Nimue feels regret?"

"I believe so. I hope so."

Artos falls silent again. Of the seven warriors who had vanquished Thunor's Disciples, now they were down to three. Owain must be on the way, but so far, the forest lay silent. Then there was Diana and Brigid. Could they be successful? Duncan had captured Alan. What if they were now captured, too?

He looked up at the old wizard and the young witch forlornly staring back at him.

"Can you stop that, you two!"

"Sorry," they both reply.

Morning. Brigid wakes in a comfortable bed, alerted by MacDuncan's snoring. He rests a few feet away in another corner of the room. Lifting Duncanna's arm from round about her, she eases out from under the warm fur cover and on to the icy floor. Duncan's bed lies undisturbed. He hasn't returned after their meeting. Something must have upset him.

There had been shouting. Brigid considers that if he was like his son, he'd be unconscious in his own vomit and urine while sleeping soundly.

Poison is the only thought in her mind as she steps carefully across the room, followed by the eyes of Duncan's dogs. They don't growl. They don't consider Brigid a threat to the family. Dragging MacDuncan to the side to get to her clothes raises no alarm. Her fingers rapidly search through the folds of the cloth until they find the small pouch that conceals an even smaller bottle. A few drops in a soup cauldron, or a large stew, is enough to wipe out those that consume the tainted feast.

Morganna had explained how the poison worked. First, the victim emptied the contents of their stomach from both ends before their kidneys and liver began to fail. Then hallucinations of their most feared demons followed, to stand and watch them die.

"Typical Morganna," Brigid says to herself.

She returns to Duncanna's side of the room and hides the poison below the bed, within easy reach.

Just then, she catches her reflection in a small mirror. The servants have scrubbed her face clean. Her skin is soft and pink. She can't remember the last time that she has seen herself. She thinks about Diana. What will she say when they meet again? Brigid's heart aches at being separated for one night. She hopes

Diana will be the same.

Morning. Duncan is so drunk he can hardly stay upright. Resting against the wall of the chapel, shoulder to shoulder with Father Andrew, he squints at the parchment that the priest is asking him to sign.

The text is meaningless to him, especially since it's mainly the religious Latin words. The only thing that is any way understandable is a very large and ornately drawn "C" followed by the letters "ontract".

"Is this legal?" asks Duncan.

"You cannot dispute the rights of the church without facing excommunication."

"Sounds painful."

"It is my lord, for then we doom you to languish for all eternity in the fires of hell."

"And I won't go to hell for swearing The Black Oath with the witch Wren Morcant?"

"My lord, this contract absolves you from all sin throughout your life, as well as breaking the witch's curse. God loves all his children."

"But especially the rich ones, yes?"

"Your lands signed over to the church will make you rich in other ways."

"And I'm allowed to keep living here?"

"Until the day you die. That is when the

contract will take effect, my lord."

"But I won't die today? I mean, that's the point of all this. All the black magic and everything."

"The witch's curse has no power over God's will. Your contract is with him. Not with the tempter."

"Very well. Get me ink and a quill to sign this thing. I want to enjoy the rest of my day."

"And a wonderful day it will be, I'm sure."

Andrew struggles to his feet, kicking through the empty flagons that litter the floor. He reaches down below his pulpit, retrieving ink and a feather for writing, as well as one last flagon of wine.

"One more drink to seal the arrangement?"

"Why not." belches Duncan.

Morning. The servants are busy in the kitchen with the last of the preparations for the day. Diana is tired as she stirs herself. They had made her work hard. Not that she was afraid of work, but all the staff had been gossiping about Duncanna and her new friend. A southern girl who Duncanna chose to be a bridesmaid. Diana hopes in her heart that it's another, but the description matches Brigid. She had quietly cried herself to sleep with painful thoughts that Duncanna might lead her friend astray.

Mona bends down over her with a kindly look.

"Do you know the girl causing the gossip? Does she come from your island?"

"My friend is Iceni."

"Well, you'll get to see your friend. There's no more preparation to be done, so I'll put you on serving duty at the top table. Since you're such a good worker. Your friend will be pleased to see you, I daresay. Though just one word of warning, Duncanna is a spider. She'll toy with who dances on her web before the kill. Now get yourself tidy. Be less unkempt to serve at Duncan's table."

Diana lets her hand trail down to the poison pouch that is hanging from the belt around her skirt. It's a stroke of good fortune, being selected to serve Duncan and Fergus. She can make sure their meals are free of contamination.

Quietly, she utters a prayer to Baba Yaroslava, and the assorted gods. She asks that her hand will be swift and steady in administering the poison, that Artos and the others will arrive with Urien's cavalry, and to keep Brigid safe from harm. So, when the day is over, they can embrace each other and rejoice in their victory.

Dun Romanach was resplendent. Every construction that stood within its walls, scrubbed, and cleaned, everywhere decorated with coloured banners and flags that displayed Duncan's emblem of the Raven's claw, dazzling in golden threads on a blood red backdrop. The weather gods had played their part, with a bright blue sky and yellow sun. The gentlest of breezes, strong enough to lift the fluttering, coloured banners to complete a perfect picture.

Roped off areas were prepared to allow the villagers to assemble without getting too near the dignitaries. Guarded by Duncan's newly formed company of overweight, eleven-year-old boys who bore spears more than double their height. Outside the Great Hall, space was allocated for the warbands of Duncan and Fergus to gather and share pre-event, event, and post-event mead.

Ifan had spent hours teaching Duncan's men how to say the word *sláinte*, the traditional toast of the Dal Riata. They had got the hang of saying it, but only after consuming several cups of mead in rehearsals. Now ironically, it was about all they could say as their party started early.

Inside the Great Hall, it was no less lavish.

They had covered all the tables in the finest linen. White was the dominant colour, dotted with plates of honeyed fruit that served as contrasting splashes of red, green, and orange. Mona was up early to run the organisation of the wedding as a military campaign. Inspecting her serving staff before the battle begins. Barking her orders, she knew where everyone should be and when they should be there.

Meanwhile, Ifan went through his routine with the Bavarian minstrels. They worked well together. The musicians had a perfect understanding of how to play each musical accent to add drama and emphasis to Ifan's words. There was talk of taking a show on the road together later that year where he would perform against a background of their melodies.

The big curtain ruffles at the far end of the hall. Someone is obviously looking for the opening. Brigid steps through, holding the curtain open for Duncanna to follow. A tense silence falls upon all the servants, the musicians, Mona, and Ifan. All pause and fix their attention on the bride-to-be. All except for Diana, who lets out a small gasp as she sees Brigid, minus her normal covering of woad. Her blonde hair is brushed out and flowing over her shoulders, her lips are red. She stands dressed in a gown that splits at each side to allow her enough movement to fight if required. As a final touch, strapped around her waist, is the belt and scabbard that carries Eochaid's old sword, Stoirm Gheimhridh.

Diana can see that Brigid is scanning the room. Is she planning to distribute her poison or looking for a familiar face? They connect with a fleeting glance as Duncanna tours around the banquet tables, examining every detail, every place setting, and decoration. The bride-to-be greets the minstrels and whispers to Ifan in the manner of a queen, complimenting her courtiers on their efforts.

Ifan bows low as Duncanna turns her attention back to Mona. The temporarily appointed head of events for Dun Romanach awaits nervously. It is the moment of success or failure that is purely in the gift of Duncanna. The bride's face lights up into a beaming smile.

"I am happy. Let the celebrations begin!"

A rousing cheer stirs the atmosphere in the room. The musicians play a flurry of notes and give a roll on the drums. Duncanna returns towards her private chambers with Brigid. Helping the bride to navigate the curtain, the Iceni turns around one last time. Looking directly at Diana, she nods and mouths the words, "I'm ready."

Meanwhile, Mona walks outside of the Great Hall and calls out at the top of her voice.

"Open the gates and let the people come

forth!"

The heavy northern and southern gates of Dun Romanach are pushed aside to let in the people from Duncan's territory. For many, this is their first visit to Dun Romanach. They are curious to get a look inside of the home of the rich and famous. Those that are more familiar to passing through on market and feast days already have their viewing spots pre-planned. They settle in early for a good view of the King of the Dal Riata and his new Queen. The older guards do their best to organise some crowd control, the new younger ones do their best to hold their spears upright.

In amongst the busy throng, not all villagers are there for the day out. Walking through the south gate alone or in pairs are the villagers of Hartriggs and the many sisters of Artos, who for once have removed their black cloaks in favour of the disguise of more standard peasant clothing.

Keeping their distance from the others and their heads firmly lowered are Artos and Hamish. The MacForres warband could recognise both, so they keep themselves hidden under the wide brimmed hats traditionally worn by local farmers while long cloaks cover their weapons. Myrrdin has also made compromises. Ordered to walk, bent over as an old man to disguise his height. The wizard's tall, pointed hat has stayed at home, uncovering his bald head, much to everyone's amusement. While Morganna has tied up her distinctive red hair, encasing it within a tightly wrapped scarf. She walks with the aid of a blackened stick, recovered from the fire at Hartriggs. A piece of Wren Morcant's staff. Now in the possession of a powerful battle mage, it has become a deadly weapon. All keep a close eye on one another, staying apart, but noting each other's positions, observing the guards and the number of Duncan's warband gathered outside the Great Hall. Most of whom are dangerously full of alcohol.

This will be a bloody fight in the end.

Artos is sure the victory is theirs. Yes, he's short of one hundred cavalry and his best friend is still nowhere to be seen, but he has magicians, including the Merlin and Morganna. All the Hartriggs villagers can fight well in a brawl, and he is being backed as potential king by no less than Nimue. Surely that counts for something. If nothing else, on this day, Duncan will fall to him. Any other result will be a loss, regardless of who lives and who dies. Whether it's a rush into the Great Hall or an ambush from the crowd, Duncan has to die.

Standing and peering through a sea of heads, Artos has a limited view. It's enough though, to spy the serving maid with fresh jugs of mead for the warband. Diana takes enough time to make her presence known, although she herself is careful enough not to make eye contact. It encourages Artos to see she is there. He has to presume that Brigid has been equally successful.

Brigid is nearby, but not where Artos imagines. Standing guard at the entrance to Duncanna's bed chamber while the maids are stitching the bride into her dress. She acts as a message relay between Duncanna and her father, who is rapidly trying to sober up in his private chamber.

Duncanna can hear the objections of her father as his servants force him to drink an unpalatable concoction of raw egg in vinegar with salt and pepper.

"This is disgusting!" he moans.

"It's good enough for you!" roars Duncanna.

"What did she say?" asks Duncan.

"She says it's very good for you," replies Brigid.

"Oh, I'll have to be sick!"

"You make me sick!" says Duncanna.

"What did she say?"

"She said she is lovesick my lord," says Brigid.

"Oh yes, yes, of course it's the wedding today. What am I doing here? I need to get my best battledress."

He shakily gets to his feet and staggers towards Brigid, who draws Stoirm Gheimhridh from its scabbard.

"Lady Duncanna has ordered me to kill any who try to enter while she is being dressed."

"What, even me?" he says.

"Especially you!" shouts Duncanna.

"You should consult a witch, my lord," says Brigid, "they will cure you."

"It was a damned witch that got me into this mess. No, no more of that. I'm a God-fearing man for good now."

Brigid toys with the pouch of potion that is now attached to her sword belt. Fate has presented her with so many chances to kill the entire family in the past few hours. She feels she is losing her touch. Just as she's weakening to temptation, she is forced to palm the poison away once more when MacDuncan sweeps through the large curtain.

"Faither, King Fergus is arriving."

"Don't let him see me!" screams Duncanna.

"Hold on I'll just get ready," protests Duncan.

"No. You will get out of here now. GET OUT

AND MEET HIM!"

"You're alright faither. I'll go right now and meet him," says MacDuncan, "what will I say?"

"Get Father Andrew," Duncan replies, "tell him they must have morning prayers or something. Anything."

"This better go well, father," shouts Duncanna.

"What my dearest daughter?"

"THIS BETTER GO WELL!"

Duncan nurses his head for a little while longer.

Outside the hall, there's a small rush of excitement going through the crowd as the groom's wedding party is climbing the slope towards the north gate. The arriving men are keen to announce their presence, two of their warriors play the pipes and raucous cheers accompany the music. Normally such a sound announces an enemy at the gate, but today it's just intended as friendly intimidation.

MacDuncan and Andrew race forward together to form a small welcoming committee at the head of the guard, but the sight that meets their eyes is not what they had expected to see.

"Father Andrew, tell me that's not," says

MacDuncan.

"I wish I could, but I know him only too well. It's the Lord Talorc and his fearsome Picts."

"ANDY!" Came the call from the approaching leader, cheerfully waving to his new friend.

"What do we do now?" says Andrew.

"I don't know. We need to buy time for faither, he'll know what to do. You take Talorc into the chapel. We can fill his men full of mead to keep them happy."

"What am I going to do in the chapel?"

"I don't know! Do the things you do. Say it's part of the ceremony. Just hold him there until I get back."

Andrew felt a tiny, hot drip of urine running down his leg. Even last night's wine wanted to make its escape.

With each step forward, the Picts grow closer, larger, and more fearsome. These were the people that turned back Rome while not wearing any pants. Fortunately for now, they've covered themselves from the waist down.

Talorc strides right in front of them, surrounded by his wild-eyed and grinning followers.

"Andy! Jesus Christ! You're a sight for sore eyes! How's the back painting?"

He tries to clinch the priest in a bear hug,

but Andrew steps back to avoid another shock of pain.

"Yes, I'm still tender, Lord Talorc, but the dragons are looking less angry now."

"Ha! that's good, I see what ye did there, and who's this neighbour?" Talorc nods towards MacDuncan.

"This is MacDuncan MacForres, heir to the estates of Galwydell and great warrior of the MacForres clan, slayer of Cadawg mac Arnall."

"Is that right, brother to be? Come and let us press our breasts together as two battle worn comrades meeting after the long years of war."

Talorc pulls MacDuncan forward into the tightest bear hug he can ever imagine. MacDuncan does his best to respond with his own pressure, but Talorc has squeezed the air and the strength out of him. Satisfied he has established psychological and physical superiority, he releases MacDuncan from his grip.

MacDuncan shakes himself to regain his composure. Mindful that the sworn enemy of the Picts is not too far away; he hurries to invite Talorc into Dun Romanach.

"Welcome eh, my brother Talorc. Your men are welcome to join with ours at the Great Hall. If you will visit the chapel with Father Andrew for the, of the ..."

"Prayers!" says Andrew.

"Aye, taking prayers, that's it," says MacDuncan

"Eh well, I suppose," says Talorc, "I was hoping to catch a wee look at the wife. I mean, Andrew brought me a nice bit of text to describe her. I'm fair excited, I've kept the parchment in my breeches all the way here."

"Oh, the prayers won't take long, then we'll introduce you to Duncanna."

"Duncanna? You said I was marrying Duncella, the good lookin' one. I hope you're not switching me to the ugly twin sister at the last minute."

MacDuncan desperately generates an extra jovial laugh to cover his mistake.

"Oh see me! I always say their names wrong. Don't worry, you're marrying the good looking one. I can assure you of that, eh, brother."

"Alright let's get these prayers done," Talorc turns to his men, "Right you lot, get tucked into the mead with these soft southern borders boys, I'll be right with you once I'm all purified and ready for the nuptials."

"Aye!" shout his men as they rush towards the lure of the mead jugs at the Great Hall.

Andrew starts to lead Talorc off to the chapel while MacDuncan silently mouths instructions.

"Keep him till I get back."

Artos squeezes through the crowd to

survey Talorc's men as they gather with Duncan's warband. His heart sinks at the sight of the painted warriors.

The Picts. What are they doing here?

A more dangerous atmosphere falls upon the celebrations. Locals begin to wonder if an invasion is underway. The reputation of the Picts partying in the villages of their victims is legendary.

The visitors with particularly young children decide that maybe it's best to leave the wedding celebrations to the adults. The crowd begins to thin out, leaving gaps and making it easier for the guards to pick out the potential threats. The peasants who are choosing to remain are the more scurrilous types, many with familiar faces from past misdemeanours, inspiring a more watchful eye from the security roaming the grounds of Dun Romanach.

Artos is uncomfortable. The sense of imminent danger is growing. Random guards are looking longer in his direction, and he can see whispered conversations between them. It's still too early to start the attack and they are well outnumbered. Urien, Owain, and Alan are nowhere to be seen. A creeping sense of imminent doom overtakes Artos. Snatched glimpses of concerned expressions between his fellow warriors reinforce the fear of a battle lost before it has even begun.

JUST MARRIED

Duncan instantly sobers up from his overnight hangover as MacDuncan delivers the bad news.

"The Picts are what?" he says, desperately hoping that he hasn't heard correctly.

"Here. The Picts are here."

"You're sure it's the Picts?"

"Painted from head to foot, hardly any clothes, and angry looking, even when they're smiling at you. Yes, it's the Picts alright. Their Lord Talorc is with Andrew in the chapel right now, for prayers."

"We'll be saying our prayers before the end of the day. What else can go wrong at this wedding?"

"What was that father?" says Duncanna as she enters the room with Brigid, "I hope I didn't hear you say that something about my wedding was going wrong?"

"I think it's more to do with being the wrong groom for your wedding," says

MacDuncan.

"Your brother speaks the truth my dear. Talorc has turned up with his men at our gates."

"That's fine," says Duncanna nonchalantly, "I'd have been marrying him next week. Might as well get it over with today. Tell the other one to go away and come back later."

"I can't tell the King of the Dal Riata to just go away! And if they meet the Picts here, there will be no later."

"We could say we've been attacked. The Dal Riata could help us beat the Picts." says MacDuncan.

"Nobody beats the Picts," says Duncan just as the large curtain is drawn apart.

"What's that you say? Aye, nobody beats the Picts."

Talorc looms large at the entrance, with Andrew cowering behind him, having failed in his subterfuge.

"I only know Our Father, so prayers don't take long. You must be Duncan. Pleased to meet you and glad to hear of your respect for my people."

Duncanna coughs lightly to draw Talorc's attention and rises from her chair. The very picture of ultimate refinement, elegance, and grace. She holds her hand out to her suitor.

"Hell's teeth! Christ Almighty! You're a wee angel! Tell me you are —"

"Duncella. Your wife to be."

"Aw here! Duncan, father-in-law. I am very pleased," Talorc grips Duncan in a tight bear hug, "very pleased. Let's get the land trade done and get on with the ceremony. I'm burning up here with —"

"True love?" says Duncanna with the sweetest smile.

"Aye, you could say something like that."

"Look the land trade," Duncan interrupts, "I'm afraid you've arrived earlier than expected. The agreement hasn't been written yet. What say we just sign a blank piece of parchment, and I'll fill in the details around your signature?"

"Aye, we rushed to get here. I don't really want to hold the ceremony up, especially with this wee charmer. Can we get on with it then? I'm dying to get started."

"Of course, we'll all go through and take our places now," Duncan agrees, "let's get these blessings done, Father Andrew."

Andrew leads Talorc back through the curtain, while Duncanna and Brigid return to the sleeping chamber to await the big entrance. Duncan and MacDuncan stay where they are to make plans.

"Get to the north gate now," says Duncan, "if Fergus turns up, tell him we're all down with the plague and he'll need to come back next week God willing."

"Even I can see through that one," says MacDuncan, "why don't we divert them? We can send them on to Tabernae Mona, tell them the wedding has been moved to there. We get them drunk on their ooshga-whatever. It'll be the next day before we need to think of something else."

Duncan suddenly eases back into something that is closer to a state of calm.

"Yes, surely, you must be my son."

"Oh eh, thanks, eh, faither."

"Take them there yourself. Make sure they stay and drink as much as possible. I will not die today."

"What?"

"It doesn't matter. Go now."

MacDuncan speeds off through the curtain, and through the increasingly busy Great Hall.

"Hello Uncle Torcaill, Uncle Gilbert, Redlead. I'm in a bit of a hurry, can't stop."

The relatives are bewildered by his exit, though Redlead can always detect a threat, and Gilbert can always detect a secret. As they view the room, now half full of Picts, both Torcaill and Redlead usher their wives to the relative safety of the women's table. An undecorated afterthought, separated from the main hall by its own small curtain.

"Which wedding is this one?" says Torcaill.

"I think it's next week's wedding," replies Gilbert.

"As long as there's a fight," says Redlead, "you can't have a good wedding without one."

"I'm sure the Picts will oblige," Gilbert confirms.

MacDuncan exits the Great Hall, just as a horn sounds again at the north gate.

"Get me a horse," he calls.

He strides forward with purpose through a crowd of villagers. Locals that he recognises, farmers and traders. One touches at his wide brimmed hat in deference which MacDuncan acknowledges with his usual kind consideration

"Get out of my way peasant," he demands, as he mounts his black steed.

The farmer draws back as MacDuncan rides to the gate, just in time to receive Fergus and his men as they arrive.

"King Fergus. Greetings from Dun Romanach. I am MacDuncan MacForres, son of Lord Duncan. He has asked me to lead you to the wedding location."

"That's why we're here," Fergus says as he rides to the head of his party, "show us to the ceremony, son."

"Eh, well we have to go back down the hill and along the road for a couple of miles."

"Back down the hill?"

"The location of the wedding has been changed. It's going to take place at Tabernae Mona."

"A wedding in a tavern? That's very modern of you."

"Oh, you know, we're very up to date here. The sixth century is just around the corner."

"Aye, and I think Duncan said to our messenger that your priest likes a good bucket."

"Eh aye he does," MacDuncan performs an impromptu mime of Andrew, drinking.

"Is the mead good?" shouts another of Fergus' party.

"Aye, it's the best, and all free, to guests of my faither."

"Free mead?" says Fergus, "that's my favourite words."

Stray shouts and occasional smashes can be heard in the background

"It sounds like there's a big commotion going on in your Great Hall. Is there anything we can do to help?"

"Oh, you know what it's like when relatives get together. That's just the bridal party sorting out who's going to sit next to who, land claims, unsolved murders. You know the way it is with close family."

"Aye, I've got two like that myself."

Fergus gestures to his two sons, who laugh

but draw one another threatening looks in the background.

"Are we going to head off then?" asks MacDuncan.

"Aye, lead the way, son. Is the food good at the tavern?"

"You'll love it. Do you like rabbit?"

MacDuncan rides through the gate with King Fergus. The small talk settling him down as the plan appears to be working with the rest of the Dal Riata following on.

As they leave, Artos, Myrrdin, Morganna and Hamish hurriedly band together in a small group.

"Does anyone know what's going on?" asks Hamish.

"The Picts have turned up unexpectedly it seems," says Myrrdin, "at least that's what I can read."

"I agree," says Morganna, "MacDuncan's mind is not a good place to go, but he thinks a lot about saving his own skin. Right now, he's planning an escape for himself."

"So, it looks like MacDuncan, and the Dal Riata are heading to Tabernae Mona?" says Artos.

The others nod.

"The Picts are already here for a wedding?"

They nod again.

"And hopefully, we have one hundred Rheged horsemen heading this way."

They nod again.

"Glad we got that sorted out."

The group is conscious of increased attention from the guards around the north gate. They separate again to make it harder for them to be followed by unwanted pairs of eyes.

A small crowd of villagers are pressing themselves up against the open doorway of Duncan's Great Hall, trying to get a look at the bride. Artos decides that's the best place for him to be to keep a check on the progress of the plan, but the tight squash of the crowd sees his hat pulled off and trampled underfoot by the people surrounding him. He has no choice but to stay amongst the throng to avoid detection.

Artos can just make out the top table through the sea of heads that are the other guests at the wedding. Diana and Brigid are nowhere to be seen, but he can spy Father Andrew standing next to Duncan who cannot hide his disgust as the Pictish warriors strip off their clothes.

"Oh, what are they doing now?" says a bewildered Duncan.

"Talorc wants full military dress for the wedding," says Andrew, "to a Pict, that's no dress at all."

Duncan screws up his face as half the room follows the example of their leader. The air fills with testosterone laced musk and wild howling from a tribe ready to party. If they weren't intimidating before, they are now.

"Let's get on with this," says Duncan.

Andrew signals for the minstrels to play music for the big entrance. Brigid appears first, holding the curtain back for Duncanna to enter. A collective "Aw!" circles the room as the guests show appreciation for the bride. Duncanna accepts every second of applause and devotion. This is the culmination of years of work, of all the backstabbing against others who would dare compete against her for the perfect husband, plus all the traditional stabbing of previous suitors who didn't offer enough land, wealth, or power.

Brigid holds the train of the bride's dress, but her bodyguard eyes scan the room for threats and friends. She feels alone and vulnerable in amongst the enemy. Her mind debates over whether she should have used her phial of poison the night before, but it's too late. She prays silently to her ancestor, for the ghost of Boudicca to lead her choices.

"The bridesmaid. Who is she?" says Gilbert.

Torcaill and Redlead shake their heads.

"There's something familiar about her. I've seen her before, but I can't put my finger on it."

"She looks as if she could be handy with

THE BLOOD OF THE BEAR

that sword," says Redlead, "maybe we should recruit her."

Brigid briefly makes eye contact with Gilbert, but then she looks beyond him and a small smile forms on her face. Gilbert follows the look over his shoulder to a group of servants gathered to watch Duncanna's entrance. One of them seems to stand out, muscular and darker skinned, she is familiar too. For Gilbert and his years of experience in dealing with the darker side of courtly matters, something doesn't feel right. If he didn't know better, then he might think that an assassination was about to take place. So best to wait and see who the intended target is before acting. After all, not all murders were bad if they helped you out on your own career.

Talorc constantly repeats the phrase, "happiest day of my life."

The unusual outpouring of emotion contrasts with the various mythical horrors and gruesome depictions of death painted across every inch of his body. Duncanna times her walk to perfection. She stands beside Talorc as the musicians stop on a flourish. She smiles coyly at her husband-to-be and, after a time, raises her gaze to eye level.

"Dearly beloved," a hush falls in the room as Andrew begins, "we're gathered here today for the marriage of the Lady Dunc ..." Andrew stops briefly, "... the Lady Duncella NicForres and Lord Talorc, ruler of the Kingdom of Fib," the crowd offers a small round of applause, "following with tradition. I need to ask if anybody else has married or undertaken an activity that would be seen as an act of marriage with the Lady Duncella already?"

The room remains silent except for Brigid, half drawing her sword from its scabbard.

"I think that's long enough now, Father Andrew," says Duncanna in a commanding tone.

"Yes, of course," continues the priest, "it says in Corinthians that love is patient —"

"Aye well I'm not," Talorc interrupts, "Andy, my good neighbour, can we not get to the do's part?"

Andrew looks over at Duncan, who is happy to speed through the ceremony, and waves his approval.

"Do you, Lady Duncella NicForres, take Lord Talorc to be your lawfully wedded husband?"

"I do," says Duncanna in her breathiest tone.

"And do you —"

"Yes, I do too," says Talorc, "is that it? Are we done?"

"I now declare you man and wife, you may kiss ..."

Talorc instantly sweeps Duncanna into his arms and runs with her to the other side of the big curtain. Lurid laughter and squeals of delight echo through the Great Hall as they race for the bed chamber.

"Play something loud!" commands Duncan.

The minstrels begin a fast and noisy reel, guaranteed to cover up any more embarrassment.

"Was that alright, my lord?" asks Andrew as he takes his place to the left of Duncan at the top table.

"Yes, faster is better today. If we can get them drunk and out of here by tomorrow, we might have a chance that we'll still get away with this."

Brigid has a place at the top table, but there's a large gap caused by the absence of Duncanna and Talorc. As she sits, Duncan leers in her general direction.

"Brigid. Find out if my son has taken our other guests to Tabernae Mona."

"You want me to go outside the hall?"

"Yes, that is what I would like you to do. Come back and tell me the news of him. On you go."

Brigid rises and starts to walk between the other tables. On her way to the door, she meets Diana coming from the other direction with plates of food for Duncan and Andrew.

"Where are you going?" says Diana in the passing.

"Duncan has sent me on an errand. I will be

back. Wait for me to return."

Gilbert watches the interaction from his seat.

"Excuse me everyone. I need some fresh air," he says as he rises and follows Brigid towards the door.

Artos catches the Iceni's eye as she emerges from the Great Hall. Brigid ignores him but signals for him to follow. He can't break his cover, but he thinks as hard as he can.

Someone follow Brigid.

Immediately, Myrrdin and Morganna emerge from different parts of the crowd and begin walking behind Brigid at a distance towards the north gate. They see her talking to the guard and then returning towards them. As she passes by, she briefly shows to Morganna that she still has the poison phial intact.

"Soon." Is all she says as she passes.

As Brigid walks back inside the Great Hall, Myrrdin and Morganna discuss their findings.

"What did you get?" asks Myrrdin.

"She's been asked to protect Duncanna and be her bridesmaid," says Morganna.

"Yes, I thought she thought that."

"I picked up that she's worried about Diana. They've been separated from one another."

"Diana is with the kitchen staff," says Myrrdin, "that's where we wanted her. Brigid is thinking that they're going to start the poisoning soon."

Gilbert is standing just in front of Artos as Brigid passes by him at the door of the Great Hall. He prides himself on his spying skills, but he hasn't spied his cousin's enemy a few feet away in the crowd. Artos is frustrated. He's trapped where he is. All he can do is watch Brigid walk back to the top table and Gilbert follow her a few steps further behind.

Brigid approaches Duncan from behind his seat and leans towards his ear. Her nerves are on edge. This is another golden opportunity to slit his throat, but she has to resist.

What would Boudicca have done?

"MacDuncan has left for Tabernae Mona with the Dal Riata. The guards think he will be there by now."

"Good, good. It's about time he did something useful," Duncan grabs Brigid's wrist, "come sit beside me my dear. You are too far away, and I should get to know you better."

The polite request is an order. Brigid has no choice but to take the seat that has been intended for Talorc. She knows that if the poison doesn't work, there may only be one choice left. If she is to die today. Duncan will die first.

The southern road that passes by Tabernae

Mona looks like a parade as the bright plaid wearing Dal Riata arrive at the hastily rearranged wedding venue. Already having shared some uisge-beatha along the way, the various members of the party are in good spirits.

As a lone figure observes them from a distance, he pats the shoulder of his white charger. One of the group interests him more than the others. Dressed differently from his drinking partners. He is clad completely in black. The mark of a member of the warband of Duncan MacForres. The man observing the scene looks down at his own clothes. He's wearing a white tunic and breeches; his leather armour almost has the look of a light gold. His spear is also adorned with pieces of copper along its white shaft. The tip itself is silver. He checks his sword in its scabbard, and his knife in his belt with its hilt of white stag horn.

As the party of horsemen disappear through the doors of Tabernae Mona, the white-clothed figure nudges his horse to walk on. As he rides towards the tavern, memories are flooding back to him. Scenes of battle, nights of celebration, great adventures with his best friend, and then the image of the beautiful Gwendolyn Nicaskill.

He dismounts in the paddock outside the tavern. His heart is calm. There is no panic. There is just a task to carry out. He grips his spear in his right hand as he pushes open the door. The tavern is already full of laughter and song. No-one reacts to him entering. Not even the man directly ahead of him, dressed in black, drinking down his mead and laughing his distinctive laugh.

"MacDuncan MacForres."

The crowd instantly falls into silence. MacDuncan has been called out in fights many times before. He recognises the threat that the voice is presenting. He draws his dagger and spins around to face his accuser.

"Alan?"

The spear tip presses hard against his chest.

"That is not my name."

"Well, you look like Alan. I should know I killed you ..."

"You did what?"

"Eh, maybe you're not Alan."

"That is not my name. And to the man that is sitting three places from my right, sheathe your dagger now or your drink will be your last, and the man that is five seats to my left. Loosen your grip on your axe for I will not hesitate to kill you should it be raised against me."

King Fergus gestures for the lowering of weapons.

"We're just here for a wedding, son. Nobody wants any trouble," says the king.

"And none you shall receive if you refrain

from any attack. I am only here to claim the life of one man," the spear presses harder into MacDuncan's chest.

"Are you sure I'm the right man. If you're not who I think you are, then maybe I'm not who you think I am. If you see what I mean."

"My name is Lancelot Du Lac. Champion and protector of the innocent. Mightiest of foes. Unbeaten in battle. I will respect all who challenge me by assuring them a quick death. My king descends from the golden line of the chosen, the rightful inheritor of this Blessed Isle, the one born to wield Excalibur, the sword of power."

"Oh, he's one of these," says Fergus, "is it the prophecy? Is the world going to end and all that?"

"Don't annoy him," pleads MacDuncan.

"We get this lot up our way MacDuncan. No sooner had the new church arrived, than all his kind followed them, bleating on that the end is nigh and we'll all burn in a big fire. What do you want to go away, son?"

"Yes, what do you want to go away?" says MacDuncan.

"I want you to go away."

Lancelot pushes his spear deep into MacDuncan's chest, covering everyone with showers of blood including himself. He looks down at his bloodstained clothes.

"Maybe white wasn't such a good idea."

"Get him!" shouts Fergus.

The Dal Riata pile on top of Lancelot, but his skills in battle are now aided by the gods. Many fall before him as King Fergus and some of his retinue decide that retreat is the better part of valour, by rushing back out of the door of the tavern. They mount their horses as hastily as they can, before riding off along the southern road at speed.

Lancelot emerges from the tavern. Dragging his spear behind him. He yanks it free of MacDuncan when the body becomes trapped across the doorway. He spends a few moments trying to wipe the smallest spot of blood from his white tunic, even although he's covered in red stains.

As he mounts his steed, he carefully positions himself in the saddle. Taking his time to hold the reins and balance his spear for greatest comfort. The sound of crows flying from the trees are followed by King Fergus and the half a dozen of the remaining Dal Riata, speeding by the tavern again in the opposite direction, quickly followed by the thunder of four hundred hooves as the cavalry of Urien comes into sight..

Lancelot rides forward to greet them as the horsemen of the Rheged pull up to a stop, outside Tabernae Mona.

"Alan?" says Owain.

"Why does everyone keep calling me that?"

"Eh, that's your name?"

"No, my name is Lancelot Du Lac. It doesn't even shorten down to Alan."

Urien laughs. "You were Alan the last time we saw you, but Myrrdin had warned me of such a thing. From now on, you will be known in the halls of all the kings as Lancelot. That is your destiny. You've had a bit of a fight here I see?"

"MacDuncan is dead, and those who chose to stand with him at his end."

"Then come Lancelot. Join us for the fight against his father. Dun Romanach will fall to our charge together."

"Aye," shout the horsemen and they all ride off, with the ground rumbling under hooves as they go.

BATTLE FOR DUN ROMANACH

In the kitchen, the food is being divided out, ready for serving. Mona's staff are drilled to perfection, flowing in and out of the Great Hall with the various parts of the feast. The next course is fish cooked with leek in white wine, a perfect choice for covering up a mass poisoning. Diana knows she won't have long to lace the bulk of the food with the black toxic oil. She scans the room. Mona stands surveying her army, but a crash of plates in the Hall distracts her. Diana moves fast, drawing the pouch into her hand and removing the phial of poison. She thanks the gods that her skill with a bow has always given her a steady hand. With a brief sweeping motion, she sprays drops of the liquid on to the communal dishes and slices of black bread.

Her own three plates have already been separated. Only the best selections for the top table remain free of the poison. She stands ready for Mona's command to serve the fish. The seconds stretch out. If only she had her arrows, she would feel better, this is not the way Diana has been trained to kill.

Mona returns, chastising the unfortunate clumsy servant with one hand and waving the order to proceed with the other. Diana grabs the three plates and makes her way into the banquet, as she does so, she bumps against Gilbert.

"Sorry sir," she says as she carries on to the top table.

Gilbert looks annoyed but does nothing more before approaching Mona.

"That girl who is serving my cousin at the top table."

"She's new," says Mona, "a very good butcher. Still learning to serve. She arrived with the one who is sitting next to Duncan. The violent bridesmaid for Duncanna."

"Violent?"

"You should have seen her battering the guard yesterday. I was worried she would kill him."

"I see."

"Is there something wrong?"

"Yes, I think there might be, but I'm not sure. Keep an eye on the one that's serving. I'll watch the other one."

The music is loud. Torches burn brightly,

along with the central fire in the room. The guests roar and laugh with one another at the tops of their voices. Diana's adrenaline courses through her in the noisy and confusing atmosphere.

She serves from over the shoulders of the guests; first Duncan, then Andrew, then Brigid. Her eyes connect with the Iceni. They can sense danger from one another. Brigid can't move from her position, but her clenched fist clearly shows she is still holding on to the small bottle of poison. Their lingering glance attracts the attention of Duncan.

"Next time," Diana mouths as she walks away.

"Do you enjoy fish, Brigid?" says Duncan, doing his best to be hospitable.

"Yes, it's delicious."

Brigid struggles to swallow even the smallest piece of food. She is nervous and nauseous at being surrounded by the enemy.

Her unwillingness to eat is spotted by Gilbert as he resumes his seat at the table.

"That fish is delicious," says Torcaill, cleaning his half of the plate shared with Gilbert, and mopping up all the juice with the bread.

"You can have mine," says Gilbert, "I suddenly don't feel quite so hungry."

"Your loss," says Torcaill as he rotates the plate to attack the other half.

Gilbert watches him devouring the meal while keeping half an eye on Brigid.

Diana stands behind Duncan, ready to remove the plates as soon as they're finished. She casts her gaze down the room. A crowd of peasants stand in the doorway, a small group of hungry looking faces that are open-mouthed at the splendour of the feast. Squeezed in amongst them is a face she recognises. Artos is leaning closer to the front. Their eyes connect, but it increases Diana's anxiety. No-one has fallen ill with the poison yet, when will they strike?

Duncan signals for her to collect the dishes. He and Andrew have cleared their plates. Brigid's remains almost untouched, but as Diana lifts it away, she can see the poison phial half hidden under a fish head. Brigid flashes a brief look at her friend and reaches with her hand to the hilt of her sword. They both know that the moment is coming.

Diana races back with the plates to apply more poison to the next course. On the way there, Gilbert extends a leg and boot to trip her up, sending her sprawling amongst the guests. The dishes come crashing down and a small phial of black liquid rolls along the floor. Mona appears the instant that she hears another clattering of dishes. She instantly starts remonstrating, while Diana struggles to pick up the spilled food and plates, amidst desperately searching for the poison. The revelry continues as the mead flows among the guests, but it doesn't stop Gilbert from acting on his suspicions of foul play.

"Would this belong to you?" he says, reaching down and picking up the tiny glass container.

"No sir," says Diana as she scrambles to her feet.

"Maybe it belongs to your friend over there?"

"I've never seen it before, sir."

"What's going on Gilbert," says Torcaill, "leave the girl alone, she just fell over."

"Mona, call Blacknail. I wish his opinion on the contents of this."

Duncan spots the incident from his seat at the top table.

"What's going on now. Gilbert has always got to complain about something?"

Brigid can't hold back much longer; she feels every muscle tense within her.

"What's Blacknail doing," says Duncan to Andrew, "he's drinking something."

Blacknail sips about half the contents and swirls it about his mouth before gargling and swallowing.

"It tastes very nice, but it is a poison and a dangerous one, too. I consumed a small measure, but ..." his words trail off as projectile vomit and diarrhoea cause him to crumple in pain. Writhing in agony on the floor, he points wildly as a strange vision overtakes. Within seconds, he is dead.

"STOP EATING NOW!"

Mona roars above the loud music, bringing it to an abrupt halt. Once again, allowing the sound of the newlywed's lovemaking to provide an inappropriate backdrop to the tension.

"Grab that girl!" shouts Mona, "she has poisoned you!"

The announcement hastens disaster as several warriors on both Duncan and Talorc's warbands begin to writhe, convulse, and eject the contents of their stomachs. Torcaill MacForres follows, scattering coin to the floor as he falls. People don't know whether to save him or just grab the money. From the sound of it, the women's table has also succumbed to the toxic fish course.

"Get her!" shouts Duncan, and within seconds, Diana is captured and wrestled onto her knees.

"That other one gave her the poison!" shouts Mona, and in the time that she takes to raise an accusing finger, Brigid has sprung over the top table, spun around in a circle, and drawn Stoirm Gheimhridh from its scabbard. She slices Mona's head clean from her shoulders, before swiftly decapitating another two men that are holding Diana down.

The victims' bodies briefly stay standing as their heads bounce and roll to a stop in the room. The whole hall sits in stunned silence, while the bride and groom reach the climactic and explosive conclusion of their passion, echoes bouncing off the walls.

Brigid pulls Diana to her feet and roars the Iceni battle cry with all her might.

Her call thunders around the walls of the room and outside across the fortress, where Artos and his warband are waiting. It reaches the villages around the hilltop fortress and causes people to bar the doors of their homes through fear. It echoes through the forest. Even over and above the earth-shaking rumble of a hundred Rheged horses.

"That's Brigid," shouts Owain.

"Charge!" calls Lancelot.

Brigid and Diana burst out of the doors of the Great Hall.

"Attack!" they both shout.

Artos pushes out of the crowd and into the doorway as they surge past, blocking the way of the first to pursue and fighting fiercely to hold the position. Small explosive bolts fly past his head. To close for comfort, but Myrrdin's accuracy is deadly.

The Great Hall is filled with screams and shouting. Many have succumbed to the toxic fish course, but others have stuck to the mead and are more than ready to fight back. Andrew is the first to retreat out of sight behind the curtain as Duncan leaps from the top table to rally his men. Torcaill and Blacknail lie dead before him, while Gilbert also seems to have conveniently disappeared. Redlead is punching many of his own side to make his way to the door where Artos stands, slicing through his opponents.

"Get him, kill him!" shouts Duncan.

The joint forces of the surviving MacForres warband and the Picts push forward as one.

"Fall back, Artos," shouts Morganna, "there are too many of them, fall back!"

Morganna and Myrrdin increase the ferocity of their explosive and icy blasts, allowing Artos to run back amongst his allies. Hamish throws off his cloak where he's been holding Diana's bow and arrows.

"Thank the gods!" says the archer as she grasps her weapon, loading it in an instant.

Then a strange silence falls like the eye of a storm. Only broken by the sound of the old guard being despatched at the watchtowers, followed by the sound of the younger guard running and sobbing back to their homes.

Duncan's voice calls out instructions. Hoots and calls build up within the walls of his

Great Hall. The familiar clang of weaponry as comrades clash swords and axes. A rumble begins to form within the building in front of them while the ground beneath their feet vibrates. Artos turns to Myrrdin, but this is none of his doing. The whole hilltop of Dun Romanach begins to shake.

Out of the Great Hall, Duncan's men and his allies pour into the grounds of the fortress while the thundering noise of Urien's cavalry arrives from the rear. The two armies clash within seconds, with Artos and his party holding the centre. They are all plunged into the thick of the battle. Soon the fog of war descends, with each warrior locked in their own combat it becomes difficult to know who is winning or losing. The smoke from the magical charges begin to obscure the vision of all. The spears of Duncan's warband hold many of the horsemen at bay, while the sheer ferocity of the Picts is difficult to counter. The painted men fight as a tight unit, not allowing their line to be broken.

Duncan stands to the rear of his army and has only one person in his sights. His last instruction to his men was clear. A bounty on the head of his opponent has influenced their line of attack. As one man falls to Artos, another fills the place. The young warrior feels himself tiring under the constant onslaught, when suddenly his strongest ally appears at his side.

"Don't call me Alan," says Lancelot.

"Your alive?"

"Did I die?"

"Doesn't matter," says Artos as they instinctively work together to force the enemy back.

The roar of battle sounds across the peaks and valleys of the Galwydell. Horses charging and rearing, metal clashing and the odd sound of a group of escaping minstrels with instruments in hand and a new band member in the shape of Ifan Gofannon.

Diana then spots Gilbert riding fast for the south gate, but the smoke obscures her aim, and he flees.

"Another day," she promises herself, before having to duck to avoid a flying axe aimed at her head.

The battle lines become less defined as various groups advance or retreat. Some of the Rheged have fallen or jumped from their mounts and riderless horses do their best to escape the battle. Artos and the others who are engaged in the never-ending melee start to become surrounded. The Picts begin to encircle their targets before attacking from all sides. Then comes Redlead, sweeping away the clouds of smoke with the mighty swing of his great sword. It causes friend and foe to leap from the path of its destructive power.

Myrrdin, Morganna and Diana are finding it more difficult to aim their various missile attacks into the heart of the battle without the risk of hitting their own. The magical blasts are increasingly used to protect themselves from the random charges of those that try to run into the barrage of explosions and ice.

"We're losing our line," shouts Myrrdin, "the Picts are fierce warriors to take on."

"The Picts are strong and organised," answers Diana.

"And the Picts are naked," calls Morganna, "protect me. I think I know what to do."

Morganna falls back behind Myrrdin and Diana. Using the piece of Wren Morcant's blackened staff, she draws a circle around herself on the ground. She speaks the ancient incantation. Only Myrrdin can understand her plan.

"The Rite of the Oak King? Yes Morganna, you can do it," he says as he renews his attacks.

A circle of ravens gather in the sky, the weather is changing, and the sun is rapidly rising higher. A sudden change in temperature is bearing down on everyone. Sweat rains from the bodies of the Picts. Weapons start to slip from the grip of the hands that wield them. Across the battlefield, Artos, Lancelot and the others also experience the heat sapping at their strength. For all the tiredness and strain, they must steady their focus and keep their determination to win, but all are struggling equally under the force of air that seems to burn around them.

Where there has been hard frost layering the ground; now there are green shoots growing underfoot. The ravens keep circling on high, the buzz of flies and bees, and then the ultimate war machine begins to rise. The hardened warriors of the Galwydell that have defeated far more than any other tribe.

Black clouds swirl between the warriors with an endless hunger for blood. Dun Romanach, surrounded by its wide flowing river and its green fertile forest and fields, is the perfect environment for the vampires of summer as they close in around their targets. No sword or shield, no spear, or axe can defeat the tiny army of millions. The Midges.

The Picts are the first to fall victim to the thousands of stinging bites, causing them to drop their weapons and join each other in a strange dance. They slap their own skin and each other's, trying to extinguish some of the agony. The MacForres warband fare little better. The tiny insects work beneath the layers of armour, cling to beards, eyes, and mouths. They force a retreat that becomes a rout.

Artos and Lancelot lower their weapons as the opposition crumbles in front of them. They are not being attacked. The savage mosquitos do not have a craving for the people of

Hartriggs or the horsemen of the Rheged.

"The midges are on our side," says Lancelot.

The black clouds thicken and pursue their targets without mercy. Chasing each victim through the fortress. They don't kill, but they drive their victims on to the swords and spears of those who do. Even the largest man in the battle is no match. Redlead desperately swings his great sword at the tiny airborne attackers, but as they turn his red hair black with their own bodies, even he has to concede defeat and falls to scratch at the endless irritation.

"Yield," says Lancelot as he appears out of a hovering shroud of insects, aiming his sword at Redlead's neck.

The battle is reaching its climax. Morganna collapses with exhaustion, but the damage has been done to the MacForres family and their Pictish allies, most of whom have fallen in battle or fled through the northern gate. Those that continue fighting are doing so to save their own lives and not for the whims of their lord.

Now Artos has an unobstructed view of the man responsible for the murder of Wren Morcant, the man responsible for the destruction of Hartriggs, the man who has used his power to oppress and abuse his own people for decades. The man that is now deciding to turn and run to save his own skin.

"Duncan!" shouts Artos as he pursues his enemy back into the Great Hall.

The first thing that hits Artos as he follows Duncan into the building is the awful smell. The many victims of Morganna's poison have variously emptied the contents of their stomachs in huge steaming piles. The next thing to hit Artos is Mona's head, thrown at him by Duncan to allow him a chance to reach the big curtain.

Duncan frantically searches for the opening, but the heavy cloth will not part.

At the other side, Talorc and Andrew work together to keep it held shut while Duncanna puts her finger to her lips in a signal for silence.

"What's wrong with this thing?" complains Duncan.

"Duncan MacForres," says Artos, "you have lost. It is time to face your fate."

"What?" says Duncan, spinning around to confront his enemy. "you dare to make demands of me."

"You know the battle is almost over," Artos begins to step forward, his sword pointing towards Duncan, "and I cannot let you live and survive those whose kin you have murdered. Do you wish to die with honour or is it to be an execution? The choice is yours."

"Strange talk from someone who should thank me for their life," replies Duncan, as he continues to grasp at the curtain with one hand, while the other holds his own sword in defence.

"Why did you return Artos? Why ruin my ambitions?"

"Because the people are under threat. My body bears the blood of Cynan who the gods ensured could rise again whenever danger presents itself."

Duncan laughs. "You? The reincarnation of a legendary king? You were never more than Uther's bastard. I left you alone to live and to grow. This is how you repay the debt?"

"You left me alone out of neglect of your own duty It is you who owes the debt to all that you have murdered, exploited, and enslaved."

"Oh, my heart bleeds!" says Duncan, "or should I say your heart will bleed."

Duncan lunges forwards, propelled by an unseen shove from the other side of the curtain. His surprise move catches Artos off-guard, and a messy scramble ensues between both men as weapons scatter and they punch, kick, and wrestle between the dead wedding guests and the scattered tables, food, and drink.

The fight rages back and forth with neither gaining advantage, each man stumbles and then counter-attacks with more ferocity than before. Both know that only one can come out of the struggle alive. It comes down to a missed swing of a fist or a pain taken from contact with the many upturned tables and chairs.

In the end, it is nothing more than a wasted

plate of oily fish that causes the downfall of Artos. Sending him off balance, he crashes down heavily, causing blood to seep out from a deep gash on his back. Duncan crushes down on his chest with a knee. and pulls a dagger from the belt of his adjacent dead cousin, Torcaill, who stares back at both of them out of lifeless eyes.

Here we go again.

Duncan lashes out with the blade, but Artos avoids each stabbing attack. Twisting and writhing below Duncan. Time slows down, the sound of battle from outside the hall begins to fade in his ears. Duncan still has the advantage, and Artos can only watch as the blade is held high above his head.

Myrrdin stands on the shoreline of Modron's Water. He faces Nimue, who stands with Excalibur in her outstretched arms. She is offering the sword to the Merlin as the prophecy predicts. Artos views this vision as if he is in the form of a bird or a dragon. He soars into the sky before swooping low over Hartriggs as he remembers it as a child. His home is still there, and the figure of Wren seems busy amongst the trees as the sun beats down. Then he turns on the wing to see a great storm approaching. A blackened sky full of lightning and thunder. He descends to once again land among the forest. Rain lashes down around him, and a wailing fills the air. He staggers, feeling an agonising pain from a wound in his back. He approaches the ford with its water rushing and swollen once more.

Then he opens his eyes.

"WASHERWOMAN! I claim my wish! Come and save me from this end!"

Duncan begins to laugh at the desperation of Artos.

"You want your breeches washed now?"

"No. It's your breeches that were washed last night!"

"What?"

Duncan shrieks with surprise as an unseen force pulls him from Artos and spins him around as if he weighs nothing. Stricken with terror, he's brought face to face with the unforgiving growl of the banshee as she plunges her skeletal hand into his chest, gripping her bony fingers around his heart and pulling it from his body. She holds the still beating organ triumphantly in the air before casting it into the fire at the centre of the Great Hall.

"I have granted your wish. Until we meet again Artos."

The banshee disappears as quick as Artos summoned her, in a powerful blast of smoke. The dead and heartless body of Duncan falls to the floor, open mouthed, as if screaming, though no sound ever emerged.

Brigid runs in to the Great Hall and straight over to Artos with Stoirm Gheimhridh drawn.

She can see the danger has passed.

"You killed him!"

"I did? Though I don't think it's my claim," says Artos, gasping for breath.

"We've won. The battle's ours," she says, " they have either run, surrendered, or died. I'll check behind the curtain, we haven't seen Duncanna."

"Be careful," shouts Artos.

"She is no match for me," insists Brigid.

As the Iceni enters the private chamber, Brigid is shocked to find that Duncanna sits alone at the table, weeping on the sleeve of her wedding gown.

"Have you come to kill me now, Brigid? Or have you come to show me a kindness in return for the kindness I showed to you?"

Brigid stands silently, deciding Duncanna's fate. Does she owe her something? One chance for her to redeem herself? She stops to consider the decision her great great great great great great great great great great great great great great great great great great great grandmother may have taken.

Without saying another word, she turns her back on Duncanna and exits back through the curtain.

"Quick there's a way out through the back," says Duncanna as Talorc and Andrew stand up from behind the table.

"Put some clothes on before you go out

Talorc. My brother's moth-eaten cloaks should cover you."

"Yes, my wee darling. Anything for you."

"Is there any wine for the journey?" says Andrew.

"Hurry, before she changes her mind," Duncanna says, as she pushes them through to the sleeping chamber.

Meanwhile Brigid races back towards Artos, who still hasn't been able to move. She notices a larger pool of blood below him and begins to lift him up from a stray axe blade that has cut through his flesh. He groans with the pain and looks up into Brigid's eyes.

"Did you see anyone?" he says.

"No, there was no-one there," Brigid looks away.

Her face is the last thing Artos sees before the world turns black.

Artos is on a boat, crossing a still body of water. Three women in cowls stand silent as it navigates towards the shore. He looks at them closely. Two he doesn't recognise, but the third is the lady. Her cold expression stares back, yet Artos now feels a hint of an emotion between them.

"Nimue?"

"Artos. You, as well as my son need to stop doing this. The Merlin ages each time he must return a life. I'm sure Morganna will not take kindly to such a price being asked when she holds the title."

"Am I dead?"

"No, not yet. You have merely rested here to recover your strength for what lies ahead. Today you journey away from Avalon, not towards it."

"Avalon?"

"You still have much to learn. Your journey has only begun. Try to stay alive a little while longer, and you will come to learn of Avalon and other such things."

Artos looks around himself. The place feels like the inside of a dream, but he can touch it and feel it. He drags his hand in the water as the boat slips towards the shore. He feels the impact as it arrives half upon land. He stands up and steps out on to the soft ground. Everything is real it doesn't feel like a vision.

"Lady Nimue?"

"Yes?" she says with a slightly frustrated tone.

"The sword. Is it time for Excalibur?"

Nimue steps into the water and the surface begins to ripple. Then the sword starts to rise. Artos notices that the water here is shallow. Excalibur is rising out of the earth itself. It sparkles and fizzes with great energy, glinting in the light of a golden dawn. Its power flows through Artos, as if it is part of him already.

"No. not yet," says Nimue.

Artos wakes up with a scream. As the room comes into view, he is suddenly surrounded by his friends, beaming with bright smiling faces.

"You've returned. My brother."

Morganna seems happier than most to see him. She clasps her hands on his before reaching out to hug

Owain. Brigid and Diana are also half in each other's arms as they cheer for Artos, returning to consciousness. They all stand back to let Lancelot and Myrrdin approach the bed that Artos is laid out on. Lancelot grabs his friend's hand.

"I'm sorry. Once again, I wasn't at your side when danger presented itself. That will never happen again my brother. We are all here to serve you.

"Have I become king?"

"No," smiles Merlin, "but you now hold Duncan's old claims, so you are a lord at least. Now that you are ready, we can begin talks with Arnall of Ynys Mon. He is prepared to drop his claim in this part of Galwydell, if of course, you promise not to attack him."

"Wait what? How long have I been, eh, asleep?"

"Over a month," says Lancelot, "Myrrdin got you breathing again, but your eyes have remained closed since that day. Though it's not the first time you've slept for days after attending a wedding."

"I think I was in, Avalon."

"That would certainly explain things," says Myrrdin, "get yourself up there's a lot ahead for you to do."

"The Rheged?"

"My father stayed for a few days," says Owain, "the cavalry did their best to clean the place up after the battle, but they're warriors first and the Angles still fight on our southern borders. They had to return, and they left a message that they hope you will return to help them too."

"Yes, of course. I'm Lord Artos then?"

"You are my lord," smiles Owain, "get yourself ready we're well stocked with food still, and the mead is plentiful."

"Your mead is plentiful," says Morganna.

Everyone leaves the room. Leaving Artos to get dressed alone. His body still aches a little, but he doesn't feel sick or wounded. Clothes have been left for him. New clothes that look as if they've been made especially for him, a new shirt, breeches, and boots, that fit perfectly.

I've never worn clothes that fitted before.

Once dressed, he sits for a moment in silence. He knows now that the next part of his life lies through that doorway. Everything he had been, is gone. A life before Avalon. Now it is about the life that is to come. He stands up and walks through to a small feast and a rousing cheer.

The party sit together for hours. Talking about their adventures in the short time they've spent together. Now their fame has travelled; they are in demand to fulfil the quests of others. Their strange mix of skills and talents set them apart. And of course, there's the prophecy. It is underway and Myrrdin will be around to make sure that they keep to the right path.

"Then she said no, not yet," says Artos, as he recounts his final part of the tale. His friends laugh at the fact that he's obviously not quite good enough yet to be the one true king.

"We'll get you there," says Myrrdin, "there's more to do to put the pieces in place. Have you been to Gwynedd?"

"No, I haven't."

"Know anything about dragons?"

"Not a thing."

Myrrdin draws long on his pipe and allows Artos to return to the conversations with the others.

"Perhaps that's for the best for now."

THANKS

A first draft may well be a solo effort, but crafting a book takes the support of many that I'd like to thank.

Thank you to Derek for the excellent cover art that brings many of the story elements together - including the humour. If one picture paints a thousand words, then you've just saved me from a lot of editing.

To my early readers, Amber, Alex, and Steven. Thank you for all your comments, encouragement, and ideas that have helped to create the finished product.

Thank you to Stacey for your professional advice and guidance. Your contribution has been immensely valuable and helped me to turn what might have been a screenplay into an actual novel.

ABOUT THE AUTHOR

Grahame Fleming

Grahame Fleming began his working life as an actor, before working in a design studio, then becoming a self-taught computer programmer and serial entrepreneur. Writing  his debut novel, The Blood of the Bear, is just another stage in his long career of "not having a real job".

Born and bred in Scotland, his fascination with all things medieval began at a very young age, and has developed into a particular passion for the history and landscape linked to the legendary figure of King Arthur.

STAY IN TOUCH

Visit www.grahamefleming.com to keep up-to-date with the rambling thoughts of the author in his blog.

Click subscribe and you'll be among the first to know about progress on new work, any forthcoming offers or other products related to The Blood of the Bear, and of course you'll be able to submit your own comments to the site.

So please drop by, subscribe, and get involved with the chat.

Printed in Great Britain
by Amazon

34208049R00314